Raider's Wake

A Novel of Viking Age Ireland

Book Six of The Norsemen Saga

James L. Nelson

This is a work of fiction. Names, characters, places and incidents either are the product of the author's imagination or are used fictitiously. Any resemblance to actual events, locales, organizations, or persons, living or dead, is entirely coincidental and beyond the intent of either the author or the publisher.

Fore Topsail Press
64 Ash Point Road
Harpswell, Maine, 04079

ISBN- 13: 978-0692880265
ISBN-10: 0692880267

To Lisa, my first mate, my only mate.
Back to the sea, where we met, where we belong.

We sailed our ships to any shore that offered the best hope for booty;
We feared no fellow on earth, we were fit,
We fought in the battle-fleet.

Saga of Arrow-Odd

The Viking Longship

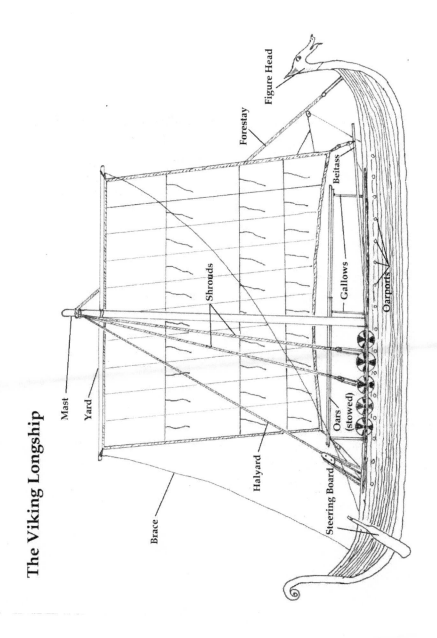

Mast
Yard
Brace
Halyard
Shrouds
Forestay
Figure Head
Beitass
Gallows
Oarports
Oars (stowed)
Steering Board

For terminology, see Glossary, page 329.

Prologue

The Saga of Thorgrim Ulfsson

There was a man named Thorgrim Ulfsson who was known as Kveldulf, which means Night Wolf. He was called that because he would often become extremely bad-tempered in the evening, despite being generally known for his even-handedness, and some people thought he was a shape-shifter and could take on the form of a wolf.

Thorgrim was a farmer in a place called Vik, in Norway, and like many such young men he spent summers raiding across the western ocean. He sailed with a jarl named Ornolf Hrafnsson, who was known as Ornolf the Restless for his love of raiding, as well as feasting and drinking. Thorgrim served Ornolf as a warrior, and as the years passed he became second to Ornolf and took responsibility for the ships and men, which was very pleasing to Ornolf as it gave him more time for feasting, and drinking ale and mead.

The two men became very close and after some time Ornolf agreed to a marriage between his daughter, Hallbera, and Thorgrim. They made a good marriage, and Hallbera bore Thorgrim two sons, Odd and Harald, and a daughter named Hild. With the help of his sons and his servants and slaves, Thorgrim became a prosperous farmer and also a man very much respected in the place where he lived. Thorgrim did not go raiding again after his marriage to Hallbera.

When Odd came of age and married, Thorgrim gave him a farm, which Odd worked as diligently as he had on his father's land. Harald, too, was a hard worker, but his fancy turned more toward raiding and battle, and he trained from a young age for the time he might go raiding as his father had. Then when Hallbera died giving birth to a second daughter, Thorgrim, in his grief, agreed to accompany Ornolf on another raiding voyage to the land called

Ireland. On this voyage he brought Harald, who was fifteen years of age.

It was Ornolf's intention that he and his men should sail his longship *Red Dragon* to Ireland and there raid during the spring and summer, returning to Vik as the season grew cold and stormy. But that was not the intention of the gods. After many adventures with the Irish king who ruled in a place called Tara, and the Danes who commanded the longphort of Dubh-linn, Ornolf, Thorgrim and those who still lived returned to Dubh-linn. It was again their wish to return to Vik, but still the gods would not allow it, and Thorgrim and the others found themselves in the longphort of Vík-ló, south of Dubh-linn, and there, after many struggles in which Ornolf was killed in a fight with a man named Grimarr, Thorgrim became the lord of Vík-ló.

The following summer Thorgrim and the other warriors at Vík-ló joined with an Irish lord and another band of men who had gone a'viking to raid the monastery at a place called Glendalough. Harald was sixteen years old at that time, and had grown big and strong as a man. Indeed, his strength was greater than that of many other men and he soon earned the name of Harald Broadarm. Harald took his place in the raiding and in the shield wall and he proved himself a brave and valuable warrior.

Thorgrim's raid on Glendalough seemed at first to be marked for great success, but it was not to be. Both the Irish lord who had first suggested the raid and the other Norsemen, who were led by a man named Ottar, betrayed them, and Thorgrim and Harald and no more than ten of their men were able to escape with their lives.

Thorgrim Night Wolf was not the sort who would let such a wrong go unavenged, and so he gathered the few men he had to him and he told them they would seek vengeance on those who had betrayed them. It so happened there were a number of Irish bandits who, seeing the chance for plunder, joined with Thorgrim and the others. They were led by a man named Cónán, who was well known among the thieves and bandits of that region.

Soon, through means of cunning and skill with sword and shield, Thorgrim had his revenge, killing the Irish lord and those others who had betrayed him. Then he reclaimed the longphort of Vík-ló and the plunder he had gathered there for himself and his men. Thorgrim killed Ottar in a *hólmganga*, which is a duel between two men, but in doing so Thorgrim was gravely wounded in his legs and was not even able to walk. But a horse was found for him and he was brought back to Vík-ló and there his wounds were tended. Soon he was all but healed and as the days of spring yielded to the full blossoming of summer Thorgrim took his place again as the Lord of Vík-ló.

Here is what happened.

Chapter One

Not on necks of oxen or cows is my champion's sword blunted,
'tis on kings that the sword in Diarmait's hand today makes a whistling noise.
The Battle of Carnn Chonaill

When the sun came up that morning, illuminating the thick blanket of gray, white and black cloud, making visible the deluge of rain that was falling and had been falling for more than a week, Bressal mac Muirchertach was still the king of a small *túaithe* to the south of Dubh-linn. And now, just past midday, he was dead.

He died in Conandil's arms, the rain pelting his pale and frightened face, the sand under his body dark and wet. The bleeding had been considerable, and from several wounds. She had done what she could to stop it. If they had been in Bressal's hall, where she might have stripped his clothing and got to the wounds in a proper way, where there would have been warmth from a great hearth fire, then she might have saved him. But that was not how it was.

They had been driven to this place by the sea, Bressal borne along by two of his men after being struck down in the first few minutes of the battle. It had been a panicked flight, and the manner in which the two bearers carried Bressal had not been gentle. That rough treatment and the cold and the wet and Conandil's inability to properly treat the wounds had all led to the old man's death on that bitter, surf-scarred stretch of shingle beach.

The attack had come just after first light and it had come from the west. The first indication that any of them inside Bressal's ringfort had of trouble in the offing was the sound of shouts and screaming, muted and far-off, and the trample of horses. It was the music of some great catastrophe and it seemed to come out of the rain itself. The distant noise had brought men to the top of the walls, straining to hear or see, but the rain blotted out most sound and the country in the distance seemed to fade into a gray nothing.

"Raiders?" Broccáin mac Bressal asked, standing next to his father on the earthen wall of the ringfort. Conandil stood beside him. She was Broccáin's wife of five months. They had both leapt from their bed to scale the walls as the sentries shouted their alarm. They had found Bressal already there.

"Raiders for certain," Bressal said. "But who?"

"Fin gall?" Conandil asked. "The heathens?" It terrified her just to say the words. She had been taken by the heathens the past summer, bound away for the slave markets of Frisia, when God had sent her the means of salvation. She knew it had to be God, because her escape was so like a miracle. Even if she did bring it about by fornicating with one of the heathens and fleeing as he slept. But that was past, confessed and forgiven.

"Could be the heathens," Bressal said. "But I would not expect them to come from the west. If they were going to raid they would come from the sea, I would think." The túaithe that Bressal ruled was on the coast, and the ringfort not far from the beach from which the local fishermen put out to sea in leather-covered boats to cast their nets.

"That whore's son Eochu, then?" Broccáin suggested. Eochu was the *rí túaithe* of the lands that neighbored Bressal's, and like all good neighbors in Ireland they were forever raiding one another. But they were cattle raids, mainly, quick forays over the border to scoop up the other's cows, the chief measure of wealth in Ireland. But what they were hearing was no cattle raid.

Through all this discussion, Conandil was desperate to point out what to her was obvious: it did not matter much who was attacking, only that the people out there needed help. But as a woman, and a woman new to the family and the *rath*, it was hardly her place to point that out.

Happily, Broccáin realized as much before Conandil could stand it no more. "Whoever this bastard is, we have to meet them," he said and those words seemed to spur everyone to move. Bressal and then Broccáin and then the sentries flew down the ladder to the grounds below, the rí túaithe and his son bellowing for sword and shield, for the house guard to turn out, for horses to be brought.

The sound of distant shouting was louder, closer, by the time the gates to the rath were thrown open and the two dozen armed men sallied forth. Bressal and Broccáin were mounted, as were a few of their chief men, but most were on foot. Some were armed with swords and shields, some with axes, but most carried shields and spears, the easiest weapon to make, the easiest to wield, and one of the most effective.

They were still coming out of the gate when the first people came running out of the fog and the mist, maybe a quarter mile away. It was hard to see what was happening. Conandil, who was trailing behind, had to wipe rain from her eyes as she blinked into the distance. She could see people running: women, men, children. She could see them stumbling, crawling, getting to their feet again. Behind them, men with spears and swords, their round, bright painted shields looking dull in that light.

This is bad, she thought. *This is very bad.* Real defense of the túaithe required the men of those lands to arm and to gather and to put themselves under the leadership of Bressal. A minor king like him, a man of no great wealth, could not afford to keep men-at-arms. He had a small house guard, but for real numbers he had to rely on those who owed him military service, the poor farmers, the *bóaire* and *fuidir*. They were no great fighting men, but they could use a spear and that was often all that it took.

But whoever had launched this attack had come in the night, waited until it was light enough to see, and fell on the people before the men could be called to arms. And now the farmers were running, fleeing in terror, and there was little chance their leaders, Bressal and Broccáin, could organize them to fight back.

But Conandil knew they would die trying, and she cursed her bitter luck and this horrible fate. She had just escaped the hell of the fin gall, had found a husband, heir to this land, a fine home, and now these bastards had come in the night to take it all. But she would not be taken, not again. Like her husband, she would die making a stand.

"Onward! Onward!" Bressal shouted, sword over his head, pointing toward the people rushing for the illusionary safety of the ringfort. It had been years since the old man had been in battle, but he had lost none of the courage that made him so loved by the people he ruled.

Together, Bressal and Broccáin spurred their horses, leading the way forward, but keeping the animals to a slow trot so the others might keep up. They had swords held high, shields on their arms. They, alone among all the men there, wore mail shirts that gleamed dully and made a jingling sound as they rode.

Conandil walked behind the column of men and off to the side so her view of the action ahead was not blocked by the soldiers. She had no idea what she might do in the middle of a fight, had given no thought to why she was advancing more or less at her husband's side. She just knew she could not stay behind in the ringfort, could not spend this time praying and worrying and wondering what was going on.

The shouting and screaming was louder now. Conandil looked off beyond the mounted figures of Bressal and Broccáin. The people were a couple hundred yards away, still running, stumbling, the women screaming in terror. Now and then one of the men would turn and raise whatever pathetic weapon he held—an ax or a pitchfork or a scythe—in an attempt to fight back. They might as well have been holding feathers for all the good it did them, the men-at-arms at their heels cutting them down with hardly a pause.

*It's like driving deer...*Conandil thought. The people were like deer being driven by the men behind, the heathens or Eochu's men or whoever it was. These men must have swept through the countryside and herded the people together and pushed them forward, the way servants will round up deer and drive them to be killed for the amusement of some great king.

And then the fleeing people of the túaithe ran headlong into the armed men who had gone out to defend them, and it was chaos. Bressal had come down from his horse and was trying to get his men to form a shield wall of some sort when the terrified people collided with his line, clawing and scrambling and fighting to get past, to put the armed men from the ringfort between themselves and their attackers.

Bressal's line collapsed under that assault, what little order he had created torn apart, and he was just trying to get the men back under command when the attackers fell on them. They came with spears mostly, and swords and their round shields. Like Bressal's men, they were not well organized, having been driving the people ahead of them, but they were not hampered by the panicked women and children, and they hit Bressal's line like a massive, breaking wave.

Conandil saw Bressal go down in that first assault and she screamed in horror and panic. She loved the old man, her father-in-law, nearly as much as she loved her husband, but now as she watched, he disappeared under the swell of fighting men, spears and swords thrusting back and forth.

Broccáin roared, a great bear's roar, a sound Conandil had never heard from him, and he charged forward, shield up, sword slashing back and forth, hacking and thrusting and clearing a swath of men away from his fallen father. His courage drove the men under his command and they, too, pushed forward, meeting the raiders shield for shield, spear for spear.

Not heathens, Conandil thought. These men, these raiders, they were not fin gall. They did not wear mail or leather armor, they did not have the pointed iron helmets and shields with their wicked pagan images painted on their faces. These were Irishmen.

"Why are you doing this?" she screamed at the top of her lungs. "You bastards, forsaken by God!" It was not as if she expected an answer, it was just that the whole nightmare was so unreal that she could not contain herself.

She reached down and picked up an ax that one of the fleeing men had dropped. Not a battle ax, but the sort used to chop kindling for the hearth or the heads off chickens. Still, it had an edge, it could kill, and that was all she wanted. She raced forward, ready to do anything, perfectly ready to die in defense of this life she had built, this fine life that she enjoyed for the first time in the twenty or so years she had been on this earth.

The nearest of the attackers was maybe ten yards away and Conandil charged for him, ax raised over her shoulder. She realized she was shrieking, but she could not really tell what shrieking was hers and what was coming from the others locked in the fight. Rain ran down her face and hair and her clothing was soaked through and heavy.

The man she was set on wore a dark green *brat* and carried a shield painted red. He held a spear over his head as if he was going to throw it, but instead he was darting it back and forth, stabbing when he saw his chance. The tip of the spear was shining bright red, and then the rain washed it clean.

He didn't see Conandil coming until the last moment. He seemed to sense the movement to his left and turned to look. What he saw likely did not impress him; Conandil stood a little over five feet and weighed maybe seven stone. The first suggestion of a smile was forming on his lips when Conandil's ax came down and split his skull, burying itself up to the handle in his head.

The man's eyes crossed and blood erupted from around the ax blade and he went down fast, driven down by the force of the blow. Conandil tried to hang on to the ax, but it was lodged firmly in the dead man's skull and the handle was wet and it pulled from her grip.

By the time the man had crumpled completely Conandil could see she had other problems. The raiders, who had been thrown back by the ferocity of Broccáin's attack, had formed up again and now they were surging forward. Broccáin's men were starting to waver and Conandil had the feeling they would break soon and start to run.

She was right. The men who were not then engaged in the fight began to fade back, and others around them began to fade back as well. Conandil saw her husband looking desperately around, looking for men to stand with him. She saw his mouth open as he shouted something—encouragement, orders, curses—but she could not hear the words.

Then everyone was running. Conandil was not aware of the moment it happened; it just seemed as if in one instant the men were fighting and in the next they were running and Conandil turned and ran as well, because there was nothing else to do. She ran with the house guard and with the few farmers who had stopped in their flight to join the battle line. She ran with the enemy at her heels and the ringfort gaping open a few hundred yards ahead.

But then there were riders. Mounted warriors with long spears sweeping in on the left, racing ahead of the running men, pushing for the ringfort, cutting off that avenue of retreat.

The rath...Conandil thought. Her only thought had been to get to the rath, the only place in all her life she had actually felt as if she was safe. And now, with the horsemen outpacing them, flanking them, driving them, the rath was beyond her reach and she felt the last bits of hope like rust flaking away.

She kept running. She ran with the others. She caught a glimpse of Broccáin, last of the men to flee, and she wished he would run faster. She caught a glimpse of Bressal, carried like some carcass by two of his men, but she had to guess he still lived or surely they would have left him on the field. But mostly she just ran.

The ringfort was half a mile from the shingle beach the fishermen used and the people were racing down the beaten road that ran to that place. Conandil had an idea that if they could get to the beach there might be boats enough for them to all get out to sea and escape. They did not have to get far, a few hundred yards would do it. Just beyond the distance of a spear throw, or a bow shot if these men had bows and arrows.

Suddenly she felt hope. She did not know if the others were thinking about the boats or if they were just in mindless flight, but it didn't matter. Once they reached the shore, saw the boats, they would think of that, too. And even if there were not boats enough for all, there would certainly be a place for Bressal and his son, Broccáin, and that was all that Conandil was worried about. She would happily die at the end of one of these bastard's spears if she could see her beloved husband safe off in a boat.

She stumbled, straightened, raced on. Her breath was coming harder, her chest burning, and she realized that Broccáin would never get in a boat if there were others still on the beach. He would be the last aboard; he would have it no other way. That was why she loved him, because that was the sort of man he was.

The land sloped away down to the water, not one of the ragged cliffs that marked much of the coast but an easy grade down to the shingle. She wanted to yell out, to tell them about the boats, to order them to get in the boats and hope they obeyed.

She crested the rise that ran down to the sea and saw the beach stretched out before her, as if it had been laid there for her inspection. A half a mile of sand and gravel from north to south, stretched out in a gentle curve and capped at either end by short, steep headlands that blocked the view of the coast beyond. The grassy meadows ended in a sharp brown line and after that there was only beach for fifty yards down to the breaking sea. There were a dozen boats there. They were floating free, three hundred feet from shore.

Conandil let out a cry of despair as she stumbled the last hundred yards down to the beach. It was as far as she could go, as far as her gasping lungs would move her. She collapsed in the sand, sucking in air, was conscious of the many people swarming around her, unsure what to do now. She heard her husband calling orders, getting men in line, setting up whatever defense he could.

She remembered Bressal, her father-in-law, their rí túaithe. She forced herself to her feet, staggered around the beach until she found where the men had deposited him in the sand. He was bloody for half a dozen wounds. His skin was very white, his eyes blinking slowly. Conandil grabbed the edges of the torn mail and pulled the tears wider to get to the wounds. She tore open his clothing underneath, pulled her knife and cut strips of cloth from Bressal's cloak. She bound his wounds as best she could, but the mail shirt made it impossible to do so with much effect.

An odd quiet had come to the beach and Conandil wondered why they had not yet been attacked. She looked up from her work. The raiders were drawn up in a line near the crest of the hill that ran up from the beach. They had swung around so they could approach from the south, why, Conandil could not guess. It would mean crossing more beach to bring the fight home. They seemed to be taking their time, getting their men in order, forming a line of shields. In front of her, on the beach, Broccáin was doing the same.

She turned back to Bressal. The old man was shivering and his eyes were wide and his mouth partway open. Conandil put her arms behind him and lifted him, surprised she had the strength, and held him pressed to her. "I love you, Lord Bressal, and I thank you for your kindness and I commend your soul to God." She heard the old man take a gasping breath, felt him shake one last time in her arms and then he was still.

Conandil laid him down gently and closed his eyes. She looked up again. The line of men on the hill was advancing now, slowly, methodically, marching in a line that hardly wavered as it came toward them, stretched out over a hundred feet.

"Stand ready!" she heard Broccáin shout. "Stand ready and murder these bastards when they come!"

The enemy came closer, and their numbers were not so much greater than those of her husband's were, and that gave her hope. Sure, the fighting men advancing on them seemed better armed, better trained. They were not just a small house guard and a handful of frightened farmers. Nonetheless, while they might be superior men-at-arms, they were not greatly superior.

But whatever happened, Conandil would not be taken. That much she promised herself. She would not be a slave again. If the battle was lost to them, then Broccáin would certainly die fighting. And she would die with him.

Bressal's sword was long gone, but he had a seax on his belt and Conandil bent over and pulled it free. She was willing to die with Broccáin, but like her husband she would make the bastards buy her life at the cost of some of their own. Maybe she and her short sword could make a difference in the fight. She had already reduced the enemy's numbers by one.

She took a step forward, ready to take her place in the shield wall, even if she had no shield. And then she heard a sound behind her, an odd sound like a shovel thrust into gravel. She spun around. The sound was the bow of a ship, a heathen longship, running up on the beach.

It had come around the headland to the north. Conandil knew that because a second one was just now appearing around that spit of land. She opened her mouth to shout a warning, but her words were cut off by the sound of the fin gall warriors screaming their battle cry as they leapt over the sides of their ship, and the hellish cries of the raiders on the hill, who were now charging down on Broccáin and his men.

Conandil took a deep breath. She raised the seax high and with a warrior's cry in her throat she charged at the Northmen leaping into the surf.

Chapter Two

He is "Simpleton" named who has naught to say,
for such is the fashion of fools.

Odin's Quest after the Song Mead

It had been raining nearly nonstop for a week. The various side roads that crisscrossed Vík-ló, and even the plank road that ran down the center of the longphort, were swamped with mud. It was early summer, yet everyone in the walled town felt the need to keep fires burning. And still the dampness pervaded everything: clothes, skin, blankets, food. The ale tasted watery, the bread was limp and soggy.

But for all that, it was the fight over the pig that finally brought Thorgrim Night Wolf to enlightenment.

He was sitting in the big chair with the carved arms and back that was set up in his hall. The fire in the hearth in the center of the room was built up high, the flames driving some of the gloom from the place. But the light could not reach everywhere, and the corners of the hall were still lost in deep shadow, despite it being early in the *undorn*, the midafternoon.

Off in one of those dark corners he could hear his son, Harald, snoring where he slept on a pile of furs. It was unusual for Harald to be sleeping during the day. He was a young man of enormous energy and he usually channeled that energy into work.

Since their return to Vík-ló following the disastrous raid on Glendalough, after their weeks in exile as they fought for vengeance and to reclaim their rightful place, Harald had hardly stopped. With a large gang of men under his command, he had repaired and expanded the plank road, built a pier out into the river that formed the shorefront of the longphort, repaired the damage that Thorgrim's hall had suffered under Ottar's brief rule, and strengthened the wall that separated Vík-ló from the Irish countryside.

It had rained on and off since their return, but Harald and his men had pressed on through the downpours, despite the added difficulty and misery of working in the wet and the mud. But then one afternoon it had started in raining and it had not stopped, and it did not seem like it would ever stop. Harald and his men had accomplished everything of use they could think to do, and anything else seemed like just killing time, which no one had much interest in doing. So the days' work came to an end, and now Harald slept.

Thorgrim shifted uncomfortably in his chair as he kept his eyes on the man in front of him. The man was speaking and Thorgrim realized he had not been listening at all, had no idea what the man had said during the last few minutes of his rambling discourse. He felt a dull ache in his legs where Ottar's sword had opened up two ugly lacerations. They were mostly healed, but they still gave him pain on occasion and he reckoned they always would. Just like the stab wound in his left shoulder. And all the other injuries he had suffered over the years.

"And so I must have told him a dozen times, lord, a dozen at least," the man was saying, "to keep the damned animal penned up." Thorgrim straightened and forced himself to pay attention. "I thought he was just stupid at first, lord, but then I realized..."

"Stupid, is it?" The second man turned on the first. "What you know..."

A knife flew across the room and bounced off the wall opposite them, its trajectory posing no threat to any of the men in the hall, and from somewhere to Thorgrim's left he heard Starri Deathless curse under his breath. It was Starri who had thrown the knife, apparently, and apparently he had intended for it to embed itself in the wall, or the man speaking, but in that he had utterly failed.

Starri was drunk, and had been for two days now. It was as odd as Harald's sleeping in midday. The Northmen, of course, were not generally adverse to drunkenness, which made Starri a great oddity, because he rarely let drink get the better of him. Thorgrim had always imagined that Starri lived naturally, every day, with the kind of liberating abandon that others found in ale and mead. Starri usually had no need for drink. But now it seemed he did.

A drunk Starri was a frightening Starri. Starri Deathless was a berserker, one of those men who lapsed into a frenzy at the onset of battle, who fought with a madness that could only come from the gods. No helmet, no mail, just leggings and a battle ax in each hand; that was how Starri chose to go into a fight. He would not follow orders, and Thorgrim suspected he could not even hear them. But any warrior of the enemy within the reach of his weapons could reckon his lifespan in seconds.

When Starri had started in on the mead he had turned predictably belligerent, challenging any who came in his way to a fight, a challenge that was quickly declined until Starri grew so frustrated he began to attack Thorgrim's men indiscriminately. Harald and the massive Godi had managed to subdue him before he did anyone much damage, but Thorgrim could see this was not going to get better soon.

As a short-term solution, and against the advice of the others, Thorgrim gave Starri even more mead, hoping that Starri would get drunk enough that he would become incapacitated. And it had worked, more or less. Soon he could hardly walk or speak, and any attempt to fight ended with him collapsing on the floor. Whenever he rallied he was given more mead. This approach was keeping everyone, including Starri, safe in the moment, but it was no solution. What the real solution was, Thorgrim did not know.

"So, he says I let the pig out on purpose, lord, but it weren't nothing like that...."

The second man was talking now, Thorgrim realized. He shook his head to clear it and once again forced himself to listen. As Lord of Vík-ló it was Thorgrim Night Wolf's duty to dispense justice. He was the ultimate arbiter, the final judge in all matters that took place in the longphort. It was a duty he took seriously. Or did. Until now.

"I thought the pig was just getting out, lord, because they're smart, as you know. But then I come to realize this one, Gellir here, he's letting him out, lord, I swear by Odin himself he's letting the pig out!"

This was not the first time Thorgrim had heard this. Ulf was the baker in Vík-ló, Gellir was a woodcarver and Ulf's neighbor. Gellir had a pig that kept getting free of its pen and rampaging through Ulf's garden and even into his house.

Or maybe the pig belonged to Ulf, and it was destroying Gellir's property. Thorgrim could not recall.

"Wait," Thorgrim said, holding up a hand. "Did you witness this? Gellir setting the pig free? Or do you have any witnesses?" He was pleased that he had paid enough attention that he could ask a pertinent question. It might make these two believe he was giving their dispute some real thought.

"No, lord, I didn't see it, but the thing of it is, I saw to it the sty was secure, lord. There's no way the beast got out on its own."

"Ah, damn the pig!" Starri cried from the corner of the hall. "I'll...I swear by the gods, I'll..." Thorgrim glanced over. Starri was trying to stand. He made it halfway to his feet, then collapsed again. Thorgrim nodded. No need to pour more drink into him yet.

He turned back to Ulf and Gellir. "Continue," he said, and the two men started in at the same time, talking over one another. Thorgrim raised a hand. "Ulf, continue," he said.

There was often a crowd of Thorgrim's lead men there when he was listening to problems such as this, the few men Thorgrim trusted to offer opinions and judgment. But there was no one now, because everyone was so sick of hearing about Gellir and Ulf and the pig.

How did we get here? Thorgrim wondered as Ulf's words moved unheard past his ears. This whole situation had an uncomfortably familiar quality.

It's the rain, he thought. It never stopped raining long in that country of Ireland, a place clearly despised by the gods. Ireland and all their Christ-God worship, no wonder Odin poured water down on their heads without mercy. That was why this all seemed so familiar, like he had lived this all before.

But that was not it, and he knew it. It was more than that. He thought back to the time just before they had headed off for the raid on Glendalough. Only a few months earlier, which was hard to believe, but there it was. They had spent the winter at Vík-ló, trapped in the longphort, working in the wet and the mud, miserable and confined. Tempers were short, fights breaking out.

Ulf was still talking and Thorgrim heard the word "pig," nothing more, but in that instant he realized three things with startling clarity. One was that the rain had stopped. The other was that he was done listening to these two men bicker over a pig.

The third was that he now understood what the gods wanted him to do.

He sat up suddenly from his slouched repose, a move so fast and surprising that Ulf stopped speaking in midsentence. Thorgrim cocked his ear toward the thatch roof overhead. He held up a hand for silence and the hall fell silent, save for the crackling and popping of the fire and Harald's snoring.

"Do you hear that?" Thorgrim asked. Silence. He answered his own question. "The rain has stopped."

There was a low murmur through the big room, but it did not reflect Thorgrim's suddenly buoyant mood. It was not so unusual for the rain to stop for a while, as if teasing them, and then set in again twice as hard as before. But somehow Thorgrim knew this was different.

"Godi, take a look at the sky," Thorgrim said. Godi stood like a bear rising from sleep and crossed over to the oak door at the far end of the hall. He swung it open and looked outside. In the gray light they could see water streaming down off the edge of the roof, and beyond that the part of the longphort that was visible, all brown and gray and black.

But there was a quality to the muted light coming in from the door that was unlike what they had seen over the past week.

"Looks like the clouds are breaking, lord," Godi reported. "Off to the east, they are breaking up."

Thorgrim nodded and he felt his sense of optimism growing now. He reminded himself that this was not the first time he had taken the end of the rain to be a sign from the gods. He had thought that just before they had sailed for Glendalough. But this was different. He felt it.

Because he knew now what he had to do. What they all had to do.

He turned to Ulf and Gellir. "This pig, the one in contention, it's still around?"

"Uh, no, lord," Ulf said, trying to be as deferential as he could be. "It's like I was saying, Gellir killed the pig when it went into his garden last and next I know he has it roasting on—"

"So the pig is dead?" Thorgrim interrupted. Both men nodded their heads. "Do you have other pigs? Either of you?"

The two men nodded again. "I have two more, lord, left after Gellir stole the one," Ulf said.

"And I three," Gellir said, grudgingly. "And some meat smoked."

"Excellent!" Thorgrim said, his enthusiasm mounting. "Here's what you'll do. As punishment to both of you for driving us all to madness with this idiocy, you will both bring your best swine to my hall when I command you, and we will slaughter them and we will roast them and all of the longphort will feast. We'll make a sacrifice to the gods and we'll feast and we'll celebrate."

"Celebrate…lord?" Ulf asked.

"Yes, we'll celebrate," Thorgrim said. "And we'll ask the gods to bless our coming voyage."

Another murmur ran through the hall, more pointed and louder this time. Thorgrim heard Harald's snoring stop abruptly.

"Voyage, Lord Thorgrim?" It was Godi asking this time, and Thorgrim could hear the hopeful tone in his voice.

"Yes, Godi. We'll sail once the ships are made ready. Fine ships, sitting on the mud and filling with rainwater. It makes the gods sick to see such things. Is it any wonder they're angry?"

"Night Wolf!" Now it was Starri calling from his far corner. His voice was still slurred, but as with Godi, there was a new and revived quality to it. "Where do we go?"

"We're going a'viking, as men were meant to do," Thorgrim said. "We're going raiding." The murmur swept through the hall once more, louder, like a building surf.

"Pray, lord, might I ask," Godi said, "where is it we'll be raiding?"

Thorgrim smiled at him. "Where there are riches to be had, Godi. Where there are riches."

Chapter Three

When edges shall be against edges, and shields against shield,
thou wilt be penitent...
The Battle of Carnn Chonaill

Thorgrim Ulfsson was not the only one pleased to see an end to the pitiless rain. Ten miles south of Dubh-linn, in a small stand of trees next to what might have been a road or might have been a shallow muddy stream, a man named Cronan and his two companions stood hunched against the downpour. The oaks spread above them, flush with their summer leaves, gave some shelter, but not much. And so, when the sound of the deluge began to taper away, and then ended completely, the men looked up with wonder and relief.

"Damn the damn sodding rain," the man to Cronan's left muttered and Cronan lashed out and hit him on the side of the head.

"Shut your fool mouth," Cronan said, even though he himself had been right on the cusp of saying much the same thing. With the sleeve of his filthy, patched and now-soaked tunic he wiped the water from his eyes.

He wiped both eyes, even though only one of them actually worked. The other was blind and had a milky cast to it, or so Cronan understood. He had only seen himself in a mirror once in his life, and he had not been much pleased with what he saw, but he thought he remembered it that way. He had seen his reflection in various pools of water, of course, but in water it was hard to get a clear picture of how he genuinely appeared.

Not that he gave a rat's turd what he looked like. The uglier, the more frightening he was, the easier it was for him to earn his living in the manner he chose.

"Come on," he said, nodding toward the barely visible path beaten between the trees. He rested his palm on the hilt of the big knife that hung from a rope tied around his belt and pushed his way through the bracken, his two fellows trailing behind.

They had spent the night in the stand of trees, drenched, hungry, cold and miserable. The night before had been spent in a farmer's hovel which, uninviting as it was, had been like some lord's great hall compared to the woods. They had slept in the company of the farmer's corpse, and that of his wife, whom they had killed soon after being let into that sorry place.

They would have liked to wait out the rain there for a few days, but there was too great a risk that some neighbors or one of the local *rí túaithe*'s men would come snooping around. When dawn came they took what they could find of value, which was practically nothing, and all the food they could carry, and left.

Cronan paused near the edge of the woods, where the thinning trees gave him a view of the road that ran beside it, a long, undulating brown band cutting through the green fields and disappearing over a distant hill. Pools of water stood in random low spots and the once dusty path was now dark brown mud, but it was not much churned or rutted as no travelers had passed that way for some time. The weather had not been particularly accommodating for travelers the past week or more.

But that would change. Unimposing as this road might be, it was one of the chief thoroughfares between the lands to the south and the ever-expanding Norse settlement of Dubh-linn, already the largest city in all of Ireland. The Irish might fear and despise the Northmen, but not nearly as much as they loved the chance to profit from them.

The foreigners in Dub-linn, the heathens, the fin gall, had silver and they had goods from the lands across the sea and they were in need of Irish meat and grains and ale. What the heathens did not buy for their immediate use they would buy to carry to trading centers in Frisia and Frankia and the northern countries. Where once only the warriors' longships made their way to the Irish coast, now more and more tubby merchant vessels were calling on Dubh-linn to fill their holds with goods rather than plunder.

And much of it flowed along this road. And so it was along this road that Cronan and his men secreted themselves, in hopes of relieving some of those travelers of their goods, and generally their lives.

"Here, Cronan, look there!"

Corcc, the one Cronan had struck moments before, was nodding to the south. Cronan squinted his one good eye in that direction. There was something moving on the road, most likely someone on horseback. Cronan suspected that Corcc could see the figure perfectly well, that anyone with proper eyes could, but he could see only a blurred figure. Despite that, he was not about to ask Corcc or his other man, Murchad, what they could see.

The three men stood silent and motionless as the distant figure approached. Finally, when Cronan was certain enough of what he was looking at, he spoke. "Rider," he grunted. "A single rider."

"Yes," Corcc said. "All by himself. Looks to me to be a monk or a priest or some such."

Cronan grunted his agreement, though he still could see nothing but a blurry figure astride a larger blurry figure. Still, that told him a lot. One man alone on a horse would be an easy target if they timed it right, sprung on him before he could bolt away. A man on a horse was likely a man with something worth stealing. At the very least the horse could be sold for something. In the unlikely event that there was a saddle as well, it would be worth considerably more.

"All right, get down, you stupid bastards," Cronan growled. He crouched down on one knee and the other two did the same. "You wait until I say the word, then it's right at him. Corcc, you get his reins."

Corcc grunted. "Ain't like we never done this before," he muttered and Cronan hit him again.

They fell silent, and soon even Cronan could see it was indeed a single man on horseback and he appeared to be a priest or a monk. At least he appeared to be wearing the robe of a priest or a monk, though it was hard to tell, as the cloth was soaked clean through and clung to the man and the horse.

They could hear the sounds of the horse's hooves now, not the soft clop of hoof on packed dirt but a squishing sound as each foot sunk inches deep in the mud and the weary animal pulled it free to take the next step.

Priest...Cronan thought. He had no concerns about killing a priest. Some did, thought that their souls would be in jeopardy, but Cronan had long ago given up worrying about that. He figured that his soul was so far beyond the possibility of redemption that he might as well take what he could from this world and not worry about the next. There were at least two priests he could recall whose fat guts had felt the thrust of his knife.

And there was the other one. The one he had never forgotten. It had been north of Dubh-linn, a year or two earlier. Just two priests on the road, and Cronan had tried to kill the one, but the priest had laid a hand on his arm, just laid it there, it seemed, but it had stopped Cronan in mid-thrust. And then he had said, simply, "Don't do that," and somehow Cronan had not been able to gut the man. It was some kind of priest magic, and it had frightened him. And then the priest had even asked for food, and Cronan had yielded that, too.

Well, I'll gut this one, if he don't do what I want, Cronan thought. *I'll gut him even if he does.*

The rider was ten feet away and still had not seen the three men concealed in the bracken. He hardly moved as he rode, just swayed with the motion of the walking horse, right up until the moment that Cronan shouted, "Go!" and sprung to his feet and Corcc and Murchad did as well.

They burst out of the brush and the man on the horse looked up and Cronan could see the shock on his face. He jerked the reins to spin his mount around, but Corcc was there as ordered. He grabbed the reins and yanked them from the man's grasp and held them tight as the horse, surprised as the man, whinnied and pulled.

Cronan was at the priest's side, his big knife drawn and held in front on him, close enough to the rider that he could easily stick it in the man's stomach. Murchad was around the other side and he, too, had a long knife drawn and ready.

"Get down," Cronan growled. "Get down easy and slow." The man nodded though his face betrayed no fear. Cronan squinted at him, trying to see if this was the same priest from years before. He could not tell for certain, but he did not think so. This one was younger, it seemed. Cronan did not think he would have the chance to get much older.

The horse had a saddle, which Cronan was pleased to see, and saddlebags which seemed full, and that was even better. The priest swung a leg over and slipped easily to the ground. His hands were held up at shoulder height as a show of supplication, though it would do him no good.

"I'm a man of God," the young priest said. "You don't want to do me harm."

Cronan cocked his head and regarded the man. He had some sort of accent, like he was from a country over the seas. "Where you from?" Cronan demanded.

"The monastery at Glendalough," the priest said.

"Before that," Cronan said.

"I am from Frankia. I am studying at the monastery."

Cronan frowned. *Monastery at Glendalough...*he thought.

He had only a vague idea of where Frankia was, and only a slightly better idea of where Glendalough was located. But he did know that Glendalough was a prominent and wealthy monastery. And that made him very curious indeed about what was in the saddlebags.

"Look, my friend," the priest said. "You don't want to injure a man of God. Let me give you a blessing and I'll be on my way."

"'Man of God'," Cronan spat. He had seen enough men of God to know he would be perfectly happy killing one if it meant getting at the riches hidden in his saddlebags. And he knew better than to let this bastard keep talking. Too much of the priest's slippery words and those weak fools Corcc and Murchad would be on their knees begging forgiveness.

"Here, man of God," Cronan growled. He took a step toward the priest and whipped his knife up in an underhanded arc meant to rip through the man's stomach and up under his rib cage. He could almost feel the familiar sensation of blade splitting flesh as his arm swept upward. And then it stopped.

Cronan looked down in surprise. The priest's left hand had grabbed his wrist and was holding it, immobile. Cronan tried to jerk his hand back, but before he put the least effort into it the priest's right hand grabbed the handle of the knife and twisted it out of Cronan's hand. The gesture was effortless and Cronan could only watch as the knife was plucked from his fingers.

The bandit looked up at the priest's expressionless face, expecting some admonition, some call to repent, but the priest said nothing as he thrust the knife forward into Cronan's belly. Cronan felt a strangled cry come from deep inside and he staggered back, hands around the blade of the knife, the warm blood already running over his fingers. The pain was radiating out from the wound, but not so much pain that Cronan could not speak or act.

"You son of a bitch!" he shouted and then grit his teeth and grabbed the handle and pulled the knife free. He had no doubt he would die of the wound, but he meant to take this bastard with him.

He held the knife tight, the handle slippery with blood. The priest had his arm up, reaching behind his back, and to Cronan's horror he drew a long, gleaming sword from a scabbard that must have been secreted under his robe.

"What in hell?" Cronan said. The sword came down in an arc and Cronan heard the swish of the blade cleaving the air and then he heard nothing more.

Louis de Roumois felt his sword's perfectly honed blade hit the Irish bandit's skull and split it with barely a pause in its downward momentum. The filthy bastard was dead but still on his feet, mouth open, eyes rolling off in different directions, as Louis pulled the blade free, spun around and drove the tip into the chest of the other one holding his horse's reins.

The second man made a strangling sound as the sword tore through his lungs. Louis pulled the blade back quick, done with that one, wanting to get at the third. He ducked around the horse's head even as the second man was staggering back. His death would not be instant, like the first's had been, but still the life was draining from him fast.

The third man, the youngest, apparently, had time enough to register what was going on, unlike the first two men. That was a great advantage, but the man did not have the presence of mind to do anything with it. Instead of turning and running as fast as he could, he backed carefully away, hands up, eyes wide, as if things would be all right as long as he didn't startle the man with the sword.

Louis took two steps in his direction. At some other time he might have taken pity on the young man, let him run off, but the past month had all but driven pity from Louis's heart. He brought the sword back over his left shoulder, settled both hands on the grip and swung it around in a powerful backhand stroke. The Irish bandit made a strangling sound, half surprise, half terror. His hands were still up and Louis's blade neatly severed the right hand, just at the wrist, barely pausing as it hit his neck and kept on going.

The sword did not decapitate the man, but near enough. His head flopped at an odd angle and he was tossed onto his side by the force of the blow. He came to rest in the mud of the road with his head just barely attached by a strip of flesh. The blood coursing from his rent neck was mixing with the standing water on the road to form a dull red liquid.

For a few heartbeats Louis remained where he stood, sword pointed at the ground; then he drew back quick to the *en garde* position and turned left and right. Prudence and training dictated that he would not drop his guard until he was certain all enemies were dead or gone.

Nothing. Louis de Roumois was alone with his horse and the three dead men scattered around him. He heard only the rustle of wind in the branches and the snorting and pawing of his mount, a well-trained animal that had not been startled by the sudden violence, but rather had stepped a few paces back and remained where he stood. Beyond that there was nothing.

He lowered the sword, rested the tip on the ground and sighed. This sort of thing was no more than he had come to expect during the few hellish months he had just spent wandering like some poor soul in purgatory around the Irish countryside.

After the disastrous attempt to crush the Northmen who had sacked Glendalough, Louis retreated with the rest of the men-at-arms under the command of Lochlánn mac Ainmire, a young former novitiate whom he himself had trained. They were bound back to Glendalough where, Louis knew, he was likely to be hanged for a murder he was wrongly thought to have committed. That was a fate he did not care to experience, so he slipped away from the weary column of horsemen and, unnoticed, he rode off north.

But he did not remain unnoticed for long. He had covered a few miles, no more, before he saw the horsemen coming up over the hill away to the south, riding as hard as their weary mounts would carry them. They were coming for him, of that he had no doubt.

He drove his heels into his horse's flanks, pushed the poor, tired animal into something like a run. He had a decent lead on the men behind him, but he knew that could change in an instant. One twist of the horse's ankle, one stone in a shoe and he was done for. He had to open up the lead while he could.

Louis charged up the next hill and down the far side, the riders coming for him temporarily blocked from view, which was good, but what lay before him was not good, not good at all. A wide river, roiling and tumbling along, a river too deep and fast for the horse to cross, Louis was all but certain. He could turn right, race off to the east, but he had an idea that the Northmen under Thorgrim's command would be found there, and they were at least as big a threat as the men behind him.

So he turned left and ran off to the west. It gave him a bit of an advantage, since his pursuers would not know he had done that until they, too, crested the hill. But it was also pretty much the opposite direction in which he wished to travel.

By the time the men behind him had come over the hill, Louis had greatly increased his lead. For another hour or so they continued this fox and hound chase over the rolling green country, but finally the men behind gave up, slowed to a stop, watched for a few minutes as Louis put more distance between them, then turned and walked their horses back in the direction from which they had come.

Louis, too, slowed to a stop, and when he was certain the chase was done, slid down from his horse, flexed his tired muscles and let the animal rest. The day was getting late and so Louis walked the horse to a nearby patch of woods in which he hid himself and the animal, and soon both were in deep sleep.

The sun was just coming up the next morning when Louis stirred himself. He was ravenously hungry and had nothing to eat. He needed to get to Dubh-linn, he knew, because that was the only place he had any hope of finding a ship to bring him back to his native Frankia and the revenge he hoped to visit on his treacherous brother. But he had only a vague idea of where Dubh-linn was, and now there was a river blocking that path.

Louis saddled his horse, climbed wearily into the saddle, rode off with the river on his right hand. His circumstances were not good, but they were not desperate, either. He had a horse. He had a sword, shield and knife. He had considerable skills when it came to combat of all kinds, honed by years of fighting off the heathen threat to his native country. He had a small casket of silver, more than enough to buy him what he needed: food, shelter, passage to Frankia.

Those things were much to his advantage, but they would not get him to Dubh-linn, and it seemed nothing else would either. He followed the river for the rest of that day and much of the next and found no way to cross. He came across the occasional small, miserable farm, its buildings enclosed by circular earthen walls, and he was able to buy food and drink from the wary farmer. He found a man who could tell him where he might ford the river, but had not the slightest idea of where Dubh-linn would be found. The days turned to a week, and then another.

Louis found a small monastery and was able to parlay his connection to Glendalough and a quantity of silver into shelter and food and a monk's robe, which he thought might do him some good. Exhausted, half-starved, Louis spent several weeks at the monastery, recovering. When he was finally ready to leave, the brothers gave him directions to Dubh-linn, but they did not sound overly confident and in the end they proved to be entirely wrong.

On the road Louis wore his monk's robe, incongruous as it was to see a monk mounted on a warrior's horse. He met bandits and he ran from some and killed others. He met traveling merchants who were better able to give directions. He met bands of men-at-arms moving across the country, and he avoided them when he could, and when he couldn't he gave them a false name and a story he had concocted during his long hours on the road, but no one seemed to much care.

Finally, after weeks of miserable travel, he was fairly confident that he was on the road for Dubh-linn and that he was not too terribly far. And then these three piles of horse dung had sprung on him, intent on taking everything and leaving his bloodied corpse in the woods. It was their bad luck that all the misery and uncertainty and frustration of the past month had stripped him of any sense of mercy he might have once possessed.

He stood there and let his breathing come back to normal. He looked up and down the road. No one coming. He considered just leaving the dead men there. It would be obvious to anyone passing by what had happened. The dead men's clothes and their crude weapons marked them as bandits, and their condition marked them as idiots who had attacked the wrong man.

But Louis knew that leaving them was not a good idea. If they were local men they might have relatives who could decide that, vermin though they might be, their deaths had to be avenged. He sighed, wiped the blade of his sword on the nearest man's tunic, then slid the blade back into the sheath strapped to his back under his monk's robe.

Louis ran his eyes over the last man he had killed, poked at him with his toe, but he did not seem to have anything on him worth the taking, so Louis grabbed his foot and dragged him through the mud and far enough into the woods that he would not be easily found. He was glad at least that he had not entirely severed the man's head, which spared him the effort of making two trips or having to touch the dead man's hair.

He did the same with the second corpse. The first man he had killed, the leader, apparently, had a filthy leather purse tied to his belt. Louis cut it free, looking inside. A few silver coins and a few copper, a tiny hunk of gold, less than the size of a pea. But it was something. And Louis liked the idea of being set on by bandits and coming away with a profit.

He dragged this last dead man off the road and dumped him next to the others. He mounted his horse and continued on as before, but now in a world that had three less murdering bastards in it, and he was glad of that. The rain had stopped and he was reasonably certain that Dubh-linn lay ahead of him, and in Dubh-linn a ship to Frankia.

He smiled. And he realized it had been a long time since he had smiled, or since he had felt the inclination to do so.

Chapter Four

Most blest is he who lives free and bold and nurses never a grief,
for the fearful man is dismayed by aught, and the mean one mourns over
giving.

Hávamál

Two mornings after the pig trial, Thorgrim woke to find the sun was
still down but his mood still high in the sky. He felt hope,
enthusiasm, feelings that had become strangers to him. But, as with
any stranger, he looked on them with caution.

Over the course of a long and often brutal life he had suffered
many disappointments and hardships. Since coming to this accursed
Ireland, a country from which he seemed unable to escape, those
misfortunes had increased threefold. For that reason, when he felt
any sort of hope kindle in his breast, he treated it like a spark that
might ignite into a great fire and consume him.

Still in his bed, he moved his head slightly so his ear was directed
at the thatch roof above. He lay perfectly still. He listened. His
bedchamber was divided off from the larger room by a wattle wall,
one of the luxuries afforded the lord of Vík-ló, and he could hear
snoring from the other side. He could hear mice moving around in
the bundles of dry reeds. He could hear nothing else.

And that was the important thing. He could not hear the drum of
rain on the thatch, that constant undercurrent of sound, the liquid
noise of water running off the edge of the roof and splashing in the
great puddles that stood like moats around the hall. Nothing. It was
not raining. Two days since the rain had stopped and it had not set in
again. Thorgrim felt the tight grip he kept on his optimism loosen
just a little.

He flexed his right leg. He had broken that leg many years before,
just below the knee, and now when it was raining, or when it soon

29

would be raining, it ached. That meant for the past few years, since his arrival in Ireland, his leg had been in near constant pain. But now it was as if the break had never happened.

Next to him, under the covers, Failend stirred a bit, made a sleepy sound and pressed herself closer to him. Neither of them was wearing anything save for the heavy fur that covered them, and he reveled in the feel of Failend's small, warm body. He rolled half on his side and wrapped an arm around her slim waist and pulled her closer and she made another sound, more awake this time, like a conscious approval of his touch.

Failend... Thorgrim mused. He was still not entirely sure what to make of her. He and his men, the few left after the raid on Glendalough, had captured her and the Frank, Louis, as they were all trying to make their escape. Failend and Louis had both been armed, both dressed in mail, a rarity for a woman, in Thorgrim's experience. He had seen a few Norse women go that way. He had never seen an Irishwoman so arrayed.

Thorgrim had assumed Louis was her lover. They seemed to be running from some situation, making their escape together when they had blundered into the Northmen's arms.

Once they were with Thorgrim's band, Louis had behaved the way one would expect a captive to behave; just cooperative enough to avoid having his throat cut, always on the lookout for a means to escape.

And escape he had. Just as Thorgrim and a few others were leading their enemies into a carefully set trap, Louis had leapt to his feet and run toward the Irish horsemen, warning them, escaping with them. In the end the fighting had gone Thorgrim's way, as the gods wished it, but Louis's actions might well have killed them all.

For that, Thorgrim would kill Louis if ever he saw him again. But he doubted he ever would.

Failend was something different.

Failend the shrew...

That was how he thought of her. Not shrew in the sense of a nagging and unbearable woman, which she most certainly was not. But shrew in the sense of something tiny, seemingly harmless, cute even, but with more strength and fight in her than a creature many times bigger.

The longer she stayed in the presence of the Northmen, the more she seemed to prefer their lives to the one she had escaped. She had shown an interest in learning the use of a sword, and because she showed nothing but cooperation with her captors, Thorgrim allowed her to have one. He even found her a smaller seax, a weapon more her size, and had shown her some techniques of blade-work.

After that she had taken every opportunity to practice, and to spar with any who would spar with her. She had learned fast, grown in skill, and even taken her place in a few scrapes they had had with the Irish who were trying to run them to ground.

Slowly Failend's Irish clothing was exchanged for clothes in the Norse fashion—leggings and tunic—men's clothing, not women's. When the need arose, she wore the mail she had been wearing when she was taken. She picked up a few words of the Norse tongue, and then more and more until she could speak the language, after a fashion. Right there, like a caterpillar to a butterfly in Thorgrim's way of thinking, Failend was turning from an Irishwoman of means into one of the hated fin gall.

It was after Louis had made his escape that Failend began sleeping by his side. That was the extent of it. They had done no more than sleep. Thorgrim was not sure why she chose to do that. Protection, perhaps. She knew by then that Thorgrim would not harm her, but she might not have been as certain about the other half-wild men in the Norsemen's company. Whatever the reason, Thorgrim had welcomed her, enjoyed the feel of her next to him. He had not asked her about it. Language was still a barrier, and anyway, Thorgrim was not the sort who was much given to talk.

Now Failend rolled over and cocked her leg over Thorgrim's thighs and reached up and ran a small, delicate hand through the thick, dark hair on his chest. She made another soft sound and pushed herself up so her face was closer to his, her cheek resting on his upper arm. Thorgrim ran his fingers along her spine, up and down, and over her bottom and the soft sounds she was making grew a bit louder, a bit more empathic.

This new twist to their relationship had occurred after their return to Vík-ló. Thorgrim had been wounded in the legs in his final, bloody duel with Ottar, and Failend had helped nurse him. She knew little about healing, that was clear, despite her having first claimed otherwise. But she learned from the Irishwoman Cara, who remained in Vík-ló to tend to Thorgrim, and soon she was able to make up and apply a poultice with as much skill as the older woman.

Failend continued to share Thorgrim's bed. Then one night, in the dim light of the moon creeping in around the wooden shutters, Thorgrim watched her pull her tunic up over her head and stand there, naked, her body thin and pale and strong. She slipped under the fur and eased herself up to his side. Thorgrim wore no clothes; they irritated his wounds; and Failend's warm body felt good pressed against his. She made him feel whole again. She made him feel young.

"Lie still, lie still," she whispered, her command of his language much improved, even though her accent sounded odd and foreign to him. Thorgrim lay on his back and Failend ran her hands and her lips over him, over his face and his neck and the rest of him. Thorgrim closed his eyes and allowed himself to get swept up in the pleasure of it all.

Then Failend eased herself carefully on top of him, eased him carefully inside her, and with her strong legs moved against him. Her hands were on his chest, her thick black hair hanging down so it nearly brushed against him until she swung it back over her shoulder, her head rocked back, her lips opened as the sensations overwhelmed her.

And so once again things between them shifted, and after that, when she came to his bed, sometimes they slept and sometimes they took pleasure in one another and then slept. And sometimes they slept and then took pleasure in one another. And that morning, when Thorgrim woke to the absence of rain and the feeling of renewal in his heart, was apparently going to be one of those times.

Failend pushed herself up so she was half lying on top of Thorgrim and began to explore him with her hands and her lips. But Thorgrim was no longer suffering from his wounds, and no longer weak from the battering he had taken during their foray to Glendalough. He rolled farther toward her, pushed her down onto her back, saw the flash of her smile in the dim light of the predawn. He leaned down and kissed her and felt her arms wrap around his neck and pull him tighter toward her as she kissed him back, her lips and tongue eager.

He did not stop pressing his lips to hers as he eased himself on top of her, taking his weight on his elbows. Failend felt small and delicate beneath him, though he knew by now she was not nearly as delicate as she might appear. He felt her legs wrap around him, her heels press into his back. He leaned down and buried his face in her hair and ran his lips along her neck and the two of them lost themselves in one another.

The morning sun was creeping in around the edge of the shutters by the time they were done and their breathing had returned to normal. Thorgrim was on his back, Failend splayed across his chest. He was running his hands through her hair. His eyes were open and looking up at the thatch overhead, slowly revealing itself in the morning light.

"You want to get out of bed and leave me," Failend said, softly. A statement, not a question.

Thorgrim smiled. "I want to get out of bed," he replied truthfully. It was the first morning in a long stretch of mornings he could recall being eager to start his day. "But I don't want to leave you."

"Hmm," Failend said. "Very well, I'll let you rise in a minute, but first you must answer a question."

"A fair price," Thorgrim said.

"You're going to sea," she said. "You won't say where you're going."

"Yes," Thorgrim said. That was true. He wouldn't say because he didn't know.

He was not sure where this was leading, but he had some ideas. Going to sea meant raiding, and that meant attacking Failend's countrymen. He could see how that notion might not sit well with her, all the violence that the Irish visited on their fellow Irish notwithstanding. "We're bound off as soon as we can. We're not farmers, you know. At least here, in Ireland, we are not farmers."

"I know," Failend said. "I know what you are. You're men and you're not so much different from Irish men. Or most other men, I expect."

"I expect you're right," Thorgrim said. He had seen a lot in his restless life, and one of the things he had learned was that men were indeed men the world over. And that could be a good thing and it could be bad.

"What I want to know is this," Failed said. She pushed herself up onto her elbows so she could look him in the eyes. "Will you leave me behind, or will you take me with you?"

Thorgrim pressed his lips together. He'd not considered this question before. In the sudden springtime of happiness he had experienced with the decision to sail, he had not thought about whether or not Failend would have a place aboard his longship. And when he considered it now he realized that the question had not arisen because there had never been a question in his mind.

"Of course I won't leave you," he said, reaching out and brushing the hair away from her face. "You're with me now. With us. Of course you'll sail on my ship. If you want to."

Failend smiled, leaned down and kissed his chest, then looked up again. "Good," she said.

"You want to sail with us?" Thorgrim asked. He was starting to sense that she was the most unusual woman he had ever known, and he was curious about what might be going on in her head.

"Yes," she said. "You...and your people...are all I have left."

Thorgrim nodded, stroked her hair. "They're your people now. You've proved yourself in a hundred ways and you're always welcome with us," he said.

Failend smiled again. "Good," she said. She threw the bear skin off of the two of them and the rush of cool morning air nearly made Thorgrim gasp. Failend leapt to her feet, her long hair spilling around her. "I have arrows to make," she said.

The sun was well above the horizon by the time Thorgrim had washed, dressed, and had his breakfast of cold beef and porridge. He and Harald stepped out of the hall and into the welcome, welcome sunshine of the summer morning.

The longphort of Vík-ló lay before them, the activity familiar and welcome. The small houses and workshops that made up most of the structures in Vík-ló were crowded all along the plank road, and from each of those places people were carrying blankets and furs and cloaks and whatever they had that had grown heavy and moist in the incessant damp. They were spreading them out on low wattle fences and on the roofs of sheds, wherever they could hope to find sunshine that would dry them out. Doors were flung open, shutters on windows swung wide to let the warm, dry air move as unimpeded as possible through the dank interiors.

Thorgrim breathed deep. He turned and looked at Harald and their eyes met and they both smiled, father and son. A good day. They were both ready to go.

Together they made their way down the plank road toward the river and the makeshift boatyard that had sprung up there. A thick plume of smoke was roiling up from the shop of Mar, the blacksmith, which was yet another good sign. The warriors of Vík-ló, eager as Thorgrim and Harald to get to sea, had wasted no time in ordering up spearheads and arrowheads and axes and even swords. Mar would be pounding out the half-round bosses that made the center part of wooden shields and the iron bands that ran around the edges. He would be making rivets for the longships and manacles for captives. To Thorgrim and the rest of the Northmen, the clanging of the blacksmith's hammer was like a call to war.

They continued on toward the water and they could see the blacksmith's shop was not the only one that had fires burning with enthusiasm that morning. The baker's ovens were being heated as the baker prepared the coarse rye bread that would be loaded into linen bags to be brought aboard the ships. The butcher had fires stoked under his massive iron pots in which he would scald the pigs he was about to butcher and salt for the voyage.

They crested the rise of ground near the end of the plank road and then, before them, lay the shipyard, busy as an ant hill, the river on which Vík-ló was situated, and beyond that the blue ocean. Thorgrim breathed deep.

"They've finally got the yard crossed on *Fox*," Harald said, nodding to the ship tied to the east side of the pier he and his men had built. Thorgrim looked in that direction. The crew of *Fox*, smallest of the four ships, had been having some difficulty with their rigging, but now it seemed they had straightened it out.

"Good," Thorgrim said. He breathed deep again. "A fine, fine morning Odin has blessed us with," he said.

"But a busy one," Harald said. "There's a great deal of work yet to be done."

Thorgrim looked over at his son, a few inches shorter than himself but broader. He took after his grandfather, Ornolf the Restless, in that way. Harald's eyes were moving from one gang of laboring men to the next, and Thorgrim could all but hear the thoughts in his head, thoughts of stowing supplies and seeing to spare oars and cordage and making sure that every man had the weapons he needed and his sea chest brought aboard and lashed in place.

*Relax...*Thorgrim thought. He wondered when his son had become so serious. Or when he himself had become less so. He wondered if all the food and ale and carnal satisfaction were making him soft.

If they are, then they will not continue to do so for long, he thought. Raiding, voyaging, those were rarely pleasant or comfortable. Salt pork and old bread to eat, spoiled ale to drink, the deck of a longship or a gravel beach for a bed, those would quickly harden any places that had grown soft. And Thorgrim was strangely eager for all that and more.

"Ah, Thorgrim!" Thorgrim and Harald looked to their left and saw Aghen the shipwright approaching, smile on his face. "I'm happy you layabeds could join us!"

Thorgrim smiled and embraced Aghen. The two men had become close the previous winter, working side by side to build two of the four longships now floating just off the sandy shore. Thorgrim had seen in Aghen a skilled craftsman who loved ships and shipbuilding as much as he did, and a man whose ideas on that subject matched Thorgrim's as much as two men could ever agree on such things. The ships they built, *Blood Hawk* and *Sea Hammer*, were two of the finest ships that Thorgrim had even seen.

Those two vessels, as well as the smaller *Dragon* and *Fox*, had sailed in the spring for the raid on Glendalough. After Ottar had betrayed Thorgrim and his men, and left them to be butchered, he had taken all the ships with him, save for *Sea Hammer*, which had been holed. They had sailed for Vík-ló, and there Thorgrim had found them after he had put his sword through Ottar.

Thorgrim had given Ottar's men the choice of remaining and swearing loyalty to him, or taking their ships and departing. Many had opted to stay, including Oddi, who was Aghen's assistant, and the other men who had been sent to hunt down the wolf that Ottar so feared. In all, more than one hundred of Ottar's former men remained in Vík-ló. Ottar, it seemed, was not very popular, even among his own people.

The rest were given leave to sail. There was some discussion of using one of the ships as a funeral pyre for Ottar, sending him off to Valhalla in proper fashion. But in truth, after Ottar's behavior in the final dual with Thorgrim, no one was sure if Valhalla was where he was bound, and no one cared enough about him to sacrifice a perfectly good ship. So instead they had burned him on shore and sailed off with all the ships that had formerly belonged to the man.

Sea Hammer alone of all the ships had not returned to Vík-ló. They had patched her and used her to escape down-river from Glendalough, but then their path had led in a different direction and they had hidden the ship as best they could and hoped she would be unmolested.

As soon as Thorgrim was able, he sent a band of twenty armed men, augmented by others from the gang of Irish bandits they had befriended, to retrieve her. They found her right where she had been secreted. And they found that some local Irish people had come upon her first. The Irish, however, did not know what to do with her, and the best they could think of was to break off some of her upper strakes to use as firewood. She had suffered no more harm than that, and soon *Sea Hammer* was reunited with the rest of the fleet and the damage done her put to rights.

"How goes it, Aghen?" Thorgrim asked.

"Let me show you," Aghen said and he led Thorgrim and Harald across the chip-strewn grass and the piles of drying lumber and the stacks of provisions waiting to take their place on board. They walked out along Harald's pier, as solid underfoot as the ground itself.

"*Fox* was not able to get their yard across because they were having all sorts of problems setting the shrouds up," Aghen explained as they walked. "I was hoping we might save the old shrouds, get some more use out of them, but there was no chance. They were near rotten. So we made up new and now all is well."

Thorgrim nodded. A half dozen men were aboard *Fox*, receiving weapons and spare lumber and cordage from the men on the pier and storing it away. *Good*, Thorgrim thought. Things were moving ahead.

Aghen turned in the other direction, toward *Blood Hawk* tied up on the west side of the pier. She, too, was taking on supplies, weapons, sea chests, all those things that a well-outfitted longship might carry off to sea. "We had some leaking down by the garboards, as you know," Aghen said. "But we had her up on the beach and really got at the seams and she seems to be tight now."

Thorgrim nodded again, but his chief concern was *Sea Hammer*, his own ship. And *Sea Hammer*, he knew, was in fine shape. Once she had returned to the longphort he and Aghen and a gang of skilled men had gone over her and repaired the damage done and set everything to rights. Now she waited only her turn to come alongside the pier and receive those things she would need.

Footsteps behind and the three men stepped aside as a half dozen men, stripped to the waist, came staggering down the dock bearing loads of provisions.

"So, Aghen," Thorgrim said, turning to the old shipwright. "Here's the question I've failed to ask. Will you sail with us?"

Aghen gave a smile, a sad sort of smile, and shook his head. "I'm not a young man anymore," he said.

"Neither am I," Thorgrim said, "but by Thor I tell you, this getting ready to sail, to see what lies beyond the bright line at the edge of the sea, it's making me feel like one again."

"I can see that," Aghen said, "and I am happy for you, my friend. But for me, my fate is to die in Vík-ló. I've known that for some time. And to hope that if a shipwright dies with an adz in his hand, Odin will welcome him into the corpse hall as if he had been a warrior wielding a sword."

Thorgrim smiled. "I have no doubt of it," he said. "Very well, I see your mind is made up. I won't try to change it. You stay here and keep watch on Vík-ló and get ready to repair the damage I always manage to do to my ships."

"I'll do that," Aghen said. "But I see you're bringing provisions and spare wood and cordage and such on board. That makes me think you're making ready for a long voyage."

"I don't know," Thorgrim said. "By the gods, I swear I do not. So I'm getting ready for whatever might happen."

Aghen nodded. "I also couldn't help but notice that you had your men load the plunder on board. All the hoard you had buried under the stack of drying lumber. All the silver and gold and jewels and such you and your men have managed to gather in your raiding."

"Ha!" Thorgrim said. "I've made and lost several fortunes since coming to Ireland. I hope to not lose it again."

"Of course," Aghen said. "But we both know your treasure is safer here than it is on board a ship. So the fact that you are taking it tells me something else, Thorgrim Night Wolf. It tells me you never intend to return to Vík-ló."

Chapter Five

What cause also moved them
From the countries of war?
To traverse the waves over the floods,
In what number of ships did they embark?

Historia Britonum of Nennius

Louis de Roumois had a choice to make, and so he stood by the side of the road in the growing twilight, stared off into the distance, and tried to make it.

Beside him, his horse nibbled at the grass, untroubled by the weight of the decision with which Louis wrestled. Ahead of him, two miles or so away, he could see the long earthen and palisade walls, the many plumes of smoke, the wide river like a band of black against the dark land that marked Ireland's great Norse longphort. Dubh-linn. He had made it at last. And now he was not sure what to do.

He turned to the horse, a good and faithful companion for these past weeks. "What say you?" he asked, but still the horse offered no opinion, just continued with its supper. Louis frowned and looked up at Dubh-linn again.

For several weeks of travel he had worn his monk's robe, and like the horse, it had served him well. In truth, the two things, a monk's simple clothing and a fine warrior's mount, made an odd combination. But there were any number of reasons why a monk might ride such a beast, and no one had shown much curiosity about it. But that might not be the case in Dubh-linn.

And that wasn't the biggest problem. Louis had managed to keep his sword secreted under the robe, strapped to his back, ready to go if he needed it. And he had needed it, a few times. Cutting down the three Irish bandits was just the last of those incidents. He had met another bandit the week earlier, but that one had had the sense to run at the first sight of the blade. And Louis, not yet entirely sick of his troubles, was willing to let the villain go.

There had been another incident when he had begged shelter from a farmer, a man he could see now had been too eager by far to offer help. The farmer had come in the night, knife in hand, when he thought the trusting monk with the fine horse was asleep. That had not ended well for the farmer. Not at all.

Keeping the sword hidden on the road was one thing, but he did not think he could continue to do so while walking around Dubh-linn. It was too obvious. But neither could he wear the monk's robe with a sword hanging at his side.

"So here's the question, horse," Louis spoke out loud again. "Is it safer for me to go about with a sword on my hip, or in the disguise of a monk?" And as soon as he put it in those terms, the answer was obvious, even without any prompting from the horse. Among the good Christian people of Ireland, a monk's robe generally offered a degree on protection. Among the heathens of Dubh-linn, it would offer none at all. Indeed, it might well invite attack.

"The sword it is," Louis said. Louis, a prince of Roumois, a trained warrior, could wear a sword well. And just as important, he had the air of one who knew how to use it, which he most certainly did, and that, more than a holy man's garb, would be most likely to keep him safe.

He tugged the robe off over his head and unstrapped the sword. He dug through the saddlebag and pulled out his crumpled, damp tunic. He considered wearing his mail shirt as well, but rejected the idea. That was too likely to draw attention, and attention was a thing he did not want. Get into Dubh-linn, find a ship bound for Frankia or some place near enough, secure passage and sail. That was what he wanted, and the quicker he could make it happen, the better.

Louis pulled the tunic on, strapped the sword around his waist, took up the horse's reins, and swung himself back up into the saddle. He nudged the reluctant beast's flanks and they headed off to cover the last few miles to the sprawling longphort.

The sun, blazing orange in the surprisingly clear sky, was hanging just above the mountains to the west when Louis crossed the bridge over the wide river and followed the well-worn road to the gates of the Norse settlement, planted there on the Irish shore. With the sun still up, the gates were still open. A few well-armed and apparently drunk Northmen were lolling around; guards, Louis assumed, but they did no more than glance up at him as he rode through the opening in the earthen walls and into the longphort itself.

From the vantage point of his horse's back, Louis looked out at the town in front of him. Born and raised in Frankia, and well-traveled, being a member of the nobility, Louis had seen a few cities, including Paris with its fine palaces and cathedrals. Dubh-linn, by comparison, was like some overgrown peasant village, like a weed of a town that had taken root and spread. There were squat homes and workshops belching smoke from the gable ends of their thatched roofs, muddy roads crisscrossing the space. There was one wide, planked road that ran downhill to the riverfront where a dozen or more ship lay beached or tied to piers built out from the land.

"Look at this, horse, will you?" Louis said. There were people and animals everywhere: horses and riders moving through the crowds, swine and cattle being driven here and there. The people crowding the streets were men, mostly. Northmen, well-armed as Northmen always were, dressed in tunics and leggings and cloaks, their hair and beards long, silver arm rings on thick upper arms. But there were women as well, and from their dress and the color of their skin and hair Louis guessed they were Irish women mostly. And that made sense. Easier to get women from the countryside thereabouts than to bring them all the way from the North countries.

*Dubh-linn...*Louis thought.

Ugly, mud and smoke filled, crowded and reeking, still it was impressive by Irish standards. In the year or more that Louis had been in that country he had never been in so big and busy a place. While there was no place in Ireland that Louis knew of that might be called a city, Dubh-linn was the closest thing he'd heard of or seen.

For a few minutes Louis remained atop his horse and took in the scene before him. Already much of the longphort was lost to him in the deepening shadows. Then with a sigh he slid off the horse and began to lead the beast along the wide plank road, searching the various buildings and yards as he did.

Down a muddy side road he saw what he was looking for, or hoped it was, anyway. A stable with a half dozen horses in crude stalls, an open thatched structure beside it, sheltering a great pile of hay. Louis turned off the plank road and made his way toward the stable, his soft leather shoes sinking deep in the mud and threatening to come right off his feet as he pulled them free.

He stopped beside the stable, looking around for whoever owned the place. He heard muttering from behind the pile of hay and a man with a massive red beard and nearly as massive arms and gut came ambling around. He looked at Louis and ran his eyes over Louis's horse, and Louis did not miss the look of appreciation that he gave the animal.

The man looked back at Louis and spoke in a rapid and guttural Norse that Louis did not understand in the least. It had occurred to him earlier that language might be a problem, but he had figured he would find some way around it when the time came. But now the time had come, and he was not sure what to do.

Louis opened his mouth to speak, but the bearded man seemed to have taken note of the uncertain look on Louis's face. He half turned and yelled something in his ugly language and a moment later a woman appeared. She was nearly as stout as the man, but she wore the brat and leine of an Irish woman.

"Is there something we can do for you, sir?" the woman asked in the speech of a native of that country.

"Yes," Louis said. He had arrived in Ireland knowing not one word of that language, but since no one else spoke Frankish he had been forced to learn it quickly. "I have a horse and saddle to sell, and I wondered if you might be interested in buying it."

The woman translated the words, and Louis watched the red-bearded man go through a wonderful series of facial contortions: excitement, and then forced restraint and then an utterly false look of skepticism as he looked over the horse's legs, flanks, teeth and saddle. He spoke at last, shaking his head.

"My husband says the horse has been ridden too hard and is near starved," the woman said, "and is quite old, too. He says he can give you five silver pieces, no more, for the horse and the saddle."

Louis almost laughed. But he did not care about fair payment for the beast, which, strictly speaking, he had stolen, so he nodded his head and thought, *I will make you one very happy thief, you whore's son.*

The man did indeed seem happy, and not a little surprised, when Louis agreed to his price with no argument. He went into his house by the stable to fetch the money and Louis took off the saddlebags and slung them over his shoulder. The red-bearded man returned and

Louis could see he was about to protest Louis's taking the bags, but he clearly thought better of it and instead handed the silver over.

Louis took the payment and tucked it into the purse hanging from his belt. The stable keeper was having trouble containing himself and clearly wanted Louis to move along before he realized his mistake in selling the horse so cheap, so Louis thanked him, thanked his wife, and trudged on down the muddy track to the plank road.

It was nearly full-on dark, but there were fires burning here and there along the road and many of the open doors in the buildings that lined the plank road were lit with fires in the hearths, providing just enough light to see, which was all the light Louis wanted. Find a ship, sail back to Frankia, and do so with no trouble of any sort; that was what he wanted, and the anonymity of the dark could only help.

Very well, a ship… he thought. There were ships to be found in Dubh-linn, he had seen them already, but he had no idea where they were going and to what end. He understood that the Northmen came to Ireland to raid, that many of those ships would be sailing off to plunder some hapless monastery. But he knew as well that merchant ships were now calling at the rapidly growing Dubh-linn, shipmasters realizing there was money to be made bringing goods from the east to Ireland and bringing Irish goods to the world beyond. And one of those mariners would no doubt be happy to exchange silver for passage.

He headed down the plank road, down the gentle sloping hill to the bank of the river. The ships and their tall masts were just visible in the fading light, and there was still a bustle of activity around them. Louis walked down along the shoreline, running his eyes over each of the vessels in turn, until at last he was forced to acknowledge he had no idea what he was looking at.

Louis had seen ships all his life, ships moving up and down the wide Seine River and tied to the docks at Rouen, in Roumois, where he had been born and raised. He had seen the fat merchant ships and the Frankish warships and the sleek, fast ships of the Northmen who came to raid. But they all looked the same to him, and he never gave them any thought. When it came to horses, Louis understood every nuance and consideration, but one ship was the same as another to him.

I will have to ask, he realized on his second pass by the idle vessels. Most of the men he could see by their appearance were

Northmen and he knew it would be pointless to speak to any of them because they were unlikely to speak Irish or Frankish. But as he stood searching among the men working aboard the ships, another came down the plank road pushing a barrow loaded with sheepskins, and he had the look of an Irishman. Like the shipmasters who brought their merchant vessels to Dubh-linn, many of the local people had figured out there was money to be made in trading with the heathens, hate them though they might.

"Excuse me, friend," Louis said, using his most welcoming voice and stepping up to the man. "Could I ask you a question?"

The man grunted and let the handles of the barrow go with evident relief. "Yes?" he asked.

"I am new to Dubh-linn. I'm from Frankia, and I'm looking for passage back," he said. "Are any of these ships bound off for Frankia, do you know?"

The man looked at Louis, looked at the ships on the riverfront, looked back at Louis. He nodded. "Most of those are longships, filled with the murdering bastards who'll be raiding the monasteries," the man said.

And stealing silver to pay you for the sheepskins? Louis thought, but he said nothing.

"But some, the squat ones there, those are merchants," the Irishman continued. "Most are bound for Wessex or Mercia. A few are bound for the eastern countries, or so I hear. A shipmaster named Brunhard. Frisian. He'd probably give you passage for silver. Don't think there's much he wouldn't do for silver."

This was exactly what Louis had hoped to hear. "Where would I find this Brunhard?" he asked. The Irishman turned and nodded up the hill toward a large building that rose above the others. It looked like a church in the way it dominated the other buildings, but Louis doubted very much that it was a church.

"The big hall there, that's where they usually are of an evening. Brunhard and all the seamen." The Irishman looked back at Louis and gave him a wicked grin. "Best of luck to you, dealing with that lot."

Louis thanked him and headed back up the plank road, back the way he had come. In the dark the hall seemed to glow from within and Louis imagined there was a great fire burning in the hearth. He had heard the din from the hall when he had first gone down to the waterfront, but now as he walked back that way it seemed much louder, the goings-on more raucous. But Louis was a soldier, and he was used to rough and bawdy scenes, and so he did not hesitate to push his way through the big oak door and into the Northmen's lair.

It was probably the biggest building in Dubh-linn, fifty feet long and thirty wide, the roof a good twenty feet overheard. As Louis had guessed there was a great fire blazing in the hearth on the floor and some creature—a sheep, he guessed—slowly turning on a spit over the flames.

There were a few heavy oak tables arrayed around the place, earthen cups and wooden platters scattered over their tops, big men with beards, tunics, arm rings, adorned with weapons, sitting on benches, drinking, shouting, singing, arguing. Louis was no stranger to such scenes, and if they had been Frankish warriors, and not the detested fin gall, he might have joined in with pleasure.

There were women as well, and Louis enjoyed women regardless of where they hailed from. In this case they seemed to be Irish, and most were scurrying around with more ale and mead and platters, attending the increasingly drunk men in the place. In other circumstances Louis might have sought out the company of one of them, but now he had more pressing concerns.

He grabbed one of the women by the arm as she hurried past, not roughly, just enough to get her attention. She turned and looked at him. Blue eyes, black hair. Very pretty.

"I am looking for a shipmaster named Brunhard," he said, speaking loud to be heard over the din.

The girl smiled, nodded her head. "There," she said, pointing across the hall. Louis looked in that direction. There was a cluster of men around one table, seated on benches, cups in hand. But one man was seated on the table itself, his feet on the bench, like some lord on a dais, and he was clearly the object of everyone's attention. He was talking loud and waving his hands as he told some animated tale.

Louis could see that the men who listened were grinning. From across the hall he could not hear the words, and he suspected the man was not speaking a language he knew, but he did not have to understand to see that his audience was very amused by the tale and were hanging on every word. Then the man on the table paused, and then he said one more thing and the listeners on the bench roared with laughter, one actually falling from the bench and spilling his ale on the dirt floor as he fell.

Just the sight of it made Louis smile as well. He turned to the girl. "The one on the table, that is Brunhard?"

"Yes," the girl said.

Louis crossed the hall, skirting the fire, enveloped by the smell of roasting meat, and approached Brunhard's table. Brunhard was drinking deep from a horn, parched no doubt by his performance. Even though he was sitting, Louis could tell he was not a tall man, but he was broad-shouldered, shaped like a small barrel. He had a thick beard, somewhere between yellow and brown in color, and it seemed like a solid thing, like it was carved from oak. He looked like a man who took great pleasure in life and found much that amused him.

Louis was still several paces away when Brunhard noticed him. He looked straight at Louis, and even across the distance Louis could see the amused twinkle in the man's eyes, the slight grin on his face, as if he already knew what Louis wanted, and intended to have some fun at the Frank's expense. He raised his horn and shouted something, but he spoke the Norse tongue and Louis did not understand.

Five feet away Louis stopped. By now all the big men on the bench, Brunhard's court, were looking at him. The Irishman down by the ships had told him Brunhard was Frisian, and Louis knew enough of the language of that country, a neighbor of Frankia, that he could make himself understood.

"You are Brunhard, the shipmaster?" Louis called out.

Brunhard's mouth formed a wry smile. His eyes never left Louis, but he said something in Norse and the men around him burst into laughter once again. Louis pressed his lips together. He had come hoping to get passage with this man, but now he wondered if he would end up killing him for his insults.

"Forgive me, friend, forgive me!" Brunhard shouted, raising his hand to Louis. There was something entirely disarming, embracing, in the way the man spoke, as if with one sentence he could prove to be your dearest friend, the sort who could joke at your expense and somehow still not give offense. "We don't see gentlemen as fine as you in here so often!"

Louis nodded. He was actually a much finer gentleman than any of them might have guessed from his dress and his sword, but that was not something he wished to make known. He was second son to the late Hincmar, the Count of Roumois. Raised in wealth that these sorry bastards could only dream about, betrayed by his brother who feared Louis would try and take his place as count after their father's death. Now bound back to Roumois to have his revenge.

"You do your friends here an injustice," Louis replied. "Sure they are fine gentlemen, one and all."

"Ha! You are quick of tongue, I can see that!" Brunhard said, all but shouting the words in his exuberance, and to be heard over the noise of the hall. "But see here," he continued. "You can speak the Frisian tongue, after a fashion, but you do not sound like a Frisian. You sound like a Frankish whoremonger."

"I am Frankish," Louis said with a shallow bow, "and my pastimes are my own affair." There was not much love between Franks and Frisians. Louis knew he had to tread carefully if he wished to get the passage he desired. "I am told you are the finest shipmaster in all of Frisia, and that I might look to you to buy passage back to my native land."

Brunhard laughed again, but there was no malice in it, just genuine amusement, as if he was enjoying their exchange. "You're a lying dog, I know it! None of the sheep biters in Dubh-linn would say that of me, though it happens to be the truth. Now, why would I help a Frankish dog like you?"

"Because I can pay you. There is no other reason," Louis said.

"Ha! You are right about that!" Brunhard roared. "I would do nothing for a Frank, save for silver. In truth, I would do nothing for any man unless he paid me. If you were a woman there might be room to negotiate, but you are not, so it must be silver. Now...what is your name?"

"Louis."

"Now, Louis the Frank," Brunhard said, "I will agree to take twenty pieces of silver and in exchange I will bring you to Frisia, where I am bound, and from there you may make your own way home. Is that agreed?"

"Yes, that is agreed," Louis said.

"Good!" Brunhard roared, and Louis wondered if the man ever spoke at any volume below a shout. "Now, Louis the Frank, you will buy me and my friends here more ale, as a gesture of your good will!"

Brunhard was smiling as he said it, but his eyes met Louis's and Louis could see there was more than bonhomie behind the words. Here was a test, Brunhard probing to see how far Louis might be pushed. Louis had known plenty like Brunhard. Wolves. Show fear and they tear you apart.

"No," Louis said. He rested his hand on the hilt of his sword. "I pay for passage, not ale."

"What?" Brunhard said, his voice thick with mock outrage. "You are so cheap you won't buy ale for your friends?"

"I am happy to buy ale for my friends," Louis said, his voice even and considerably less loud than Brunhard's. "But I see no friends here, just a fat Frisian whore's son."

The Frisian nodded and he held Louis's eyes and the two of them stared at one another as the rest waited for the reaction, whatever it might be. And when it came, Louis was not too terribly surprised.

Brunhard laughed.

"Well said, you Frankish swine!" he said. "You buy your ale and I'll buy my ale, and when you give me the silver for your passage I'll buy more ale still! You there!" Brunhard called to one of the serving girls. "Ale for the Frank here! Come, drink with us, Louis, and we will drink to a swift and profitable voyage."

Louis nodded and dropped his hand from the hilt of his sword. He cared not in the least for Brunhard's profits, but a swift voyage was something to which he would gladly raise a cup.

Chapter Six

I have travelled on the sea-god's steed
a long and turbulent wave-path...
Egil's Saga

*Dubh-linn...*Thorgrim thought, looking out over the water between himself and the distant shoreline, the flashes of white on the ragged blue surface of the sea. *This sorry bastard must have sailed from Dubh-linn...*

The sun was just past the midday mark, the day all but cloudless. The distant sail, gray and bellied out from the yard, stood out sharp against the blue sky and deeper blue of the sea. The ship beneath plunged along, tossing up wake that seemed like tiny shards of silver at that distance, a mile or so to the northeast of *Sea Hammer.*

It was Starri Deathless who had seen the ship first, of course, Starri with the sharpest eyes among all of them. He had been at the masthead since the first glimmer of light had appeared in the east, not long after they had got underway. With the sun just above the horizon he could see nothing to the eastward, but the ship had appeared to the north, making its way east, toward the rising sun. She had been under oars, and only Starri could have seen so tiny and distant a shape.

The vessel was several miles off when Starri first called down from aloft. The four ships in Thorgrim's fleet were in a fairly tight group, also driving along under the power of their oars, the morning breeze having yet to fill in.

Sea Hammer had the lead, and astern of her, not more than half a cable away, was *Blood Hawk*, *Sea Hammer*'s near sister. *Blood Hawk*'s first master, Bersi Jorundarson, had been cut down at Glendalough. Now she was commanded by Godi Unundarson, who had been at Thorgrim's side for many fights now. Godi was quiet but he was smart and bold and loyal. The men respected him, and if there were any who did not, they knew to keep that to themselves.

Off *Blood Hawk*'s stern and a little behind was *Dragon*, a bit smaller than the two leading ships. Nearly all of *Dragon*'s former crew had also been killed at Glendalough. They had died fighting, and Thorgrim had no doubt they were now feasting in Odin's corpse hall.

Thorgrim had given command of that ship to a man named Fostolf, who had been one of Ottar's men but had chosen to stay in Vík-ló and swear loyalty to Thorgrim. They had been enemies once, his men and Ottar's, but now they would fight side by side, and old animosities had to be left in the past. Thorgrim figured the best way to show that he was sincere in that belief was to give one of Ottar's men command of a ship.

Aghen had told him that Fostolf was a good man, one who had come to despise Ottar once he saw what sort of a man Otter really was. Aghen thought Fostolf could be trusted with command of a ship, and, after coming to know the man, Thorgrim agreed. Fostolf was not a young man; Thorgrim guessed he had seen only ten fewer winters than he himself had. He did not seem a rash and heedless fool, and Thorgrim was so far pleased with the way he managed himself and his crew.

Last in line was *Fox*, the smallest of the longships. She was commanded by Thorodd Bollason who, like Godi, had been with Thorgrim for some time now, and had fought many battles at his side. Thorodd was younger than Godi, and more intemperate, more prone to being impetuous. That was not necessarily a bad thing; he was like a dog straining at the leash, which was fine as long as the leash held.

Still, before Glendalough, Thorgrim would not have trusted Thorodd with a command. After Glendalough, he had so few men left that he felt he had no choice.

He considered giving *Fox* to Harald. Harald was respected and he was a good seaman and was proving to be more clever than Thorgrim had ever given him credit for. But he was young, and to give command to one's own son when he was one of the youngest of all the ships' crews would not have sat well with the men. Being a leader did not mean being free to do whatever he wished. Ottar had found that out when his men had turned their backs on him.

Now Harald was coming aft, moving easily on the rolling deck. "See here, Father," he said, stepping up onto the small after deck where Thorgrim stood gripping the tiller. "*Dragon* has fallen off a bit and *Fox* is following her. You can see they're moving like their asses are on fire."

Thorgrim grunted and nodded to the tiller. Harald took hold of the thick oak bar so that Thorgrim could turn his attention to the other ships. He leaned over the larboard side, looked astern. And he saw Harald was right.

All of them, Thorgrim's four ships and this vessel they were chasing, had been driving under oars in the calm of the early morning, and all had set sail as soon as the breeze had filled in from the northeast. The breeze had continued to blow, and now the ships were plunging along, sails straining against the ropes that reinforced the wool cloth, bows rising and coming down in a welter of spray. It was a beautiful thing.

The chase had been going on for hours already. The ship, Thorgrim was certain, had come from Dubh-linn, one of the large and growing number of *knarrs*, wide, heavy-built merchant vessels that were calling on the longphort, bringing goods from the east and trading for leather and sheepskins and dried fish and wool cloth and any of the many things that Irish merchants wished to bring to the markets beyond the horizon. As such, it would make a fat prize.

Or so Thorgrim hoped. If the ship was from Wessex, or Frisia or Frankia, as so many of those merchantmen were, he would have no concerns about plundering it. If they were Northmen, that might be a different situation. But in any event, they had to catch the vessel first.

The merchantman had not seen Thorgrim's ships at first, since he did not have Starri Deathless and his hawk's sight, and because the rising sun was in his eyes. When he did spot them he turned north, moving as directly away from the four ships in pursuit as he could. It was too late for him to get back to Dubh-linn where he might hope to find some sanctuary among the other merchants; Thorgrim's ships would cut him off before he made it. So now his only choice was to remain on the lawless sea, run to the north and try and shake off the wolf pack on his heels.

"They're moving faster already," Thorgrim said, looking at *Dragon* and *Fox*. All of the vessels had the wind coming over their starboard bows, their yards hauled around as fore and aft as they could go, the windward clews hauled tight to the end of a massive pole called a *beitass*, thrust out over the starboard side. On such a point of sail the ships bucked and rolled and kicked like wild horses. But still the merchant ship kept out of their grasp.

He bent over, looked forward under the edge of *Sea Hammer*'s straining sail. The knarr's sails stood out against the green shore beyond it, the big headland that jutted out to the north of Dubh-linn and formed a wide bay into which ran the Liffey, with the longphort on its banks.

Thorgrim's ships had been following the merchantman's wake, skirting close to the headland north of Dubh-linn, keeping between their quarry and the land. They had stayed close together at first, but now the distance between them had opened up, and there was no way to communicate from one ship to the other. *Dragon* and *Fox* had turned to the west, toward the land, just a bit. By falling off, turning their bows a little further from the direction the wind was blowing, the ships were no longer sailing directly at the prize they were chasing, but they were moving faster through the water. It was a tradeoff, a gamble, but it might well give them the edge they would need to overtake the vessel they pursued.

"They'll pass by us, catch this bastard," Harald said and Thorgrim could hear disappointment in his son's voice, and the hint of a suggestion that *Sea Hammer* should also fall off. Even though they would all share any plunder equally, Harald did not like the idea that another ship would beat them to the prize.

"We'll see," Thorgrim said, straightening. He had been watching the situation carefully—not just the ships, as Harald had been, but the sea and the sky and the clouds, gauging the feel of the air, the strength and steadiness of the wind. This was a more complex game than Harald quite realized, more than the captains of *Dragon* or *Fox*, or even Godi aboard *Blood Hawk*, realized either.

It was two days now since they had sailed from Vík-ló. When all was at last ready, when all repairs had been made, the ships loaded with their gear and provisions, weapons stored aboard, rigging set taut, figureheads set in place, they had feasted.

In obedience to Thorgrim's command, Gellir and Ulf had each brought a pig, both of which were slaughtered at a place down by the water, and Thorgrim used their blood to bless the ships and to bring good luck on the voyage. Then they roasted the pigs and two sheep as well. They broke open barrels of mead and ale; they had bread and honey and whatever greens could be gathered. They sang songs and those with the talent to play the skald recited poetry. Among those was Thorgrim Night Wolf, who was a good skald, though few knew it, since it was a talent he rarely displayed. They feasted late into the night and all of Vík-ló took part and they imagined it was just how Valhalla would be.

The next morning they were underway. They had no destination in mind; Thorgrim meant to sail wherever the gods made clear they should sail. He had hoped that would be south, that they might run along the shore and then, if the gods willed it, cross the sea to Wales, or Wessex, and then around and back to Norway.

But it was not what the gods had planned. The four ships rowed out of the mouth of the river that made the harbor at Vík-ló, and soon the wind filled in from the south and no one much felt like rowing against it, and since they were determined to go where the gods blew them they raised their sails and stood north, skirting a coast that Thorgrim had come to know well.

As they left Vík-ló astern, Thorgrim stood on the small afterdeck, Harald at his side, and watched the mouth of the river and the familiar headland receding in the distance. A few columns of smoke could be seen rising up from the shore, visible long after the earthen walls surrounding the longphort had disappeared from sight.

"Mar is hard at work, looks like," Harald mused. There was an almost wistful quality to the young man's voice, and Thorgrim knew why. He felt it himself, and for a moment he did not dare to speak. They had been through brutal combat in that place, they had seen good friends die so that they could retain possession of Vík-ló. They had fought their way back there after the slaughter at Glendalough, and as they filed through the big gate in the earthen wall they felt the relief that comes with being home.

But Vík-ló was Irish land; it was not their home. Growing fat and complacent in such a place, ignoring the call of the sea and the lure of plunder and places unseen, that was not what had brought them all those sea-miles from the northern country. It was time to go.

Thorgrim had not even thought about it in any meaningful way when he had ordered the treasure they had accumulated stowed aboard for the voyage. It was only when Aghen made mention of it, what it implied, that they elected to take all their wealth with them, that Thorgrim understood his own truth: he was not going back.

And so they ran north in a wind that slowly veered to the west, pushing them farther and farther offshore, until at last the day grew late and the coast more distant. Then Thorgrim ordered the ships to come around on a starboard tack and they stood in toward the shore because Thorgrim knew from his several voyages up and down that coast, from Dubh-linn to the places to the south, that there was a good beach on which to ground the vessels for the night.

The sun was nearing the distant mountains when the four ships ran their bows up into the shingle and the men hopped down into the surf and pulled them further up and ran lines ashore to secure them. They built a fire. They broke out the ale and mead and roasted some of the fresh meat they had and they had another feast to celebrate their having freed themselves from the weight of the land.

They were underway again the following day, moving under oars when Starri spotted the merchantman. They began the chase, and continued on under sail once the wind had filled in. And now they were north of Dubh-linn and the mouth of the Liffey and they were chasing still.

Thorgrim looked forward, past the bow. The merchant ship and the headland were just in sight around the edge of the sail, and *Sea Hammer*'s bow seemed to be swinging a bit to larboard. Thorgrim smiled. Harald, still at the tiller, was falling off, turning the ship a bit, just as *Fox* and *Dragon* were doing, hoping to keep ahead of them, not daring to broach the issue with his father, hoping the old man was too addled to notice.

Thorgrim turned to Harald. "I think we'll tack," he said. It was the last thing Harald expected and probably the last thing he wished to do. By tacking the ship, turning the bow through the wind, they would be sailing almost due east, away from the land and, more importantly, away from the ship they were chasing. Thorgrim could see the dismay on Harald's face and he almost laughed.

"Tack?" Harald said.

"Yes," Thorgrim said. Harald nodded. He was too disciplined to protest. Thorgrim stepped up to the edge of the afterdeck. "You men, get ready to tack!" he shouted.

The order was as unexpected to them as it was to Harald, but like Harald, they knew better than to argue. Instead they moved quickly to their places: some men to the braces, some to the sheets, some to shift the heavy beitass from the starboard side to the larboard.

"Put your helm alee!" Thorgrim called and he heard the creak of the steerboard as Harald pulled the tiller back. *Sea Hammer* began to turn up into the wind, the headland on the horizon beyond sweeping past. Forward the men watched the edge of the sail for the moment it would start to shake with the wind coming down either side of the cloth. Everyone was alert, but no one moved. The ship was all readiness and potential.

Sea Hammer was a nimble ship, she responded well to the steer board's bite in the water, and she spun quickly up into the wind. The leading edge of the sail began to quiver and then the entire sail, so solid-looking with the wind filling it, began to ripple and twist, and then men on the deck moved at once, like a flock of birds all suddenly lifting from a field.

The tack and the clew, the lines holding the lower corners of the sail, were cast off as the ship's momentum carried her around through the wind, and the sound of water rushing by the hull was replaced with the crack of the oiled wool cloth as the sail snapped and flogged. The beitass, like a smooth log twenty feet long and ten inches thick, was lashed to the starboard sheer strake, but now a gang of men cast it off and hefted it over to the larboard side, running the larboard tack through the notch in its end.

Sea Hammer continued to turn, and now the wind came around the front of the sail, pressing it back against the mast, striking it on the wrong side, but helping push the ship around. Hands stood at the braces, ready to haul the yard around to get the wind on the proper side of the single square sail.

Thorgrim felt the breeze on his cheek, ran his eyes over the sail. *Sea Hammer* had lost nearly all of her forward momentum, the wind both aiding the ship in the turn and killing her headway. The trick was to get through the wind while losing as little speed and distance as possible.

"Steady now," Thorgrim called to Harald and Harald pushed the tiller forward. "Haul the braces!" Thorgrim shouted so his voice would carry to the men forward, and with a collective grunt they leaned into the leeward brace. Overhead the long tapered yard began to swing around through nearly one hundred and eighty degrees. On the starboard side, now the leeward side, men hauled the sheet aft. Forward, to larboard, the corner of the sail was hauled foot by foot down to the end of the beitass.

"That's well! That's well!" Thorgrim called. And it was. For men who had not been to sea in some time, who had been living and fighting ashore for the better part of a year and had not voyaged much beyond Vík-ló, their seamanship was still passably good.

Then Thorgrim heard a voice, a small voice, to larboard. "What happened? Why is the ship leaning the other way now?"

He looked down. Failend had come staggering aft. She was wearing a tunic and leggings, a belt around her waist. Her skin was pale, paler than usual, with perhaps a tinge of green. Her hair had been tied back with a leather cord but some had escaped and Thorgrim could see what he guessed were flecks of vomit in it. She had spent the past few hours either heaving over the leeward rail or getting ready to do so. Thorgrim had forgotten about her and he felt a momentary flash of guilt.

"We tacked," he said. "Turned the bow through the wind." He could see from her expression that none of that made sense, nor was she in any condition for a lesson in ship handling. "If you think you'll be sick again, you'll have to go to the other side of the ship."

Failend nodded. "Why did we...tack?" she asked.

"We're still chasing this poor bastard," Thorgrim said, nodding over the larboard side toward the distant merchantman. "This will help."

Failend looked in the direction Thorgrim had indicated. The other three longships were still directly astern of the merchantman, getting closer to shore all the time, but *Sea Hammer* seemed to be sailing almost directly away from their quarry. She looked forward. None of the men who were now sitting on their sea chests seemed very happy with the situation. She glanced over Thorgrim's shoulder and Thorgrim imagined that Harald did not look too happy, either.

Whatever was happening, Failend clearly did not have enough energy or interest to pursue the issue. She just nodded and then staggered down to the new leeward side, flopped down on an unoccupied sea chest and leaned on the sheer strake, ready to commit anything that might be left in her stomach to the deep.

They stood on, the distance between *Sea Hammer* and the other ships growing greater, the discontent growing deeper as Thorgrim's crew saw their chance of being the ones to capture the prize, and the honor that went with it, slipping away. The wind continued to veer to the east and *Dragon* and *Fox* and even *Blood Hawk* continued to draw closer to the merchantman, closer to the headland north of Dubh-linn. The grumbling aboard *Sea Hammer* continued.

"We'll tack again," Thorgrim announced to Harald who was still at the tiller. He called forward, sent the men to their stations. They moved more slowly, with less will. They were much farther from the knarr than the other three longships, thanks to Thorgrim's inexplicable change of course.

Sea Hammer came about on a starboard tack once more and Failend found herself back on the windward side, the side from which she had been told she should not vomit. She pushed herself off the sheer strake but she remained sitting on the sea chest, looking blankly around. There was a bit of color back in her cheeks, a touch of pink rather than green.

A sharp gust struck *Sea Hammer* and she heeled a bit harder to larboard, and then suddenly the wind backed to the north, a change that a landsman might not even notice but to a sailor was an abrupt and startling shift. Thorgrim heard Harald grunt in surprise and push the tiller to compensate. He watched the men forward as they registered this shift in wind direction. They looked to the west and Thorgrim could practically see them realize what this meant.

"Look here," Thorgrim heard one of his men call out. It was a man named Armod who had fought with them at Glendalough. Armod was pointing toward the other ships, now a good two miles away. "They'll never weather that headland!"

The knarr was close to the headland north of Dubh-linn, but the other three ships, *Blood Hawk*, *Fox*, and *Dragon*, were closer still. If the wind had stayed where it was they could all have sailed easily past the point of land. But now, with the abrupt shift, the three longships would not make it around the point. They would have to tack, stand farther out to sea, then tack again. The merchantman would leave them far astern by then, having effectively scraped them off on the shoreline to the west. He would have had nothing but open ocean in front of him. But he didn't. Because now, thanks to Thorgrim's decision to sail away from the land, *Sea Hammer* was there to stop him.

"Fall off a little, Harald, make right for him," Thorgrim said casually. He could see the men of *Sea Hammer* were in low and passionate conversation, and he knew they were debating whether he, Thorgrim, was a genius with regard to wind or just lucky.

It was both, but Thorgrim would not admit as much. He always kept an eye on the weather, noting signs and trends. As a seaman, even as a farmer, it was a crucial skill. In the years he had spent in Ireland he had seen that late day shift of wind frequently. It tended to happen when the sky was clear as it was that day and clouds were building to the west.

And so he had guessed the wind would give him the shift he wanted. But he was not sure, because things like wind shifts were never a certainty. They were the province of the gods, and there were none as capricious as the gods. So he kept his thoughts to himself and hoped and this time he would be rewarded.

They're pleased we've sailed from Vík-ló, Thorgrim thought. *The gods are happy we are doing what men should be doing.*

This was a sign, an omen, that he had done the right thing, and even as *Sea Hammer* swept down on the struggling merchant ship, he took pleasure in that knowledge. But not an excess of pleasure. He knew the gods might be happy now, but soon they would get bored, and they would begin to toy with him once more. Because they always did.

Chapter Seven

I will steer the reins well
Of the sea-king's horse...
Egil's Saga

A mile and a half to the west the merchantman tacked and Thorgrim thought, *This will be easier than I imagined.* And then he chastised himself for thinking such a thing and inviting the gods to make a fool of him.

Still, it was hard not to think it. The other three longships had tacked to get around the headland, and the merchant ship had tacked as well, the master apparently fearing he was getting too close to land. Perhaps there were rocks just below the surface that he knew about but Thorgrim did not. Whatever the reason, he was wasting a lot of time and sea room coming about, and that meant *Sea Hammer* would be on him all the quicker.

"Everyone, up on the weather side, come on," Thorgrim called down the length of the deck. Most of the men were already sitting up on the high side, sitting on sea chests or on the deck with their backs against the side of the ship, but others were sitting amidships. With the sail set and drawing well and the vessel holding steady on her course, there was not much for them to do. But they might get a bit more speed out of the ship if they put all the weight up to weather and flattened her out a bit. It was worth the effort, certainly.

Fore and aft men jumped to their feet and moved up the slanting deck to the starboard side. They moved with alacrity, now that they could see they would have the honor of taking the prize because they, collectively, the Sea Hammers, had made the right call when it came to the vagaries of the wind. That at least was how they would perceive it.

The merchantman tacked again and soon she was racing north once more, running in a direct line away from *Sea Hammer*, a race she would not win. *Sea Hammer* was a fast ship. She was freshly cleaned and fitted out and not loaded down with cargo, and so it was not long at all before she was only a few ship-lengths behind her quarry and quickly closing the distance. Even Thorgrim, whose eyes were not what they had once been, could see men moving about on her deck.

"I see eight men of her crew," Starri called down from aloft. There was a grudging quality to his voice; this was not his idea of action. Thorgrim might love the challenges of seamanship as much as he loved the challenges of battle, but Starri Deathless certainly did not feel the same.

There would be no fight here. These men on the tubby merchant ship would be fools to put up any resistance. The best they could hope for now would be to get away with their ship and their lives, but even those might be forfeit to the Northmen.

Yard by yard *Sea Hammer* continued to overhaul the merchant ship. Thorgrim could see the details of the vessel now, the steering board, the white foam rolling down the ship's side, the straining shrouds leading from the weather side to the masthead. This ongoing chase was pointless—the merchantman could not escape—and Thorgrim was suddenly tired of it, though he knew that he would have done the same thing had he been master of the knarr.

Thorgrim looked over at Failend, who was still sitting on the sea chest ten feet away. Her eyes were open and she seemed to be watching the distant ship and even taking some interest in the world outside her misery, and that he took to be a good thing.

"Failend," he called and she looked over at him. Thorgrim nodded toward the merchant ship, now little more than a hundred feet away. "Do you think you can stick them with an arrow, show them the folly of trying to flee?"

Failend looked back at the merchant ship, studied it a moment, looked back at Thorgrim and shrugged. But then she got to her feet and shuffled forward, stepping carefully on uncertain legs, to where she had stowed her bow and arrows in a place safe from the rain and spray.

It was some time after they had arrived in Vík-ló that Failend mentioned her proficiency as an archer. She had just made note of it in passing, some comment about how she had always loved to shoot, how she had spent hours at it as a young girl, how she seemed to have a natural, God-given talent for it. Thorgrim could not even recall how the subject had come up, but he had been impressed with the sincerity and enthusiasm of her words, the humility with which she spoke.

There were any number of bows in the longphort, but they were made for the warriors who sailed on the raiding voyages and Failend was too small to draw any of them. So Thorgrim asked Aghen to make a bow that was her size, and he did, out of seasoned yew, a beautiful example of the woodworker's craft.

Failend was delighted, wiping tears away when Thorgrim presented it to her. "Now you have no more excuses," he said to her. "Now you must show us if you are as skilled as you say."

A bale of straw was set on the ground one hundred feet away from where Failend stood with bow and a full quiver. Dozens had turned out to watch, having heard about her supposed prowess.

The first two arrows went wide of the mark, sailing off beyond the bale to stick like windblown saplings in the ground. The watchers were quiet, uncomfortably so. They liked Failend, and they certainly would not mock the woman who shared Thorgrim's bed, but her failure was on painful display.

Thorgrim watched Failend, watched her face. There was no suggestion of trouble, no indication she thought she had done poorly. Her expression was calm, thoughtful. She picked up another arrow, sighted down the length of the shaft, spun it in her fingers, then nocked it on the string. She raised the bow as she had the first two times, drew the arrow back, paused as she looked past the arrowhead to the bale beyond.

Then she loosed the arrow and dozens of heads swiveled and tracked its flight, straight and true and right into the middle of the bale. Thorgrim heard a murmur of approval. Failend's expression did not change. She picked up another arrow, examined it, nocked it, aimed and loosed. The arrow drove into the straw not even a hand's breadth from the first, so deep that just the feathers and the last five inches or so were jutting out.

At that Failend nodded. She picked up another arrow and sent that one into the narrow space between the first two. "There, I think I have the feel of the bow now," she said, as much to herself as to the gathered watchers. She put a fourth arrow into the bale.

There were a dozen arrows in her quiver and she put ten of them into the straw bale, grouped so close their ends could have been covered with a bowl. As the crowd began to drift away she retrieved the arrows and did it again.

After that, a day did not go by that Failend did not spend some time putting arrows through bales of straw. Rain, wind, none of that mattered. In fact, she took particular care to practice in all conditions. She moved the bales progressively farther away, arranged them so she had to shoot up at them and then so she had to shoot down. She shot from behind obstacles and by firelight and in every situation she could imagine. And she was as good as she had said. Better, in truth. Much better.

Now she came aft again, bow and arrows in hand, moving a little easier as she found her sea legs. "Do you want me to kill that fellow steering?" she asked as she drew an arrow from the quiver. No need to check how true it was; she had personally selected every arrow she had brought with her.

"No, not at first," Thorgrim said. "Just show him you can. Unless he's a complete madman that should be enough to get him to heave to."

Just as Thorgrim said the word "madman" he noticed Starri coming down the aftermost weather shroud, hand over hand, his feet dangling below him. He dropped to the deck, grabbed the hem of his tunic and pulled it over his head and tossed it aside. Around his neck he wore an arrowhead on a leather thong, nearly identical to the one on Failend's arrow except it was split nearly in two from the tip to notch. It had been shot at Thorgrim moments before a battle and had split itself on his sword. Starri had worn it since then, a sign, he was sure, that Thorgrim was blessed by the gods.

Thorgrim's glance moved up to Starri's face. He had that look in his eyes Thorgrim knew well, one that usually meant someone was about to die.

"I don't think we'll see any fight today," Thorgrim called out to him. Starri looked back and nodded, but Thorgrim was not certain he understood the words. He turned to Harald. "We'll have to keep some men by him, see he doesn't run mad over these poor bastards," Thorgrim said. Harald nodded.

Failend had her bow out of the sheepskin cover she kept it in, an arrow on the string. She had gone down to the leeward side, where the sheer strake swept up into the tall sternpost, making the side of the ship high enough for her to brace herself against it. From there the knarr was just visible around the edge of the sail.

She raised the bow and drew the string and stood as motionless as she could on the heaving vessel, her arm swaying up and down in counter to the pitching of the ship. The men were quiet, fore and aft, watching. There was only the sound of the wind in the rigging, the water on the hull.

And then the twang of the bowstring. The arrow sailed out over the water, making a bright streak in the air and coming to a stop as it drove itself into the sternpost of the merchant ship, a few feet above the helmsman's head. Cheers broke out along *Sea Hammer*'s deck.

Failend turned to Thorgrim. "This is something I've never done, shooting at something moving while standing on something moving. And with so much wind."

"Well, you did very well, for all that," Thorgrim said.

Failend frowned. "I was aiming for the…the pole…what do you call it?"

"The mast?"

"The mast."

Whatever she had been aiming at, the arrow sent an unmistakable message, and the master of the merchant ship did not mistake it. It was him, apparently, at the helm and Thorgrim saw him look up at the arrow, look back at *Sea Hammer* and then begin to wave his arms and shout to his diminutive crew. The men began to run in various directions, taking up the sheets that held the sail taut and casting off the halyard.

"Stand by to cast off and lower the yard away!" Thorgrim shouted to his own men, but by then they were already moving. He glanced astern. The three other ships in his fleet had tacked again and were struggling to get up with them, but they had half a mile of hard, upwind sailing before them. Thorgrim's men would have plundered this prize by the time they even arrived.

The knarr had turned up into the wind, her sail cast free and flogging and the yard came sliding down to mast. *Sea Hammer* surged up alongside, and her sail was cast off as well as the last of her momentum brought her up alongside the merchantman.

Starri Deathless leapt up on the sheer strake, a battle ax in his hand. He teetered there for a second, poised to leap, but before

Thorgrim could even give the order three men grabbed him and pulled him back, thrashing and screaming, to *Sea Hammer*'s deck.

Grappling hooks flew across the gap of water, grabbing hold of the tubby knarr, and hands aboard *Sea Hammer* hauled the two ships together. Thorgrim finished buckling on his sword belt and strode forward, stepped up on the sheer strake where Starri had been making ready to jump, waiting for the ships to rise together, and stepped over onto the deck of his prize. Behind him he heard others follow him over.

The merchantman's crew were on the far side of the deck, standing in a sullen and frightened knot. They had no way of knowing what these Northmen would do, and if they were Frisians or Franks, no way of communicating. There was nothing that Thorgrim could see that would indicate from where this ship hailed.

And then the master of the merchantman spoke, his voice loud and betraying no fear, the words, even the accent, perfectly familiar to Thorgrim. "Pray, lord," he called, "I beg you leave my men unharmed. I won't waste my breath giving you leave to take what you want, since you'll take it anyway, but there's no need to harm my men. They were willing to heave to and put up no fight."

They were willing to heave to when they saw Failend could pick them off like birds on a branch, Thorgrim thought, but he did not say the words. Rather, he crossed the deck, eyes on the master, stopped ten feet from where the man stood, broad chested and defiant, his black and gray beard jutting out from his face.

"You speak my language," Thorgrim said. "Where are you from?"

The master straightened a bit. "I am from Vik," the master said. "In my younger days I went a-viking with a jarl named Ornolf the Restless. If you're from that country you may know of him."

Thorgrim took another step forward, squinted at the man, tried to peer through the thick and graying beard, the weathered and lined face. Tried to see through twenty years of hard life to the man this man once had been. "Kalf Hrutsson?" he said.

The master leaned forward and squinted the way Thorgrim was squinting. Then he straightened and smiled and exclaimed, "Thorgrim Ulfsson?" Then Thorgrim smiled too and the two men stepped quickly toward one another and embraced.

"Thorgrim Night Wolf!" Kalf exclaimed again, slapping Thorgrim on the shoulder. "By the gods, I can hardly believe it! As I heard it you have been gone from East Agder for a long time. Gone a'viking again, with Ornolf, I heard."

Kalf, Thorgrim recalled, did not live in East Agder but had a farm several leagues from there.

"There are stories that you were all killed by the Irish," Kalf continued. "But you live!" He glanced at the men behind Thorgrim. "Is Jarl Ornolf here as well?"

"Ornolf was killed last year. Killed by Danes. As for me, I still live." Thorgrim turned and beckoned a confused-looking Harald over to him. "This is my son, Ornolf's grandson, Harald. Harald, this is Kalf Hrutsson. He and I used to go a'viking with your grandfather. Many, many years ago."

"Many years ago," Kalf echoed. "But you still have the strength for it, I see. Me, I am reduced to this." He gestured to his fat, wallowing merchant ship. "This life, master of knarr, it's as exciting as pushing a barrow of vegetables to the market. But it earns me a living and it frees me from my wife, for the summer anyway."

Thorgrim smiled. "I don't know that I have so much strength, Kalf Hrutsson," Thorgrim said. "I would like nothing better than to return to Vik, and my farm, but the gods have not willed it. How about you? Are you sailing for Vik now?"

"No," Kalf said. "The season is young. I'll sail to Hedeby and then maybe to Frankia if I hear word that the trading is good there. I'll return to Vik at *Haustmánudur*, when the harvest is coming in."

"I see," Thorgrim said, and he felt a jab of envy. The gods seemed pleased to let this man come and go as he wished, while he himself seemed unable to ever leave this accursed Ireland. He knew what Starri would say about that: the gods did not care about this fellow Kalf who would rather haul wool cloth and barrels of fish and whetstones to trade rather than go into battle as a real man should. And Thorgrim guessed he was right, hoped he was right, but it did not make him feel so much better.

And of course, he could not plunder Kalf's ship.

"You're a lucky man, Kalf Hrutsson," Thorgrim said. "There are longships full of warriors hungry for plunder all along this coast, and you meet up with an old shipmate and neighbor."

"I am lucky. That's why I'm still alive," Kalf said. "But you're lucky too, Night Wolf."

"And why is that?"

"Because of all the merchants in this sea, I am the only one who will tell you this news. In a day or two, three great merchant ships will sail from Dubh-linn for Frisia. Not pathetic tubs like this, but fine ships loaded with wealth worth the having. I don't know what the cargo will be. I've heard only rumors. But the master of these ships is a Frisian named Brunhard, and I know that wealth follows him wherever he sails."

Chapter Eight

This once I felt when I sat without
in the reeds, and looked for my love;
body and soul of me was that sweet maiden…
Odin's Love Quests

It had not rained in three days, the only good thing that had come to Conandil since the morning on the beach when Bressal mac Muirchertach had died. She opened her eyes in the pre-dawn light. The sky was dark, with just a hint of light in the east, and it was hard to tell if it was clear or covered with a uniform blanket of cloud.

She lay on the ground, wedged between two others, but the warmth of their bodies felt good, and the rough cloth pulled over her gave her some protection from the morning chill and she did not want to move. She did not want to rise and face whatever horror awaited. She wanted to stay right where she was, warm between the men on either side of her. She wanted to remain there, motionless, and let death come softly for her.

But it would not work that way, and she knew it. Death would not come, not yet.

She had tried chasing death, flinging herself at death, but it had done no good. She had raised her Lord Bressal's seax over her head and charged headlong at the Norse raiders as they leapt off their ships. She had shouted her battle cry, meant to warn Broccáin and the others of this new threat at their backs. She had meant to die and, if she was cunning and quick, to help a few of the heathens die as well. She did not intend to be taken as a slave. Not again.

But she could not make the heathens kill her, and that was something she had failed to understand. They had not come to kill. They had come to take slaves, maybe the most valuable plunder to be found in Ireland. Certainly the most abundant.

The Northmen had allied themselves with Eochu, Bressal's perennial enemy. That was why Eochu's men had taken pains to drive them down to the beach, where the Northmen could come from the sea. The partnership offered benefits to both parties. Eochu was free of Bressal, the Northmen gathered slaves, they all enriched themselves with silver. It had worked out very well.

None of this Conandil knew when she charged at the heathens, her every thought aimed at killing or being killed. She headed straight for the nearest of them, a man who had been watching her approach for a minute at least. He stood with a grin on his face and Conandil could only think of using the seax in her hand to cut that grin away, along with half the man's face. It would be easy. The heathen had his shield down at his side, the point of his sword resting on the sand.

Conandil was still shouting when she brought the seax back over her shoulder and slashed at that infuriating grin. She saw the polished blade come around and then the Northman's shield was up in front of him and the seax hit the wooden face with a deadened thump.

She felt the shudder of the blow ripple through her arm and then the shield dropped again and she saw the man's fist come swinging around wide. She was just starting to react when the fist connected with the side of her head and she lost focus and balance and any connection that she had to the world around her. She was aware of falling sideways but was unable to do anything to help herself. She was aware of coming to a jarring stop in the wet sand, and the feel of hands rolling her over and sharp cords cutting into her flesh as her wrists were bound tight.

What little she could see—the sand, the surf beyond, the back end of one of the longships—seemed to swim in her eyes, blurred and unreal. She felt herself pulled to her feet, spun around, and then the world turned upside down and she had a vague thought that this heathen had thrown her over his shoulder, and then it had all gone dark.

She was in the bottom of the longship when she woke, tossed on the rough deck like a sack of oats, her head pounding, wrists burning in pain. The steady rain had given way to a light mist, but Conandil was as soaked through as if she had been thrown into the sea.

The wooden boards beneath her were not steady, but seemed to be heaving and rolling. She thought that sensation was due to the blow she had taken to the side of her head, and it took her some time to connect the motion with the fact that she was on a ship. Which was apparently at sea.

With that realization she felt a wave a nausea overtake her. She was a captive again, a slave, a *thrall*. This was not supposed to happen. She was supposed to die fighting the heathens. But now she understood that for one such as herself, not a warrior but a woman, and a small one at that, she was not going to die if her enemy did not wish her too.

And then another thought came to her and it swept the nausea and the horror and the fear away. *Broccáin!* She tried to sit up and failed. Lying on the deck, wrists bound, it would take some maneuvering to shift her position.

She glanced around. She could see men she recognized lying tossed around like the dead after a battle. They were also bound, and most were bleeding. Conaill and Dímmai, two of her husband's house guard, were just feet away. Conaill's face was covered in blood, but he was moving, and moaning slightly.

They would not have taken dead men on the ship, Conandil thought.

She rolled onto her back, shuffled backward until she found something solid to push against. The side of the ship, she guessed. She wedged her shoulder against it and pushed herself into a sitting position and looked around.

The big square sail was set and the ship seemed to be moving fast. Conandil was too low to see over the side so she did not know if they were near land or miles out to sea, and at that moment she did not really care. Her eyes moved over the dozens of men who crowded the deck, lying on backs and sides and stomachs, some squirming, most lying still. Broccáin had been wearing a mail shirt when she had last seen him, one of the few Irish so equipped, but Conandil guessed the Northmen would have stripped him of that.

What was he wearing? She tried to picture him, standing on the earthen wall of the rath, before he donned his armor. *A red tunic, rust red...* She looked desperately around. Nothing. No one wearing a tunic such as that Broccáin had been wearing, not even any of the fifty or so Northmen who crowded around the windward side of the ship, laughing, joking, swilling ale.

Conandil leaned her head back and closed her eyes and felt herself being swept deeper and deeper into the nightmare. She would not live as a slave. She certainly would not live without Broccáin. She missed her chance to die in honorable and just battle. Could she kill herself? No, that was a mortal sin, unforgivable. Years of hell on earth were still better than an eternity in hell itself. What if she let herself starve? Was that the same as hanging herself or cutting her wrists?

Then she remembered something else that made her eyes open, made her sit up. There had been more than one ship. Two at least that she had seen and maybe more. She craned her neck to see over the edge of the ship she was on, and was rewarded with a glimpse of the top of a red and white sail not too far away. The second ship. If there were more she could not see them, but that did not mean they weren't there.

She leaned her head back once more and again closed her eyes. There was nothing she could do. She was floating, literally, figuratively. But at some point the ships would come ashore and then she would know if Broccáin was aboard one of them, and then she would figure out what next, and what next after that.

The wait was not as long as she feared it would be. She thought they might have been bound directly for the slave markets across the seas to the east, and she had no idea how long that voyage might last. But the sun was still up when the Northmen lowered the sail and tied it in place and pulled out their long oars and began to row. Soon Conandil could see land passing by over the side of the ship, green hills. Irish hills, she was certain.

She could smell wood smoke and food cooking and mud flats and animals. She could hear the sound of many, many voices, a cacophony of activity. And then the ship came to a stop and the Northmen came along the deck, dragging the aching, stiff, wounded prisoners to their feet. A man with a massive red beard grabbed Conandil and lifted her as if she weighed nothing at all and set her upright, and for the first time since coming to she was able to see beyond the side of the ship.

Dubh-linn… she thought. She was no stranger to the longphort. Her father was a merchant and she had accompanied him on his travels around that part of Ireland, and that had certainly included Dubh-linn because any Irish merchant who wished to gain wealth came to Dubh-linn. Dubh-linn was where the wealth was to be found.

She could recall seeing on those visits the Irish captives who were bound off to the slave markets. She had looked at them through the gaps in the thick boards of the enclosures in which they were held, remembered feeling sick about it. She remembered swearing she would make her father stop trading with the heathen swine. But she had not, and now she was receiving a just punishment for that cowardice.

Heathens? she thought bitterly. That bastard Eochu, a good Irishman, a *rí túaithe*, a Christian, supposedly, had played as big a part in this treachery as the heathens had.

She turned in a half circle. There were two other ships next to them which were also run up on the mud bank, the men aboard stowing their long oars and carrying ropes ashore. Those ships were crowded like the one she was aboard, packed with the captives from that short, brutal fight on the beach.

She ran her eyes desperately over the sullen, shuffling men, their torn and bloody clothing, blood-streaked faces and matted hair and beards. And there, at last, on the second ship, she saw him. Broccáin. His red tunic was torn in a great gap down the front, dried blood like brown dirt covered his scowling face. Like all of them, his hands were pinned behind his back, his wrists lashed tight. He seemed to limp a bit with the few steps she saw him take. But he was alive. And that meant there was hope.

A heavy board was run from the ship to the edge of the muddy bank. The captives were forced to clamber over it, no easy task with bound hands, and when any of them tumbled into the mud the heathens laughed and left them lying there until they were in danger of drowning, and only then, and reluctantly, they hauled them out and set them on the solid ground.

The captives were herded up a road made of wooden planks, with the heathens like drovers on all sides. One by one the lashings on their wrists were cut free and they were shoved into the very enclosure in which Conandil had seen those other captives, years before. Dozens and dozens of men and women, the people of the túaithe once ruled by Bressal mac Muirchertach, the survivors of a bloody and nameless fight on a shingle beach.

And finally the last of the Irish prisoners was inside and the heavy door was closed and barred. Through the gaps in the planks they could see the guards who walked the perimeter. Getting over the wooden walls would have been little problem, even high as they were, but anyone who tried would be dead before they touched the ground on the other side.

As soon as she was pushed into the pen, Conandil made her way to Broccáin and threw herself into his arms. She hugged him and to her immense relief he hugged her back. She had feared that her husband, having fallen so far in a single day, would be too despondent to care about her, or anything. But he pressed her tight, and buried his face in her hair, and again she felt just the smallest sliver of hope.

"Come, sit, let me look at your wounds," she said, pushing him over to the plank wall and making him sit with his back to the boards.

"It's nothing, no great injury," Broccáin said. "Most of us, we're not so badly wounded. Those who were, they killed on the beach. But the bastards saw to it we were not badly hurt." He paused. "The same way you take care not to harm any animal you intend to sell," he added, and that time he could not hide the bitterness and despair.

There were other women besides Conandil who had been swept up in the raid, but only half a dozen were in the enclosure, and Conandil did not like to think what had become of the others. Those who were there took it upon themselves to tend to the men's wounds, but the wounds were not so bad, mostly shallow sword cuts or blows to the head. Broccáin was right. The heathens and Eochu's men seemed to have taken pains to inflict little harm on the captives.

They spent the night in the enclosure, and the next day the rain stopped and the sun broke through and it brought the smallest amount of relief to the miserable captives. They remained there that day and the next and the next and still it did not rain, but their hunger and thirst grew harder to bear with the meager food and water that was provided. The Irishmen speculated about where they might be bound, what fate might befall them over the seas. But mostly they were quiet, each lost in his or her own private misery.

And then, after three days in the enclosure, they came for them. In the early morning, while Conandil lay between Broccáin and the man on her other side, wishing she could stay where she was and let death take her, the slavers came in death's stead. She heard the bar of the door open and then the door swung open and two men stood there.

One was short and broad, with a thick beard and wearing the clothing of a stranger from across the water. The other was broad as well, but tall, a massive man with huge hands, hands that Conandil noticed right away. Monstrous, obscene hands. That one, the big one, was dressed like an Irishman.

Conandil heard the short man speak to the big one, though he didn't so much speak as snap orders at him. Just a few words.

"Here, get these swine going," he said, but he was not speaking the Irish tongue.

Frisian, Conandil thought.

In the years she had accompanied her father she had heard many languages, and as it happened she had a certain gift for learning them, along with an insatiable curiosity. She was not fluent in any, save for Irish, but she had picked up enough of the Frisian tongue, and the Norse and the Frankish and the Angles, who spoke much like the Frisians, that she could converse tolerably well. It was a skill she kept to herself. She had learned, as a merchant's daughter and later as a thrall, that there was considerable advantage in understanding what others were saying when those others thought you did not.

Now the big Irishman was speaking, bellowing at the captives, his countrymen, who did not speak Frisian. "Up, up on your feet, you pigs. Up and don't think you'll try any tricks!"

Conandil looked past the two men filling the enclosure's entrance. There were at least a dozen more behind them, men with spears held ready. There would be no rushing the door. These men were not strangers to this business.

The captives stood slowly, sullenly. The big Irishman grabbed the man closest to him, jerked him toward the door and thrust him through. The shorter man with the beard had stepped out of the way, out of the pen, and now Conandil could see men waited with chains and manacles on the other side. An iron collar went around the neck of the first man, a chain threaded through the hasp to keep it shut. And then the next was pushed out of the door and a collar placed on him as well, the length of chain running between them.

One by one, quick and efficient, the men were pushed out of the enclosure and chained by the neck. A dozen were bound together then marched away, and then the slavers started in on the next dozen.

The next to go was a man standing five feet from where Conandil stood. He was one of the farmers, the fuidir who had come to the defense of the rath, and as he stepped up he growled to the big Irishman, "I know you, Áed, you traitorous bastard, and I'll have your heart."

Áed did not respond, at least not verbally. He took two steps toward the man and smashed his massive fist into his face, a move far quicker than Conandil would have guessed was possible for the great lumbering beast. The farmer's head snapped back, but before he could fall Áed had a fistful of his tunic. He jerked him back to his feet and drove a fist into his stomach, and as he doubled over, another to his face. This time the man went down, moaning and twisting on the ground. Áed turned to the two Frisians standing near the writhing man.

"Get that pile of shit up and get him out there," he said, the words like a snarl, and with not the least hesitation the two men lifted the prone man to his feet. His face was nearly covered in blood and his nose was hanging off at a strange angle. He gasped in pain as they half carried him through the door and supported him as the collar was secured around his neck.

Broccáin was next. Mouth set in a scowl, he stepped through the gate and paused as the collar was affixed. Conandil watched with revulsion and fear. She was terrified that Broccáin would do something rash, decide he would rather die than suffer the humiliation of being bound like an animal. And that would only lead to worse humiliation and pain, because they were not likely to kill him, just beat him until he could resist no more. Young, strong, Broccáin was too valuable to be thoughtlessly slaughtered.

It tore Conandil apart to see the collar go around her husband's neck, to see the agony in his face, but she was nonetheless relieved that he did not fight. As long as he lived, he could still escape.

She and the other women were the last to be brought out of the enclosure. They were not chained as the men had been, just forced at spear point to walk behind the shuffling lines. They made their way down the plank road they had come up a few days before. The sun was warm, the sky bright, the gentle wind sweeping the noxious smells of the longphort away. Some of the people crowding the narrow streets and trampled yards of the workshops along the way glanced up as the parade of frightened men and women marched past, but most did not. This was not, apparently, a particularly unique sight.

They came at last to the river's edge and the ships tied up there. Conandil knew nothing of ships. She had spent a total of six days on ships over the course of her life, and that had been as a captive of Northmen, this time and the last. She had been too miserable to take note of anything during those times.

Now she stood on the riverbank and looked at the various vessels tied up there, as well as those tied to a solid-built wooden wharf that jutted out into the stream. Some of the ships were big and some not so big. Some had high, sweeping prows on which could be mounted the frightening dragons' heads and other beasts with which the Northmen adorned their ships, though most did not have those carvings in place now. These, Conandil guessed, were the warships, the raiders who put out to sea and fell on hapless monasteries, plundering the wealth and enslaving the people.

The other ships had none of the swift, threatening quality of the longships. They were smaller, generally, and wider and deeper. The middle part of these ships was more open and Conandil guessed that was so cargo could be put down there. These would be the merchant ships, the traders, the ones who brought the goods of Ireland to the world, and brought the fine things of the world back. The Irish, not a seafaring people, were coming to appreciate the opportunities for long-distance trade that the far-ranging Northmen brought with them.

The lines of chained men were brought up short at the base of the wharf. There were four lines of a dozen men, and two more with six men each, more than sixty captives, including the women. Conandil did not think any of the ships she was looking at would be big enough to fit all those men aboard, certainly not for a voyage over the ocean. But she had no idea. The whole thing seemed so unreal, unfathomable and dreamlike.

The big Irishman, Áed, was speaking again. "Listen to me, you worthless creatures," he said. The chained men looked up and Áed stepped quick to the nearest one and hit him hard across the face with the back of his hand. "Don't look me in the eye, don't any of you miserable turds look me in the eye!" he shouted, and his voice had a hysterical tone to it. "You don't look any of us in the eye! You look down. That's what a slave does, he looks down, and so that's what you'll do."

He paused, ran his eyes over the men, looking for any defiance. Seeing none, he went on. "There are three ships here, and they belong to your new master, Brunhard. They are the finest ships in the western ocean. You will each get a bench on one, and when the wind blows we will sail and when the wind does not blow you will row. And if the wind never blows, you will row all the way to Frisia. And when you get to Frisia, then you will dream of the fine time you had aboard the ships, because then you will know what hell really is."

Áed paused again, waited for some reply, some sign of defiance. Again, there was none. A knot of men were standing off to one side, arms folded, watching with a detached sort of amusement. These Conandil took to be the ships' sailors. Áed looked over at them and nodded.

That gesture prompted the men to action. They ambled over to the various lines of slaves, led them out along the wharf and down the precarious planks to the decks of the three ships tied there, the chains of twelve men each taken aboard the larger ships, those of six men to a smaller one. Conandil followed behind, careful to keep with the line that included Broccáin.

This is it, she thought. *This is it, this is it, this is it...* In a moment she would no longer be on Irish soil. She would be on the deck of a Frisian ship, a Frisian slaver, and there would be nothing but water between her and Broccáin and the slave markets in that foreign land. She felt her stomach turn, she felt like she wanted to run, to scream, to do something as this last chance slipped away from her.

But there was nothing she could do, so she stepped silently down the rough plank and onto the deck of the ship rocking in the small swell from the sea.

Chapter Nine

[N]ever in speech with a foolish knave
shouldst thou waste a single word.
From the lips of such thou needst not look
for reward of thine own good will...
                    The Counseling of the Stray-Singer

The weather was fine and Louis was wearing a sword and he was standing on the deck of a ship bound off for Frisia, from where he could easily make the journey south to his home in Frankia. Escaping the dull life of a novitiate at the monastery at Glendalough, returning to his native land, taking vengeance on the brother who had betrayed him, these were all things that Louis de Roumois had been dreaming of for a year and more. And yet he was not entirely pleased with the situation.

Brunhard stood next to him on the afterdeck of his ship, the largest of his three ships. The vessel was called *Wind Dancer*, which suggested a sort of nimbleness that Louis doubted she would display. They were watching the captives come aboard, the sailors shoving them to the rowing benches, encouraging them with punches and lashes from the short lengths of rope they each carried. There was one woman aboard, Louis could see, but she was not chained to the others. The sailors seemed to ignore her and she in turn tucked herself up against the side of the ship, tying to remain as inconspicuous as possible.

"You see, here, this is how I do things, and it is a brilliant way!" Brunhard was saying. He had been keeping up a nearly unbroken monologue since he had returned to *Wind Dancer* at the head of the columns of chained men. "Why should I hire sailors, who will cost me far more than they are worth, to sail my ships, and go only when the wind blows, when I have ships loaded with the strong men I bring to the slave markets? Why should these pathetic creatures enjoy a carefree voyage across the ocean?"

"You'll have them row clear across the sea?" Louis asked.

"If the wind will not do, yes, I will," Brunhard said. "I buy strong slaves, and I teach them to row, and if the wind fails, out come the oars. While all the other traders are drifting around at sea like toy boats, we are on our way to Frisia. A shorter trip means I need buy less food to feed these sorry creatures, and by the time we arrive they are even stronger still. So I sell them for more silver than any other trader there."

"Hmm," Louis said. That explained a number of things about which Louis had been vaguely wondering. In his experience, limited though it was, merchant ships tended to be decked over only in the bow and stern, with the midsection open for stowing cargo. There tended to be only a few oarports, and the oars, worked by the small crew, were used mostly to maneuver in harbor.

Brunhard's ships were not like that. On either side, the decking ran bow to stern, with just the center open, and rowing benches were mounted by each of the oarports, a dozen per side. Such an arrangement made sense now, in Louis's mind. Louis had never bothered to ask Brunhard what cargo he would be carrying across the sea. It never occurred to him to care one way or another. But again, it never occurred to him that Brunhard would be carrying slaves.

Louis had come to like the Frisian over the course of the past few days. They had spent nights drinking in the hall, along with Brunhard's crew and various other hangers on. Brunhard rarely stopped talking, which would be insufferable in most men, but he had a gift for telling a tale, and a sharp sense of humor, and he was a very entertaining fellow, which was why a crowd generally gathered around him. He spent freely, kept the food and ale coming, laughed easily and welcomed nearly all. He was well known in Dubh-linn, and well liked.

"Now, most of these slavers who come to Dubh-linn," Brunhard continued, "they're willing to buy whatever sorry cripples those thieving Norse bastards sweep up from the countryside or the churches. But not me. I make deals, you know, the best deals. These men here, they were taken in battle. They're men-at-arms, house guards, in the main. Sure, some are just farmers called up for service, but most are fighting men. Strong and well fed."

"Really?" Louis said. This was more interesting. "How do you happen to get them?"

"These Irish, they are always going to war with one another. It's not hard to find some Norse chieftain willing to join with one of these Irish lords to attack his neighbor. The fighting men turn out to defend their land, the other lord overwhelms them with the aid of the Northmen, and my ships are full of good, strong slaves."

"I see," Louis said. It made perfect sense to him. He had been in Ireland long enough to know that what Brunhard was saying was the truth. The easiest thing to do in that country was to get one minor kingdom to go to war with another, and the Northmen, who had allegiance to none of them, were always happy to wade in.

Still, Louis had not been so comfortable when he learned that slaves would be their cargo, and he was less so now. He had no quarrel with slavery; trading slaves was not so different from trading wine or ironwork or hides or any of the thousands of things that were traded all over the world. He had slaves at home; most people he knew had slaves. They were no less a part of his world than cows or dogs.

But for all that, Louis could not quite ignore the fact that these were men, and worse, they were fighting men. His people. He had known many Irish warriors and fought beside them and even come to love a few of them. Fighting men deserved honor, even in defeat.

"Excuse me now, my Frankish friend," Brunhard said. "I must get these lazy bastards to work." The last of the slaves had been seated on the rowing benches and Brunhard headed toward the bow, making his way down the centerline with his odd, waddling gate.

Louis watched him go. He moved his eyes over the men at the rowing benches, a dozen per side. The slave trade was like the butcher's trade, he figured. It was a part of life, and he was happy to enjoy its benefits, but he did not particularly wish to see how the whole thing happened.

Brunhard stopped at the bow and turned to look at the slaves on the benches, who were dutifully looking at the deck at their feet. They were battered and sullen men, just what Louis might have expected. But they were not broken. There was still a spark of defiance in them, he could see that. He was happy that it was there. He did not like to see such men crushed, though of course any defiance would only mean trouble for Brunhard and his men, and that could mean trouble for him.

Next to Brunhard stood the big Irishman, Áed, and him Louis did not like. Capturing fellow Irishmen on the battlefield and selling them into slavery was one thing, in his mind. That was part of the warriors' world. But serving a Frisian master like Brunhard by brutalizing his own countrymen, that was closer to treason than Louis could countenance.

And beyond that, there was just something repugnant about the man. He was the sort whose presence made your skin crawl. Even Brunhard did not like him. Louis could tell. But he imagined Brunhard kept him around because he was damned good at his vicious work.

Louis heard Brunhard say something, low, and Áed shouted, "Okay, you bastards, look up!" On both sides of the ship heads lifted, looked forward. "This man is Brunhard," the big Irishman continued. "He is your lord. He owns you, all of you, and will do with you as he wishes. And the first thing he wishes is that you miserable turds learn to row this fine ship so you may row it clear to your new home across the sea. So you will do as you are told, and if you do not, you will get the end of a rope, and if you do wrong again you will get much, much worse. Do you understand?"

On either side, heads nodded. The sailors, grinning, lifted the oars from the deck and handed them to the bewildered slaves, then cast off the lines that held the ship to the wharf. *Wind Dancer* drifted clear of the pilings and Áed shouted out orders for the men to run their oars through the row ports. He paced fore and aft, swinging a rope end in his hand, screaming at the men on the benches, which did nothing to make their job more comprehensible.

The other sailors stationed themselves around the ship, ropes in hand, eyes on the rowers. But they were Frisians, Louis knew. They could not speak the Irish language, and could only give directions by pantomime and brute force.

Louis looked out over the side of the ship. Brunhard's other vessels were also getting underway, oars run awkwardly through the row ports. Brunhard came ambling back along the deck, his eyes everywhere, his face still locked in that great, wide grin. He stepped up beside Louis.

"So, Louis the Frank, you never did tell me how long you have been in this country. Do you speak the language of these Irish curs?"

"No," Louis lied. "Not much. I have a few words here and there, enough to get me to the mead hall in Dubh-linn."

"Why did you come to Ireland?" Brunhard asked. Brunhard liked being the center of things; he did not spend much time inquiring about the lives of others.

"I came with some fellows of mine. Franks. We thought to make our fortunes, but we did not. And now I am the only one left alive." Louis fabricated the story as he spoke, but he felt sure that Brunhard did not care enough about anyone other than Brunhard to doubt his words or even make further enquiry. And he was right.

"Ha! Well, that doesn't surprise me. Franks are too ignorant to make their fortunes in such a country as this. And not just Franks. Most men are, beside me. Now, watch this," he said, nodding forward. "This is always a fine amusement."

The Irish slaves had the blades of their oars down and they were holding them motionless as the current swirled *Wind Dancer* and Brunhard's other ships down the river and out toward the sea. Áed was up in the bow, the rope end in his grotesquely large hand held at his side, his mouth in a scowl. "When I say stroke, you bastards pull the oars!" Áed shouted.

"What's he telling them?" Louis asked.

"He's giving a lesson on how to row," Brunhard said. "I don't speak this barbarian language. I just leave it up to Áed. Cruel, filthy bastard he is, he knows how to do this job."

"Now stroke!" Áed shouted and the men at the benches leaned back and *Wind Dancer* gathered way. "Lift your oars!" Áed shouted next and all but one of the oar blades came dripping from the water.

The one man, two benches back from the bow, larboard side, had apparently not understood and Áed was on him like a bolt of lightning. The rope end came down hard on his back and he gasped and his eyes went wide, but he had the look of a hard man and did not flinch. "Lift your oar, what do you think that means, you stupid whore's whelp?" Áed shouted and this time the man understood and lifted his blade from the water.

Áed continued to prowl aft, stopping a few feet in front of Brunhard and Louis, then turning so the rowers, facing aft, could see him. "Once again, you sorry turds," he shouted. "Stroke! Lift your oars!"

It was smoother that time, more coordinated, the oars coming down, pulling, lifting nearly as one. "This is no great art," Brunhard said to Louis. "Even these brutes can learn it quick, with a little practice and the right motivation. We'll row clean out of the river and once clear of the land we'll try backing and turning and such as that. If we get into some sort of trouble we may need these animals to know their business well."

"What kind of trouble might we get in?" Louis asked.

Brunhard looked at him and smiled. "You Franks really are as stupid as I thought, aren't you? This is the sea, Louis, the sea. There is trouble to be found all over. Rocks, winds, storms, fog. And that's not even reckoning with the bastard Northmen who'll steal the last crust of bread from an honest merchant such as myself. Even if all goes well you'll be lucky to arrive in Frisia with your life. I can guarantee you not all of these bastards chained up forward will."

Áed continued to shout and the Irishmen chained to the benches quickly picked up the rhythm of the oars and *Wind Dancer* settled on a heading for the open sea. Brunhard's crew moved along the centerline, keeping their eyes on the men at the oars, lashing them with their rope ends on occasion and for no reason that Louis could see. Just to keep them from growing too confident, he guessed.

The shoreline seemed to slip past at an amazing speed, the ship driven by the pull of the oars and the ebbing tide that swept it along. On either side, Brunhard's other two ships kept pace, the slaves on their benches also falling into the rhythm of the stroke. The mouth of the river moved past, and Louis could see nothing but the headland to the north, and to the east and the south, only the open sea. The wind was light and the seas rolled in a moderate swell. The afternoon was warm, the sky blue overhead.

Once again, Louis felt his spirits buoyed. Here was an unbroken, watery way back to Frankia. He knew it was not that simple, that there were many hundreds of treacherous miles between him and his home, but he was now clear of Ireland, and nothing but sea between him and the revenge of which he dreamed.

"Now we teach these whore's sons about rowing," Brunhard said to Louis, then took a step forward. "Áed!" he called. "Set these bastards to it!"

Áed nodded and turned to face the rowers, who had now settled into a regular stroke. "Now we teach you whore's whelps something about rowing a ship!" he shouted in Irish. "This is the starboard side," he said, pointing to that side with his rope end. "This the larboard. Any man who forgets that will wish his mother had drowned him, do you hear me?"

He continued in that vein, instructing the rowers how to hold their oars on one side and pull on the other to make the ship turn in her length. He instructed them in backing their oars to give the ship sternway. He showed them half a dozen other ways to work the oars to move the ship in various directions. He and the sailors doled out curses and beatings with the rope ends as the bewildered Irishmen on the benches slowly learned the tricks of moving the ship to Áed's command.

Louis looked out beyond *Wind Dancer*'s deck. One of the other two ships was half a cable length off to the north, the other off to the south, and they were doing the same thing: turning and backing and stopping under the power of their oars.

"How long have you been at this trade?" Louis asked Brunhard.

"Years!" Brunhard exclaimed. "Many years! Sure, I've made mistakes, lost several fortunes. Clever as I am, it took me some time to come up with this way of doing things." He made a sweeping gesture to indicate the slaves arrayed before him. "But now I have it all worked out, and I know every damned inch of the coastlines from here to Frisia, know every trick of the winds and the tides. Now the money rolls in with every voyage and soon I will give it all up and buy a great hall filled with ale and whores!"

Louis nodded. He had no doubt that Brunhard would do just that. It seemed to him he had never met a man who took a bigger bite out of life than Brunhard the Frisian.

"Áed!" Brunhard shouted. "That's well. Let us make way now!"

Áed nodded, shouted out a few orders and then the slaves began to pull together, driving *Wind Dancer* in a straight line, and the man at the tiller eased it over so the ship settled on a southerly heading, the coast of Ireland stretched out along the starboard side.

"We follow the coast south," Brunhard said to Louis, "and when we come to the great headland, and if we have not all been murdered by the bastard Northmen who swarm around here like flies to shit, then we will sail east to Wessex and along that coastline and see if *those* bastards don't cut our throats. Then we will cross the sea again to Frisia and then you may be on your way to Frankia where you may copulate with goats, as you Franks are so fond of doing."

"That's sounds like a fine thing," Louis said. "The goats in particular. So you've trained these poor bastards at the oars well enough?"

"Not quite," Brunhard said. "All I have left to do now is to kill one of them."

Louis paused before making reply. He was not sure he had heard Brunhard right, or if he had, whether or not the Frisian was making a joke. "Kill one of them?" Louis asked.

"Yes, of course," Brunhard said. "Look at them. I teach them to row, they learn, they think that they have done a good thing. They become confident, forget that they are my property, no more, of no greater importance than the whetstones I bring to sell. So, I kill one, and it reminds them that they are nothing at all."

Louis frowned and thought about that before he spoke. "You just pick one and kill him?" he said at last. "Sure, there must be a better way to keep them in line?"

Brunhard turned and met Louis's eyes. A hint of the smile was still on his lips but any trace of amusement was gone from his eyes, and his voice. "Don't tell me my business or question what I do, you Frankish turd, or it's over the side with you. You may not have the balls for this kind of work, but do not question those who do."

"I'll keep that in mind," Louis said. He took care to put no deference into his voice, no tone that would suggest he was cowed by Brunhard's words.

He did not fear Brunhard, though it did occur to him that there was nothing keeping the man from tossing him overboard at any time. When he had first come aboard *Wind Dancer*, carrying all his worldly goods in a sack over his shoulder, Brunhard had taken careful note. The man's eyes had lit up when Louis paid him silver for the voyage. Brunhard, he was sure, had guessed there was more of that to be had in Louis's sack, and he was right. If Brunhard told Áed and a few of the brutish sailors to grab him up and toss him over the side, then the contents of the sack were his.

Louis understood that he would not be sleeping soundly until he stepped ashore in Frisia.

But he was not thinking about that at the moment. He was still mulling Brunhard's casual resolve to kill one of these slaves. Louis was a warrior; he was not shy about killing. But he was also a Christian and a gentleman, and he despised senseless brutality. Now he was wondering if the Frisian would indeed do it, and if so how bad it would be.

It was not long before he had his answer.

Chapter Ten

[T]o the heedful comes seldom harm,
for none can find a more faithful friend
than the wealth of mother wit.
Hávamál

Starri Deathless called out from his perch at *Sea Hammer*'s masthead. "They still have not seen us!" he shouted. "By the gods, they must be blind!"

He had been up there on and off since dawn. All told he had spent more time that day clinging to the top of the mast than he had on deck. He came down to eat and drink on occasion, and to relieve himself over the side. That last business he had in fact tried to do from the masthead, and only the outraged shouts of his fellow warriors and an unequivocal order from Thorgrim had brought him grudgingly to deck.

Thorgrim had no idea how the man could stay up there so long, alternately clinging to the shrouds or with his legs wrapped around the mast or actually seated on the very top of the mast. In his best days, years before, Thorgrim could have tolerated that position for an hour at best. But Starri, like a bird of prey, liked to be up high, ready to swoop down.

"What are they doing, Starri?" Thorgrim called out.

"They are just rowing, rowing," Starri called down. "Like they haven't got a care in the world! And from what I can see, they have no great skill with the oars!"

"Rowing?" Thorgrim called back. "Banks of oars on both sides?"

"Well, Night Wolf," Starri called down. "Even I can only see one side of a ship at a time, so I know only that there are oars on their starboard sides. But since they are not going in circles, I would guess there are oars on the larboard sides as well."

Thorgrim nodded to himself. *Odd*, he thought. Merchant ships rarely carried men enough to man banks of oars. Too much cost. Generally they had only a few oars for use in harbor, and relied only on the winds the gods provided for free when they were out at sea.

Well, no matter, Thorgrim thought. *They are here now, and soon they will be ours.*

They had been waiting a day and a half for this moment, since catching Kalf Hrutsson and then letting him go. Waiting for this Brunhard and his three fine ships laden with goods which Kalf swore to the gods would soon sail from Dubh-linn.

Thorgrim decided that they would remain at sea through the dark hours of night. If they did not, if they sailed off to find a beach and hauled the ships ashore, there was a good chance they would miss their quarry.

As the sun fell in the west the four ships had gathered and lashed themselves together and the captains met aboard *Sea Hammer*. Fostolf of *Dragon* had been the most vocal in his opposition to Thorgrim's plans. In truth he had been the only one in opposition.

"We're too far south of Dubh-linn here, we might still miss him," Fostolf argued. "We should get right in the mouth of the river, anchor there and wait."

Thorgrim shook his head. "This Brunhard, he's a Frisian, according to Kalf. I wouldn't hesitate to plunder a Frisian merchant. I'd do it just for the pleasure of it. But there are some in Dubh-linn...many, in truth...who we should leave alone. It will not go well for us to be lurking like thieves in the mouth of the river."

The other two, Godi and Thorodd Bollason, nodded in agreement with Thorgrim's words. They had been with Thorgrim a long time, and through many fights, and were more willing than Fostolf to follow Thorgrim's plans without question. And they knew, and Fostolf did not, that Thorgrim had a great aversion to Dubh-linn and would avoid it at all costs. They knew he would never have sailed north from Vík-ló if the winds had not dictated it.

They also knew that while Thorgrim was always careful to ask the opinions of his chief men, it was less certain that their council had any effect on the decisions he made.

And so with the winds calm and the seas no more than a gentle swell and the ships bound together, they lowered an anchor on all the rope they could tie together, hoping that would at least slow their drift. They posted watches through the night and they slept.

Failend came aft and sat on the edge of the afterdeck where Thorgrim had laid out some furs for a bed. She was moving easier now, and her color was back to that of a living human. She had eaten two meals that day, and really eaten, not just picked, and Thorgrim was glad of it. What Failend did not realize, or so Thorgrim guessed, and he could not bring himself to tell her, was that she would likely have to run this gauntlet at the start of every voyage.

"Has someone cast a spell on the men?" she asked.

"Why do you think that?" Thorgrim asked.

"No one is drinking ale. No one is gorging himself. No one singing or telling filthy jokes. I might think I was back in the monastery at Glendalough."

Thorgrim smiled. "It's the ocean. And the night. The men don't like being on the ocean at night."

"Why not?"

"There are strange creatures in the water," Thorgrim said, as if explaining a common fact to a child. "And spirits as well. Some are good spirits, but some are very bad. You never know. And of course, we're strangers here, and the spirits of Irish waters would have no love for us."

Now Failend smiled. "You heathens, you truly are an ignorant and barbaric lot," she said. But then she crossed herself and snatched up the silver crucifix she wore around her neck and kissed it, which Thorgrim knew were the ways the Christians warded off spirits. Then she lay down beside Thorgrim and closed her eyes.

Soon after, Thorgrim could hear her gentle and rhythmic breathing as sleep took her away. He lay back, eyes open, and felt the motion of the ship under him, heard the slapping of water on the hull and the creaking of the mast and rigging, and watched the great sweep of stars moving back and forth overhead.

The night was long but it was gentle. They heard the sound of whales, and once something splashed nearby the ship and startled Harald so much he jumped and those who saw him do it laughed. But there was a forced quality to their laughter. They were no more sanguine about the dark and the deep water than was Harald.

Dawn came and the men were grateful for the gathering light in the east. They unlashed the ships, spread out over a wider patch of sea, ate their morning meal. They saw several vessels leaving Dubh-linn that day, some heading north, some south, one to the east. But none were the three fine vessels of which Kalf had spoken. It was not until after midday that those ships made their appearance.

They came slowly around the headland, moving under the power of their oars, and they seemed to be making a clumsy job of it. Starri called down from aloft as he saw them to the north. Thorgrim's ships were closer to land now, tucked in where they would be more difficult to spot against the hills to the west.

It was not until sometime after Starri's report that Thorgrim saw them as well, their hulls low in the water, their sails still furled and lowered, and their masts, bare like winter trees, difficult to see against the sky. But he did see them, at last. Three ships, just as Kalf had said. If they were fine ships, if they were crammed with goods worth having, that was yet to be seen.

He heard some bustle of activity across the water, the squeal of a rope through a block. He turned and looked over the larboard side. Fostolf's *Dragon* was hoisting its sail, the men heaving on the halyard as the yard came up off the gallows.

"Fostolf!" Thorgrim called. *Dragon* was a couple hundred feet to leeward in the gentle breeze from the north. "What are you doing?"

He saw Fostolf standing on *Dragon*'s afterdeck, his eyes moving from Thorgrim to his men at the halyard and back again. Finally he called, "We are setting our sail! Do you not see the merchant ships we've been waiting on?"

"Too soon!" Thorgrim called. "We'll let them get farther out to sea, farther from Dubh-linn!" He would have thought that was obvious. You didn't leap at the hare when he still had the chance to scurry back into his burrow.

"We'll lose them!" Fostolf called back. "Night will be on us!"

Thorgrim's eyebrows came together and he frowned. It had been a long time since anyone had questioned his decisions. Had he and Fostolf been face to face he would have set the man right, and quickly, but he did not want to start shouting out a chastisement over that stretch of water. But in the end he did not have to, because Godi did it for him.

Blood Hawk was just to leeward of *Dragon* and about fifty feet from the smaller ship's stern. Anyone with lesser lungs than Godi might not have been heard, but the big man's voice could carry the better part of a mile if he wished it to, and in this case he did. "Fostolf!" he called. "Don't argue! When you have sailed as many miles as Thorgrim Night Wolf, then you can question him. Except by then you'll be dead!"

That brought spurts of laughter from the four ships and Thorgrim felt the tension collapse like a sail deprived of wind. But he did not forget Fostolf's back talk. And he did not think he had heard the last of it.

Chapter Eleven

A twelfth I know: if I see in a tree
a corpse from a halter hanging,
such spells I write, and paint in runes,
that the being descends and speaks.

The Song of Spells

Brunhard had taken a seat on a small chest on the larboard side of the afterdeck, directly across from the man stationed at the tiller. He had fallen quiet, an uncharacteristic thing as far as Louis could tell. Then he stood quickly, as if suddenly remembering something he had to do. He looked forward to where Áed stood leaning against the mast. He nodded and Áed nodded back and that was apparently all the communication needed.

Áed pushed himself up and moved slowly down the middle of the ship, running his eyes over the men at the oars. He stepped all the way aft, turned, moved forward at a slow and contemplative pace, as if assessing each man's efforts. He passed a big man with a torn, rust-red tunic, a man's whose face was set and expressionless, his eyes looking aft, fixed on nothing. Áed paused for a beat, then moved on. The man on the next bench forward was in bad shape, his nose broken, blood smeared on his face and half wiped away. His eyes flicked up at Áed as he approached, then back down again. But that, apparently, was enough for Áed.

"What are you looking at? What?" Áed screamed at the man. "I asked what you're looking at!"

The man opened his mouth to answer, but before he could speak Áed hit him hard on the side of the head with the rope end. The man's head snapped around and he half fell on his oar, breaking his stroke and fouling the oar behind him.

"Why aren't you rowing, you useless whore's son?" Áed screamed and hit the man again. The other oars were in confusion now, the rowers darting glances at the fray, then looking quickly away for fear of getting the same attention.

"Look at what you've done!" Áed shouted. The man at the oar made another attempt to speak and Áed hit him again and yelled, "Keep your damned mouth shut!" He straightened and turned toward the afterdeck and called, "Master Brunhard, this man will not row properly and he shows us all disrespect!"

Áed spoke in the Irish language, which as far as Louis knew Brunhard did not understand, but it didn't matter. Like players on a stage, each man had his part and they were well rehearsed. Everything that Áed said was directed at the slaves, even if he pretended to speak to Brunhard.

"You know what to do with such men," Brunhard yelled, the words in Frisian but their meaning unmistakable. He pointed to the ship's yard, swung fore and aft and resting on the gallows as the ship was driven by the men at the oars.

Louis could see the sailors grinning now. They knew this act as well, and apparently they liked it. Several of them moved to the base of the mast and one lifted a great coil of rope that hung from a cleat and dropped it on the deck. Three more grabbed onto the rope, and with a guttural order from the first, they heaved away and the yard rose off the gallows a foot, then two, then ten. Another order and the rope was tied off to the cleat once again, the yard hauled part way up the mast.

Along the benches men were glancing up at the yard, glancing sideways, then quickly down again to avoid attracting attention. Áed hit the man with the broken nose once again, and another sailor unhooked the chain that ran through the rowers' iron collars and removed the ring from the man's neck.

"Master Brunhard, maybe all should see what happens to these worthless swine when they do not obey!" Áed called.

Brunhard nodded. He stepped over to the side of the ship, cupped his hands around his mouth and called out across the water, "Come and see the show!" But Louis noticed the other two ships were already pulling for *Wind Dancer*'s side.

There seemed to Louis to be a great tangle of ropes hanging from the yard, but the sailors apparently could tell them apart. The man who had untied the first line now cast off another and eased it away. The rope ran through a block that hung from a shorter, stouter rope attached to the end of the yard nearest the bow, and Louis had a pretty good idea of how this would play out.

Áed and another of the sailors jerked their victim to his feet and pulled him toward the bow. The man stumbled and was half-dragged forward and Louis heard him shout, "Áed! You whore's son bastard, I'll…"

He got no further in his threat. Áed hit him hard in the face, then hit him again. The man's head slumped over and then lolled back. There was fresh blood on his face. He was still conscious, but barely.

Brunhard's other ships drew up on either side of *Wind Dancer*, their oars held motionless in the water, the three ships riding easily over the long low swells, sitting on their spot of ocean.

"Look here, all of you!" Áed bellowed, his voice carrying over *Wind Dancer*'s deck and the other two ships as well. "All of you sorry bastards, look here, now!" The men at *Wind Dancer*'s oars, and the one woman who was huddled forward, turned and looked at Áed, the sailor, and the bleeding man. None of them, none of the watching captives had any expression on their faces—not horror nor revulsion nor anger. They just watched.

One of the sailors grabbed up the end of the rope that hung from the end of the yard. There was a loop tied in it and he slipped the loop over the bleeding man's head, tightened it around his neck. "Your lives are not yours," Áed called, his volume undiminished. "Understand that. Your lives belong to Master Brunhard alone, and if you dare to disobey, even in the least, as this man did, see what will happen to you!"

He stepped back and as the man, now unsupported, began to slump to the deck a gang of sailors hauled away on the rope. The man was pulled straight, but before his feet came off the deck the sailors stopped, leaving him twisting, his toes just touching the planks below.

The man made a strangling noise and struggled to lift himself with his toes and clawed at the rope around his neck. His eyes went wide as his fingers tried to get under the noose. Then the sailors eased the rope and the man came down on his feet. Louis could hear him suck in a breath as his fingers went back to the rope to loosen it now that he could.

And the second his fingers touched the rope the sailors hauled again, laughing this time, pulling him clean off the deck so he swung forward in a great arc and then back again, legs kicking, arms flailing. The yard was hauled around so the end from which the man hung was now over the water. He twisted and swung back and forth and kicked and then as his movements began to slow the sailors let go of the rope and the man plunged down into the sea.

For a moment there was only a foaming circle of water where the man had disappeared, and then the sailors hauled again and the man came up from below and once again hung kicking from the rope at the end of the yard. Three times the sailors did this, letting the man float so that he might regain his breath, only so they could choke it out of him again. Louis felt furious, he felt sick, he felt helpless watching this grotesque spectacle.

The third time the man was hauled from the water he was not let down again, but left to kick at the rope's end. "Watch this!" Brunhard said to Louis. Louis pulled his eyes from the dying man, looked at the stout shipmaster. There was a bright look in his eye, a bit of a smile on his lips, and it was genuine. Brunhard was enjoying himself.

"Sometimes there are sharks," Brunhard said, "but I guess we will not be so lucky today."

Forward, one of Brunhard's men had pulled a bow and a quiver of arrows out from some safe place. He nocked an arrow and aimed it at the hanging man as he drew back the string. He paused, just a beat, then let the arrow fly. It flashed across the short distance and embedded itself in the man's shoulder and the man let out a scream, as much as he could scream, and kicked harder still.

"My man did not miss, in case you wondered," Brunhard said. "He was aiming for the shoulder and he hit what he aimed at. Excellent archer, he always does."

And as if to demonstrate that fact, the archer loosed another arrow which hit the Irish slave in the opposite shoulder. The man kicked some more, but the strength was going out of him now.

The archer nocked another arrow. He looked aft at Brunhard and Brunhard nodded to him. He drew back the bow and fired and the arrow came in under the hanging man's chin and the tip erupted in a jet of blood from the back of his skull. He twitched a few times and then hung limp.

For a long time there was silence aboard the three ships as all eyes were on the horror at the end of the rope. Then Brunhard nodded at Áed. The Irishman gave a brusque order and the dead man was lowered down and swung inboard, the noose taken off his neck and his body tossed into the sea.

"Any one of you bastards say one word, do one thing that does not please your master," Áed shouted in his big voice, "and that will be your fate!"

No one spoke, which did not surprise Louis in the least. The yard was lowered back to the gallows, the oars manned, the three ships began to gather way once again.

"You see," Brunhard said to Louis, the familiar jovial tone in his voice. "I give these sorry bastards some entertainment, they are good and docile the rest of the voyage!"

"I see," Louis said. And he did, more than he wished to see. He saw what he wished he had seen before taking passage with this Frisian madman.

Then one of the sailors, who had climbed up on top of the yard resting on the gallows, called out. "Master Brunhard, there are three…no, four ships to the west of us!"

Brunhard looked up sharp at the man. "Are they making for us?"

"No, Master Brunhard. They're just lying there. No sail set. Hard to see against the land. Oh, one of them is setting sail!"

"Ha! More of these Norse dogs, I'll warrant!" Brunhard said. "You see, Louis the Frank! More fun for us!" But this time Louis could hear a different tone in the man's voice, and the amusement did not sound quite so genuine.

Chapter Twelve

Hew wood in wind, sail the seas in a breeze,
woo a maid in the dark, for day's eyes are many...
Maxims for all Men

The hunters lay in wait for some time longer, watching the merchant ships crawl south. Like the gray wolf that is hard to spot in the shadows of the forest, Thorgrim's ships were not easily seen against the land, and as the sun moved to the west, seeing them became harder still. Nothing about the way the merchantmen moved suggested alarm.

"Hold a minute!" Starri called down from the masthead. "They've stopped now... They've gathered together...like women at the fence exchanging gossip!"

Thorgrim waited for more, but Starri said nothing else. The three ships had all met up, not sailing, not rowing, just drifting in a little clump. Thorgrim could see that much from the deck. They were two miles away, perhaps a bit more, from where Thorgrim's fleet lay inshore of them.

He waited for what he thought was a reasonable time, and then called up, "What now, Starri?"

"They're still..." Starri began, and then stopped. "No, they're underway again, and..." He paused, apparently trying to figure what the merchant ships were up to, then called out again, his voice bright with excitement.

"They're rowing now!" he shouted. "Oh, they've seen us, and they're rowing like the great serpent Jörmungandr is biting their asses! Ha, ha!" Starri laughed in that particular way he did, just on the edge of hysteria. "No, wait...ah, now they're setting sail, the cowardly dogs!"

Starri, Thorgrim knew, was hoping for some bloody fight across the decks of the ships, but once again he was pretty sure the man would be disappointed. Merchants tended to run until they could run no more, and then give up and wish for the best.

"They can run as fast as they like," Thorgrim called, "but they cannot run fast enough." Then, in a louder voice, one calculated to be heard aboard *Sea Hammer* as well as the other three ships lying near, he said, "Make sail! All hands make sail! Let us run these frightened rabbits down!"

The afternoon had been quiet, just silent watching and anticipation, but with those words the silence was trampled by a hundred and fifty warriors swarming over four ships to get the sails set. It did not take long. The men had been anticipating this order for hours, once the afternoon breeze had filled in. They had cast off the lashings that bound the sails to the yards and the yards to gallows, had stretched out the halyards ready for hauling. There were men standing by the lines and more making ready to dip the ends of the yards under the shrouds and swing them around so they would set perpendicular to the ship's centerline.

"Heave!" Thorgrim heard Harald say and the men at the halyard pulled the rope aft with a short, hard jerk, readjusted their grips and heaved again. Foot by foot the big yard moved higher on the mast, the red and white oiled wool sail tumbling free as the spar rose.

"That's good!" Harald shouted. "Swing her around!" Eager hands grabbed onto the brace, the line that ran from the end of the yard, and pulled down, tilting the yard nearly vertical and then swinging the low end forward and around the shrouds, before easing it back to the horizontal. The breeze ran down the length of the cloth, making it ripple and gently snap, and Harald called for the men at the halyard to heave again.

He wears his command well, Thorgrim thought. He was with Harald every day, nearly, and had been for two years or more, since they had first left Vik to go a'viking with Ornolf. It was difficult, sometimes, with such proximity to see the changes in the boy. But every once in a while he felt as if the gods gave him a chance to catch another view of his son, like noticing a new vista in an otherwise familiar landscape. This was such a moment, and he liked what he saw.

Sea Hammer's yard reached the top of the mast and Harald ordered the halyard made off, the leeward brace hauled aft and the yard swung around until the breeze filled the sail. It rippled once then filled again and stayed filled, bellied out in a gentle curve. The wind was light, just enough to keep the sail full, but *Sea Hammer*, like all Norse longships, was narrow and sleek and responded well to even the light pressure of the wind. Thorgrim felt her heel a bit, felt her gather speed, heard the growing murmur of water running down her side.

He looked to leeward. The other ships, *Blood Hawk* and *Dragon* and *Fox* were setting sail as well, each a little behind *Sea Hammer* because Harald had made certain *Sea Hammer* would have her sail set first. That sort of thing was in his bones; he could not tolerate his ship not being first. Likewise, he could not tolerate not being the first man into a battle, though he never was, because, try as he might he could never get into a fight quicker than Starri.

Thorgrim felt his spirits soar. The fleet was gathering way, stretching their legs as they built to a run. They were a pack of wolves, just like a pack of wolves, patiently waiting and then coming on with a frightening burst of speed. *This is why those poor bastards will not run from us for long*, he thought.

By the time he looked back out to sea the merchant ships had their sails set as well, the wind nearly right astern of them and they seemed to be moving at a decent clip, faster than Thorgrim would have thought a wallowing, heavy-laden merchantman might sail.

Harald had taken the tiller now and Thorgrim turned to him. "Head right for them, right for their wake," he said. "But stay to windward, don't let us get down wind. I think this breeze will hold steady now. We want to keep them between us and the shore, don't want them running off to sea."

Harald nodded and his eyes moved from the distant merchantmen to *Sea Hammer*'s sail to the ships near astern, watching everything at once, like the good sailor he was. In the same way, Thorgrim's eyes were everywhere, and he gauged the manner in which the other three ships were being handled, the set of their sails, how steady a course they held, and he found nothing wanting.

Already *Sea Hammer* was stretching out a lead. She was the longest of the four, and probably the best built, though *Blood Hawk* was nearly her equal. Godi's ship was only a hundred feet or so astern of *Sea Hammer* and seemed to be matching *Sea Hammer*'s pace, or nearly so. The others, shorter on the waterline, were dropping behind yard by yard. But if it came to it, if they left the others far astern, *Sea Hammer* and *Blood Hawk* alone should be enough to take three merchant ships with their small and frightened crews.

They settled into the chase, Harald ordering all idle hands up to the weather side and calling out for small and probably pointless adjustments to the trim of the sail. A long wake stretched out behind *Sea Hammer* and the other ships as they plowed along on the tail of their prey.

Starri was still at the masthead and he let out a long whoop of exhilaration. "The hounds have a fair race now, after the fox!" he shouted. "There's a fire under this bastard Brunhard!"

Thorgrim frowned. Starri was giving voice to something that Thorgrim himself was thinking, something that was starting to irritate him, like a pebble in a shoe. These merchantmen were fast.

We should have halved the distance with them by now, Thorgrim thought as he looked at the three ships ahead. They did not appear appreciably closer than they had when the chase had first begun.

Maybe Kalf was wrong, he thought. *Maybe they are not heavy laden with cargo.* There were two things that made a merchantman slow. One was the shape of its hull, wide and deep, designed to carry as much cargo as it could. The other was the cargo itself, how much there was and how much it weighed. A fat ship loaded down with casks of ale or whetstones or ingots of iron would not sail fast. It certainly would not sail as fast as a longship.

"Starri's right," Harald called from his place at the tiller. "These bastards have some speed on them."

"Yes," Thorgrim said, stepping aft. "Kalf said they were fine ships. Maybe he meant they were fast ships." From that distance they could see only the three square sails and the dark hulls below, the occasional flash of white water at their bows. Even Starri with his hawk's eyes, perched at the masthead, would not be able to see enough to gauge their quality with regard to seaworthiness and speed.

"He might have meant that," Harald agreed. "Or maybe they're sailing light. Or even unladen."

Thorgrim grunted. That could well be. And if they were unladen, carrying no cargo, he would look and feel like a fool. He and his men would have chased these ships all over the sea only to find there was nothing on board.

But there was only one way they could discover the truth of that situation.

"We'll see," he said at last.

Thorgrim Night Wolf was known as a man of few words. That was his nature and it was also his choice. He had learned as a young man that the less you said, the less chance there was of saying something stupid or just plain wrong. For that reason, he did not promise Harald or anyone that they would catch the merchantmen. Because he knew he might not. And as it happened, they didn't.

The hours crept past and the water slid under their keel and the coast of Ireland sunk lower on the western horizon. Somewhere off to the west was Vík-ló, and as the day wore on Thorgrim was certain they had finally passed south of it.

At least we're going in the direction I wanted to go, he thought.

They were gaining on the fleeing ships, he could see that, but gaining slowly, and the sun was sinking in the west much faster than they were overhauling their prey. Brunhard, if it was Brunhard, was heading offshore. Not directly out to sea, just tending away from the land. But Thorgrim did not think they would keep on that heading.

He'll be lost if he goes out to sea that way, Thorgrim thought. *He needs the headland to mark where he should cross the ocean.*

A merchantman sailing to Frisia would generally sail south until he reached the great headland that jutted out to the east. That would tell him when he should turn and run for the coast of Britain. Thorgrim had spent enough time sailing those waters to know that. Just heading blindly out to sea, as Brunhard seemed to be doing, was an invitation to be lost or swallowed up by the sea, or something worse.

He only wants me to think that's what he's about, Thorgrim thought. *Hopes I'll give up the chase.*

And this time Thorgrim was right. The coast of Ireland was becoming a low and indistinct line on the horizon, and the men of *Sea Hammer* were starting to throw worried glances that way, when the merchant ships suddenly spun on their heels and began racing back for the protection of the land. They were still a mile ahead of Thorgrim's ships, still nearly matching them knot for knot. The sun was now low enough that it was difficult to look to the west, which made it hard to see the ships they were chasing.

But still they raced on, and now Thorgrim could see Brunhard was making for a headland to the south and he realized what they were about.

Oh, you bastard, you dog! Thorgrim thought as he watched the merchant ships running for the shore. Brunhard had led them away from land as the sun was going down, but now with night coming on he was heading back. He was playing a close game, trying to time this thing perfectly.

Thorgrim scowled in frustration. He said nothing, but he did not have to. Every man aboard was mariner enough to see how this would play out.

Failend stepped up beside him. "What is he doing, this Brunhard?" she asked. "Why is he sailing toward land? Won't that give us a chance to catch him?"

Thorgrim smiled, despite himself. While every man aboard might understand, Failend, a stranger to ships, did not. "You see that point of land, sticking out from shore?" he asked, pointing. "Brunhard's trying to get in around the headland and disappear from our sight just as night falls. He's guessing that we won't dare follow him in close to shore. That we'll think it's too dangerous to risk chasing him in the dark."

"Well, he guessed wrong, didn't he?" Failend said.

"No," Thorgrim said, "he guessed right. I've never sailed this stretch of coast, never been this far south. I don't know what's around that headland. But I know there are ugly rocks enough off the Irish coast that I don't wish to go blundering around where I can't see."

"But if Brunhard can sail there safely, can't we?" Failend asked.

"Not necessarily," Thorgrim explained. "If Brunhard knows that stretch of coast well he might be able to get through a channel, or he might know some clear passage. Once he gets around that point he'll be out of sight to us, so we won't know what course he sails. It would be madness for us to try and go after him."

"I see," Failed said. For a moment the two of them watched the three merchant vessels, a mile ahead. Then Failend spoke again. "That's very clever of him, isn't it?"

"Yes," Thorgrim said, grudgingly. "Yes, it's very clever. This Frisian bastard is a better seaman than I had expected."

They stood on, Brunhard's ships, and in their wake and a mile behind, *Sea Hammer*, with *Blood Hawk* only a cable length astern and the smaller ships, *Dragon* and *Fox*, now a half mile behind them. The sun touched the horizon and the western sky grew orange and red. The distant mountains seemed to blaze and Brunhard's ships reached the point of land jutting out to the east and disappeared from view.

"We'll stand on," Thorgrim said to Harald, loud enough to be heard across the deck. He wasn't ready to give up yet; he would at least get around the headland and see what was there. He looked to the west. The sun was half gone behind the hills. There would probably be light enough for them to make it around the point and see if they might still get at Brunhard's ships.

Then the sail fluttered and snapped and then filled again. *Sea Hammer* sat up on a more even keel and then heeled again as the sail bellied once more. "Oh, by the gods..." Thorgrim muttered. The evening breeze was dying away.

Sea Hammer was just regaining her momentum when the breeze failed again, puffed and then failed for good. The ship sat upright, her sail hanging limp. Darkness was spreading out over the water, the sun lost behind the mountains, the brilliant reds and oranges fading quickly.

"The wind has gone," Failend observed.

If any of the men had said that, Thorgrim would have taken it as irony and in his present mood might have punched him in the head. But Failend, he knew, thought she was making a sincere and insightful observation.

"Yes," he said. "Yes, it has."

"So now what do we do?" she asked.

Thorgrim looked at the shore of Ireland, quickly being lost in the gathering dark. He looked out to sea. The horizon to the east was just visible, the sea and sky fading to a deep, deep blue that would soon be black as tar.

"We go out to sea," Thorgrim said.

Chapter Thirteen

The miserable man and evil minded
makes of all things mockery...
Hávamál

Louis de Roumois stood on *Wind Dancer*'s afterdeck looking back along the ship's track to the four Norse raiders sailing in their wake. The longships had been clumped together when the chase began, sometime after midday, but now they were spread out, the two largest ships in the lead, the others trailing behind.

It was exhilarating, this effort to run away from a powerful enemy, knowing that losing the race would mean a bloody fight to the death. The thrill of the thing had almost blotted out the disgust Louis felt watching Brunhard murder the Irish slave.

Almost, but not entirely. Louis had been genuinely disgusted. But he had also seen enough of the cruelties that men inflicted upon men, and enough of the pointless violence that went on in the wicked world, that he was not particularly shocked. And, grotesque as it was, he understood why Brunhard had done it.

And so, when the Northmen had appeared to the west, Louis's attention had shifted to this new threat. He had watched with interest as Brunhard fought to get every bit of speed he could out of his ship and those in company with him. He would not have thought the insouciant Frisian would have been good at much of anything besides drinking and whoring and telling lies, but as far as he could tell, the man was a damned good sailor.

Not that Louis really knew enough to judge. But he watched Brunhard's focus, and the careful adjustments he made to sail trim and the steering of the ship, and he was impressed by how exacting the man was. And the final proof of his skill was the fact that

Brunhard was able to keep out of the clutches of the notoriously fast longships.

"You still see them, Louis the Frank?" Brunhard called from where he stood by the ship's mast. "Those Norse swine, they're still there?"

"Yes!" Louis called. He could still see the lead ship, the big one with the red and white sail. The others, farther behind, would soon be lost to sight behind the headland that Brunhard had rounded after turning back toward shore. And even the closest of the Norse ships was nearly swallowed up in the increasing dark of twilight.

Wind Dancer turned slightly more to the west. "Oh," Louis called, "now I've lost sight of them! Behind the land, there!"

"Good!" Brunhard called. "They won't have the balls to follow us here, witless curs. No one has balls like Brunhard!"

Louis turned and looked forward. The sun was starting to disappear, but there was still light enough for him to see a number of massive, jagged rocks jutting like dragon's teeth from the water close to shore, the swells breaking white around their bases.

Aren't we going to wreck on those? Louis thought to himself. He opened his mouth, called, "Brunhard! Aren't we..." and then thought better of it. He knew nothing of such things and Brunhard clearly did. Asking that question would only make him sound like a fool, and Brunhard and the sailors already considered him an idiot, as all sailors did anyone who didn't follow the sea.

I'll just hope Brunhard wishes to live as much as I do, he thought.

The wind was failing, the sails starting to flog and go limp, but the sailors had apparently expected this. They were already lowering the yard away and passing the oars to the slaves seated on the rowing benches and chained by their necks to one another. The yard was swung fore and aft and lowered to the gallows and Áed stepped to the afterdeck.

"Run out your oars, you swine!" he shouted, and the rowers, accustomed now to this work and this treatment, did as they were told.

"Now you listen," Áed shouted next. "We're running in through those rocks and every one of you had better row like the devil has you by the throat, because by God he does! Make one mistake and every one of you is dead, right to the bottom with the chains around your necks! Now pull!"

The slaves leaned forward as one, set the blades of the oars in the water, leaned back, and *Wind Dancer* began to gather way. Astern of them, the other two merchant vessels fell into line, their sails stowed, oars run out.

"Pull!" And once again the rowers moved in near perfect unison and the ship moved faster still.

Brunhard was up in the bows now, one hand on the tall stem, looking forward. Louis could not see his face, but from what he had seen that day he could picture the furrowed brow, the slight frown all but lost in beard, the squint of his eyes as he turned his attention like a spear thrust toward the problem at hand.

He could hear the surf breaking around the rocks. *Wind Dancer* seemed to be heading for two of the pillar-like outcroppings, the space between them hardly wide enough for the ship to pass through under oars. To the south there was a wider gap between rocks, and Louis nearly called out to bring that to Brunhard's attention, but again he thought better of it and kept his mouth shut.

"Starboard, hold your oars!" Brunhard called in Frisian, the volume and pitch of his voice suggesting he was not as calm as he looked. Áed translated the words into Irish, even louder and more pointed than Brunhard had spoken them. Louis had been nervous before, but now, realizing how tense the mariners were, he was lapsing into genuine fear.

"Pull! Pull, you bastards! Pull together!" Brunhard shouted next and Áed was translating even before Brunhard was done speaking. The sailors prowled the centerline of the ship, smacking the rowers with rope ends, a pointless and even stupid gesture in Louis's mind, but still he said nothing.

Wind Dancer leapt ahead and the rowers, seeming to sense as Louis did the danger of their situation, pulled again and pulled with a will. The ship began to slew sideways and Louis heard the creak of the steering board and the helmsman pushed the tiller over. The ship straightened, but not entirely, and Áed screamed, "Pull!" even without Brunhard's having given the order.

The rocks were like great sea creatures, barely visible in the gloom, rising up from the sea, and *Wind Dancer* plunged into the gap between them. A wave broke against the base of the nearest one and Louis felt the cold spray whip against his face. He sucked in his breath and then the ship was through, the great beastly rocks astern, the water calmer, the motion of the vessel easy.

"Hold your oars!" Brunhard shouted and Áed translated and the rowers stopped with their blades trailing in the water.

Louis looked astern. The ship behind them was running the gap now, the seas turning her partially sideways but not enough to run her up on the rocks. And then she was through and soon after the next in line. The sound of the surf slamming against the rocks filled the night, but the three ships were safe inside.

Brunhard came ambling back to the stern and Louis could see the grin was back on his face. "Well, Louis the Frank, did you shit your trousers when we came through the rocks?"

"Of course not," Louis said. "I have nothing but faith in Frisian skills, you know that."

"Ha! You lie like all Frankish dogs lie! But no matter. We're safe in here. We'll spend the night like we are on a boat in a mill pond. Those Norse swine won't follow us in here, and if they are gone in the morning, we are on our way!"

Forward some of the sailors were wrestling with something, and when Louis heard the splash he realized it was an anchor.

"Was it luck that you found such rocks as these here?" Louis asked. "Or did you know about this place before?"

"Any man who relies on luck will be dead within the year, sailing these waters," Brunhard said. "Of course I knew how these rocks were set, and I know the only pass between them. Just to the south it looks like there's more open water, if you don't know that the reefs come up to a foot or so below the surface. Tear the bottom right out. Once when I ducked in here with some Northman on my ass, the dumb bastard tried to follow me and he broke his ship's back on that reef. Sweetest sound I ever heard was the screaming of those drowning idiots."

"I can imagine," Louis said.

"I know a dozen ways to rid myself of these damned Northmen along this coast, believe me. Either you learn, or you die. And most die. Because, and I'm willing to say it, these Norse are good seamen. Luckily, no one is better than Brunhard."

Once the anchor was down and holding and the ship made ready for the night, a barrel of ale and a barrel of dried fish and a sack of bread were opened and food handed out to the sailors and to

Brunhard and Louis. Louis sat on the edge of the aft deck and ate and drank with relish. He had not quite realized how tired and hungry he was.

No food was given to the rowers, at least not the food that Louis and the sailors enjoyed. Áed gave sharp orders to the Irish woman, the slave who had come aboard with the rest, and she set about distributing food and water to the men chained to the benches. The slaves' food came from a different barrel than the one used to feed the sailors, one that had been around much longer, Louis imagined, its contents rancid, something Brunhard had picked up at a good price.

In the light of a lantern hoisted partway up the mast he watched her moved fore and aft. She was not chained like the others, and Louis guessed she was considered no threat and was better left free and set to work. No one helped her as she handed the rations out, working as quickly as she could. She spoke to the rowers in low tones until Áed saw her and told her to keep her mouth shut.

She was young, and for all the dirt and the tangle of hair and torn and filthy clothing Louis could see that she was pretty. He had assumed at first that she was of the lowest class, of the bóaire, one of the poor farmers who owned all but nothing. But looking closer at the clothing she wore, the way she carried herself, made him think perhaps she was something more than that.

Her face had some color to it, the face of a woman who worked out of doors. She handled her duties with authority and competence, not like one accustomed to being waited on by servants. But still she had none of the cowed, fearful deference of a servant or a slave. She had more dignity than that. More bearing.

Louis tracked her as she moved from man to man. She paused to speak quickly to the one in the torn red tunic, but only briefly, a few words, despite Áed's warning to keep still. There was some connection between them, he could see it. *Lover? Husband? Brother?* Louis wondered.

He liked the way she moved, the way she held her head up while all the other captives were looking down at the deck, terrified of Brunhard and Áed, frightened by the brutal death of the Irish rower. His murder, apparently, had had just the effect Brunhard had predicted. The man did know his business.

Finally the Irish girl was done with her work and she retreated up to the bow, found a spot farthest from any of the sailors, and sat and had her own supper.

She reminds me of Failend... Louis realized. That was why she had caught his notice. She reminded him of his former lover, Failend. They were about the same size and had the same sort of physique, their short stature and thin frames hiding a surprising amount of strength. They had the same look of pride and dignity.

More reason to think she's no dairy maid, Louis thought. Failend had been married to one of the wealthiest men in Glendalough before she had apparently murdered him. Before she had taken up with the Norse heathens who had captured them. She was supposed to be with him now, on their way to Frankia, but instead he had been forced to take their silver hoard for himself and leave her, after she lost her mind and joined willingly with the Northmen.

He felt himself flush with guilt when he thought on that. He was still not certain he had done the right thing. It was not like him to abandon a woman in dire circumstances. But she would not listen to reason, would not understand that the heathens were an enemy not to be trusted.

Louis wondered where she was now. *Sold as a slave, I would imagine.* He had an idea that he might find her in Frisia, in the slave market, and buy her freedom. That thought pleased him. Certainly the heathens had appeared to welcome her in as one of their own, but they were like mad dogs and could turn at any moment.

Finally Louis finished his scant meal, stood and stretched. He looked out over the side of the ship. It was full night now, but in the light of the stars he could make out the vague shapes of the other two ships anchored nearby. He could hear the sound of the seas breaking against the treacherous dragon's teeth rocks, but where *Wind Dancer* lay it was calm, the ship just rocking gentle as a cradle.

Before they had left Dubh-linn Louis had purchased a soft leather sack large enough to fit inside, meant for sleeping in the chill night air aboard a ship at sea. He pulled it out now, found an unoccupied stretch of deck plank and crawled inside. The saddle bag with his other belongings he used as a pillow, not so much because he needed a pillow as to keep it out of Brunhard's hands. Brunhard certainly knew by now that there was silver hidden in the sack, and he was no doubt very curious as to how much.

He took off his belt and knife and laid those next to him, where he had already set his sword. He had been uncertain at first if he should wear his sword when they were at sea. His inclination was to do so; if there was ever a doubt he would always opt for wearing the sword.

But no one else on board was armed, save for the sailors with their sheath knives, and it was damned awkward to move in that tight, crowded space with the long blade hanging from his belt, so he decided against it. But he always kept it near.

Now, with his things arranged, Louis closed his eyes. Now that he was lying still the cradle effect of the ship's rocking was even more pronounced. It was soothing, as was the gentle sound of the water on the hull and the lap of it running up on the distant beach. It was not very long at all before he was asleep.

He dreamt of Failend. He had dreamt of her before, and generally they were warm and good and usually lustful dreams, but not that night. In his dream he saw her backed against a tree and he had a spear in his hand and he was thrusting the spear into her, pulling it free, thrusting again. Any of those thrusts should have killed her, but they did not and so he kept at it, not wanting to kill her but doing it anyway, wanting her to die so that he did not have to keep impaling her.

Failend was screaming and he was screaming, but the sounds were muffled, like there was something over their mouths, and try as he might he could not manage to scream at full volume.

Then he woke, eyes open, mind flailing around to make sense of where he was, what he had just been dreaming. He could see the stars overhead and the upper edge of the ship's hull. He could feel the hard deck and *Wind Dancer* rocking in the swell.

And he heard the screaming, the muffled screaming. It was still going on. Louis blinked, unsure if he was awake, and if he was, unsure why this part of the dream world had followed him into the world of men and night.

There's someone screaming, Louis thought, and it was like a great insight. Not a dream, someone was actually screaming.

He pushed out of his sleeping sack and grabbed up his sword, instinctively pulling it free from the scabbard as he did. A woman was screaming, but not aboard *Wind Dancer.* Nearby, on one of the other ships. And then he heard someone sobbing, off in the other direction. And then he heard the muffled screams from forward, the sound of voices, low, some with menace, some with amusement. He heard thrashing like there was some sort of fight going on.

He had taken two steps along the deck when he heard Brunhard's hoarse voice behind him, calling, "Here, you Frankish dog, what are you about?" But he ignored the man, stepped quickly down the deck, past the rows of chained captives larboard and starboard. They had been sleeping as best they could in their awkward positions, but now they too were starting to stir.

The muffled screaming, the struggling, had not stopped, nor had the screams from the other ships, and in the moments since coming awake Louis had realized what was going on. The sailors, apparently, had been given free rein to do with the slave girls as they wished, and now they were.

He could see a knot of men forward, and in the light of the stars could make out individuals. He was not thinking now, just moving, reacting in the way that dozens of conflicts great and small had taught him to react. There was a fight going on forward, and so forward he would go.

He grabbed the shoulder of the nearest man, spun him around and shoved him hard. Surprised, off balance, the sailor fell back and took the next man with him. Louis kicked the man to his right in the small of the back and he arched back and Louis grabbed his face and pulled him the rest of the way until he collapsed to the deck.

Áed was there. He loomed over Louis. His leggings were around his ankles and his left hand held a mass of the Irish girl's hair, his fist half the size of her entire head. He was forcing her down and back. Her brat was torn and Louis could see the white skin underneath. He could see a thin line of blood coming from the corner of her mouth.

Louis's sword came up, the tip just under Áed's chin, and he said, "Stop." He spoke in Frisian and he knew Áed understood the language. He certainly understood the point of the sword under his chin.

But he was not afraid of it. In one move, faster than Louis would have thought the man able, Áed let go of the girl's hair and knocked the blade aside with his left arm as he lunged forward with his right and grabbed Louis by the throat. He tried to step in close, press himself against Louis so that Louis had no room to raise his sword again, but with his leggings around his feet he could not move fast enough.

Louis brought the sword up once more and held it under Áed's chin, giving it just enough pressure to press into the skin, not enough to break it. Áed, however, did not let go of Louis's throat. The fingers of his massive hand nearly encompassed Louis's neck and he was exerting enough pressure to let Louis know he could crush his neck if he wished.

And there they stood. Louis could hear the sound of the sailors picking themselves up off the deck, those who had remained on their feet pressing in closer. He could hear the soft sound of knives being drawn from snug-fitting sheathes.

Across the water, aboard the other two ships, Louis could still hear the screams and sobs of the slave girls whom no one had foolishly rushed in to rescue. And he himself stood motionless, sword pressed to Áed's chin, Áed's hand around his neck. With one easy thrust he could push the tip of his sword up through the Irishman's chin, through the roof of his mouth and up into his brain. A quicker death than Áed deserved, certainly, but a death nonetheless.

And then what? Half a dozen Frisian sailors were huddled around him, ready to plunge their knives into his back the second he moved. Why they had not done so already, he could not guess. Likely they were waiting to hear Brunhard's pleasure.

And Louis could imagine what Brunhard's pleasure would be, if he killed Áed.

Very well, Louis thought. *Now what in all hell should I do?*

Chapter Fourteen

I counsel thee, Stray-Singer, accept my counsels,
they will be thy boon if thou obey'st them,
they will work thy weal if thou win'st them:
seek not ever to draw to thyself
in love-whispering another's wife.

The Counseling of the Stray-Singer

Áed did not flinch, he did not even seem aware of the steel sword tip at his throat. He spoke in an ugly, guttural growl, and he spoke Frisian which made it uglier still. "Put the sword down, you miserable shit, and go aft. This is not your affair."

"I'll shove this blade through your thick skull. I can do it faster than you can crush my throat," Louis said, truthfully.

"Go ahead. And my mates here will take you apart piece by piece and they won't be quick about it," Áed said, also speaking the truth.

And so they stood, the water lapping along the sides, the men gathered around breathing hard, the women on the other ships still sobbing, still screaming. And then Louis heard the unmistakable sound of Brunhard's feet stamping forward.

"All right, you whore's sons, all right!" he shouted as he walked. "Louis, you miserable dog, put that sword down. Áed, let go of the dog's throat!"

Louis and Áed looked into one another's eye for a few seconds more, then each did as Brunhard had instructed because they could not think of any other way to end this thing. They each took a step back and Áed took the moment to crouch and grab his leggings and pull them back up around his waist.

"Good, Áed," Brunhard said, stepping into the gap between the two men. "Pray keep that disgusting thing well hidden. Save it for the Irish bitch."

Louis lowered his sword, enough so it did not look to be a threat, not so much that he couldn't kill any man around him with a quick twist of his wrist.

"What the hell is going on here?" Brunhard demanded, his eyes moving between Louis and Áed.

You can damn well see what's going on, Louis thought, but before he could speak Áed did.

"This bastard Frank, he's sticking his nose in business that ain't his," Áed said. Brunhard nodded, looked at Louis.

"That true?" he asked. "You getting into my men's business?"

Louis took a deep breath. He had acted without thinking and now he had put himself into an untenable situation. This was, indeed, none of his business. What was about to happen to this Irish slave happened to women the world over. It was happening to the women on the other ships, just a few rods away. Was it his place to try to stop it? Because all he could do now was die trying, and then these animals would do it anyway.

Louis fixed his eyes on Áed. Anything he said about coming to a woman's rescue would be lavishly mocked, so he said, "I couldn't let this pile of shit have his way. I would puke for a week just thinking of it."

"Ah, you are a fine gentleman!" Brunhard said, loud, smirking as he spoke. "So very noble. Such a sensitive stomach. But this bitch is my property to do with as I will."

"You'll ruin her," Louis said. "She'll be worthless in the slave market when these beasts are done."

"My choice," Brunhard said. "My decision. And sometimes I decide that pleasing my men is worth more than one scrawny slave."

Louis frowned. Every second his situation grew worse. Because now he had stepped in and that meant he could not back out. Honor would not allow it. He had stopped them from raping this girl and now he could not simply abandon her, throw up his hands and let them do as they wished. If he was killed in defending her, which he most certainly would be, then there was nothing for it. He could not back down.

He thought of his brother in Roumois, sitting on their father's throne. He thought of running a sword through the man's guts, the dream that had been driving him all this time. He was finally on his way toward making that happen, and now he never would, and he felt regret mix with all the other things boiling in him.

And then he had an idea.

"I want to buy her," he said.

Brunhard was quiet. Áed was quiet and so were the sailors. Then Brunhard said, "You want to buy her?"

"Yes. She's a slave, is she not? For sale? Be worthless by the time we reach Frisia. Let me buy her now."

"Right," Áed said. "You buy her so we can watch you hump her all the way to Frisia?"

"What I do with her is my business," Louis said. "She'll be my property, and I'll do as I please." He took his eyes from Áed for the first time since the fight began, looked directly at Brunhard. "I have Frankish silver, *sceattas*, and hack silver. Not much," he lied, "but enough."

"Silver, eh?" Brunhard said. "I'll take twenty ounces for her."

"Twenty ounces? You old criminal. Ten."

"Fifteen."

Louis pretended to think about it. He could have paid twenty easily enough, but he did not want Brunhard to know it. "I think I could pay fifteen," Louis said at last.

"Done!" Brunhard said, loud, and he laughed with pleasure. He reached over and took the girl's arm and jerked her toward Louis. "Áed, tell the bitch she's Louis's now!" But Áed was too angry about how the affair had played out, and he just stepped back, leaned on the stem and glared at Louis, Brunhard and the girl.

"No matter!" Brunhard said. "She understands, and if she doesn't you'll make her, even if you don't speak their damned language. I'm sure you can show her something that's understood the world over!" He laughed again and pushed Louis and the girl toward the after end of the ship.

Louis looked at the girl and for the first time their eyes met. Louis did not see fear in her eyes, or anger or confusion or gratitude. They were expressionless, blank. The eyes of someone who was simply bracing for what would come next.

He jerked his head toward the stern of the ship and walked off in that direction, threading his way between the rowing benches and around the mast. He could hear her light footfalls as she followed him. He could hear Brunhard talking in low and animated tones to his men forward and he could well imagine what reassurances he was giving them.

They came to Louis's leather sleeping sack and Louis pointed to the girl and then to the deck beside it. The girl looked out over the water, then up at Louis. "You are a God-forsaken fool," she said. She spoke softly, and in Irish, a language she had no reason to think Louis would understand.

"I am," Louis said. "But I am also a fool who speaks your tongue." With that he saw a flicker of surprise in her eyes, a thing he counted as a great triumph. But there was still an unforgiving tone in her voice when she spoke.

"Since you're a fool," she said, "you don't understand that that Frisian bastard will just take your silver and then throw you overboard and let his men have their way with me."

"He could have done that just now," Louis said.

"He's toying with you. It's what he does, can't you see that?"

"Yes, I see that," Louis said. And he did. Maybe better than this girl, though she was already proving more insightful than Louis would have expected. No poor farmer's daughter, this one. "But if he toys with me for a day or two, then that buys time to figure some way out of this."

He looked forward. In the light from the stars he could make out Brunhard coming aft, having no doubt assured his men they would have their fun in the end, that they needed only wait a few days more.

"I don't want Brunhard to know I speak Irish," Louis said, soft. Then he grabbed the girl by the arm and jerked her close and pointed to the deck. "You sleep there, you understand?" he said, loud and insistent and in Frankish. The girl looked confused, as well she might be, but she kneeled down and then she lay on the deck.

Louis had first thought to let her use the leather sleeping sack, to take the deck for himself. But he realized that they had roles to play now, and a slave did not sleep in greater comfort than her master.

Brunhard seemed to materialize out of the dark. He looked down at the girl on the deck and then up at Louis. "Very well, you Frankish prick, you have your slave," he said, his mouth set in its usual grin. "Now, will you keep me awake humping her all night?"

"No, I think not," Louis said. "It's been a tiring day."

"Ah, you disappoint me. You won't even have her share your sleeping sack?"

"She looks as if she might bite and scratch. Wild cats, all these Irish girls."

Brunhard laughed. He was certainly having fun. "Maybe she's not for you. Would you like to buy one of the boys at the oars? Half the price you paid for her."

"She'll be enough for me, I think."

"Ah, but will you be enough for her? I doubt it. But if not, my men can help," Brunhard said, and then his voice took on a more serious tone. "But see here. Since you are so damned tired I won't make you drag out your silver tonight. But first light...fifteen ounces, you understand?"

"I understand," Louis said. He understood very well. He understood that he was the mouse, and Brunhard the cat, and Brunhard was having his fun until he decided the mouse had lived long enough.

Louis shuffled himself into his leather bag and fell into a fitful and broken sleep. He would doze, dream strange dreams, and then wake suddenly, aware of the presence of danger. He would listen, and as the hours passed he heard the night settling down around him. The sounds of the horrors being committed on the other ships died away, the muted conversations aboard *Wind Dancer* faded until all was silent. Then Brunhard's snoring started in, and nothing could be heard over that.

It was sometime deep in the night when Louis woke again, eyes flicking open, tense and alert. He lay still, listening, but could hear nothing now, save for the liquid sounds of the water overboard. Even Brunhard's snoring had become less pronounced.

He heard a voice at his side, the words as soft as a breath. "I don't think they'll come for us tonight."

Louis turned his head. The Irish girl was lying on her side, facing him. Her eyes were open and the light of the moon that was now rising was reflected in them. Her great tumble of brown hair was pushed back off her face. Her expression was relaxed. Stoic, even. A pretty girl, a little more than two decades old.

"No," Louis agreed, speaking just as soft as she had, softer than the sound of the water along the hull. "We have a day or two before Brunhard tires of this."

They were quiet, the girl looking into Louis's eyes, unblinking, her face still without expression. "Thank you," she said at last.

Louis gave a slight nod, acknowledging the thanks. He would have been annoyed if she had not thanked him, but he was embarrassed now that she had.

"You've done more than any man would likely do, more than any man on this wretched ship would do," she said. "You've thrown your own life away to help me."

"Not yet I haven't."

At that the girl gave a ghost of a smile. "Tomorrow, tell Brunhard you've changed your mind. Tell him to give me back to his men. He'll do it anyway, and that way you might spare yourself."

"You are not the daughter of some *thrall*, some slave, or some miserable landless farmer, are you?" Louis asked.

"No."

"Then you know I can't do that."

The girl nodded.

"What's your name?" Louis asked.

"Conandil," the girl said. "And I heard Brunhard call you Louis. Louis the Frank."

"I am Frankish," Louis said. "I am Louis de Roumois."

The girl nodded again. For some time they were quiet, eyes open, listening.

"That man in the torn red tunic," Louis said. "On the third bench back, on the left side. Is he someone special to you?"

Conandil smiled a bit more at that. "You are very observant, Louis de Roumois. I hope there are no others here with such keen eyes. Yes, that is Broccáin mac Bressal. My husband. His father was the rí túaithe of a small kingdom south of Dubh-linn. Do you know what that is, rí túaithe?"

"Yes," Louis said. "A king of some sort."

"Yes, a king who owes allegiance to one above him, the *rí ruirech*. The rí túaithe to the west of us, a miserable bastard named Eochu, betrayed us. Joined with the heathens to attack our rath and take us all, and the people in the countryside as well. Those who lived were sold. I tried to not be one who lived, but they took me anyway."

Louis was quiet, thinking about this. "You told your husband to keep silent, to not let on that you were husband and wife," he said. It was not a question.

Conandil nodded. "The men here are very cruel. If they knew he was my husband they would see that as a chance for great fun. I made him swear he would keep still, no matter what."

Louis looked up at the stars. He could hardly fathom the agony the man must have felt, chained to a bench, sworn to silence, as the crew of the slaver made ready to take turns with his wife. He felt a bit better about having likely tossed his own life away.

He guessed that when Brunhard and his men came for him, Conandil would throw herself in the sea, take her chances with a merciful God rather than a vengeful crew. At least he had given her that choice.

Louis turned back to Conandil and her bright eyes. "Maybe we'll find some way out of this," he said.

"Maybe," she said.

Chapter Fifteen

"Consider, noble Norsemen," said the banded goddess,
"how many fires burn brightly here…"
Gisli Sursson's Saga

Louis closed his eyes and soon sleep had him in a firm grip at last, deep and without dreams. He slept through the rest of the dark hours, and when he came awake again the morning light was just making itself visible to the east and he was aware that something was happening and it was not good.

He sat up quick, eyes open, his hand reaching out for the sword at his side. The only thought that could form in his groggy mind was, *Already?* He looked left and right to see where the attack was coming from, how many, how they were armed. It was still mostly night, with just the first gray vestiges of dawn. There were men getting to their feet, the sounds of some grand commotion, but it was all happening forward, in the bow. No one seemed to be paying any attention to him.

Conandil sat up at his side and her eyes were also wide with surprise. "What is it?" she asked in a whisper.

"I don't know," Louis said. He studied the chaos forward and saw there was more order than he had realized. The sailors were moving along the rowing benches, waking the dozing slaves with kicks and lashes from their rope ends. The long oars were coming down off the gallows and men were handing them along. More hands were gathered up in the bow, Áed among them.

"Louis!" he heard Brunhard bark. He turned and looked aft. The master was standing by the tiller, arms folded, looking like the trunk of a tree that had been cut down at shoulder height. "Get your sorry hide off the deck, and your new whore, too! We have work to do!"

Louis kicked his way out of his sleeping sack and stood and Conandil got to her feet as well. Louis pointed to the sack and said in Frankish, "Roll that up!" and Conandil nodded and got to her knees and rolled the sack, good thrall that she was.

"What's happening?" Louis asked. He was not sure if Brunhard would answer, but the Frisian could not resist the chance to speak.

"Damned wind has come around out of the east," he said and then took a moment to spit over the side. "We're on a lee shore and the worthless shit anchor is dragging already."

Louis nodded, though he was not sure what all of that meant. But now that Brunhard had mentioned wind he realized that it was brisker than it had been the night before. Not blowing hard, really, but steady and strong enough to kick up small waves that broke on the shingle beach a cable length away.

He looked forward. The bow of the ship was pointing straight out to sea and he understood that was because the wind was blowing from that direction. If the anchor did not hold them in place, the wind would push the ship onto the shore.

*Anchor is dragging...*Louis thought. *Maybe that's what that means.* But he could see even Brunhard was not feeling too talkative, which meant the situation had to be serious. He stepped out of the way and watched as the rowers ran their long oars out through the row ports and held them horizontal. Áed prowled the center of the ship, his mood apparently even more foul that was his wont, but that was no surprise. He would take the night's frustrations out on the helpless men chained to the benches, but there was nothing Louis could do about that.

"Listen to me, you sorry turds!" Áed shouted with particular vehemence. "We are rowing out against the wind, and by God you had better pull for all you are worth or I'll rip the lungs out of each and every one of you! Do you hear me? By God you'll pray for death if I have to put my hands on you! Now, stroke!"

Nearly as one the rowers leaned forward, put their oars in the water, leaned back and pulled. *Wind Dancer* moved ahead, not with the nimble speed Louis had seen the day before, but fast enough. Up in the bow the sailors there pulled in the rope tied to the anchor as it came slack.

"Stroke!"

The rowers leaned into it again. More anchor rope came on board.

"Stroke!" Four more pulls of the oar and then one of the sailors forward called, "Anchor's up!"

Now it was Brunhard's turn to shout. "Keep them at it! Keep them at it!" he called forward to Áed, and there was no amusement in his voice now, and that told Louis that things were serious indeed. Brunhard turned to the man at the tiller.

"Right through there!" He pointed to a place just to the left of the bow. "You see?"

"I see, Master Brunhard!" the man at the tiller yelled. The wind was blowing stronger, the waves a little more pronounced. The men at the oars leaned into them, driven by the sailors' rope ends and unmistakable sense of urgency aboard the ship. It was nearly the inverse of the night before, Louis realized, but now the wind was stronger and apparently the danger greater.

"Stroke!" Directly ahead of them the sun broke the horizon with a blinding flash, the light falling on the water and the shore beyond and the wicked dragon tooth rocks through which they were threading their way.

Beautiful! Louis thought. An amazing scene, the green water breaking white around the rocks, the brown gravel beach, the sandy cliffs running up to the shore beyond, all bathed in the morning sun. They could not ask for a more gorgeous place in which to die a watery death.

"Stroke!"

Now they were among the dragon's teeth, rocks jutting up on either side, and even Louis could see how one false stroke, one mistake with the oars or wrong twist of the rudder could put the ship up against them, where the seas would slam them without mercy and the frail shell of *Wind Dancer* would be crushed like wheat on a thresher's floor.

And suddenly they were through. With one pull the ship slipped through the gap and there was only open water and the brilliant sun ahead of them, but Áed did not slow the pace at which he was driving the men at the oars.

"Stroke!"

Louis looked astern. *Wind Dancer* had led the way and now the second of Brunhard's ships was making its way through the gap, and seeing the maneuver from a distance it looked more frightening still. The surf hit the dragon teeth rocks with great spumes of spray and the seas knocked the ship's bow side to side, threatening to turn it one way or another and smash it to kindling.

The oars worked furiously, though from the angle at which Louis was watching they seemed to just go up and down, up and down, rather than sweeping fore and aft. They looked far too inadequate to drive the vessel against the incoming seas, but, like *Wind Dancer*, the second vessel shot through the gap and into the open water.

The third ship came through, and *Wind Dancer* was about two or three cable lengths clear of the rocks before Áed began to slow the pace of the rower's stroke. The morning was cool, but the men on the benches were sweating hard. Conandil, unbidden, had gone forward and found a ladle and was bringing water to the men, one at a time. No one told her to stop.

The three ships fell into line, pulling directly away from the coast, the sea beyond the bow winking and glinting in the light of the sun that was hanging just above the horizon. Louis looked over at Brunhard. He appeared more relaxed now.

Brunhard, in turn, seemed to sense that Louis was looking at him. He turned and grinned, then nodded toward Áed, standing by the mast, calling the stroke. "I'm glad you didn't shove your sword through his skull, Frank," he said. "Áed may be a great filthy beast of an Irishman, but he knows how to keep the rowers at it."

"He seems to have a talent for shouting and beating men," Louis admitted. Then, wishing to change the subject, said, "Will you make these poor whore's sons row all the way to Frisia, or will you set the sail soon?" They were already quite far from the coast and Louis could not understand why they were still driving under oars when there seemed to be a fair amount of wind blowing.

Brunhard shook his head as if Louis had asked the stupidest of stupid questions. But Louis knew he would explain because Brunhard could not resist explaining. "You see how the wind comes from the east?" he said. "You see the shore, including rocks and such, are to the west? If we set the sail, the wind will blow us onto the rocks."

"Why don't you set the sail and steer the ship to the south? Where there are no rocks?" Louis asked.

Brunhard grinned wider, shook his head again. "Why don't you keep to buggering sheep, or something else that you're good at and leave the sailing to me, eh?" he said. "We can steer to the south, but the wind will still blow us to the west. Not directly, true. If we steer south then we will actually be heading southwest because of what is called 'leeway.' Eventually we'll be on the rocks. So, we set sail only when we are far enough away from the shore. But that is not the only reason."

Louis was about to ask what the other reason might be when Brunhard stepped forward and called for Áed to pass word for the rowers to rest on their oars. Once the rowing had stopped and *Wind Dancer* was no longer moving through the water, just rising and falling on the swells, Brunhard turned to one of his sailors. He gave no order, just pointed to the masthead. The sailor nodded and scrambled easily up the rigging, settling himself in at the top with legs twisted around the thick ropes.

For a long time there was only silence. The slaves at the oars looked down at the deck, grateful for the brief reprieve from their work. The sailors leaned against the sides of the ship and stared expressionless out to sea. Brunhard maintained his tree stump-like stance, his head swiveling side to side as he slowly scanned the horizon.

"Master Brunhard!" the sailor at the masthead called. "I see nothing! All is clear to the horizon in every direction!"

"Good!" Brunhard shouted. He turned to Áed and nodded and with a shout Áed set the rowers to work again. The man aloft slid down one of the ropes to the deck.

"That was the other thing," Brunhard said. "Before we get too far from shore we make certain none of those Norse swine are lurking anywhere. But it seems they've lost interest. They're like spoiled children who quickly tire of a plaything."

"Let us hope," Louis said.

For some time more the men at the oars rowed and the three ships, with *Wind Dancer* in the lead, pulled away from the Irish coast, their bows turned a bit more southerly as they distanced themselves from the dangers of the rocky shore. Finally Brunhard ordered the oars run in and the sailors stepped up to do their part, casting off the lines holding the sail to the yard, hoisting away on the halyard, swinging the end of the yard forward to duck it around the shrouds, and finally setting the big square sail to the wind.

More hands heaved in the lines made fast to the corners of the sails and the great square of cloth flogged and then filled with wind. *Wind Dancer* heeled to leeward and the note of the water running down her hull rose in pitch and volume. Louis had to shift his stance to keep from stumbling, and forward he saw Conandil catch herself on one of the rower's shoulders before she went right over.

"There, you soft-hearted prick!" Brunhard said. "Now the wind drives us, and you don't have to worry about your beloved Irish slaves getting all tired out from rowing!" Louis had to marvel at how Brunhard could use his great, embracing smile to say the most outrageous and offensive things and still seem like one's dearest friend.

Louis sat on the deck, rested his back against the side of the ship. "Whatever gets us to Frisia the fastest," he said. "Whatever gets me off this damned ship the fastest."

And he was indeed eager to reach Frisia, and Frankia, but still there was something marvelous about being on the ship under sail. Even Louis, a stranger to ships, had to admit it. The motion was regular but easy, smooth, not like the jarring of a trotting horse. They were moving fast but with no effort on their part, save for some minor turning of the rudder, a few pulls on ropes here and there. All the considerations of the land seemed far away. The sea was a moat now, separating them from the troubles of the shore.

Louis let his body sway with the motion of the ship and stared off idly forward, past the edge of the sail. In that direction there was nothing but water beyond the confines of the ship, but as Louis understood it there was a great headland somewhere beyond the horizon, and once they reached that they would turn east and make the crossing to Wales, spending hopefully not more than a single night at sea.

It will not be so long before I am back in Frankia, he thought. And then he remembered Brunhard. The jovial Brunhard. The man who would kill him when the time was right, take his silver, give Conandil to his sailors. Good Master Brunhard. Louis did not doubt that the man was just waiting for the right moment to toss him overboard.

"Say, Louis," Brunhard said, as if he could hear Louis's thoughts. "Don't you have some silver to give me?"

Louis sighed and stood, but before he could even take a step toward the place where his bag was stowed they heard a cry from aloft, a lookout who'd been sent to the masthead a few moments before. The same man who had been sent up earlier, but his voice did not sound so calm as it had that morning when he reported an empty sea.

"Master Brunhard!" he called.

"What?" Brunhard shouted aloft.

"The sun has climbed higher now, well clear of the horizon," the lookout called, and even Louis understood that he was making excuses for what would come next.

"Yes, it does that, you stupid bastard!" Brunhard shouted. "What do you see?"

"Four sails, master! Off to the east and just coming over the horizon."

There was quiet fore and aft. No one dared say anything until Brunhard had spoken, and Brunhard was busy staring off toward the east. Finally he looked aloft again.

"Is it those bastard Northmen? The ones who chased us yesterday?" Brunhard shouted.

The man aloft hesitated. Maybe to look again, to be certain. Maybe because he was afraid to report what he saw.

"Yes, Master Brunhard!" he shouted at last. "Yes, the same four ships!"

Chapter Sixteen

Old age does this to me,
but youth to you,
you've hope of better,
but I none at all.

The Saga of the People of Laxardal

Earlier, Thorgrim's men had not been happy about spending the night at sea a mile or so offshore, south of Dubh-linn. They had been even less happy when he informed them that they would once again spend the night at sea but this time beyond the sight of land.

Once the three merchant ships had gone around the point, disappeared from view just as the sun was going down, Thorgrim knew they were beyond his grasp. The wind died away, the sails came down and the oars came out. Thorgrim turned *Sea Hammer* more southerly, rounded the point, and in the fading light he could make out the terrible rocks that jutted from the sea like giant teeth looking for a ship to devour.

He did not have to study those rocks long to know he did not want to get in among them after dark. Probably not in full daylight, either.

So he had swung his ship around to the east and headed offshore, the other three vessels rowing dutifully astern. The mast and the gallows and the tall stem and sternpost glowed a warm orange color as they caught the setting sun on their after sides.

As the last vestiges of light faded in the west, Thorgrim ordered the ships together. Lines were passed from one to the other until all four ships were tied together, as if they were getting ready for a sea fight. The masters of the vessels stepped from one to the other until they were gathered around *Sea Hammer*'s afterdeck, where Thorgrim stood leaning against the larboard side.

He was not in a good mood. He stared out over the stern and the jagged dark line on the horizon, the shadow of Ireland, and he frowned as his dark thoughts swirled around. He felt as if the black mood was coming on him, that foul temper that sometimes came in the evening, and often led to his wolf dreams in the dark hours. What happened then, he did not know. No one did. Some thought he took the shape of a wolf and prowled the night. They called him Kveldulf. Night Wolf.

But he was never so sure that was true.

He knew only that sometimes the black mood came on him, and sometimes he dreamed that he was moving through the world, through Midgard, the realm of man, like a wolf. Sometimes he saw things that proved to be true.

The wolf dreams had never come on him when he was at sea, however. This was new. But it might not be the black mood, either. He might just be in foul temper. He had every reason to be.

Thorodd Bollason was the last to make his way to *Sea Hammer*'s stern, but Fostolf was the first to speak. "Do you mean to have us keep to the sea a second night?" he asked. "My men are not happy about this. Yesterday we were not so far from shore, but now we can drift to places only the gods know of."

Thorgrim turned and fixed Fostolf with his eyes. Someone had lit a lantern so there was light enough to see that Thorgrim was not in the mood for debate. Even Fostolf could see that, and whatever further protest he was about to launch died on his lips.

No one spoke. No one dared. They shuffled nervously and looked away and waited for Thorgrim to speak.

Save for Starri Deathless, who was generally oblivious to the mood of any gathering he was in. There was, of course, no reason for Starri to be there—he did not command ships as these other men did—but just as none of the company dared cross Thorgrim Night Wolf, they did not care to cross Starri either. One could never tell how a berserker would react. So if his presence was all right with Thorgrim, it was all right with them.

"Thorgrim Night Wolf has some plan," Starri said, "and you can bet it's a clever one, because the gods speak to him. Some of you men have not been with us so long. Do you know the tale of this?" He held up the arrowhead he wore around his neck, the one that had split itself on Thorgrim's upraised sword.

The others mumbled their acknowledgement. They had seen it, and heard the tale. Anyone who had been in Starri's company for more than half a day had heard the tale.

"Listen to me, now," Thorgrim said, forcing himself to speak in a steady and measured way. He did not want Starri to start in on the story of the arrowhead. He did not like it when Starri insisted that he, Thorgrim, was blessed by the gods. He did not think it was a very lucky thing to say.

"Those whore's sons slipped through our fingers, but they won't do it again. They might expect us to wait nearby, like a cat crouching by a hole, ready to leap on a mouse. If they see us they'll stay put until we tire of waiting. And they'll likely expect us to be waiting to the south of them. They might even sail north for that reason. But we'll wait out here, too far offshore for them to see, especially with the rising sun in their eyes. They won't expect that. Once they're too far from shore to get back among those rocks, we pounce."

He looked from man to man. They were all nodding their heads, some with more enthusiasm than others. Harald looked the most pleased. This was the sort of thing he loved, and while he, too, was wary of a night at sea, he seemed less bothered by it than most. Godi, too, seemed pleased. The others, if they were not so happy as that, at least hid it well.

They went back to their ships, but they kept them lashed to one another, riding up and down on the swells like bits of jetsam entangled together. Most slept, and soon the sounds of their snoring was the loudest thing to be heard on that still night.

Sleep did not come to Thorgrim so easily. He stood against the starboard side of the ship, then sat on the deck, his back against strakes. Failend came aft and their eyes met and neither spoke. Failend knew Thorgrim well, and she knew better than to speak to him then, so she lay down on the fur on deck and closed her eyes and soon she, too, was sleeping.

Thorgrim tilted his head back, looked up at the stars, marveled at them, wondered about their nature, as he so often did. He had always considered the stars to be one of the few things the gods had ever done that was just for the benefit of man. They were beautiful, and they gave off a subtle, almost magical light. When the earth was dark and all references to land lost, they were like markers in a narrow fjord, guiding the way. And now, drifting on the ocean, Thorgrim could see that his little cluster of ships was not being swept away by the currents or driving toward the rocks. The stars told him that.

Sleep came at last, but not for long. It was still dark when Thorgrim awoke. He had slept deep, had not dreamed of wolves or anything he could recall. His dark mood was a bit lighter now, but even before he sat up he knew there were other concerns.

The wind had come up during the night and it was starting to blow from the east and Thorgrim was pretty sure it would continue to build. He looked up at the stars, up at the fixed star to the north, and felt sure they had been blown closer in to shore. Not too close, he hoped. It was time to move.

He climbed out from under his fur blanket and found Harald, sleeping with his mouth gaping, and he shook him gently. Harald's eyes snapped open, but Thorgrim could see that his son was not sure what was happening, or even where he was. He gave the boy a moment to collect himself, then said, "I am going over to *Fox*. We'll get to a place where we can see the shore. The rest of you stay below the horizon, but make sure you can see us still. You'll have to row east a bit, against the wind. When you see us set the sail on *Fox*, then the three of you set sail and follow. Bring *Sea Hammer* alongside *Fox* so I can get back aboard. Do you understand?"

Harald nodded and Thorgrim guessed by the look on the boy's face that he was fully awake now and had understood the instructions. He left Harald there and moved forward, looking close at the sleeping men until he found Starri Deathless. He nudged Starri with his toe, then stepped back quick as Starri sat bolt upright, eyes open, though still not entirely awake. It was prudent to keep clear of Starri when he was roused in so unexpected a manner. One never knew.

"Starri, come with me," Thorgrim whispered, and Starri nodded and climbed out of his makeshift bed. He followed Thorgrim over *Sea Hammer*'s sheer strake onto *Blood Hawk*, tied alongside, and then across *Blood Hawk* to *Fox* at the far end of the raft of ships.

Thorodd Bollason, the man Thorgrim had set as master of *Fox*, was awake and, having seen them coming, was waiting at the place where his ship touched *Blood Hawk*. Thorodd was a young man of about twenty-five winters. Loyal, sometimes too eager to please.

The master of a ship sailing in company with others had to strike a fine balance, in Thorgrim's opinion. He had to be willing to do the bidding of the commander of the fleet, but he needed initiative as well. The one commanding was not always there to give instruction. In truth, he more often was not. A shipmaster needed the balls to make decisions on his own and the brains to make the right decisions.

Thorodd Bollason was not yet that man. He was close, but he seemed a bit lacking yet in both balls and brains. Fostolf, master of *Dragon*, on the other hand, seemed to Thorgrim to be fully outfitted with balls, but maybe a bit shy with regard to brains.

But they were good men. If they lived long enough, they would learn.

"Thorgrim Night Wolf," Thorodd said by way of greeting as Thorgrim stepped down on a sea chest and then down on the deck. "Starri. What's acting, at this time of night?"

"We're going to get underway," Thorgrim said. "We're going to go west, far enough to see the coast well. We'll watch for these merchant ships. I brought Starri, keenest eyes in the fleet. Since *Fox* is the smallest, she'll be the hardest for our quarry to see. The others will stay back until we set sail."

Thorodd thought about that and nodded. "We could unstep the mast, make us even harder to see," he suggested.

Thorgrim considered that, weighed the advantage of Starri's being able to watch from higher up against the disadvantage of being more visible.

"Good idea," he said. "Let's cast off from the others and get the mast on the deck."

Thorodd moved among his men, waking them, not too gently but not too harshly, either. Moments later, hands were casting off the lines that bound *Fox* to *Blood Hawk*. As the two ships drifted apart, others cast off shrouds and stays and eased the mast down from its vertical position to the horizontal. The oars, lashed to the gallows, were untied and handed out to the men at the sea chests that served as rowing benches.

Soon they were pulling through the dark, a slow, steady stroke, *Fox* cutting through the swell. Thorgrim stood aft by Thorodd. After the expanse of *Sea Hammer*, *Fox* felt more like a boat than a ship.

As they rowed slowly west Thorgrim watched the stars on the western horizon. Finally he said, "That's far enough. Let the men rest on their oars." Thorgrim thought they were the proper distance from the coast, but there was no way to know for certain. Better to wait there for the first hints of sun to tell them where they were.

They did not wait long. Soon after the oars had come in Thorgrim looked astern, looked toward the east, and he could see the black yielding to gray as the sun began its slow climb to the rim of the earth. The wind was building a bit, easterly, unusual for the predawn hours that tended to be calm.

"We'll have a lee shore this morning," Thorodd observed. "Let's hope we're not too close to land now."

"We're not," Starri said with certainty, but if this was because he could see something the others could not, or because he had an excess of faith in Thorgrim's navigation, Thorgrim could not tell.

But Starri was right. Soon the gray spread across the skies to the east and stars began to fade and the long, black coast of Ireland separated itself from the black expanse of ocean and sky and they could see they were still miles away from land.

"Close enough for you to see, Starri?" Thorgrim asked.

Starri frowned at the distant shore. "I am like the hawk, you know," he said, "but even the hawk cannot see forever. And since you seem to lust after Brunhard and his ships the way a drunkard lusts for drink, I dare not miss them. So let's get a bit closer."

The oars were run out again, the rowers pulling with more enthusiasm now that they knew they would not hit anything. The men who were idle took down the carved oak figurehead of a fox with teeth bared that arched up above the bow, and the carved tail on the stern, all to make the ship more invisible from shore.

You seem to lust after Brunhard and his ships... Thorgrim toyed with the words in his head. Once again Starri, in all his madness, seemed to understand something about Thorgrim's motives that even he, Thorgrim, did not realize. He did indeed want Brunhard and his ships. They should have been his the day before. He should have snatched them up as easily as picking something up off the ground. But they had escaped—not through luck but through skill—and that was a goad to Thorgrim Night Wolf.

He had no idea who this Brunhard was, but already he wanted to capture him and strip him of everything he owned and kill him if he resisted in the smallest way.

"He won't get away again," Thorgrim said, just loud enough for him and the gods to hear.

The men rowed and the sky grew lighter and finally Starri said, "This is close enough."

The land was still a few miles away, a long, low, irregular black shape stretching from south to north. Thorgrim knew that he himself would never be able to pick out a ship at that distance, but Starri seemed confident that he could. And soon he would have the assistance of the sun, that would break the horizon and illuminate the sea and the land with its brilliant light, and blind anyone looking toward the east where *Fox* lay in wait.

Thorodd ordered the oars run in, save for the two amidships which, with the occasional pull, were used to keep the ship pointed toward the west. Next he ordered *dagmál*, the morning meal, handed out. It consisted of dried fish and bread and ale and it was received gratefully by the men who had already spent considerable time at the oars.

Starri ate quick and then climbed up onto the stem, now the highest perch aboard *Fox*. He remained motionless, facing the land, his eyes like a bird of prey scanning the distance for any sign of motion.

Thorodd, standing at Thorgrim's side on the afterdeck, nodded forward. "Starri makes a fine figurehead," he said. "I think I'll keep him in place of that bit of carved oak."

Thorgrim smiled despite himself, despite how humorless he felt at that moment. "He's far more frightening than anything else you could put there," he agreed.

The sky grew lighter still, pale blue in the east, dark blue in the west. And then the sun broke the horizon and lit up *Fox* like a blazing fire sprung to life, casting long shadows down the deck. It touched the highest peaks on the land to the west, lighting them up, creeping down the high ground to the coast and then to the sea. Thorgrim sat a little straighter, half expecting Starri to call out that he had seen the ships right ahead and underway. But he did not.

Rather, Starri was silent and remained silent for a maddeningly long time. The men finished their meal. Some dozed leaning on the ship's sheer strake. Others stared off north or south. There was no looking to the east, into the brilliant morning sun.

Thorgrim Night Wolf had many strengths, but waiting patiently was not one of them, which was unfortunate because both seafaring and raiding often required just that. But try as he might, and he did try, he could not avoid growing irritable as the sun climbed higher in the sky and Starri stared silently forward. And so when Starri at last sung out, "There they are, Night Wolf! They're coming out at last!" he felt palpable relief.

The men on the sea chest sat upright, smiled, looked past the bow. Good cheer swept over the ship just as the first brilliant rays of sunlight had done that morning.

Thorgrim, who had been leaning against the side of the ship, straightened and headed forward, Thorodd at his side. He stepped up to the foredeck and stood to the starboard side of the stem. Starri was standing with one foot on the starboard sheer strake, one on the larboard, hugging the stem like it was his lover and staring out toward the shore.

"Where are they, Starri?" Thorgrim asked.

"You see that high peak, just a little off the starboard bow? The odd-shaped one? Look just in front of that and you can see them, like little ducklings paddling out to sea."

Thorgrim looked. He squinted, he looked sideways, he looked with one eye and then the other. "If you say so, Starri, then I'll believe you," he said at last. "Are they under sail?"

"No, they're rowing away from the land," Starri said. That made Thorgrim feel better. It was reasonable, and not a sign that his eyes were failing with old age, that he could not see ships with their sails furled. Thorodd could not see them either.

"They're likely anxious to get off this lee shore," Thorodd said and Thorgrim nodded his agreement.

"They'll row away from land until they have sea room enough and then set sail," Thorgrim said.

"Should I set the sail now?" Thorodd asked. "Signal the others to get underway?"

"Not yet," Thorgrim said. "We're invisible to them now, with the sun behind us. We'll let them get as close as we can before we leap on them. But you may as well get the mast stepped again."

Thorodd turned to oversee that operation and Starri continued to watch the ships approach and Thorgrim continued to stare in that direction in hope of seeing something. And finally he did. Just the smallest of specks, moving across the water, but distinct from the land behind them. Moving fast.

"Why do they have so many men for the oars?" Thorgrim wondered out loud. Every merchantman he had known carried a small crew, five or six men. But these ships seemed to have oars manned like a longship.

"I can't imagine," Starri said. "They're not warriors, we know that. They ran like rabbits from us. But they each have full banks of oars. Madness."

"Or maybe not," Thorgrim said. "It means they're faster than other merchant ships when the wind fails. And they seem faster when the wind is up as well."

Soon the merchant ships were more visible still, and even Thorgrim did not doubt his eyes. One by one they hoisted sail, the cloth lit up golden by the sun which was still low to the horizon. They set a course roughly south, but still tending away from the coast. They had not yet seen the fox lying in wait. They would not have set that course if they had.

"Very good, Thorodd!" Thorgrim called aft. "We have them now! Set the sail!"

There were smiles down the deck as the men tailed into the halyard. The big yard rose up to the top of the mast and the corners of the sail were pulled aft. The wind was almost astern of them now, which was good for *Fox* or any longship. Soon they would swoop down on Brunhard and his little fleet and help themselves to whatever they might find.

Thorgrim looked astern, held his hand up to his forehead to shade his eyes from the sun. The other ships were off to the east, but not so far that he could not see them. They had seen *Fox*'s sail go up, the signal for them to do the same. He could make out *Sea Hammer*'s red and white sail and he smiled. He knew Harald would have had his eyes fixed on *Fox*, waiting for the very second *Fox*'s sail appeared, determined to be the first of the fleet to respond to the signal. And he was.

Underfoot Thorgrim felt the ship heel to the pressure of the sail, felt the life come back into her timbers as she stopped her wallowing in the sea and gathered her determined and powerful momentum. He stepped aside as three of Thorodd's men hurried forward bearing the figurehead, which they proceeded to return to its place on the stem. Waiting and watching were over.

As smallest ship in the fleet, *Fox* was also the slowest and soon the others began to come up with her, *Sea Hammer* in the lead. Thorgrim knew that Harald would be constantly adjusting course and the set of the sail, probably driving the men to madness as he tried to squeeze every bit of speed out of the already fast ship.

But Harald did know how to drive her, and soon she was ranging up along *Fox*'s side. Thorodd took charge of *Fox*'s tiller and the two ships inched closer to one another. Harald sent one of *Sea Hammer*'s more nimble men up aloft to tie a rope to the leeward end of the yard which was swung over to *Fox*. Thorgrim grabbed hold of the rope, climbed up onto *Fox*'s sheer strake and swung across the gap between the two ships. He landed back aboard his own vessel with all the grace he could muster and tried not to show his relief that he had not plunged into the sea.

They swung the rope back and Starri took it up. He swung across the gap, but rather than landing on the deck, he swung into the shrouds and grabbed hold of the heavy, tarred line and raced up to the top of *Sea Hammer*'s mast where he could get the best possible view of their quarry. He wrapped his legs around the masthead, looked west and whooped with delight.

"Oh, Night Wolf!" he shouted. "Now they've seen us, and now they're running, but it's too late for them!"

Chapter Seventeen

A fifth I know: when I see, by foes shot,
speeding a shaft through the host,
flies it never so strongly I still can stay it,
if I get but a glimpse of its flight.

The Song of Spells

Brunhard seemed angrier, and more unnerved, than Louis had seen him anytime during their brief acquaintance. He snatched up an earthenware cup that he had set on the deck and flung it against the side of the ship, smashing it into bits, spraying Louis and the helmsman with shards. He swore a terrible stream of oaths, cursing the lookout and the Northmen and the Irish and God.

Up above, the lookout remained in position at the masthead, apparently not eager to return to deck, and Louis could well imagine why. No one else on board made a sound.

The Northmen must have done something clever, Louis thought. He stood and looked inconspicuously out to sea but he could see nothing of the raiders the man aloft had spotted.

He understood in a general way what Brunhard had done the day before to escape the pursuers. He knew that Brunhard considered it the most clever thing devised by man, and himself the cleverest of men for having pulled it off. But now, apparently, the Northmen had done something clever in their own right, and Brunhard was not taking it well.

Well, those heathen bastards can be clever, that's for certain, Louis thought. He had seen Thorgrim Night Wolf pull off more than a few clever tricks. He had even been Thorgrim's victim on more than one occasion. So he knew the heathens were not to be underestimated.

And then another thought occurred to him and his stomach tightened. He tried to dismiss it. It was, of course, ridiculous. The coast of Ireland was swarming with these Northmen. The odds against the man hunting them being Thorgrim Night Wolf were too much to calculate.

Ridiculous! Louis thought. But he could not shake it.

And then yet another thought came: it did not really matter. If the Northmen now in pursuit caught them and overwhelmed them, then Louis was going to die fighting, and it didn't really matter if it was Thorgrim who killed him or some other blood-hungry savage.

That thought did not bring him much comfort. Nor was it much comfort to realize that if the Northmen didn't kill him, then Brunhard certainly would.

"Ah, damn them!" Brunhard shouted. "Damn them all to hell!" He crossed to the leeward side and spit a great globule of spit into the sea. He stepped back to the middle of the afterdeck, arched his back, slapped his hands against his broad stomach. He looked down at Louis and grinned his great grin.

"There! I feel better now! Now I'm ready to bugger these Northmen the way you Franks bugger your goats!"

Louis shook his head. A moment before, Brunhard had been shouting his anguish and despair into the morning sky, and now he was grinning like there was some great feast laid out before him. Louis was starting to wonder if the man was a complete lunatic.

Brunhard stepped over to the windward side, looked out to sea. He stared for some time, not moving, not speaking. Then he looked over at the shore to the west, then up at the sail, bellied out taut in the stiff breeze.

"Helmsman! Fall off now, fall off!"

The helmsman pulled the tiller toward him, just a bit, and Louis could see *Wind Dancer*'s bow swing to the right, turning toward the land.

"Silef!" Brunhard called forward. Silef was one of Brunhard's Frisian crew, the one he trusted most, as far as Louis could tell. When it came to driving the Irish slaves, Áed was Brunhard's man. But for anything that had to do with seamanship, it was Silef.

Now Silef, who was nearby and apparently expecting Brunhard's summons, called, "Yes, Master Brunhard?"

"Get some of these lazy whore's sons to the sheets and braces! We'll have the wind on our larboard quarter soon enough!"

Silef turned and began to shout orders that Louis would not have understood even if he spoke better Frisian than he did. A great bustle ensued, during which this rope was pulled and that rope was slacked and the yard overhead moved a bit and then everything was pronounced correct and set back as it was. On the thwarts the Irish slaves looked warily around, unsure of what was happening, risking a beating with their curiosity.

And now *Wind Dancer*'s bow was pointed back toward the land. Not directly, they were approaching the shore at an oblique angle, but they were, without question, approaching the shore.

"Now, see here, Brunhard," Louis said. "This very morning you lectured me about the importance of keeping away from the land, and now you are clearly sailing right for it again. I wonder at what you are thinking. Did the heathens trick you in some way?"

Brunhard turned quick and Louis saw the anger on his face and just as fast he saw it brushed away as the Frisian fixed his grin like a mask. "Heathens!" he said, spitting the word. "They waited for us offshore, hid behind the rising sun. It's as clever as heathens get. But now I'll do for those bastards."

Louis nodded. But Brunhard had not answered his question, and he wanted an answer. Louis de Roumois was naturally curious, but there was more to it than that. He knew that his fight with Brunhard and the others was not over, that the incident with Conandil and the stash of silver he had in his bag had not been forgotten. And this ship was a foreign country to him, ground not of his choosing. The more he knew about it, the better he could fight.

"But you haven't told me, Brunhard, why are we going back toward the land?"

"Ah, you ignorant Frankish cur, you try my patience!" Brunhard shouted. "Yes, the shore is a great danger, particularly with the wind as it is. But if it is a danger to us, it is a danger to the heathen as well. And the heathen is not as great a seaman as I am, and he is not as clever as I am. So I will get him to a place of danger and then I will play a trick on him and we'll see the end of his miserable existence. Now do you understand?"

"Yes, I think so," Louis said. "But what is the trick you will play on him?"

"It's a very clever trick," Brunhard said. "It's a trick blessed by God, who has given me just the right conditions to play it. Because

God loves Brunhard as much as everyone else does. And you, Louis the Frank, will have to wait to see what great, clever trick I pull from my bag!"

Once again *Sea Hammer* stretched out a lead over the other ships in Thorgrim's fleet, five ship-lengths ahead of *Blood Hawk*, which was also fast and well-handled, and much more than that over the smaller ships. Brunhard's merchantmen, still a mile and a half ahead of them, were running with their tails between their legs. They were fast. For merchant ships. But Thorgrim could see their lead visibly dropping away.

He stood on *Sea Hammer*'s sheer strake, on the weather side, one hand on the aftermost shroud. The tar on the rope was sticky against his palm, the line bar-taut and quivering with the pounding of the ship in the sea. With every third or fourth plunge of the bow, *Sea Hammer* would send spray aft, as if she was splashing him in a playful way. He breathed deep. He loved this, every bit of it.

But that feeling, he knew, was based in part on his certainty that they would catch this son of a bitch Brunhard. He would not slip through their fingers again. That would be too infuriating by half.

"He's running like a rabbit for the shore," Harald said, standing nearby. With the hum of the rigging and the pounding of the ship in the waves and the rush of the easterly wind Thorgrim had not heard his son step up to his side.

"Nowhere else for him to go," Thorgrim said. "If he tries to run in any other direction he only shortens the distance between us."

Harald was silent for a moment, and then asked, "Do you think he'll try what he did yesterday? Tuck in through some treacherous place where only he knows the safe passage?"

"No," Thorgrim said. "That was a good trick, but it only works if all things are just right, and this dog Brunhard had luck with him."

"How's that?" Harald asked.

"Recall, it was just sunset when he closed with the land," Thorgrim said. "And he had the headland to block our view of the passage he took. Plus, the wind had died away, so he had little chance of being driven ashore."

"I see," Harald said.

"I'm not saying the bastard isn't clever. He had the perfect conditions, sure, but he also knew how to make use of them. But now I think luck will be with us."

They were quiet for a moment, and Thorgrim could feel a creeping discomfort. He wondered if he was tempting the gods by suggesting he and his men would be lucky today. So he decided to explain further, aware that he was making his case to Thor and Njord as much as he was to Harald.

"Even if Brunhard knows another passage in through some rocks, he would not try it in this wind," Thorgrim said. "Not with such a dangerous lee shore. Besides, that only works if it's getting dark and we can't see the passage he takes, so we can't follow him in. We'll be up with him well before dark."

"Of course," Harald said. "I wonder how close he'll dare get to this lee shore." Instinctively the young man turned his head into the wind, felt the breeze on his face. He swiped a long strand of yellow hair from his mouth and turned back to look in the direction that Thorgrim was looking, toward Brunhard's ships.

"We'll see," Thorgrim said. "It may be his plan to try and get so close to shore that we dare not follow. If so, it's not much of a plan. Our ships are more weatherly than his, and there is no Frisian merchantman can match us for seamanship."

Thorgrim remained where he was for a little time longer, then climbed down from the rail and headed aft. The men of *Sea Hammer* were gathered up on the weather side, some sleeping, some sharpening weapons, all silently grateful for the wind that drove the ship faster and easier than the oars would have done.

Starri was sitting on the edge of the afterdeck, sharpening the long knife he wore on his belt. The two battle axes he always carried into a fight were waiting their turn.

"Once more I say, don't get your hopes up, Starri," Thorgrim said. "They're just merchantmen, you know. I don't think they'll put up a fight, once we catch them."

"Maybe not," Starri said. "They used trickery last time, but I don't know that it will work again. But I've been thinking about this, Night Wolf."

That's never good, Thorgrim thought, but he said, "About what?"

"Well, you were the one who asked why they had so many men at the oars. So that makes me wonder if maybe they are only merchantmen for part of the time. Maybe this Brunhard has his mind set on some raiding as well, or gathering cargo by taking it from other merchant ships. Maybe he has warriors on board. Maybe this time they fight."

"Hmm," Thorgrim said. "Maybe."

That was in fact an uncharacteristically reasonable thought. And it gave Thorgrim some hope. Because he wanted to drive his sword, Iron-tooth, through Brunhard's chest, but he was not the sort who would butcher a man who was posing no threat. If Brunhard did him the courtesy of offering battle, however, then he would happily cut the man down.

Thorgrim looked forward, along the length of *Sea Hammer*'s deck and beyond, to where the three merchantmen were pitching and rolling and struggling and failing to get clear of their pursuers. "We should know soon enough," he said.

The coast of Ireland, earlier no more than an irregular blue-green line on the horizon, began to resolve itself into details as hunter and prey raced southwest. Thorgrim could see the line of brownish beach where the shore met the water, and in places high cliffs with the surf breaking white at their feet. He could see the rolling hills further inland and the mountains beyond that. He could make out green fields and stands of trees. Here and there he could see more of the deadly rocks standing just offshore like sentries guarding the vulnerable land.

Brunhard's ships were about a mile from the shore now, and *Sea Hammer* less than a mile astern of them. Thorgrim looked hard at the coastline beyond, but he could not see any particular place that the Frisian might be sailing for, no place that appeared to be a refuge from his pursuit. As far as Thorgrim could tell, he was just running.

Another half a mile and Thorgrim could make out more details of Brunhard's ships, the high stem and sternposts, the straining sails. The largest of the three, Brunhard's own vessel, Thorgrim imagined, was not in the lead but rather was behind the two smaller ones. That must have been by choice. The larger ship should have been the faster ship. Thorgrim wondered if Brunhard was purposely hanging back, giving some bit of protection to the other vessels, willing to take the initial attack on himself. It's what he would have expected a warrior chieftain to do, though not necessarily a Frisian merchant.

"Not long now," Harald said. He had been walking fore and aft, checking every little thing, then coming back to stand at Thorgrim's side, then walking fore and aft again. He had Thorgrim's lack of patience mixed with his own youthful energy, and that made for a restless combination.

"Not long," Thorgrim agreed.

Brunhard's ship was less than a quarter mile ahead and had closed to just a couple of cable lengths from the Irish coast when they finally turned more southerly and shaped a course roughly parallel with the land. Thorgrim had to wonder how well Brunhard knew that stretch of water. The coast of Ireland was a treacherous one, like his own Norway, with plenty of rocky shoals just below the surface, eager to tear a ship's bottom out. He himself had never been that far south of Vík-ló, had never sailed those waters. It was all new and unknown to him.

Well, Brunhard should serve as a good warning to us, he thought. If there were hazards under the sea, the Frisian would hit them first, and hopefully with time enough for *Sea Hammer* to change course.

The sun reached its midday point and began the long slide to the west and the seven ships raced south, *Sea Hammer* coming closer to Brunhard's beamy merchant ship with every sea mile they covered. Now even Thorgrim and his aging eyes could make out individuals on the deck, men sitting on the thwarts down the length of the vessel.

Failend was sitting on a sea chest just forward of the afterdeck, half sprawled over it, her face turned up toward the sun, her eyes closed. Her complexion looked good, not the sallow, greenish hue she had sported at the onset of the voyage, and Thorgrim knew she was adjusting to the motion of the ship. She had eaten dagmál, eaten a substantial amount, which pleased him.

Looking at her now, Thorgrim had an idea.

"Failend," he called and she opened one eye and rolled her head toward him. "Pray, come here."

She pushed herself off the sea chest and came aft with her usual light step, like a dancer. She stepped up onto the afterdeck.

"Here's this Frisian merchant we've been chasing," Thorgrim said, pointing forward.

"Oh, yes," Failend said. "That would be the same ship we've been staring at since soon after daybreak. And all of the day yesterday. I'm glad to see we've nearly caught him."

"Do you think you could put an arrow through the man steering her?" Thorgrim asked.

"Not from here."

"No. But we'll be closer soon."

"Closer, I might," Failend said. "It's tricky work, shooting at a rolling ship from a rolling ship. I'm not much accustomed to it."

"Then I'll get you closer," Thorgrim said.

Failend went forward to fetch her bow and quiver of arrows. Thorgrim moved his eyes back to the Frisian, no more than a cable length ahead now. He could see no excitement on her deck, no sign of panic.

You may not be in a panic yet, he thought. The ships had the wind on their beam, and they were skirting close to a treacherous lee shore. One mistake and they could be set down on the rocks or the unforgiving beach just a few hundred yards to leeward.

If Failend could put an arrow though their helmsman so he let go of the tiller, the Frisian ship would probably fly up into the wind, her sail would come aback, she would be in danger of being driven ashore. They would just have time enough to sort it out by the time *Sea Hammer* came down on them and Thorgrim's warriors poured over her side. He was ready for that. He was growing tired of the chase.

Failend found her bow, strung it and picked up a quiver of arrows. She made her way forward and the men followed her with their eyes, part from lust, part from curiosity. She stepped onto the small foredeck, one hand on the tall stem, and looked forward.

Thorgrim turned to the man at *Sea Hammer*'s tiller. "Failend is going to shoot the Frisian's helmsman," he said. "You'll fall off a bit, come up on his starboard side so she may have a clear shot."

The helmsman nodded and Thorgrim made his way forward and stood at Failend's side. They were coming up on the Frisian now; maybe a hundred yards separated the two ships. *Sea Hammer*'s bow swung off the wind a bit as the helmsman followed Thorgrim's instructions, steering to come up on the Frisian's starboard side, giving Failend an unobstructed view of the man at the steering board.

"Well?" Thorgrim asked.

Failend shrugged. "I'll do my best," she said. "A better than even chance I can put an arrow through some part of him."

"Any part should do for our needs," Thorgrim said. He walked aft, called, "Harald, come here!"

Harald came over, quick and eager. "Failend is going to shoot their helmsman if she can," he explained. "If she drops him, their ship will fly up into the wind. It will be madness aboard. We'll come alongside with *Sea Hammer*. You take thirty men and go aboard. Starri will be with you. There's no chance he won't be. Just make sure he does no great slaughter if they don't fight. I'll keep *Sea Hammer* alongside, see that the Frisian does not get driven ashore. But you must do your work quick and get the ship under control and sail her off to safety, far from the shore."

Harald was nodding and suppressing a smile as Thorgrim spoke, delighting in the thought of carrying out his father's bold plan. He already had his sword belted at his side. Now he turned and began calling out the names of the men who would follow him on board the Frisian.

Thorgrim smiled. He knew what would happen. Harald would be first over, or at least he would try, but he could never get there faster than Starri. Starri did not do it out of malice, he was not even aware he was doing it, he just could not hold himself back. It drove Harald mad.

As for Thorgrim, he was too old and had been in too many fights to worry much about whether or not he was first into the fray. He could not move as swiftly as he once could, and he accepted that. As to questions of his own courage, that was another thing to which he gave little thought. Courage, in his mind, meant doing something despite the fear, and he had long ago stopped being afraid, at least of any hurt that could be doled out by men.

He stepped back to the foredeck. Failend had an arrow nocked, her fingers resting gently on the bowstring, the arrow still pointed at the deck. Forty yards between the ships, and now *Sea Hammer*'s helmsman had turned so the longship was aiming for the Frisian's starboard quarter and the broad back of the helmsman was plainly visible.

The wind had continued to build, the ships were heeling to starboard, their sails full, rigging straining, the water rushing white along their sides as they plunged along on near parallel lines. Just a few hundred yards to leeward, here and there, jagged rocks reached up from the surf, the seas crashing at their base.

Thorgrim ran his eyes along that hazard. *Harald had better do his work fast*, he thought. If the Frisian ship was out of control, if she could not use her sail to keep off the rocks, then she would be blown down on them in short order, and torn apart as if she were made of cobwebs.

Once things began to happen, they would happen fast, and there would be precious little time separating triumph from disaster.

Thirty yards. Thorgrim was still calculating time and distance. Shoot the helmsman, the Frisian flies up into the wind. *Sea Hammer* closes the distance in the time it takes them to get back under command.

"Whenever you think you have a shot, Failend," he called.

Failend nodded, stepped forward and raised the bow. No one on the Frisian ship seemed to be looking back at them. The few men he could see were focused on something else. Thorgrim thought he could see wisps of smoke coming up from some place forward of the helmsman and blowing away in the breeze, but he knew he might be wrong. Probably was. Lighting a fire on a ship, particularly in such conditions, was madness.

Failend drew the bowstring back and held it and kept holding it as her legs moved with the ship and the point of the arrowhead moved up, down, side to side as she got the feel of the ship's motion and the way the Frisian was moving in relation to *Sea Hammer*. On shore, Thorgrim knew, she would have released long before this, and put the arrow though whatever she was aiming at, but this was a much more complicated situation.

And then her fingers let go and the bowstring twanged and the arrow shot out over the water, a straight, bright line from her bow to a point right between the Frisian helmsman's shoulders. Thorgrim saw the man arch back, his arms fly up, thought he could hear his strangled cry of agony. He reeled aside and the tiller whipped over and, with no one steering, the Frisian merchantman began to turn wildly up into the wind.

The space between the two ships was closing up fast. Thorgrim looked aft. Harald and his men were gathered at the larboard side, ready to leap across onto the Frisian's deck. Starri was whirling around and making jerking motions with his arms.

Thorgrim looked back at the Frisian, in time to see a thick set, bearded man grab the wounded helmsman and pull him aside like he was made a straw, and then grab the tiller and haul it aft, reacting quicker than Thorgrim had hoped they would. The ship's bow, which had been spinning up into the wind, began to turn again, but it didn't matter. *Sea Hammer*'s bow was almost up with the Frisian's stern, and in no time at all Harald and his men would be pouring over the side.

Then another man appeared on the Frisian's afterdeck, and this one was looking aft, looking at *Sea Hammer*. He had a staff of some sort in his hand—Thorgrim was not sure what it was—but an instant later he recognized it as a bow, like the one Failend was holding. There was an arrow nocked, and the end of the arrow was engulfed in a ball of flame, a fire as big as a man's head.

Now, what by the gods...Thorgrim wondered. Fire on shipboard was a danger, to be sure, but if this fellow meant to set *Sea Hammer* ablaze with his flaming arrow he was dreaming. It would be hard to get the thick oak planks burning, easy for Thorgrim's men to put it out.

And then the man raised the arrow and pulled back the string and Thorgrim realized what he intended.

"Oh, Thor strike you dead!" he shouted, then turned aft and called, "Up into the wind! Come up into the wind!"

He never knew if the helmsman heard or not. Certainly the man did not react before the flaming arrow came sailing overhead and lodged itself in *Sea Hammer*'s sail. The oak that made up the hull might not ignite easily, but the wool sail, well-oiled to protect it from the weather, certainly did. The flames spread out from the arrow, building and climbing up the cloth. Then another arrow struck, further down, and a second part of the sail ignited.

Thorgrim felt *Sea Hammer* come up on a more even keel as the wind spilled through the burning cloth. He turned and raced aft, past men looking up with stunned expressions. He had no thought for them, no thought for the Frisians. Because now it was *Sea Hammer* that was out of control, his ship that was being driven down onto the rocks by the merciless wind.

Chapter Eighteen

There is mingling in friendship when man can utter
all his whole mind to another;
there is naught so vile as a fickle tongue;
no friend is he who but flatters.

The Counseling of the Stray-Singer

Thorgrim had not even reached the stern before Harald and the other men began to react. He heard Harald's voice call out, "Lower the yard! Lower the yard!" just as he made the step up onto the afterdeck.

The helmsman saw Thorgrim coming and he stepped aside as Thorgrim grabbed the wooden tiller bar and whirled around so he was facing forward. The sail was fully engulfed in flame, black smoke rolling off the cloth and blowing away to leeward, bits of flaming wool dropping to the deck where they were stomped out under the feet of frightened men.

One of the older hands, a man named Vali, was the first to the halyard. He tossed the coil of rope aside and took the heavy line off the cleat, but he knew better than to just let it go. With a turn still around the cleat he slacked the halyard away fast. The yard came down in a controlled plummet and Vali checked it when it was five feet above the deck.

From where Thorgrim stood the yard looked like nothing but a great shaft of flame, the fire wrapping itself around the spar, bits of flaming rope and cloth falling onto the deck and the sea chests and into the sea. The men had all strapped on swords or taken up axes or spears in anticipation of fighting the Frisians and now they used those weapons to impale bits of flaming material and heave them over the side. Others were grabbing up buckets and scooping seawater where they could and tossing it on the flames.

Thorgrim devoted the space of a few heartbeats to the scene, no more. He knew that the fire was not the greatest danger to *Sea Hammer* and her men. With the sail gone the ship could make no headway, and if she made no headway she could not be steered. Already the wind had her and was driving her down toward the murderous rocks rising up from the ocean bottom.

"Ahh!" he shouted in frustration and pulled the tiller hard, leaning back as he did, putting all his weight into it, and was rewarded with the sight of the bow turning to leeward. There was no stopping *Sea Hammer* from being driven ashore, but maybe he could thread the ship through the rocks before she was torn apart. If he couldn't, then anyone who was not a strong swimmer was dead, and those who could swim were likely dead as well.

The tall prow came around and Thorgrim could see open water between two rocks and he pushed the tiller forward to steady the ship's swing. "Oars!" he shouted. "Ship some oars!" he called again. The men forward were thinking only of the fire. Thorgrim knew well how easy it was to forget about everything that was happening beyond the rails of the ship. "Oars!"

The cry broke through at last. Hall and Bjorn, two of Ottar's men, but good men, reliable, grabbed up two of the oars off the gallows and turning to larboard and starboard ran them through the nearest oarports.

"Pull!" Thorgrim shouted. As long as the sea was driving them the steerboard was nearly useless. The oars would give more steerage, more control. Hall and Bjorn leaned back, faces turning red with the exertion. Forward, more hands lifted oars from the gallows and thrust them through row ports.

A roller came in from the east and lifted *Sea Hammer*'s stern and then set it down, then lifted the bow in turn. The surging water slammed into the rocks ahead, racing through the gap for which Thorgrim was aiming the longship. The seas poured through the space and Thorgrim saw them boil and break over a ledge that lay all but submerged between them, a rock that seemed to be crouched in hiding, ready to rip *Sea Hammer*'s bottom clean out.

"Oh, by the gods!" he shouted. "Back! Back your oars! Back!" He saw looks of confusion forward, but just a flash, because these were men with many sea miles behind them. Hall and Bjorn and the three men forward of them who had also managed to ship oars now leaned back, dropped the blades, thrust their arms forward as they leaned into it. They were too few to move *Sea Hammer* astern, but they stopped her forward momentum, checked her headlong drive into the rocks.

They moved together, as best they could, Hall setting the stroke, the others following. Back, down, thrust the loom of the oar forward, *Sea Hammer* hung on her patch of ocean as more men ran the oars out and joined the effort.

Another sea came and lifted the stern and *Sea Hammer* spun to starboard, caught in the grip of the surf. "Larboard, stroke! Starboard back!" Thorgrim shouted and the men obeyed, mostly, two oars on the starboard side fouling as the rowers mistimed the stroke. Slowly, painfully, the ship twisted in the sea until her bow was once again pointed more or less at the beach.

"Back!" Thorgrim shouted.

He had thought, just for an instant, they might actually be able to back the ship away from the rocks, get clean of the shore, get sea room enough to keep off the beach, but he could see now that would not happen. The seas rolling in from the horizon had them now, and at best his men could keep the ship where it was for a brief time more. But in the end they would be flung onto the rocks. There was nothing for it.

He looked off to the north. *Blood Hawk* was charging down on them, her sail set and drawing, the foam curling up under her bow, and Thorgrim had a sudden terror that Godi would do something foolish, would try to come to their aid under sail and get caught as they were with the seas driving them ashore.

But Godi was no fool. He was still a quarter mile away when Thorgrim saw the longship's yard come whipping down the mast, hands gathering the sail up as it came, more hands running oars out through the row ports. Godi would come in under oars, pass a line, tow them free. If he had time enough. Which Thorgrim knew he did not.

Very well, Thorgrim thought, his mind racing through the possibilities. They could not row clear, could not remain where they were, and Godi would not reach them in time.

Through the rocks then, and onto the beach... He could see it, a quarter mile away, the long stretch of shingle beach, an easy landing if they could get past the irregular and half-hidden rocks.

He ran his eyes along the various hazards, the waves breaking at their bases, or sending up sprays of foam where rocks were hidden just below the surface.

There... Just to the south, a cable length away, a gap where the water seemed to flow unimpeded, a spot where a narrow and shallow draft ship might just safely pass. But could they work their way down to that spot, line *Sea Hammer* up to drive on through?

Maybe.

"Back! Back! When I give the word, starboard will pull!" He braced, felt the lift of the wave under the ship, called, "Starboard, pull!"

Along the starboard side the men leaned into the oars, driving the ship forward, while to larboard they drove the oars back and *Sea Hammer* seemed to spin like a dancer. But now the seas were on her beam, catching the ship full on her broadside, making her roll in a frightening way and driving her fast toward the rocks.

"Pull!" Larboard and starboard they pulled together and *Sea Hammer* shot forward, even as the seas lifted her like an offering to the gods and tossed her closer to the rocks, then let her wallow in the trough.

"Larboard, back! Starboard, pull!" Thorgrim shouted, but now the men knew what he was doing, working the ship yard by yard along the shoreline to find a passage through the rocks. They knew what needed to be done, and they obeyed fast and well. *Sea Hammer* spun back, her bow once more pointing toward the beach, and they were halfway to the gap that Thorgrim had seen.

"Back! Back!" The men at the oars thrust the looms away and *Sea Hammer* crawled painfully away from the rocks, making up some of the sea room she had lost in that last maneuver. Thorgrim could see the red faces, the open mouths, the hair drenched with sweat as the men heaved on the oars. At a steady pace, long strokes, they might go for a few hours at the oars. But this was brutal, a fight between ship and sea, mortal combat, at least for the frail men aboard their wooden ship. Thorgrim knew they did not have much more of this in them.

"Now, one more, and then we ride the seas in like a sled on ice!" Thorgrim shouted. "Stand ready! Now, starboard, pull!"

Once again the men obeyed, starboard heaving on their oars, larboard backing, and once again *Sea Hammer* spun on her keel and they shot forward even as the seas tried to dash them on the rocks. Thorgrim gave the order and the ship twisted back and the seas lifted her stern and dropped her bow and he had a vision, a clear view of the water racing through the rocks to larboard and starboard, churning and rolling but not breaking on any submerged obstacle that he could see.

"Now, pull!" he shouted, and there was a mad, reckless tone to his voice that matched the wildness roiling in him. He remembered how Ornolf the Restless used to taunt the gods and now he knew why, and he wanted to do the same. *Take me if you will, you bastards, I'm Thorgrim Night Wolf and I'll meet any man or god wherever they choose!*

The rowers leaned into the oars. *Sea Hammer* shot forward, the seas lifting her stern as the momentum built. They pulled again and Thorgrim leaned into the tiller to drive her bow around. They were careening toward the rocks now and either they would find a clear path through or they would hit a ledge and tear the bottom out and spill men, weapons and treasure all over the ocean floor, but there was no stopping the momentum now.

Thorgrim leaned back with the tiller and saw *Sea Hammer*'s bow come around and knew it was as lined up as it would get. The rocks loomed above, larboard, then starboard, and twenty feet off either side. He saw panicked faces looking up as the breaking sea crashed against them and flung spume back over the ship. And he wanted to laugh with the madness of it.

Then he felt *Sea Hammer*'s bottom hit, a jarring blow that made the ship shudder, made him stagger and grab fast at the tiller to keep from falling. He grit his teeth and waited for the ship to come to a grinding stop, to swing broadside as her keel caught on the rocks below, to see the strakes torn out of her.

But that didn't happen. She hit again, less hard that time, and then she was through, the rocks astern, clear water ahead, as far as he could see, clear to the beach.

Still he wanted to laugh, to shout, to curse the gods, but instead he shouted, "Stroke!" and the stunned men remembered themselves and leaned into the oars again. They had to run up on the beach, assess the damage, set things to rights as best they could. And then get underway once more. There was work to do. In the next day or so, Brunhard would die or he, Thorgrim Night Wolf, would die. There was no other option.

The men were pulling with an easy stroke, the need for frantic heaving at the oars over, the beach only a few hundred yards away. Thorgrim turned and looked back over the larboard quarter. Brunhard was well clear now, half a mile off, heading out to sea, having sprung his trap by luring *Sea Hammer* in among the rocks. Thorgrim felt a rage building in him such as he had not felt in a long, long time. And he felt like a fool, and he felt ashamed of the trick for which he had fallen, and that all seemed to open up a vicious, gaping wound for which blood was the only salve.

He turned and looked over the starboard side. Godi in *Blood Hawk* was under oars, standing off from the rocks, clear of the surf's grip. As Thorgrim watched, *Blood Hawk* spun around and headed the other way and Thorgrim guessed that Godi was looking for a way to reach the beach as well, a less treacherous way than the one Thorgrim had been forced to take. And further off, still under sail, *Fox* and *Dragon* were racing to catch up.

Thorgrim looked back at *Blood Hawk*. Part of him wished Godi would go after Brunhard, for fear the Frisian might slip away. And part of him did not wish Godi to do that, for fear Godi or one of his men would kill the man and deprive him, Thorgrim, of the pleasure. But what Thorgrim wished did not matter. Godi had apparently decided to stay at *Sea Hammer*'s side, and, with half a mile separating them, Thorgrim had no means to tell him different.

Two more strokes and *Sea Hammer*'s bow ran up onto the sand with a gentle grinding sound. The oars came in, men leapt over the sheer strake into the surf and hauled the ship further up the beach. Thorgrim let go of the tiller and hopped down off the afterdeck and lifted some of the loose deck planks.

There was water in the bilge, as there always was, but no more than usual. He could see no strakes stove in, no gaping wounds where the ship had struck rock. He guessed that the keel itself had struck, maybe taken a nasty gouge, but nothing worse than that. Silently he thanked the gods, and worried that in his madness he may have offended them. At least he had not said any of the taunts out loud. He was not sure if that made a difference.

Men were already swarming over the blackened yard, cutting away the last charred bits of sail and the short lines that lashed it to the spar. Starri was scurrying up the rigging to assess the damage the flames had done to the rope. Others were stacking the oars back on the gallows.

"It's not so bad, Father," Harald said, coming aft. Thorgrim could hear the hesitation in his voice. Harald would not know what his father's state of mind was, but he could guess it was not good, and he was likely concerned about the reaction he would get. But Thorgrim only grunted, so Harald went on.

"The yard got blackened, but it didn't burn, really. I think it's still strong enough to hold a sail. Or would be if we had a sail, which we don't. Nothing but a few charred bits of that left."

Thorgrim grunted again. Of everything aboard the longship, the sail was the most difficult and expensive to replace. That was why there was no spare. Thorgrim could replace any other part of the ship by cutting down a tree and using the tools he had on hand to shape it and fix it in place. There was spare rope to replace damaged rigging and spare clench nails and all the tools needed. But when it came to weaving cloth for a sail, he would not know where to begin even if he had a loom, which he did not.

He looked north up the beach. Godi had found a way in through the rocks and was pulling for them, closing the distance quickly. Thorgrim made a decision. "We'll take the sail and standing rigging from *Blood Hawk*," he said.

"Ah…." Harald said. "Certainly, we could do that… Her mast and yard are near enough the same length as *Sea Hammer*."

Thorgrim could all but hear the arguments in Harald's head, the first being that swapping out the sail was not necessary. *Blood Hawk* was nearly as big and fast as *Sea Hammer*. The expedient thing to do would be to leave *Sea Hammer* on the beach, load the men aboard *Blood Hawk* and go, rather than waste the hour or more they would need to move sail and standing rigging. Also, Godi would not be happy about this, not happy at all.

Thorgrim did not care about any of that. He was in command here, *Sea Hammer* was his ship, and he would not give any Frisian whore's son the satisfaction of knowing he had forced a Norseman to leave his fine ship behind.

He heard Godi's big voice, heard the splash of *Blood Hawk*'s oars and turned just as the longship ground up on the beach thirty feet away. Godi was over the side even before his ship came to rest, making a big splash as he hit the water and waded ashore.

"Thorgrim!" he boomed, coming up the beach, covering the distance with his long strides. "By great Odin's ass what happened? Was it Thor set your sail on fire?" His expression was half amused, half uncertain.

"No, it was that goat turd Frisian. He let us get close up and then put a couple of flaming arrows into the sail. Burned like dried thatch."

"Hmm," Godi said, and Thorgrim could hear that the man was impressed with the cleverness of the trick, but knew better than to say as much. And well he might be impressed. Thorgrim was calm enough now to also see how clever it was. He would be impressed if he had seen the trick played on someone else, if he personally had not been so humiliated by it.

"Look, Father," Harald interrupted. "*Dragon* is coming ashore, too."

Thorgrim and Godi turned to look north. Fostolf was following the path Godi had taken around the rocks and was heading for the beach.

"Seems Thorodd is the only one to go off on his own," Thorgrim said.

"He's young," Godi said. "Rash."

"Yes," Thorgrim agreed. He was surprised by this. If he had had to wager, he would have bet Fostolf, not Thorodd, would have been the one to strike out on his own. He wondered if Thorodd would be any match for the Frisian, Brunhard. He did not think so.

"So what do we do now?" Godi asked. "My guess is that you have a plan already to get revenge on this Brunhard bastard."

All three of them—Thorgrim, Godi and Harald—turned and looked to the south. Brunhard's ships were barely visible now, and in their wake, but still a few miles astern, was Thorodd's *Fox*.

"Yes," Thorgrim said, turning back to the others. "Yes, Godi, I do have a plan. And I fear you will not like it very much."

Chapter Nineteen

[B]rief is wealth, as the winking of an eye,
most faithless ever of friends.

Hávamál

Like the sun breaking through a thick layer of cloud, so Master Brunhard's mood improved as the Frisian ships put distance between themselves and the Northmen. Louis was hardly surprised.

The biggest of the longships had all but run them down, come so close that someone on their deck was able to drop *Wind Dancer's* helmsman with an arrow. An impressive shot, to be certain, but not a long one as the Northman was nearly alongside. At that moment Louis was certain the situation would end in a bloody and one-sided fight on the Frisian's deck.

But Brunhard had surprised him. Again. And even more impressive than the Northman's bow shot was the Frisian's trick with the flaming arrows.

Louis had been watching the ships astern so closely he had not even seen the preparations. When he finally noticed the archers stepping aft, thick twists of oiled cloth lashed to their arrow shafts and blazing away, he had thought they meant to shoot the arrows into the Northman's hull, and he knew that would be pointless. He didn't even think of the sail until the first arrow pierced the cloth and hung there, well out of reach of anyone on the Northman's deck, igniting the cloth before anyone could react.

Another arrow struck, and another. The sail seemed not so much to burn as to melt, so quickly was it consumed. And then the seas had the Northmen it their grip, hurdling them toward the shore.

They could not see, from *Wind Dancer's* deck, if the Northmen had wrecked or made it to the beach. The distance between the ships opened up and the Northman was lost from sight among the rocks as the Frisian ships continued south as fast as they could sail. Any sound they might have heard of the ship breaking up or the drowning men screaming was lost to the wind and Brunhard's booming laugh, his shouting with glee, his boasting and recounting of what he had just done, as if all the men around him had not also witnessed his triumph.

"Ha! Louis! Did you see that?" Brunhard shouted, though he and Louis had been standing nearly shoulder to shoulder through the whole of the affair, from the moment Brunhard had pulled the wounded helmsman aside and grabbed the tiller himself. "I could practically smell those Norse pigs shitting themselves! And now they are dead on the rocks, and the crows will feast when they wash up on the beach."

Brunhard, of course, did not actually know if that was true or not, but that would not stop him from saying it, and Louis knew better than to point it out.

"Very clever, Brunhard, very clever indeed," Louis said instead. It was one of the few sincere things he had ever said to Brunhard.

"Of course it was clever, I told you it would be!" Brunhard roared. "And see, the other Norseman, he's going into the beach, too! No doubt to chase the crows away from the bloated corpses of their fellows!"

Louis turned and looked aft. The big ship, the one with the red and white striped sail that had nearly run them down, was lost to sight. Half a mile or so behind it was the second of the longships, a slower vessel, apparently, since it was always trailing behind. Now they had their sail down and oars out and seemed to be looking for a way to get past the rocks and onto the beach where the first ship had been driven.

The image of that red and white striped sail played in Louis's mind. For weeks he had been a prisoner of the Northman Thorgrim Night Wolf, carried down the Avonmore River aboard Thorgrim's longship. They had never set the sail, only used it as an awning, but Louis was sure it, too, was striped red and white.

No, that's ridiculous, he thought. *This coast is filthy with these Norse pigs and no doubt half of them have sails of red and white stripes. It's not possible that this is Thorgrim Night Wolf...*

Thorgrim, he was sure, would wish to kill him on sight. It would be absurdly bad luck if this, of all the Norse raiders in Ireland, was indeed Thorgrim Night Wolf. But then, his luck had been running about as foul as luck could run.

After some time Brunhard seemed to grow tired of bragging to Louis, or perhaps ran out of additional things to say, so he wandered off forward to find another whom he could regale with a retelling of the events they had all just witnessed. Louis sighed and looked astern once again, not looking at anything in particular, just letting his eyes rest on the far shore. It was the view he preferred, looking aft, and he suddenly understood why. Looking astern meant he did not have to look on the wretched slaves on the thwarts and the gloating, vicious crew. It was the only direction in which he could look and not be reminded of the awful situation in which he remained.

And he was indeed still in a bad circumstance. The reappearance of the Northmen had taken the Frisian sailors' attention away from him, and Brunhard's delight in his victory had distracted him from the vengeance Louis was certain he intended, but those things would not last. Brunhard would soon grow bored and look for a new victim and happily for him he did not have to look far.

He heard a soft footfall beside him and knew it was Conandil because she was the only one aboard who moved softly. "It seems the Northmen are not done with us," she said. Louis turned and looked down at her, her pretty, expressionless face, her thick hair unkempt and tied behind her head. She, too, was looking astern and Louis wondered if she did so for the same reason he did.

"What do you mean?" he said. They spoke softly, backs turned to the others, so no one would hear or see them converse. No one knew that they could.

"See?" Conandil said, nodding toward the horizon to the north. "There's another ship, still coming after us."

He looked in the direction she was looking. He saw nothing, nothing but the east coast of Ireland off to his left, and directly behind them, and stretching all the way around to the right in a great half circle, the bright line of the horizon.

"Where?" he asked.

"There."

Louis squinted, leaned forward until he realized how absurd a thing that was to do and straightened again. And then he saw it. Just a white speck, really. But the more he looked the more he saw it was not a white speck. The rectangular shape slowly resolved itself, the slight wobbling motion left and right. Another ship, right in their wake.

"There were four of them, weren't there?" Louis said. "Four of these heathen longships."

"Yes," Conandil said.

"Brunhard wrecked one, the other went in after it. Two left, and here's one of them, at least, still coming after us." He glanced over at the sun hanging in the west. "He won't catch us, I don't think, before it is dark."

For a moment the two of them stared at the distant sail. "For us, I don't know which is the better fate," Louis said. "Taken by these Norse dogs or left to suffer Brunhard's will."

"There's only one Norse ship, and we are three," Conandil said. "Do you think they could take us still?"

"Certainly," Louis said. "There are likely more men on that one raider than there are sailors on all Brunhard's ships. And the Northmen are warriors, armed and trained. The sailors are not."

"The prisoners are," Conandil said.

"What do you mean?"

"The prisoners. The Irishmen at the oars. They are warriors mostly, taken on the battlefield." Conandil, apparently, could not bring herself to use the word "slave."

Louis nodded. He remembered now. Brunhard had bragged of it. The Northmen and the rí túaithe of some little kingdom had conspired to launch an attack on those poor bastards so that they might be taken and sold, slaves being one of Ireland's most abundant and valuable resources.

*Now there's an irony…*Louis thought. They had men enough to put up a real fight, maybe even defeat the attacking Northmen, but those men were in chains. If the raiders did manage to run Brunhard's ships down, those men could do nothing but watch as the Frisians were slaughtered, and then wait to see how their new masters disposed of them.

Or maybe not, Louis thought, as a new idea began to form itself out of the swirling fog in his head. He was about to speak when he heard the heavy thump of Brunhard's feet as the master came aft again, heard the booming voice.

"Louis the Frank! Are you staring at your beloved Ireland? Sorry now you left it?"

"No," Louis said. "I am looking at the Northman who is still chasing us. It seems you did not frighten them all away."

"Bah!" Brunhard said, waving a dismissive hand, though Louis was all but certain the Frisian had not seen the ship in their wake. He himself had barely seen it, and he reckoned his eyes were better than Brunhard's who had ten years on him at least. "I'll find some way to bugger this one as well."

"Will we sail through the night?" Louis asked. "Try to get clear of this fellow?"

"No," Brunhard said. "I'm tired of sailing. There's a fine beach a few miles ahead of us. We sail until it's dark enough that this bastard following cannot see where we go, then we'll run her ashore. Have a decent meal, sleep on solid ground. Does that suit you, Louis the Frank?"

"That would be fine," Louis said. "As ever, your ship seems more like a royal barge than a slaver."

"Well said!" Brunhard yelled. "I swear, it will break my heart when I finally slit your throat!"

Just as Brunhard had said, *Wind Dancer* and the other ships continued on south, skirting the coast a little less than a mile off, as the sun dropped toward the western mountains. Once it was gone they used the last of the light to turn landward and Brunhard brought his ships through the dark water and onto a stretch of beach as easily as if it had been midday.

Wind Dancer ground up onto the sand and the other two went aground on either side of her and the sailors leapt over the sides and took ropes and anchors up the beach and secured them. A gangplank was put over the side and the slaves, still chained neck to neck, were led off the ships for the first time and set under guard. A fire was lit with the ships mostly blocking it from sight from the sea.

"So, Louis," Brunhard said later, sitting on the sand by Louis and facing the tall and exuberant flames, "I hope tonight you're planning on humping that little Irish bitch you bought. You know, my men are sore disappointed they didn't get a chance at her. At least they should be allowed to hear you doing it, don't you think?" The words came out as humor, and there was a smile on Brunhard's face, but as was so often the case there was something ugly just below the surface.

"What I do with my slave is my affair," Louis said. "But it will not be for the amusement of your men. But see here, Brunhard, I had another idea, one that might be of great profit to you."

As Louis suspected, there was no word that could grab Brunhard's interest more than "profit," though he did a good job of looking as if he did not much care. He stared off into the fire, put his fingers in his mouth and fished out some detritus from his dinner and pitched it into the flames.

"What idiot idea have you come up with, Frank?" he asked at last.

"Here's the thing," Louis said. He had practiced this talk in his head and tried now to not sound too prepared, as if he had just thought of it. "Your trick with the flaming arrows was brilliant, but you know that."

"Of course I know that. Even the damned Northmen know that!"

"The Northmen that are still alive, at least," Louis added. "So, it seemed you wrecked one ship and the second went to their aid and no doubt wrecked as well, or at least are so far behind they'll never catch us now."

"That's true, very true," Brunhard said. His eyes were on Louis now, his feigned lack of interest dropping away.

"But there's still one of the Northmen following us. You saw that. One of the smaller ones, we know, because the two big ones were the ones that went up on the beach. We lost him in the dark, but come morning he will be after us again, I have no doubt."

Brunhard waved a dismissive hand. "That sorry bastard will never catch us now," he said.

"But maybe we should let him," Louis said. "Those raiders, if they've been at it long, they could be stuffed with silver, gold, jewels, all the things the heathens have plundered. Take the ship and you take the plunder. And the Northmen still alive, well, they can be sold as slaves as well as any Irishman."

Brunhard was nodding but frowning. "This is true, what you say. But those heathen bastards are warriors, and there are many of them. My men, they're tough as old leather, don't get me wrong, but we don't have half as many men on my three ships as the heathens have on the one. And my men are sailors, not warriors. They'd butcher us."

"Yes, true," Louis said, leaning a little closer to suggest he was now reaching the crux of his argument. "But here's the best part. These Irish slaves, they *are* warriors. You said so yourself. Taken on the battlefield. And…I did not tell you this, but I was head of the house guard for the Count of Roumois. Most of my time was spent fighting these heathens as they came up the Seine. I know how to fight them and beat them."

Louis could see he had Brunhard's full attention now, so he went on. "Here's what we do. We take one of your ships…not *Wind Dancer* but one of the smaller ones, and we make it seem as if there is something wrong, as if it cannot keep up. Let the heathen come up with her. I'm on board, and a few of your sailors. Those archers who shot out the other ship's sail as well. And the Irish slaves, but armed, their arms hidden. When the heathens come aboard, thinking they've made an easy catch, we go at them. We'll kill half of them before they know what's happened, and their ship is ours."

Brunhard frowned and looked away and Louis could almost hear his thoughts, the temptation, the skepticism. "You arm the slaves?" he said at last. "They'll kill you before the heathen has come a mile closer."

"We don't have to unchain them. They can fight with the chains around their necks, but they would not be able to take the ship from us," Louis said. "You could promise them their freedom if they fight and win. You don't have to mean it. They don't really have to believe you. Hope alone would drive them. Plus, if they don't fight, the Northmen will kill them. If they really are fighting men, they won't let that happen."

Brunhard nodded. "An interesting idea," he said.

Louis nodded as well. He had struck the right tone so far, he thought, and did not want to seem too eager.

"You would lead this?" Brunhard asked next.

Louis nodded again. "You saved me from your men, from Áed who wanted very much to cut my throat. I appreciate that. And I expect a share of the plunder."

"Of course you do, you greedy Frankish turd," Brunhard said.

"We would need to make certain the slaves we have on the ship are really fighting men, not farmers," Louis said. "You can pick the sailors who'll go with us. If we win, it could make us very rich. If we lose, you lose only a third of your slaves, a few men, a ship, and my company. A risk worth taking, I think."

"Maybe it is, maybe it isn't," Brunhard said. "I'll sleep on it, if you and your Irish bitch don't keep me awake all night making the beast with two backs, and I'll tell you in the morning what I think." He stood abruptly and walked off to where the men of *Wind Dancer* were bedding down.

"In the morning, then!" Louis called out. But he did not need to wait until morning for Brunhard's reply. The plan Louis had laid out was a good one, the risks to Brunhard small, the potential for profit great. He had seen the avarice shining in the Frisian's eyes. He knew what the answer would be.

And that in turn gave him hope. Because it meant that now there was at least a chance that he and Conandil would not be butchered by the time the sun rose and set once more.

Chapter Twenty

Never a whit should one blame another
whom love hath brought into bonds...
Hávamál

Louis spent the night with Conandil at his side and his sword, unsheathed, between them. But he slept soundly, and as the dark hours rolled past he did not feel the need to touch either of them. It was not until he realized something was poking at his shoulder that he came awake with a start.

He opened his eyes. It was still dark. His hand moved reflexively for the hilt of his sword. His fingers wrapped around the wire-bound grip and he heard Brunhard's voice, gruff but speaking low, say, "No, no, you idiot, you have no need of that. Get up and follow me."

Louis sat up and looked around. There were small flames flickering in the fire pit, enough to illuminate the Frisian's face and beard with a soft orange light. Brunhard had been poking Louis's shoulder with the toe of his shoe.

"Where are we going?" Louis croaked.

"To talk. Come on. Are you some sort of Frankish princess? How long are you going to sleep?"

Louis kicked his way out of his leather sleeping sack and climbed to his feet. He picked up his sword as he did and slid it into the sheath hanging from his belt, a belt he had not bothered to remove. Brunhard was already walking away and he stumbled after. He was surprised Brunhard had made no bawdy jokes about Conandil. He guessed the Frisian had other things on his mind.

They stopped by the fire where half a dozen men were gathered around. Áed was one and the sailor, Silef, was another. The rest Louis did not recognize so he guessed they were from the other ships in Brunhard's fleet.

"This is Louis the Frank," Brunhard said to those others, jerking a thumb in Louis's direction. "He says he's some sort of fighting man. Louis, this is Merulf, master of the *Galilee*, which is the smallest of my ships."

Louis nodded his greeting and Merulf, whose slight scowl was visible though a scraggly and unkempt beard, nodded back, a gesture that carried not the slightest welcome.

"We have been talking among us about this plan of yours," Brunhard went on, "and we agree it's a good one. Surprising, coming from the likes of you, but good, still. Merulf has stepped up and offered his ship as the one we will use to bait the Northman."

Merulf did not speak, and Louis suspected that he had offered nothing of the sort. Brunhard had referred to *Galilee* as Merulf's ship, but of course it wasn't. It was Brunhard's ship, and Merulf was simply a master hired on, a man who was easily replaced if he did not yield to Brunhard's wishes.

"What do you have for weapons?" Louis asked.

"The archers, as you said," Brunhard replied. "We have a few swords, axes, but we also have two dozen spears. They're cargo, I was bringing them to Frisia to trade, but we could put them to use."

"Good," Louis said. "Perfect. Since we mean to keep the slaves chained, even as they fight, so they don't turn on us, spears are the best weapons for them. Pole arms. Gives them reach, even if their movement is limited."

"Yes, that's right," Brunhard said. "Now, Merulf will have command of the ship, as he does now. His word is law. You, Louis, will be in command of the slaves and the others who are there to fight. And you had better know what the hell you are about. You better not be lying when you say you're some sort of warrior. Áed will go with you as well."

"No," Louis said. The last thing he needed was that great Irish beast standing behind him with a weapon in his hand. "If Áed is there, then there is confusion as to who commands. That could be the death of us all."

"Áed can speak to the slaves. You cannot," Brunhard said, which was not true but Louis did not want Brunhard to know that.

"I'll bring my slave. Conandil. She speaks Frankish."

Louis saw the surprise on Brunhard's face. "Really? The little bitch speaks your language? I wonder what other skills she has that I don't know about. You make me sorry I sold her to you."

"I must also look over the slaves who are on *Galilee* now," Louis went on, ignoring the remark. "Not all of these Irish are warriors. Some are farmers who were called up to fight. We cannot afford to have any man who isn't good with a weapon. I'll need to replace any like that with better men. And I'll need to take others as well. *Galilee* doesn't carry near as many men as *Wind Dancer*. We must have more if we're to beat the heathens."

Louis looked from man to man. None of them looked happy to have this Frankish interloper making demands, but neither did they look as if they wanted to argue with him or Brunhard.

"Very well," Brunhard said at last. "It will be as you wish. And either you'll make me wealthier still, or you'll be dead, and either way I'm a happy man."

"I'm sure," Louis said. He wondered if Merulf felt the same, given that if he, Louis, was dead then Merulf would no doubt be dead as well. He wondered if he should be concerned that Brunhard had not put up more of an argument.

Well, there's nothing for it, he thought. If they did this thing, there was a good chance he and Conandil would die at the hands of the heathens. If they did not, then he would most certainly die at Brunhard's hands, and Conandil, he guessed, would find herself praying for death.

Most of Brunhard's sailors and the Irish slaves were still asleep, but those who were awake began to fan out among the heaps of slumbering men, delivering kicks just hard enough to wake them and elicit the occasional curse. Soon they were up and shuffling around, the few women among the slaves set to stoking up the fire and getting oat porridge on for breakfast. Someone had pulled out the spears from among *Wind Dancer*'s other cargo and put them aboard *Galilee*.

Louis roused Conandil and led her over to where Brunhard and the sailors chosen for this task stood by the chained Irishmen, still sitting on the ground

"Now, Frank," Brunhard said, "Merulf and me, we figure *Galilee* will bear forty of these Irish dogs, no more. Will that be enough to beat the heathens?"

"Yes, it will be," Louis said. "If those Irish are good fighting men."

He turned to Conandil. "I need to pick out the best warriors of this lot. Forty of them," he said. He spoke Frankish. Conandil nodded her understanding, but of course Louis already knew that she understood. They had talked all of this through, in the dark, lying side by side, their voices no louder than breathing.

"Why are you talking to her about this business?" Brunhard demanded.

"Because she's one of them. She lived in the rath of the rí túaithe where these men are from. You know what that is, a rath?"

"Yes, I know what that is, do you think I'm as stupid as you?" Brunhard snapped.

"Then you understand she knows better than you or me which men here can fight."

When Brunhard did not reply, Conandil said, "Shall I tell you, master, which are the best of the warriors?"

"Yes," Louis said.

Conandil stepped forward, walking slowly down the line of chained men. She pointed at those she deemed the best of the men-at-arms. Two of Brunhard's men followed behind her, and as she chose they removed that man from his neck chain and placed him in another. Louis and Conandil stepped up to Conandil's husband, Broccáin in the red tunic, and she pointed to him without the slightest hint of recognition, and he in turn showed no recognition of her.

For ten minutes they moved down the line of men and finally they had selected forty and Louis told her that was enough. They seemed to be good men, tall, strong, well-formed. They had some pride left; he could see that in their bearing. They had not given themselves up to despair, and that was important, because men who were in despair were not men who would fight well.

"Very well, Brunhard, these men will do," Louis said at last.

"We'll see soon enough, won't we?" Brunhard said. "Now, Merulf and his men have been told of your plan, and you can see they're damned pleased about it all. *Wind Dancer* and *Two Brothers*, we'll get underway now. Just as the sky is turning gray in the east *Galilee* will get underway. Merulf will have the yard cocked and the sail hanging like it's torn, some nonsense like that. Let the Northmen think she's disabled, somehow. They're like wolves, they'll likely shit themselves they'll be so excited."

"Good," Louis said. "We'll be ready for them. Once the Northmen are our prisoners, then we'll set sail and catch up with you. But you must not hover too near. If the heathens think you can come to our aid they may not attack."

"Yes, I'm not some Frankish simpleton, I understand that," Brunhard said. "You just fight like you mean it, and if you try any tricks to betray me, you'll wish the heathens had cut your heart out, trust me."

With those words of encouragement Brunhard took his leave, ordering *Wind Dancer* and the other ship, *Two Brothers*, pushed back into the water. Soon they were no more than vague shapes in the light of the stars, and then they were lost entirely.

Louis found Merulf sulking by the bow of *Galilee*. "Brunhard told you what we have in mind, what your part will be?" he asked.

"Yes," Merulf said. "Can't say I'm much in favor of it. Didn't intend to be fighting heathens when I come on as master of this ship."

"You won't be fighting heathens. I will. Me and these other men. You just do your part, see to the ship, and by nightfall you'll be a considerably richer man."

Merulf only grunted at that, so Louis left him and stepped over to where the slaves, the chosen men, were sitting on the sand, still chained to one another.

"Listen to me," he said and the forty men looked in his direction. He spoke in Irish because Brunhard and Áed were not there to hear him, and because it did not matter anymore. He would be free by nightfall or he would be dead, and it did not matter who knew what languages he could speak.

"You're all warriors, fighting men," he said. "That's what Conandil told me. We are going out to sea now, where the heathens are lurking like wolves. The heathens who sold you into bondage. They'll attack our ship, but they will not think it's filled with armed warriors. When they come aboard, on my command, you'll grab up your spears and we'll kill them all. Some of you might die, but you'll die like men. If we're victorious, then Brunhard had promised you your freedom."

Nearly all of the speech, rousing as it was, was nonsense and Louis suspected that the Irishmen in chains knew it. But it probably did not matter. Faced with heathens launching a mad attack against them, these men would fight rather than be cut down like sheep sent to slaughter. They probably understood that Brunhard would not give them their freedom no matter what they did, but the outside chance that he might was motivation enough.

And later, when she had the chance to move quietly among them, Conandil would explain their real purpose, the plan beyond the plan. And that would most certainly motivate them.

Louis turned back to the ship. Merulf was still standing sullen by the bow. "Merulf!" he called. "We can get underway now, whenever you are ready."

Merulf shouted a few orders. His men retrieved the ropes and anchors that held the ship fast and then climbed aboard. Merulf told Louis to get the slaves heaving the ship out into the surf, which they did. Then they waded out, waist deep, and climbed aboard, an awkward trick with their necks chained one to the other. Finally Louis and Conandil waded out, and Louis helped Conandil aboard, then climbed over the sheer strake himself and made his way aft.

The night was still dark, no hint of dawn, but the great spread of stars overhead gave off light enough for the men aboard to do what needed doing. The sailors passed the oars to the slaves, now seated on the thwarts, and they thrust the blades out through the oarports. Merulf took a step forward and shouted, "Back your oars!" He spoke Irish, but his pronunciation was so bad that Louis guessed that the rowing commands were the full extent of his fluency. Merulf, Louis suspected, had worked with Brunhard before, and was accustomed to the Frisian's clever plan to make his Irish slaves row themselves across the sea.

But those few words of Irish were all that Merulf needed. The oars came down and were thrust forward and *Galilee* moved slowly away from the beach. Three more strokes like that and then the ship was spun in her length and they headed bow-first out into the dark water.

Conandil, Merulf, the helmsman, the after end of *Galilee*, they were no more than dark and barely distinguished shapes to Louis. The rest of the ship forward was all but lost in the dark, and beyond that there was nothing at all. But Merulf did not seem concerned about rowing through the darkness, and Louis recalled that night before, when they had run up on the beach, there had been no threatening rocks or shoals in the waters offshore.

Merulf drove his ship seaward, calling in his crude Irish for the rowers to keep pulling, giving commands to the helmsman to do this and that, things Louis did not understand. He felt the motion of the ship change, just a bit, as it moved into deeper water, but beyond that he had no idea of what was going on.

For some time they pulled through the dark in that manner, Merulf keeping the Irish rowers at a steady though undemanding pace, the ship forging ahead with an easy rocking and pitching motion. The air was filled with the scent of brine and a hint of grass and earth from the land, not so far off. And soon Louis became aware of the growing light, realized he could see nearly to the *Galilee*'s bow and could make out the rolling water over the side.

Merulf called forward to his sailors. "Cast off the starboard gaskets and we'll hoist the yard cockbilled, about halfway to the masthead." The words were meaningless to Louis, but apparently not to the ship's men, who moved to comply. They did not move fast, or with any great enthusiasm, no more pleased about any of this than Merulf was. But they did move.

Some of the men took a heavy rope down from a cleat and laid it out straight, others reached up and untied a thinner line that was lashed around the yard. A few moments later they grabbed onto the heavy rope and pulled and the yard rose up the mast, then rose again as they continued to haul. When it was partway up they dipped the larboard end down and around the shrouds, then let it go when it was square to the ship's centerline. Another line was hauled on, and rather than setting neatly horizontal, the yard was now tilted at an odd angle, and half the sail was hanging limp and flapping in the light breeze. It looked as if some great misfortune had taken place.

Perfect, Louis thought.

It was lighter now, the sky to the east growing gray, the men pulling at the oars entirely visible from the afterdeck. "Merulf," Louis said. "We must distribute the weapons and I must have a chance to drill the men in what we'll be doing. I don't need long, but if we're to avoid being slaughtered I'll need some time for this. Now, before we're visible to any heathens who may be lurking."

Merulf grunted, which Louis realized was most of the man's communications. But it seemed an affirmative grunt, so Louis walked the length of the ship to the foredeck and addressed Brunhard's men who were loitering there, the sailors and archers and the few others more skilled in weapons.

"I need you men to hand out the spears," he said. "Set them on the bottom of the ship, one by each of the men at the oars." As they shuffled to obey, Louis walked back aft, addressing the rowers in Irish. "The sailors will be putting spears next to you. Don't take your hands off the oars. Make a move for a spear before I tell you and you'll be cut down where you sit."

The men at the oars looked up at him, never pausing in their rhythmic stroke, their faces without expression, but Louis was confident that they understood.

Merulf's men seemed less confident in the slaves' good behavior. Louis could see the caution and wariness with which they handed out the spears, while the archers stood with arrows nocked ready to drop any Irishman who made a move for a weapon. But the Irish understood how futile such a gesture would be, and they kept their hands on the oars as the spears were placed out of sight beside them.

Louis switched back to his rough Frisian and addressed Brunhard's men once more. "You men know what we intend. One of the heathens is still chasing us, and we mean to turn things around and capture him instead. He'll see a helpless-looking merchant ship and he'll attack. When he comes alongside, he'll see a small crew and a gang of slaves chained at the oars. The timing is the crucial thing. I've fought many fights like this, and I'm still alive, so if you want to stay alive as well, listen to me. We must let the heathens get aboard; we must not let them think we have any fight in us. Let them drop their guard and then we attack."

Brunhard's men and Merulf's did not seem any more enthusiastic, but they gave desultory nods so Louis knew at least they had been listening. Now he could only hope they would obey as well. He turned to Merulf. "Could you tell the slaves to stop rowing?" he asked.

Merulf give a harsh order and the men at the oars brought the blades up from the sea and rested their arms on the looms, holding the oars above the water. Louis ran his eyes along the lines of men on the thwarts. *Galilee* had ten rowing benches per side. To accommodate forty men they had double-manned each oar and the small merchantman looked crammed with rowers. Louis hoped that would not make the Northmen suspicious. He had no idea how odd it might look to them. But Brunhard and Merulf knew of such things and they had said nothing, so he guessed it would be all right.

He told the rowers pretty much what he had told Brunhard's men. They had to wait for the precise moment, the moment on which Louis would decide, and then they were to snatch up their spears and drive them into the heathens.

"Only throw your spear if you have no other means of killing one of them," Louis said. "When you throw your spear you disarm yourself. Use them to impale the bastards."

From the starboard side a man spoke up, his voice belligerent. "How can we fight if we're in chains?" he demanded. One of Merulf's sailors took two steps toward him, rope end raised, but Louis called for the man to stop.

"It will be no easy thing, fighting with the chains on, I know that," Louis said. "But you know why Brunhard insists they remain. You must do the best you can, or the heathens will cut you down like dogs."

This was met with a muttered response, which Louis ignored. "Now, when I shout 'weapons,'" he continued, "that is when you snatch up your spears, rise and fight. We'll drill with that move now."

For some time after, as the sun came closer to the horizon, they ran through the steps they would take to spring their trap on the heathens. The Irishmen at the oars took up the stroke until Louis called for them to cease rowing. He explained that the heathens would then come alongside, and the men on *Galilee* would wait for them to come. He told them how the heathens would jump aboard, unsure of what was happening, wondering if the men of *Galilee* would fight back.

"Weapons!" Louis shouted, and at that signal the Irish whipped the spears out from under the benches, leapt to their feet and thrust at the imaginary enemy. It was awkward at first, but they tried it again and again and the movement became faster, more fluid, as the slaves became accustomed to the action and learned how to work together so their chains did not inhibit them.

The sun had broken free of the horizon, the sky clear once again, by the time Louis was as satisfied as he was likely to be. In truth, he could have spent an entire day drilling the men and still not have been completely satisfied, but this would have to do. And he could see that Conandil had chosen well; the Irish slaves were indeed warriors, men used to handling weapons. They were men who could be trusted to fight to the death, even as the heathens came screaming over the rails.

He turned to Merulf who was standing behind him and off to one side. "I think they're ready," he said. "Ready as they are going to get."

"Well, that's a damned good thing to hear," Merulf said in his grunting tone. "'Cause that heathen son of a bitch is not more than a couple miles astern and he's running right up our arse."

Twenty-One

There we felled three
skillful helmet-trees
of rare renown.
                The Saga of the People of Laxardal

Louis stepped to *Galilee*'s side, looked astern. Sure enough, about two miles behind them he could make out the grayish white rectangle of a sail, set to the light offshore breeze. It might have been the heathen or it might have been the Holy Ghost for all Louis could tell, but if Merulf said it was the heathen, then he was most likely right.

He watched the distant ship for some time. Behind him, he heard Merulf step forward and call out the order to row, the Irish words barely discernable through his Frisian accent. And then came the creak of the oars in the oarports, the steady swish of the blades through the water. Merulf called for them to pull easy. They were not trying to escape, only to look like they were.

Louis turned back to Merulf and nodded past the bow. "Do you see anything of Brunhard and his other ships?" he asked.

"No," Merulf said, giving full vent to his irritation and resentment. "Just us. Just us and this murdering bastard in our wake."

"But only one murdering bastard?" Louis asked. "You see only the one heathen ship astern?"

"Yes, just the one," Merulf said bitterly. "That's how we know God's blessing is upon us."

Louis ignored the master's sarcasm. "The men must not be thirsty for this fight," he said. "They've been drilling for some time. Can I have my slave give them water now?"

Merulf considered that and apparently could find no objection, so he nodded and looked away. Louis called Conandil to him. "See each of the men get a dipper-full of water. Understand?"

Conandil nodded and gave a shallow curtsey and headed off forward to where the water barrel and dipper stood. Soon she was moving back and forth between the barrel and the seated, rowing men, tipping water into their mouths as they rowed, whispering a few words with each drink given.

Louis's eyes moved from Merulf to Brunhard's other men, but none of them seemed to be paying any attention to the Irish slave girl. And that was good. Because the words she was saying *sotto voce* to the slaves were most certainly not for the Frisians' ears.

He ran his eyes up the *Galilee*'s mast. The sail hanging limp and crooked gave a credible impression of a ship in distress, or so he thought. He looked astern once again. The longship seemed closer now, but he could not be certain.

"When the heathen has drawn nearer," Louis said to Merulf, "we should see that the rowers do a poorer job of their task. Row a little clumsier. That will make us look even more unprepared."

Merulf gave a grunt of a laugh and spat over this side. "I don't know how these sorry creatures could look any clumsier, but I'll see what I can do."

The sun rose and the ships crawled on over the gently rolling sea and it dawned on Louis that this was not going to end quickly, that this chase might go on for some time. After the morning drilling with weapons, the excitement of seeing the enemy in their wake, Louis had been ready for the fight to commence, and had lost sight of something he had come to understand: sometimes things happened very slowly at sea.

Louis de Roumois had been a horse soldier, head of a troop of mounted warriors. They had used their speed to counter incursions by the Northmen in the River Seine that ran through Frankia to the sea. He was used to plunging into battle in an instant, to seeing a threat and moving to counter it at the speed of a running horse. He was not accustomed to such things as wind and tide and current imposing their will on his movements and it drove him to distraction.

He sat and drew his sword and pulled a stone from the pouch he wore on his belt and began to run it along the blade. The men at the oars continued their slow pull. The breeze off the land died away and a stronger breeze filled in from the sea, but *Galilee*'s sail only flapped like a broken wing and looked more pathetic still.

Merulf stepped over to where Louis was seated. He had been looking astern, Louis noticed, but Louis made a point of not asking him about the heathen ship. But he knew Merulf would tell him anyway.

"The Northmen, they're making use of this sea breeze, moving right along," he said. "They'll be up with us soon enough." Much of the bitterness was gone from his voice, and in its place was something that sounded more like concern. Fear, maybe.

Louis stood and sheathed his sword. "Let me take a look," he said. He stepped aft, leaned on the shear strake and looked astern. The longship was indeed closer, a bit more than a half a mile away, heeling in the breeze, the white foam around its bow visible even from that distance. Louis felt a stirring of passion, like that moment when a woman he hoped to bed begins to remove clothing. Here was some real excitement in the offing. He was ready. To fight, to win, to die, whatever it was, he was ready.

"Good," he said, straightening. "Good. Let's get on with this and spill some heathen blood." Merulf nodded and Louis sensed the shift in power aboard the ship. When they had been sailing, Merulf was the master; it was his ship entirely. Louis was nothing, not even a mariner.

But it was different now. Soon, very soon, this would not be a ship. It would be a battleground, a killing field. It would be Louis's world. Not Merulf's. It would be a world that Merulf did not know and apparently did not care for. And already Louis could see that the Frisian master was yielding to him.

Good, Louis thought.

"Everything should be ready, but I'll see again," Louis said. He stepped forward, past the cluster of sailors and bowmen aft, down the center of the ship between the double-banked oars, the men pulling with an easy stroke. The Irishmen kept their eyes down, as they had learned to do, but Louis could see something new on their faces. A hint of defiance, an eagerness for the coming fight.

His eyes moved to the deck and the spears resting there. They were not easy to see, the wooden shafts against the wooden deck, and Louis was counting on the heathens not spotting them until it was too late.

He continued toward the bow, eyes moving larboard and starboard, looking at the men and the weapons. Forward of the rowing benches there was another cluster of sailors keeping watchful eyes on the slaves. Conandil was there too, sitting off to the side, trying to look as inconspicuous as possible.

"The slaves have had water and what they need?" he asked her, his voice harsh, a master addressing a slave.

"Yes, master," Conandil said. Louis still did not know if any of the sailors spoke Irish at all, but he made certain that if they did his words would cause no alarm.

He turned quickly and strode aft again, and once more looked astern. The enemy was a quarter of a mile astern and closing the distance fast, the sail full, if not straining.

Louis turned to Merulf. "I want the rowers to row faster, but do a bad job of it. Will you give me leave to instruct them?"

Merulf nodded. Louis stepped forward. "The heathens are coming up fast," he said in a voice that could be heard all the way to the bow. "We must look as if we are panicked. I'll need you to row faster, but foul your oars on occasion, seem as if you have no skills. We do not want the enemy to think there's any fight in us. Go!"

The Irish, who were actually becoming rather skilled rowers, leaned into it and pulled together, then again, and *Galilee* moved noticeably faster through the water. Two more strokes and then Broccáin swung his oar out of time with the others, knocking it into the oar ahead of his, fouling that one, which was struck by the next ahead. On the larboard side they pulled as the starboard became more entangled and *Galilee* began to turn helplessly.

"Hold, starboard!" Merulf shouted and the starboard oars came up as the larboard rowers sorted themselves out, an even harder job now that they were two men on each oar. Louis could hear Merulf cursing under his breath, impatient and frightened, and he wanted to point out that they were not in fact trying to escape, but he kept his mouth shut. He was enjoying the master's discomfort.

"No, pull, you fools!" Merulf called as the oars were got in line again. "Pull!"

Louis looked astern. The longship was close enough that he could see the figurehead now, some sort of animal with a long snout, mouth open, teeth bared. He could see men on her deck looking back at him. A lot of men, to be sure, but not as many as, say, Thorgrim's ship would have held. This was not as big a ship as that.

There would not be many more men than Louis commanded, though the heathen's men would not all be chained together at the neck.

There were no shields mounted on the longship's side. In Louis's limited experience he found that sometimes the Northmen did that and sometimes they did not, and he was not sure why. Now, he imagined, the shields would just get in the way of their climbing from their ship onto *Galilee*. He wondered if they would bring shields into the fight. He had guessed they would not. It would be very awkward climbing from ship to ship with shields on their arms.

He hoped they left the shields behind. Shields were a good defense against spears, and the Irish slaves would have difficulties enough in the coming battle.

He turned and looked forward. "It will not be long now!" he called. He turned to the archers standing nearby. "You, wait on my signal. Keep your bows hidden. Most likely I won't tell you to shoot until the heathens are on board." The archers nodded. They did not look any happier than Merulf.

The Northmen were close enough astern now that they could hear them yelling. It was nothing intelligible, Louis guessed, though all of their barbaric language was a garble to him. They were just shouting and beating their weapons on the side of their ship. They were hoping to frighten their intended victim, and judging by the looks on the faces of Merulf and his men, it was working. Only the Irish slaves seemed more determined than frightened.

Then the shouting and banging stopped and Louis heard a single voice carry over the water, loud and insistent. He suspected it was one of the heathens calling for them to surrender. Probably offering not to harm anyone who did not fight. Louis did not understand the words, but that did not matter because he would never have trusted the word of a Northman in any event.

Instead, he climbed up onto the edge of the ship and balanced himself with a hand on the sternpost and shouted back. He called in Irish, since that was the least likely language to be understood on the heathens' ship. "Come on aboard, you dogs! You swine! Come aboard and we will gut you all like the pigs you are!"

He hopped back to the deck. He figured that was all the verbal intercourse they would need.

Soon the shouting and banging resumed and Louis felt a grin spread across his face. He was fond of battle, maybe over fond of it, the way others were overly fond of drink. It was something he had not tasted in some time, but he remembered now how much he liked it.

The Northmen were nearly on them, the bow of their ship only thirty feet away off the starboard side and a bit down wind. The leering figurehead and the line of men at the ship's side were perfectly visible. Louis saw something streak through the air and an arrow hit the *Galilee*'s side with a thump, and then another, just a few feet forward of the helmsman.

"They're aiming at me!" the man at the tiller shouted, his voice carrying shock and outrage and not a little fear.

Of course they're aiming at you, you fool, Louis thought, but he said in his brightest voice, "There's no chance they'll hit you. Not from one moving ship to another."

That was not true at all, of course, and Louis knew it. But even if the helmsman was killed it would not matter much. They did not have long now, no more than the time it would take for two or three more strokes of the oars. Louis had noted how the ship behaved when the oars on the larboard side had fouled and it gave him an idea.

He looked back at the longship. Thirty or forty feet away, no more, and starting to turn to run right up along *Galilee*'s side. He took a step forward and addressed the rowers.

"When I give the word, the rowers on the starboard side will foul their oars, as larboard did before. Then the heathens will be on us. Make ready..."

He looked back at the longship. *Now!* he thought.

Merulf stepped closer. "What did you tell them?" he demanded.

"You'll see," Louis said. He turned back to the rowers and yelled in Irish "Now! Now! Starboard side, foul your oars!"

It was chaos, lovely chaos. Half the oars went forward, half back and they locked one against each other in a great tangle of wooden shafts and dripping blades. The larboard side, however, pulled with a nice, clean stroke and *Galilee* spun around to starboard, right across the path of the on-rushing longship.

"Ahh!" Merulf screamed. "You idiot! See what you've done!"

Louis smiled. He could see what he'd done. It was exactly what he wished to do. He heard shouts from the longship, what he guessed were orders flying back and forth. The Northman turned hard to starboard to avoid slamming into *Galilee*. Her sail was hauled up and she slowed, and slowed more as her hull struck *Galilee*'s starboard side oars and snapped them off, then drove hard against the merchantman's hull.

"Ready, ready, wait for my word..." Louis shouted forward, calling in Irish and again in Frisian. The heathens were shouting and waving axes and spears and swords, massing at the side of their ship as the two vessels ground together. Grappling hooks flew and caught in *Galilee*'s side and the lines were hauled taut as the ships were lashed together. An arrow whipped across *Galilee*'s deck and embedded itself in one of the Frisian sailors' guts and the man fell shrieking and writhing to the deck.

"Steady, steady..." Louis shouted again, in both tongues. This was the hardest moment of all, and the most crucial. If they let the heathens see now they had a fight coming, there would be a terrific effusion of blood, and it would not be heathen blood.

The ships were bound together, spinning slowly in place. The shouting from the longship had not stopped, but the men aboard the *Galilee*, the Irish rowers and the sailors and Brunhard's men, stood watching as if struck dumb.

The first of the Northmen came over the rail, screaming in his ugly language, a great battle ax over his head, his long beard braided in a few places. But he was not holding a shield, to Louis's relief. He vaulted over the side, landed on *Galilee*'s deck, and still screaming swung his ax in a wide half-circle and cut one of the slave's heads nearly clean off, the spray of blood lashing the man beside him as his body toppled over.

"Steady, steady!" Louis called and the Irishmen proved their worth, remaining fixed in place, no one panicking, no one moving before his time. The first heathen brought the ax back again, ready to meet any new threat, and then paused. Because no one was moving. No one was fighting back.

More and more of the Northmen came over the side, weapons in hand, landing on *Galilee*'s deck in the spaces between the rowers. They came ready for a fight and they got none, and one by one they lowered their weapons, partway at least, as they looked around. Louis could see the growing confusion.

"Who are you?" he called, loud and demanding. He spoke in Frisian, which was a tongue the Northmen were most likely to understand.

The first of the Northmen to come aboard looked over at him. He was younger than Louis had first thought, about Louis's own age. "I am Thorodd Bollason," he shouted back.

Louis's next words were in Irish, and they were loud, emphatic, and anticipated. "Weapons! Weapons! Now! Now! Kill them!"

Fore and aft, in four rows, sat the oarsmen, and they looked like pathetic, beaten and cowed men, chained to the benches, presenting no kind of threat to the Northmen. And so, as the forty Irish warriors bent down and snatched up spears in a move they had practiced over and over again that very morning, the Northmen were too surprised and confused to react.

Louis saw the one named Thorodd Bollason turn to see what was happening, this sudden activity. A shout was just coming from his lips, his ax was just going up again when he died on the points of three spears thrust into him by the three slaves nearest where he stood. The command on his lips turned into a scream, his back arched, blood erupted from his mouth and the three Irish warriors pulled their points free and let Thorodd Bollason drop to the deck as they turned to other victims.

"Archers!" Louis shouted, but the Frisian bowmen already had their bows out from where they had been concealed, already were nocking arrows, and even as the word left Louis's mouth the first arrow twanged off its string and sent one of the heathens back over *Galilee*'s side, tumbling back aboard the longship, clutching at the shaft jutting from his chest as he fell.

The Northmen were recovering from the surprise, but even the few heartbeats they took to do so was too long for many of them. The Irish warriors' spears reached through the press of men to tear into stomachs and chests. Most Northmen did not have mail, Louis knew, and he guessed that those who did did not care to wear it when fighting on shipboard, lest they go over the side. Certainly none of the heathens he saw now were wearing mail, and that just made it easier for the Irishmen to cut them down.

And the Irish were doing their work well. The rows of men farthest from the heathens reached through those in front of them and rammed their pole arms into the first rank of the enemy, while those closest to the Northmen reached past them to get at the heathens behind, some still aboard their longship. Men were falling screaming, clamping hands over wounds that would bleed them out if the Irish did not throw them overboard first.

The Northmen, however, were not the sort to stand and let themselves be cut down. The first few seconds of the fight had been one-sided, but the Northmen recovered quick, and swords and axes swung and parried spear blows and lashed out at the men chained one to another.

Now those chains became a problem. The Northmen leapt fore and aft, looking for advantage, and the Irish, so hindered in their ability to move, could do little to counter them. A Norse ax came down on one man's skull, nearly splitting it. A sword opened a great wound in another man's arm. And each man was a link in the chain, and each one who was disabled only further hindered the others.

Louis pulled his sword and he shouted, loud as he could, wishing to draw attention, to distract the Northmen, even for the briefest instant. He leapt forward, sword sweeping at the nearest man, who held his ax up to stop the blow. Louis turned his wrist, altered the course of the blade just the smallest bit, and the edge of the sword cut into the heathen's hand that was gripping the ax.

The man screamed, blood burst from the hand, the ax fell and Louis brought the sword back and drove the tip through the man's throat, turning the scream into an ugly gurgling sound. From the corner of his eye he saw movement and he leapt aside as a sword scythed past in a downward stroke. Louis stamped his foot on the blade, but he was too close to make use of his own sword so he hit the man hard in the face. The Northman staggered back and Louis slashed at him as he did, opening up a gash in the man's leather armor, but doing no worse hurt than that.

Then Merulf was there, screaming like a lunatic. He had an ax in his hand, not a fighting weapon, per se, but an ax used in repairing the ship. Still, it was effective, particularly in the hands of someone who seemed to have gone mad. He chopped the blade into the man Louis had punched, jerked it free, turned and flailed at the next man forward. Merulf seemed furious at the idea that heathens might sully his precious ship with their unholy presence, and he would not tolerate it.

Fine, Louis thought. He did not care what drove Merulf, only that he was driven.

The archers at the bow and stern were still keeping it up, picking off the men in the back while the Irish slaves continued to wreak havoc on the others. There were wounded and dead among the slaves now, men who had half fallen and were held part way up by the iron collars around their necks, doing a macabre and grotesque dance as the men to whom they remained chained continued to fight.

Merulf was pushing his way forward, his ax flailing. A Northman in front of Louis was engaged with one of the Irish warriors, parrying his spear thrusts, looking for an opening to use his seax on the man.

The Northman saw Louis coming at him, understood his dilemma, threats from two sides. He turned quick to face Louis, realized his mistake, and died on the end of the Irish spear before he could correct it.

Some of the heathens were starting to tumble back aboard the longship, but there was no safety for them there, because once they were clear of the tumble of fighting they were easy targets for the archers, who dropped them like sitting birds on the deck of their own ship.

Then, almost as suddenly as the fighting had begun with Louis's call to arms, it stopped. The few heathens still alive, nearly all of whom were wounded, were throwing weapons aside, and some were cut down with the wicked points of spears even as they did.

An odd quiet swept over the two ships, still bound one to the other, a quiet punctuated by the groans and cries from the wounded. The madness seemed to abandon Merulf. He lowered the ax to his side and came stumbling aft. The fight was done. The first fight was done.

Louis took a step forward, ran his eyes over the Irish warriors still holding their spears at the ready. This was the moment when they were supposed to lay the spears down, when the weapons would be collected by Merulf's men. That was what the Frisians expected them to do.

It was not what Louis expected them to do. It was not what Conandil had whispered for them to do as she distributed the ladles of water to each man. Now was the time to bring their weapons to bear once again.

Louis had let his sword arm drop, let the tip of his sword rest on the deck in the most unthreatening manner. Now he lifted the blade, turning as he did, looking for Merulf who was standing behind him. When he cut the master down, that would be the signal for the Irish who would turn on the others.

He spun around and saw Merulf standing just where he had anticipated, just as he had pictured it, save for one thing. Merulf was not standing still; he was swinging his ax around in a big horizontal arc, the iron head on a course to strike Louis right on the temple. Louis had less than a heartbeat's time to register this surprise before the ax made contact with his skull and something seemed to explode in his brain and then he was aware of nothing more.

Twenty-Two

*Silent and thoughtful and bold in strife
the prince's bairn should be.*
Hávamál

Harald Thorgrimson, known as Harald Broadarm, had learned many good lessons in the two years and more he had gone a'viking with his father. He learned much about seafaring and shipbuilding, which he had not learned growing up on the family farm. He had learned a great deal about fighting, despite believing, before sailing from Vik, that he already knew pretty much all one could know on that subject.

He had learned about death in its many facets, and the ways of men: Norwegians and Danes and Irishmen. He had learned about women, several hard-earned lessons about women. He had learned to think in strategic ways, and in ways of which he was not even aware. And, perhaps most useful of all, he had learned when to speak, and when to keep his mouth shut.

That part of his education was paying off on the beach on the east coast of Ireland, where *Sea Hammer* and *Blood Hawk* and *Dragon* were run up in the gravel. Men were swarming over the two larger vessels. Harald, as usual, was in the thick of the work, laboring harder than any two men because he so feared having anyone feel he was not doing his part. But all the while he could not help but think, *This is madness…*

Thorgrim was not about to let the Frisian merchant who had so cleverly driven them ashore get away with it, not for long. Harald understood that, and he agreed with that sentiment with all his being. Indeed, there was not one man on the beach who did not take it for granted that they would get bloody and thorough revenge on this Brunhard, even if they had to chase him to Frisia and beyond.

But Thorgrim also insisted he would go after him with *Sea Hammer*, despite the sail having burned to ash, the rigging damaged in the flames. In order to use *Sea Hammer* they had to shift the sail from *Blood Hawk* and bend it to *Sea Hammer*'s yard, not a huge task. But they also had to unstep the masts of both ships and remove the rigging from each, shifting *Blood Hawk*'s undamaged rigging to *Sea Hammer*'s mast.

Thorgrim had explained that that was what they would do. Godi frowned but remained silent. His ship, his *Blood Hawk*, would be stripped of her ability to move any faster than the men could row her. She would be out of the fight.

But even that was not Harald's biggest worry. "That will take some time, Father, shifting the sail and rigging." He looked out to sea, to the south, the direction in which Brunhard's ships, with *Fox* in pursuit, had disappeared. The glance was involuntary, Harald had not meant to imply anything by it, but the implication was there nonetheless.

"We'll lose some time this way," Thorgrim said, the words coming out sharp. "But *Sea Hammer* is the faster ship. If we're going to run this Frisian bastard down, we'll need *Sea Hammer*'s speed."

"Yes, or course," Godi said. Godi was a man whose loyalty was absolute. His frown, his glance at the ground, was the most strident protest Harald had ever seen from the man.

Harald, too, was not one to argue with his father. Thorgrim Night Wolf was the boldest and the cleverest man he had ever known, and Harald's obedience went far beyond the simple loyalty owed by a son to his father. In his mind, Thorgrim was never wrong. And those times when he had thought Thorgrim was wrong, the mistake had generally been Harald's. But this time he was not so certain.

"I had thought, Father, that we would be better off getting underway with *Blood Hawk*. We could push off the beach now and…"

"No," Thorgrim said. "We'll go after them in *Sea Hammer*."

And that was an end to it. Thorgrim's tone made that clear, and Harald's hard-earned lessons in when to speak and when to remain silent paid off then. He said nothing more, just unbuckled his sword belt, which he was still wearing, having put it on thinking there was a fight coming, put the belt and weapon in a safe spot and went to work with the others, casting off the lashings that held *Blood Hawk*'s sail to her yard, moving the heavy wool cloth to *Sea Hammer*'s deck, bending the sail on again. And when that was done, the hard work began.

The yards, which were resting on their respective gallows, were cast off from the ship's masts in preparation for lowering the masts to the deck, which had to be accomplished before the rigging could be removed. The base of each mast was set in a step designed to allow the mast to pivot as it was lowered from the vertical to horizontal and back, but that did not mean the task was necessarily easy. The masts were substantial pieces of timber, forty feet in length and more than a foot thick at the base. Their descent had to be carefully controlled by men tailing on to the shrouds while others supported the mast, reaching as high up as they could. If they lost control and let the masts plunge uncontrolled to the deck, they would destroy half the ship before they came to rest.

But for all that, this was a task the men knew well, and soon the masts were nearly horizontal, resting on the ships' sheer strakes. On board *Blood Hawk* men used hammers and spikes to pry the rigging free, while aboard *Sea Hammer* the charred shrouds were cut away, the undamaged parts carefully coiled and stowed down. Rope was a precious material; not a bit of it that was still usable would be wasted.

Harald kept an eye to the west as he worked. They had spent all of the morning hours and part of the afternoon chasing the Frisian. More time had been eaten up by his father's insisting that *Sea Hammer* be set to rights rather than simply sailing in *Blood Hawk*. Harald guessed that his father had planned to sail in pursuit before the sun set, but he had not dared ask. And now it seemed unlikely that would happen whether Thorgrim wished it or not.

At last they were ready to bring *Sea Hammer*'s mast back to the vertical. Harald, standing next to the massive timber, now lying horizontal, ran his eyes over the preparation. "There, you have two after shrouds crossed!" he called to two of *Sea Hammer*'s men, standing ready to haul in the lines. "Get those untangled!"

The men did as Harald instructed and Harald nodded, then called, "Heave away!" The men at the lines began to pull and Harald and the half-dozen men beside him got their hands under the mast and began to lift. The muscles in Harald's arms and his back and gut strained as he heaved, his lips pressed together with the effort. He was one of six lifting the mast; he did not have to put that much effort into it; but he did anyway, because he loved it. He loved the feel of the power in his arms and back, he loved pushing through the hurt, loved to feel the massive weight yielding to his strength of arm.

Harald Broadarm.

The mast lifted higher and higher and Harald and the others stood straighter and soon their arms were over their heads and they were pushing on the mast rather than lifting. And then as the mast came more vertical they were doing nothing at all and the shrouds, looped over the masthead and pulled aft by the others, did the last of the work. The mast fell into the shallow step with an audible thump and Vali secured the wedge that would hold it in place and the others brought the shrouds over to where they would be made fast to the side of the ship.

Harald looked again to the west. The sun was not high above the horizon. He looked to the east, at the treacherous rocks that lined the shore. And those rocks were the least of their worries, because those were hazards they could see. It was the things they could not see, the half-submerged rocks and reefs and shelves just off the beach, that were the real danger.

He looked at his father, standing off by himself, arms folded and frowning and looking out at the water. *Anger will cloud a man's mind...* he thought.

As a young boy Harald had thought of his father as some sort of god, but another thing he had learned in their voyaging together was that he was not that. He was a man, just like any other man. That realization had not diminished Thorgrim in his son's mind. If anything it had raised him higher in Harald's esteem. Because it was no great feat for a god to do all that Thorgrim had, to survive all he had and vanquish all he had. But for a man it was extraordinary indeed.

But men also made mistakes. And Harald feared his father was making one now. And if it got much darker, and Thorgrim decided he would put to sea nonetheless, to thread his way through the hazards near shore, then he might be making his final one, and they might all pay the *wergild* for that mistake.

Even as these thoughts were running through Harald's mind, he saw Thorgrim's arms drop, saw his father seem to slump a bit in his stance. Thorgrim leaned his head back, looked straight up for a moment, then looked forward once more and walked over to *Sea Hammer*'s side.

"Bjorn," he called to one of the men who had just finished coiling down a charred shroud. "Get a few men together and gather up some wood and get a fire burning. We'll be spending the night here."

Bjorn nodded to Thorgrim and Harald nodded to himself. His father, he knew, was not going to say anything more about his decision, because the decision itself, in Thorgrim's mind, would be an admission of defeat. Temporary defeat. But Thorgrim Night Wolf, Harald knew, would not ultimately be defeated until he was cold and dead, and even then he would somehow manage to have his revenge.

They were well into twilight when Bjorn's nascent fire began to grab hold of the wood he and the others had stacked into something like a cone shape. Failend, whom Harald had not even noticed was gone, returned about that time with the six men who had gone with her. Between them they carried a dozen geese and two sheep on poles, animals which had, unfortunately for them, wandered within range of Failend's bow. The men were relieved of their burdens by others who eagerly set in to plucking and skinning, the thought of fresh meat rather than dried fish or salt pork being a great motivator.

Once it was full dark, once they had all eaten and had a few cups of ale, Thorgrim called Harald and Godi and Fostolf together. Starri, of course, joined them as well.

They sat on large rocks near the head of the beach, a dozen rods from the fire. "You men, you and all the men, you did good work today," Thorgrim began. "I hoped to get to sea again before the sun went down, but there was nothing for it. All hands worked as well and as fast as they could, but we could not get the ships ready in time."

Not that we had to, Harald thought. *We could have sailed in Blood Hawk...*

"I made the decision not to sail in *Blood Hawk*," Thorgrim said, as if he had read Harald's thoughts, and Harald felt himself flush. He hoped his father would not be able to see that in the dim light. "I made that choice because I think we will need *Sea Hammer*'s speed for what I plan. Maybe I was right, maybe not. We'll see."

Godi spoke up. "I don't think the Frisians will be so far ahead of us," he said. "I don't think they'll care to sail after dark, so they would have put ashore not so long after us. And Thorodd in *Fox* will still be on their asses."

The others nodded at that. "That's what I hoped," Thorgrim said. "I hoped they would not get so far ahead. Because this is what I have in mind." He leaned back, took a deep drink of ale. He started in again.

"I've never sailed these waters, but I have spoken to many who have. They've all told me the same thing. To cross the sea to the land of Wales you sail south until you reach a long cape stretching far to the east, south of which the land tends off to the west. From there it's a day's sail east with a fair wind to Wales. Once land is reached in Wales, you sail south across the mouth of a great bay, a day's sail or more, and then you are in the kingdom of Wessex and can run east along the coast."

He paused again, let the men consider this. Then he said, "That means this Brunhard will continue south until he reaches the cape that points east. I don't know how many days' sail it is, but we could not see it today, so it's at least another day, probably more. I mean to take *Sea Hammer* out to sea, sail south as fast as I can, sail through the night if I must. I mean to be there before him. If he reaches that place first and crosses the sea we may lose him, and then we'll have to chase him clear to Frisia. I want to be there first and let him sail into my arms."

The others nodded as they listened. "But why so sneaky, Thorgrim?" Starri asked. "Why the fox and not the wolf? Why do we not just chase him down, kill them all?"

"Brunhard knows this coast, knows it very well," Thorgrim said. "He's shown us as much, twice now. I fear if we just chase after him he'll have some means of disappearing. But if we let him get far from land, and then spring on him, he will have no place to run."

"*Sea Hammer* might reach the cape first," Godi said, "but *Dragon* will not keep up with her. And *Blood Hawk* is under oars alone until we get a new sail." There was no bitterness in his voice, and Harald was surprised by that. He was not sure he would be so even-tempered if his ship had been reduced to a rowing boat.

"*Sea Hammer* will sail alone," Thorgrim said. "*Dragon* will sail after Brunhard as if trying to catch him. *Fox* is already after him, if Brunhard has not tricked Thorodd into running up on a rock, or something of the kind. Those two ships will follow Brunhard, like driving deer. If he tries to go to sea before he reaches the cape, they'll cut him off. They'll drive him into *Sea Hammer* and the three ships together will tear him apart."

Again heads nodded. All the men there could see the sense of this. Thorgrim turned to Godi. "Godi, you've made no protest about me taking *Blood Hawk*'s sail. I appreciate that, and your loyalty. You may stay with *Blood Hawk* as her master, or you may sail with me in *Sea Hammer* to try and catch this Brunhard. I leave the choice to you."

The choice? Harald thought. There was no choice. Crawl pathetically under oars along the coast, or drive south under a billowing sail into a near certain battle? There was no choice.

"I'll sail with you, Thorgrim Night Wolf," Godi said. "Just like before."

"Good," Thorgrim said. "And when this is done you will be master of *Blood Hawk* again." He turned to Harald and gave a weak smile. "Congratulations, Harald. You have your first ship to command. You are now master of *Blood Hawk*."

Harald squinted a bit and cocked his head to the side as he did when he was not sure what was happening, which was more often than he cared to consider. He heard "congratulations" and "ship to command" and "master" and those were good things. But put all together there was something not right.

And then he understood.

"You...want me to take command of *Blood Hawk*?" he said. "Which has no sail? What am I to do?"

"We'll give you men enough to row and you'll follow down the coast. We'll meet up by the cape when you reach it."

"But..." Harald began. He was not sure where to start. "But the fighting will be over by then. Brunhard will be killed, his ships taken."

"If the gods favor us," Thorgrim agreed. "Look, son, we can't leave the ship here on the beach. I need a man I can trust to be in command of it. I've taken Godi's sail, so it's only fair I should give him the choice of which ship he wants to sail in."

For a moment Harald said nothing. Finally he said, "Of course." He could think of nothing else to say. Nothing else that would be of any use. His thoughts were tumbling like a river running over stones.

It was not until sometime after that, standing alone down by the edge of the sea, looking out into the dark, that his thoughts began to settle and he could truly understand the terrific injustice of it. He was being given command of a ship. Which could barely move. Which would not be part of any of the upcoming fight. And which would be given back to her true master once she was made whole again.

He heard footsteps on the beach behind him and he knew it was his father, but he was too furious to turn or even acknowledge his approach. He was aware of Thorgrim standing beside him, but he did not look at him or speak at all. His only thought was, *I am nearly as tall as he is now.*

For some time Thorgrim stood beside him, a presence, no more, not speaking or moving. Looking out over the water as Harald was doing, but Harald would not turn and look at him so he did not know. Finally Thorgrim spoke.

"Do you know about this Christ God? Who the Irish worship?"

It was such an unexpected question that Harald nearly forgot he was supposed to be angry. "Some," he said. They had been more than two years in Ireland, had spent considerable time with men and women who followed that religion. Harald, unlike most Northmen, had even learned the language. He knew a bit about the Christ God.

"Failend is forever telling me about him," Thorgrim said. "Mostly I don't understand. But she said something once about how the Christ God sacrificed his son. I'm not sure why. But he did it to show men that he loved them. That's what Failend said."

They were quiet again, listening to the sound of the waves lapping over the sand. "What is it you're trying to say, Father?" Harald said at last. "You show love for your men by sacrificing me?"

"No," Thorgrim said. "I don't know why I said that about the Christ God. Except this. You're my son, but I command all these men. I must worry about all of them, see they're all ready to fight. If I do an injustice to a loyal man like Godi, then the others wonder if I'll do the same to them. But if I force the one man they know I love the best, my own blood, to do the thing he does not want to do, the thing that will make him most angry with me, then they know they can look to me for justice."

"And what about me?" Harald said, and there was more anger and despair in his voice than he had intended. He turned and met Thorgrim's eyes. "Is it justice to me that I have to crawl along after you like some sorry creature while you and the others do the fighting?"

Thorgrim held his son's gaze. "Who would you have me put in your stead?" he asked.

"Anyone!" Harald said. "Any of the others."

"No," Thorgrim said calmly. "That's no answer. Pick one. Who should I put in your place? Pick the man and I'll do it."

Harald stood his ground and let the images of the others float through his thoughts. And as he did that, he understood why his father had done the thing he had done.

He, Thorgrim, as lord of all those men, could not come behind with *Blood Hawk*. He had to lead the men into battle. And of all the men there on the beach, Thorgrim would most want his son by his side. Which was why he risked Harald's anger and chose him to stay behind.

Harald saw that he was thinking only of himself and the sacrifice his father was forcing on him. But Thorgrim was making a sacrifice too, and he was doing it for the good of all the men.

"Fine," Harald said. "I'll take *Blood Hawk*." Because now he understood, and the understanding eased his mind. A bit.

But do not for a moment believe I will stay out of the fighting, he thought.

Chapter Twenty-Three

I pray thee be wary, yet not too wary,
be wariest of all with ale,
with another's wife, and a third thing eke,
that knaves outwit thee never.
  The Counseling of the Stray-Singer

At first, Louis de Roumois did not know what had brought him back to the waking world. It was through no choice of his own, and as he became aware of the agony in his head he wished he could go back to where he was, but he could not.

Something was prodding him to wakefulness, something gentle but insistent. And then he realized it was a tapping on the back of his head. Something was tapping him—slowly, rhythmically, repeatedly.

He remained motionless and let the tapping continue. He was lying on something solid, but that thing was moving, rocking gently. He kept his eyes closed and tried to make sense of that but the pain in his head was making all thought nearly impossible, like trying to talk over a howling storm. If he had had an iron bar driven through his temples, he guessed this was what it would feel like.

He wondered if perhaps an iron bar *had* been driven through his temples.

Ship…

The thought came floating up from someplace beyond the pain. He was on a ship. Lying in the deck. The ship was rolling in the waves and his head was rolling with it and with each roll it thumped against something behind him.

Ship…

The images ghosted through his head, but he was having a hard time sorting them into any kind of storyline. There were heathens with weapons. Irishmen with spears. Conandil.

Conandil...

The two of them had had a plan. Get weapons in the hands of the Irish warriors. Kill the heathens. Kill the Frisians. Row the ships to shore. But what had happened?

Louis considered opening his eyes, but the thought alone brought a fresh wave of pain. He thought maybe if he moved, just a bit, he could stop his head from knocking against whatever it was knocking against. He pressed down with his arm, shifted his body to the side, and the pain was so great he moaned despite himself.

Then he heard a voice, close by. "Master Brunhard! Master Brunhard!" There was more, but Louis could not hear it and did not care. The sounds around him were becoming more distinct. He could make out the usual clatter of a ship rolling in the waves, the sound of men moving about, this and that being shifted and dropped. There was a heaving grinding sound as well. Not continuous, but every once in a while.

Louis wished with all his soul it would stop. He would have lifted his hands to his ears if he had had the strength.

Then he felt the deck jar under him as someone apparently hopped aboard. He heard quick steps coming his way and then the loud, bemused voice of Brunhard above his head.

"So, the Frankish prince is awake, is he? You may thank God, Merulf, you did not kill him. I would have been furious. All that fun, thrown away?"

Louis felt two strong hands grab his tunic and then he was being lifted up off the deck, up onto his feet. He might have screamed with the agony of it, but he could not muster a scream so he groaned instead. He blinked his eyes open. The light was like another iron bar to the skull. He closed his eyes and felt Brunhard's rough hand slap him on the side of the head.

"Wake up, Louis the Frank!" Brunhard shouted. He slapped him again, shook him. Louis opened his eyes. It was the only way to make it stop.

Brunhard's ugly face was less than a foot from his. The Frisian was grinning through his massive beard, his strong hands wrapped in the cloth of Louis's tunic.

"Ah, Louis, there you are!" Brunhard said, loud enough for the words to be painful. "Please, stay awake! I have a question I must ask you." He hit Louis again.

Louis's head lolled but he forced himself to stiffen his neck and look Brunhard in the eyes.

"Here's my question, Louis," Brunhard said. "Do you think I'm stupid? Do you?"

Louis said nothing. Brunhard hit him again.

"I said, 'do you think I'm stupid'?" Brunhard said, even louder.

"Yes," Louis croaked, the words coming out weak and pathetic. "Yes, I think you're a fool."

Brunhard grinned even wider. "You're an honest man, I'll give you that," he said and hit Louis again. "But you're wrong in this, my friend. Because I am not so great a fool as to think you would defeat the Northmen and then come bounding back to me like some loyal dog."

It would be pointless to try to argue, Louis could see that, so he said, "Of course I came back. I still have to drive a sword through your guts."

"Ha! Good for you!" Brunhard said, sounding genuinely pleased. He gave Louis a push and Louis fell back, too weak to stop himself, and came to rest still standing half upright, his rear end resting on the sheer strake.

"But of course, you did not come back," Brunhard continued. "You were making ready to kill poor Merulf and then run away. Good thing I gave Merulf warning that you would do that. He's far too trusting a soul."

Louis's eyes moved past Brunhard. He realized he was still aboard *Galilee* and the grinding was the heathen's ship, still bound to *Galilee*'s side and working against the merchantman's hull. The pain in Louis's head was still excruciating, but his mind was starting to clear a bit. He wondered how long he had been lying passed out on the deck. Long enough for Brunhard's other ships to turn and make their way back to *Galilee*'s side.

Brunhard, Louis knew, was waiting for a reply, the next thrust in the dual of wits they had been fighting since they first met in Dubhlinn, but Louis was in no state of mind to keep that up. He looked forward. The Irish slaves were where they had been before, seated on the rowing benches, though now there were gaps in the rows of men, iron neck bands hanging empty where dead men had been removed and their bodies no doubt tossed overboard.

Some of the Irishmen had ugly gashes and contusions. Most were blood-smeared, but if it was their own blood or that of the Northmen Louis could not always tell. They had heads down, looking despondently at the deck. They had come within a spear-trust of freedom, and it had been snatched away again.

Louis looked beyond the side of the ship. He could see bodies floating nearby, naked bodies stripped of clothing, jewelry, weapons and armor. The dead heathens. And Irish as well. There was a long line of bodies drifting off toward the Irish shore, a few miles to the west.

"Well, see here, Louis," Brunhard started in again. "I don't want you to think yourself a complete fool. Because, I'll be honest…and I am an honest man, you know…your plan to defeat the heathens was brilliant! And such riches! Come with me!"

He reached out a meaty hand and once again grabbed Louis by the tunic and jerked him upright. He half turned and crossed the deck to where the heathen ship was tied up alongside, pulling Louis behind him. They stopped at *Galilee*'s rail, right where the two ships were butting against each other.

"Here, have a look for yourself," Brunhard said and he pulled Louis closer and then shoved him hard. Louis's legs hit the side of the ship and he tumbled forward, right off *Galilee* and onto the captured ship alongside. He had a vague notion of what would happen next and then he slammed hard down on the longship's deck. The impact jarred him, went right through his body like a bolt of lightning and he gave a strangled cry of pain.

He heard laughter in response. Not just Brunhard, but the others as well, the Frisian sailors who were enjoying the show. He felt Brunhard land on the deck beside him and once again lift him to his feet by his tunic.

"Come on, you Frankish whore's son, look here!" Brunhard shouted in Louis's ear. He half pulled him aft where a handful of his men had been emptying the Northman's hold.

"Look! Look!" Brunhard shouted. "At first it was just casks of water and dried fish and that sort of shit, but below? Look what we've found!"

Louis looked down at the deck. The light made his eyes water and his head pound like a war drum, but he could see what Brunhard was pointing at. Four small chests, opened and brimming with silver and some gold and jewels as well. Several leather bags, the drawstrings untied, the glittering wealth inside visible through their mouths. It was a fortune.

"These heathen scum, they must have been plundering the monasteries here for years!" Brunhard exclaimed. "And all that wealth, years' worth, all stowed aboard this one ship! Louis, you've made me a very wealthy man! With this fortune, and of course that casket of silver I took from your bag, I'll be rich as Crassus! I could kiss you. I won't, but I could."

Louis looked up into Brunhard's eyes and resisted making reply. He knew the tears were streaming down his cheeks, and though it was from the light, and nothing more, he knew Brunhard would not let it go.

"Ah! I see you are weeping with joy for me!" Brunhard said. "As well you might. But there's more happy news! I was going to kill you, you know. But then I thought, what a waste that would be! So instead I am going to set you in chains with the rest of this Irish filth and I am going to make you row to Frisia and then I am going to sell you to the first man who promises to carry you away to the Moorish countries where you will be set to work in a salt mine or some such."

At that Louis could remain silent no longer. "You had better kill me now," he said, his voice still weak and pathetic. "Because if you don't, I will certainly kill you."

"You don't sound so very frightening, Louis the Frank," Brunhard said, the smile never leaving his face. "But there may be something that will save you from the Moors." He leaned closer, in a conspiratorial way. "You see, I never believed that you were the wandering soldier you claimed to be. I can smell royalty," he said, and tapped the side of his nose, "and I have an idea you might be from some very wealthy house of Frankia. And so I might hold you for ransom. That would be a good thing, wouldn't it?"

"There's no one would pay a goat turd for me," Louis said and he suspected he was telling the truth.

"Well, you're not worth a goat turd," Brunhard said. "But we have yet to discover what some fool might be willing to pay for you. But see here, we can't spend all day floating around. There were more of those damned Northmen than just the two I have dealt with, and they may be coming yet. And to make matters worse, some of my rowers were killed by the heathens, and now I have another ship to row! So we'll get you in your chains and seated on your rowing bench and you can earn your keep for once."

Brunhard looked over at *Galilee*, still grinding against the longship, and nodded his head. A couple of Merulf's men reached over and grabbed Louis and before he could make a sound they dragged him back aboard the merchant ship. With a kick to the backside they directed him toward an empty rowing bench. He sat down, hard, his head on fire, his vision blurred, as he felt the cool iron ring clamped around his neck.

His mouth was open, he was gasping for breath, when Brunhard came ambling up. "Very well, Louis the Frank," he said. "You've seen enough rowing I think you know how this works. And do a good job, because I'm thinking Merulf and the others are just looking for a reason to beat you senseless."

He turned and took a step away, then turned back again. "Oh, yes, one other thing," he said. "We'll put ashore tonight, and then I think I will let my men have that slave girl of yours. Well, mine, now. Either way, I'll see you get a good view of the festivities."

He turned and walked off at his frenetic pace, leaving Louis to watch his back and burn with loathing and fear and humiliation. He felt the iron bar turning in his skull.

For the next few hours they rowed, and Louis's entire being was concentrated on the oar in his hands, the back of the man in front of him, the steady lean forward, dip the oar, draw it back.

It was not as easy as it had seemed, and just as Brunhard had suggested, Merulf and the others were looking for their chance at him. So when his stroke was off, when the blade of his oar skipped over the surface rather than dig into the water, when he came close to fouling the man in front of him or behind, he was struck. A rope or a fist or a foot, they used them all, but they did not miss a chance to deliver punishment.

They pulled through much of the day, the wind having failed them, and only as evening came on did a breeze fill in, enough for them to set the square sail and give the exhausted rowers a rest. They stuck close together, all the ships of Brunhard's fleet, including the captured longship, not much bigger than *Wind Dancer*, but much finer and faster.

Conandil had been taken aboard *Wind Dancer*, but Louis gratefully took a ladle of water from the slave girl who was left aboard. She was battered, dirty, and she looked as if she was stunned, as if she, and not Louis, had been hit hard in the head. But she delivered the blessed water, quickly and silently.

As the ship heeled slightly in the breeze, Louis leaned against the sheer strake, hunkering down so he would not be choked by the iron collar around his neck. He felt sleep washing over him. He wondered if Merulf or the others would beat him if he dozed off. He decided they probably would, but he was too far gone to care.

Then he woke with a start, aware that something was happening, something sending a ripple through the ship. He opened his eyes and looked around. Merulf and the others were looking aft, peering around the tall sternpost. He heard their low talk, heard mention of Northmen. He leaned over as far as he was able, looked aft himself. He scanned the horizon. Nothing there that he could see.

And then there was. So far off it was little more than a speck, lit up orange in the late day sun. A speck that held steady, seemed stationary. A ship's sail. Another of that fleet of Northmen, in their wake.

The sight moved Louis not in the least. It meant nothing to him, made no difference. Irish, Northmen, he was a slave now, property of whoever owned the ship to which he was chained.

It did make a difference to the Frisians, however. They moved quickly to take in the sails, despite the fair wind, since the sails were what made them visible over so great a stretch of water. The oars were passed along to the rowers, and soon Louis found himself once again at the monotonous work of rowing.

But not for long, this time. The light was failing as the day ended, and *Wind Dancer* turned her bow toward the shore and the other vessels followed her in, the Norseman lost in the gathering dark. Soon the little fleet was once again run up on the sand, food, water, ale off-loaded, a fire built where it was mostly shielded by the ships from view from the sea.

Louis sat on the beach, still chained to the others, and greedily ate what little food he was given, drank the water that was brought in a ladle. The pounding in his head was mostly gone away, but every other part of him ached. And deep inside, at the core of him, beyond the physical, he felt despair, complete and all-consuming. He no longer cared what happened to him, or to anyone else.

And so, when he heard Brunhard coming over to him, he did not even bother to look up.

"Louis! You look tired!" Brunhard said. Louis did not respond.

"I'm talking to you, you Frank bastard," Brunhard said, and there was more menace in his voice now. He put the toe of his shoe under Louis's chin and lifted his head, forcing Louis to look up at him. "I promised you some entertainment," he continued, "and now you get it."

He saw a struggle to his left, off by the light of the fire, a muffled shout, and then he saw Áed and a couple others wrestling Conandil to her feet. Conandil fought like a wild animal, but she was a small one, and strong as she was her strength was nothing compared to that of the sailors. It was not a hard fight, or long. They half carried, half dragged her over toward where Louis and the other slaves sat in their chains.

"I'm a kind man, Louis, you know that," Brunhard said. "So I'll give you a choice. Either I have her first, or Áed does. But you get to choose."

Louis looked up at the Frisian. He thought nothing, felt nothing.

"Choose," Brunhard growled. "Or by God I'll see it's worse for her than you can imagine."

Then another voice called out, from farther down the chain of slaves. A bold voice, strong and commanding. Irish.

"No," the voice said.

Broccáin mac Bressal, Louis thought. *Conandil's husband.*

Áed was already moving, closing the distance to Broccáin, ready to punish the man for the outrage of uttering that single word, but before Áed could reach him, Broccáin said, "We can make a bargain, you and me."

"Hold!" Brunhard said, raising a hand to stop Áed before he reached the Irishman. He turned to Louis. "What did he say?"

"He said he wants to make a bargain with you," Louis said.

Brunhard turned to Áed. "Is that what he said?" Áed nodded. Brunhard laughed, a loud and genuine laugh. He stepped away as if Louis was already forgotten, moved toward where Broccáin was seated. "And what possible means do you, a pathetic slave, my own property, have to bargain?" he asked and Áed translated the words.

"The heathen ship we took today," Broccáin said, "it was loaded with plunder. I saw it, we all did. A fortune. And now there's another following us. And it, too, is probably filled with plunder. Why have one ship when you can have two? You and your men, keep your hands off the girl and we'll take this second ship for you."

Brunhard listened to Áed's translation, but he kept his eyes on Broccáin, as if evaluating the man along with the words. "If I want to take the heathen ship, I'll take it. I don't need to bargain with you," he said. "Who do you think you are?"

"I am Broccáin mac Bressal. I command these men. Or I used to," Broccáin said. "If I tell them to fight, they will fight. If I tell them not to fight, then you will not have men enough to defeat the heathens."

For a long time Brunhard was silent, staring at Broccáin, evaluating the situation. Then he said, "Why do you care so much about this girl?"

"She's my wife," Broccáin said, and Louis knew he was taking a terrific gamble in admitting that. He was handing Brunhard the one thing he could hang over the Irishman's head. But Broccáin understood that as well, and so he continued to speak.

"You say I have nothing with which to bargain, and you're right. But neither do you. You've taken everything from us. We're slaves. If you take our lives you'll do us a kindness. But the girl, Conandil, she's something I'll make a bargain for. Keep her safe, and we'll deliver the second heathen ship."

Again Brunhard was quiet as he considered this. Louis could practically hear the thoughts churning in the Frisian's mind. Could he believe Broccáin? Was Conandil really his wife, would he really do this to save her? What was the risk to Brunhard and his men? What were the rewards?

And Louis was pretty certain he knew what the stout, greedy, big-mouthed shipmaster would decide, because the same considerations that led him to attack the first ship were now persuading him to attack the second. There was no risk to *Wind Dancer* or Brunhard's own hide. He did not even have to risk *Galilee*. He could send the captured longship. If he lost that, and the slaves with it, it was no great thing, not with the heathens' plunder he now had. And if they took the second Northmen's ship, the potential reward was enormous. The first longship had taught them that.

"Very well," Brunhard said to Áed. "Tell this Irish bastard he has a deal."

Chapter Twenty-Four

[W]ork a ship for its gliding, a shield for its shelter,
a sword for its striking, a maid for her kiss...
Maxims for all Men

Harald stood at *Blood Hawk*'s bow, looking forward, south over an empty sea. Behind him, the steady, monotonous creak of the oars in the oarports, the occasional soft murmur of the rowers speaking to one another. They had been rowing all day. And they would row all night. They just didn't know it yet.

There was nothing to see ahead of them. For a few hours that morning they had watched *Dragon* slowly opening up the distance as she sailed south, searching for Brunhard's ships, getting ready to play her part as sheep dog, herding the merchantmen into *Sea Hammer*'s open jaws.

Sea Hammer, too, had been in sight for some time, standing offshore, running a little east of south, but she had disappeared from Harald's view before the sun had reached its high point in the sky.

Thorgrim intended to get far enough out to sea so that Brunhard would not see him pass by, would not know *Sea Hammer* was waiting off the great cape to the south. Thorgrim planned to sail all night, if need be, but Harald knew he hoped to reach the cape before the sun went down. If they spent the night racing south through the dark, there was good chance they would pile up on the cape before they ever saw it.

The wind was from the west now, the quarter from which it most often blew in that particular stretch of ocean. That was good for Thorgrim, as it let *Sea Hammer* run away on one of her best points of sail. It was good for *Dragon* as well, allowing her to drive on under sail with no danger of being blown ashore. It was presumably good for *Fox*, somewhere ahead of them, and even for Brunhard and his ships. For Harald and the men of *Blood Hawk* it did almost no good at all, other than saving them from the additional misery of rowing into a headwind.

Harald turned and looked up to the top of the mast. He had insisted that the mast be restepped, even though Thorgrim had pointed out, tactfully as he could, that it was unnecessary given that *Blood Hawk* had no sail. But a mast made a good lookout perch as well, and Harald wanted it up. A few temporary shrouds were all that were needed to hold it vertical, since it had only to bear the weight of a man, and not a yard and sail and the extreme pressure the wind would place on the rig.

The man aloft was Starri Deathless, keenest eyes among all of them. Harald had not expected to have Starri with him. Thorgrim had not expected it. In truth, it seemed even Starri had not expected to be with Harald aboard *Blood Hawk*.

It had been decided on the beach that morning. The men had been roused well before dawn. They had breakfasted on the last of the fresh meat Failend had brought in, along with rough oat cakes and ale.

"Father, I need more men," Harald said as they gathered on the beach, breakfast done, the food and cooking gear being stowed away. Thorgrim had picked men at random to go with Harald, knowing none of them would be any more enthusiastic than Harald was at the notion of rowing rather than sailing, of tagging along rather than being first into the fighting.

"More men?" Thorgrim asked. "You have men enough."

Blood Hawk was pierced for fifteen oarports per side, a total of thirty oars. She needed thirty men to row her, and if she had been going to sea as part of a raiding fleet she would have had at least another twenty men on top of that, for fighting and for relieving those at the oars. But Thorgrim had picked just twenty-four men to join Harald in driving the ship south.

Harald knew perfectly well why he had done that; Thorgrim wanted to use the minimum number of men possible to limit the discontent, and, more importantly, to provide himself with the maximum number of warriors on board *Sea Hammer*. But Harald would not stand for it.

"The men aboard *Blood Hawk* can do nothing but row, and yet you won't give me enough hands to relieve the men at the oars?" he said, trying to sound reasonable, not bitter. "The gods alone know how far we will have to row. I need at least enough men to man all the oars."

"You make a good argument," Thorgrim said. "But I must have men enough aboard *Sea Hammer*..."

You mean that Sea Hammer alone will be doing anything worthwhile, Harald thought, and in the silence of his mind he gave free rein to his bitterness. Then he said, "Still, there are dangers everywhere, and *Blood Hawk* can't sail away from any of it. You are only looking at taking some slow merchant ships. I don't know what I will be up against, me and my men."

After a lifetime as the son of Thorgrim Ulfsson, and the past two years a'viking with him, Harald knew perfectly well what sort of arguments would work on his father. Any suggestion that he was being unjust, any implication that he was taking the best for himself, would have an effect more powerful than the strongest drink. Thorgrim, Harald knew, already felt bad about stripping *Blood Hawk* of her sail and Godi of his command, of putting Harald in charge of the impotent vessel. And he knew he was on the right tack with this argument.

"Very well," Thorgrim said. "You may have fifteen men more. And I will let you choose them." Thorgrim framed that last part as if he was doing Harald a favor, but Harald knew it was anything but. His father had had his fill of telling men they would be left behind for a day or more of backbreaking rowing just to catch up. Now, if Harald wanted more men, he could tell them.

Fair enough, Harald thought. The victory this time might not be unequivocal, but it was his.

Harald chose his men, then they loaded the gear back aboard the ships and shoved the ships out into the water so only the very forward-most curve of their bows rested in the sand. It was still not yet light enough for them to wend their way through the rocks to the open sea, but Thorgrim Night Wolf meant to be ready to get underway the very second it was feasible.

He and Harald and Godi and Fostolf gathered together on the sand for one last discussion before they climbed aboard their ships and headed off in their separate directions. Starri was there as well, as usual, though he said nothing, and just seemed to stare out toward the east.

"*Sea Hammer* will get far enough from the cape that the land is partway below the horizon," Thorgrim said. "We'll wait with our sail down so we're better hidden. Then when *Dragon* is able..."

"Night Wolf," Starri said, interrupting as if Thorgrim had not been speaking at all. "I think the gods are whispering to me."

The four others were quiet as they turned toward Starri. They were all accustomed to his madness and the wild things that came out of his mouth. On the other hand, not one of them doubted that the gods whispered to him as they did to all berserkers, who saw and understood things that other men did not. Sometimes that was good, and sometimes it wasn't.

"What do they say?" Thorgrim asked.

"They say I should sail with young Harald. Would that be all right with you?"

At that, Starri pulled his eyes from the black eastern sky and looked at Thorgrim. The split arrowhead around his neck, the sign that the gods had given him, showing that Thorgrim was favored by them, was polished to a dull silver from Starri's constantly rubbing it, and now it seemed to glow as it picked up the faint light of the stars.

Thorgrim nodded a bit as he seemed to consider this. Harald tried to read his face: worry, irritation, disappointment? But divining Thorgrim's thoughts was no easy business. Harald was more proficient than any of them at that task, and even he could rarely see past the stolid mask. And he could read nothing in Thorgrim's emotionless response.

"You can sail with whoever you want to sail with, Starri," he said. "If that's all right with Harald, I mean."

"Fine with me," Harald said, as surprised as any by this. Starri would always choose to go where there was the best chance for fighting, and *Blood Hawk*, trailing behind under oars, did not seem to be the place for that. But they also knew that arguing with Starri was pointless, and Harald would indeed be happy to have him aboard.

The first gray light was appearing by the time they climbed back onto their respective ships, and soon after that it was light enough to make their way to sea. Thorgrim led the way in *Sea Hammer* with *Dragon* coming astern of her and *Blood Hawk*, oars fully manned, Harald at the tiller, coming last. They made their way past the rocks that littered the seas just offshore and out into the clear, open water. For some time they were all under oars, and *Blood Hawk* was actually foremost, making her way south, with *Sea Hammer* shaping a course offshore.

As the light grew Harald took advantage of Starri's presence and sent him up the mast, but even when daylight had come full-on he could see nothing of any of the ships for which they hunted: Brunhard's ships or *Fox* which had gone ahead the day before.

It was not so long after the sun rose that the breeze started to fill in. *Sea Hammer* and *Dragon* set their sails, flogging and filling in the wind, and Harald felt a stab of irritation and even envy at the sight. Soon *Dragon* passed down their larboard side and drew ahead and *Sea Hammer* grew more and more distant as she stood off toward the horizon.

The day settled into its monotonous routine. Once it was clear the other ships were pulling away, Harald relieved some men of their duty at the oars. He had already calculated the fairest system by which he could rotate men through that work and still maintain steady progress south. He would not ask Starri to row. That was pointless. But he himself would pull an oar just the same as any other man aboard. He would not have it any other way.

He was just off his shift, could still feel the strain in his arms, as he stood at the bow and looked south and looked up aloft at where Starri had affixed himself to the masthead. He was certain that Starri would have called out if he had seen anything, and that it was pointless to ask, but he could contain himself no longer.

"Starri! What do you see?" he called.

"Water, Broadarm!" Starri called. "Water and Ireland. Just what we've been looking at this past year and more."

"Very well," Harald called. He looked out at the sun, setting toward the west. "You may as well come down to deck."

He walked slowly aft and Starri came down the mast, half climbing, half sliding. He stepped up on the small afterdeck and turned forward. The men were moving with an easy rhythm, having fallen into the stroke so completely they were probably not even aware of what they were doing, just letting the muscles in their arms and backs move as they had learned to move.

"Listen up, you men," he called and he was aware that the way he spoke, the words he used, the tenor of his voice, were all those of his father's. But he did not know of any other way to speak to men such as these, and, still angry as he was, he supposed Thorgrim Night Wolf was not a bad one to imitate.

"You've been rowing hard, I know," he continued when he had the attention of everyone on board. "We all have. Save for Starri, but he's played his part. In any event…" He was losing the train of the thing and he knew it and he struggled to get back to it. "The others, who have been sailing, they've pulled well ahead by now. So I…"

He was about to say *I would like to row through the night*, but he caught himself. Instead, he said, "We will row through the night. Every man will take his place at the oar, me included. But if there is fighting to be done, plunder to have, we will only be part of that if we're bold enough to do this thing. Are you with me?"

When he had played this out earlier in his head, Harald had envisioned cheers at this point, fists held aloft in solidarity. That was not the reaction he received. But neither was he greeted with any sort of protest. Instead he saw nodding heads, grim but determined looks.

That would do.

Harald ordered some of the idle men to roust out food and water. When the others had served themselves, Harald took his share and sat on the edge of the afterdeck. He ate and looked up at the sky. A moon was hanging in the east and he was glad of that, as it would help keep him from piling the ship up on the Irish coast. It was too early yet to see any stars, but when he could he would take note of them and they would also help him fix his position as well as mark the time when he should change the men at the oars.

"Broadarm," Starri said, appearing at Harald's side. "That was well said. Like your father would have done."

Harald grunted. "Thank you," he said. It was not exactly the compliment he might have hoped for.

"What would you have me do?" Starri said. "I can pull an oar as well as any man, but sometimes I don't think people believe that."

No, they don't and with good reason, Harald thought. Starri was strong and nimble, but he lacked the attention necessary for the long and monotonous job of rowing. Most men, in that situation, could let their minds wander off, while their bodies maintained the steady, rhythmic motion. But not Starri. Once his mind was off somewhere beyond the ship, it was as if his body tried to follow, and soon he was out of rhythm and fouling the oars of the men in front and astern and a great mess ensued.

"Sure, you are a fine oarsman," Harald said. "But we need your eyes more. No need to go aloft. Just place yourself in the bow and look out every once in a while. Make sure we are not going to hit anything, or row into some trap laid by Brunhard."

Starri nodded, fine with that arrangement, and he headed off to the bow. Harald slept some, then woke and looked at the stars, then slept some more. He was confident that he would wake when he needed to, and he did, sitting up and looking about and recalling where he was.

He stood and stretched and in a soft voice rearranged the men at the oars, taking his own place at the aft, starboard side. And they pulled on through the dark. The seas, at least, were calm: long, low rollers coming in from the northeast, lifting *Blood Hawk* with a gentle motion, twisting her a bit as they set her down, then lifting again, as steady and regular as the rowers' strokes. Occasionally something would jump from the water nearby, but Harald found it was much less disconcerting with the ship underway. Somehow, lying motionless, they seemed more vulnerable. But now they were moving, active, ready to fight. Or so it seemed.

The moon passed overhead and the men hauled on the oars, then rotated again, and sometime later rotated one last time. Those not rowing slept where they could, crammed near the bow and stern, but there were fewer than there would normally have been, and *Blood Hawk* was a tolerably large ship and they found room enough.

Starri did not sleep, which was not unusual for him. A few times during the night Harald made his way to the bow to see what Starri was seeing, but it was not much. Water, and the dark outline of Ireland off the starboard side. Harald looked out at the coastline, a dark presence against the starlit skies. *Dragon*, he was sure, would not have sailed on through the night. They would be hauled up on a beach somewhere, and not so far away.

If *Blood Hawk* had stopped for the night, then *Dragon* would be many miles ahead by now. But as it was, they would not be so far behind Fostolf's ship. They might even have overtaken her, but he doubted that.

They pulled on, and finally the dawn came again, spreading gray along the eastern sky and then red and orange, and the sky itself growing to a pale blue as the blackness retreated to the west. Harald had been sleeping, but he woke as the first hints of light began to appear on the horizon.

"Starri," he called, once he was sure there was light enough to see some tolerable distance. "Up to the masthead, if you would."

Starri Deathless, eager as Harald, went hand over hand up the temporary shroud, clutching the rope with his bare feet, then climbed squirrel-like up the last ten feet to the top. The day before he had rigged a loop of rope around the mast to serve as a sort of chair and now he settled himself into that and began to systematically scan the horizon.

Harald wanted to dance from foot to foot with anticipation, he wanted to call out to Starri and ask what he saw, but he did none of those things. Instead he remained fixed in place, looking off at the distant shoreline, doing his best to imitate Thorgrim Night Wolf, who always seemed unmoved even when everything was collapsing around him.

Starri will call out if he sees anything, Harald assured himself.

"Broadarm!" Starri called down.

"Yes, Starri?" Harald called. *Here we are,* he thought.

"I see nothing!" Starri called. "No ships, anyway."

Of course... Harald thought, chastising himself. *What did you think, that the sun would find us right in the middle of Brunhard's fleet?* Even rowing all night they could not hope to cover anything like the distance a ship under sail would make. *Dragon, Sea Hammer, Fox,* Brunhard's ships, they had all left him well over the horizon. He felt the bitterness creeping back.

His mood did not improve as the morning wore on and the men had their breakfast and then switched out their places at the oars. Harald was pulling once again, his body moving with the oar, his mind racing, wallowing in the unfairness of it all. He toyed with the idea of just beaching the ship, lighting a fire, having a grand feast ashore, letting all the men get roaring drunk. Why not?

Then Starri, who had remained silent and aloft since dawn, called out again. "Broadarm! I see something! Ships, it looks like! Right ahead!"

Harald felt something jump inside him. He swiveled around, trying to look forward while still maintaining his stroke, an awkward motion. Then one of the men named Gudrid was standing beside him and said, "Let me take the oar, Harald, so you may look."

Harald nodded his thanks, more grateful than Gudrid could have known, and slipped out from under the loom as Gudrid slipped in. Harald moved quickly to the bow, stepped up onto the foredeck, craned his neck around the stem. He could see water and land. And something else. Something on the water. At least he thought he did. But it was very far and he did not have the advantage of Starri's height of eye and vision.

"What do you see, Starri?" he called.

"It looks to be two ships!" Starri called down. "They're not under sail, so it will be hard for you to see them. Two ships and they may be lashed one to the other. They are very close to each other, anyway."

Harald frowned and looked forward again. *Fox* and *Dragon*? That was the most likely. Brunhard's ships? Perhaps. But if they were Brunhard's ships, then where were *Fox* and *Dragon*?

We'll know soon enough… Harald thought. This was one lesson a man learned from seafaring: sometimes there was nothing you could do but wait. You learned that, and accepted it, or you went mad.

Harald walked aft again. Not all of *Blood Hawk*'s oars were manned; some he had had to leave unattended to see that the work was fairly distributed. Now he said, "Let's get all the oars manned, close as fast as we can." He stopped short of ordering specific men to the oars, but he did not have to. The warriors' blood was up now, their curiosity fully engaged, and they were as eager as Harald to find out what was going on. Harald had hardly finished speaking the words before the remaining sea chests were occupied, the missing oars run out through the oarports.

"Ah, they're underway now, Broadarm!" Starri shouted down from aloft. "Two ships, and they are pulling apart and…" All hands waited, ears cocked toward the masthead. "And they are pulling for us! They are coming toward us!"

Harald felt a little quickening. He stood a little straighter, stared more intently ahead. He felt like Starri felt, perhaps, when the gods where whispering to him. And he thought the gods were saying, *There is danger here…*

And he hoped that he heard them right.

Chapter Twenty-Five

Nothing of that which was gained by fraud can go to the liberation of his soul.
Emperor Charlemagne the Just

They were spread out over many miles of ocean, Thorgrim's ships and Brunhard's ships, like pieces on some board game of the gods.

When the sun had come up that morning, Harald Broadarm had been standing at *Blood Hawk*'s bow and staring hopefully south after a long night of rowing and keeping the other men at the oars. He had seen nothing. All the things he had hoped to see were happening more or less as he imagined, but well beyond the range of his eyes.

Sea Hammer, his father's ship, sporting the sail that should have been set on *Blood Hawk*, was driving along south, not just out of Harald's sight but out of sight of anyone watching from the Irish shore.

The longship *Dragon*, under Fostolf's command, was just pushing off the beach where they had gone ashore for the night. They had spent the afternoon of the previous day in chase of a cluster of ships, which Fostolf took to be Brunhard's. Fostolf was trying to do as Thorgrim had instructed, drive the ships south to where *Sea Hammer* waited, but whether he was driving them or they were just sailing he did not know. In any event, he had lost them in the dark and hoped now to find them again.

And ten miles south of Fostolf and *Dragon*, the longship *Wolf* was also put off from the beach.

At least, Louis de Roumois guessed that the ship they had captured from the Northmen was called *Wolf*, judging from the leering, sharp-fanged, canine look of the figurehead. But he did not know for sure, and anyone who could have told him had been killed and tossed over the side the day before. And he did not really care.

He thrust his oar through the oarport and sat waiting for Áed's orders. He had hope the way a man hanging over a cliff clinging to some scrubby bush has hope; he had not fallen to his death yet, and as long as he lived there was a chance, tiny as it might be, that he would continue to live, and find his way back to *terra firma*.

"All right, you bastards, row," Áed growled. He spoke low, for no rational reason that Louis could divine, but idiots like Áed, with no experience or sense for the sort of work they were about to undertake, always did things like that.

Louis dipped his oar and pulled. He was used to the task now, and he did not make a mess of it. He felt the hope glow brighter.

Brunhard had kept his word, kept his filthy crew off Conandil, for the one night at least. Not an easy task; they had been denied their go at her once, and they were not happy to be denied again. But they feared Brunhard more and so they went away grumbling.

Brunhard had ordered Broccáin released from the chains and had called him and Áed over so they could discuss how he, Brunhard, might be further enriched. But Broccáin had insisted that Louis be included in the discussions, said Louis had been the clever one who had tricked the heathens the first time. And so Louis, too, was unchained and brought over by the fire.

The plan was simple enough, not much different from the way they had taken the first Northmen's ship. In fact it would be easier this time because they would be using the captured longship. The second heathen ship would see a vessel they knew well, and assume it was manned by their friends. The Frisians could make right for the Northman, rather than let the Northman catch up with them. The heathens would think nothing of this ship coming alongside. They would not become suspicious until it was clear that the men aboard her were strangers and the arrows began to fly.

It was still dark when they loaded the weapons aboard. Louis suggested they dress the slaves in the clothing taken from the dead Northmen. Brunhard was not very enthusiastic. Louis was sure Brunhard was planning to sell the clothing and he did not want it bloodstained and torn. But he relented. Having the Irish dressed like Northmen could mean another half a minute's confusion on the part of the heathens, and that could make the difference between Brunhard's getting his hands on their plunder or not.

Once again, archers, sailors, and slaves were set aboard the ship. Broccáin was allowed to be free of the chains, but Louis was not. Broccáin argued that Louis, as one of the leaders, should not be encumbered, but that was not a point on which Brunhard would yield, and so Broccáin gave it up. And Louis was denied the tiny sliver of satisfaction he might have gained from going into a fight a free man, or something like a free man.

Brunhard's merchant ships put to sea, heading south, and the captured longship followed in their wake, but turned north, intending to be well clear of Brunhard's fleet when they intercepted the Northman still trailing them. That was Brunhard's wish. When the fighting started he did not want himself or his precious ships to be anywhere nearby.

The coast of Ireland was on their larboard side now as they retraced their course of the day before. Louis recognized none of it; from two miles away every bit of the shoreline looked pretty much the same to him, and he wondered how the sailors could tell where they were. But of course they were not looking for a point on land, they were looking for a ship at sea. And it was not long before they found it.

One of the Frisian sailors was positioned up at the bow and he called out just a little while after sunrise that there was a sail to the north and making for them. That was repeated in Irish this time for the benefit of Broccáin and the Irish warriors.

Louis, facing aft on the rowing bench, tried to crane his head around to see, but he could not. The wind was from the north, which meant he and the other slaves had to row against it, while this newcomer could run down on them under sail. But that did not matter. Soon the distance between them would close, and then they would all be in a fight for their lives, and there was not much point in thinking beyond that.

Perhaps I'll die a quick death with a weapon in my hand, Louis thought. It seemed the best he could hope for now.

Broccáin came aft from his place at the bow, stood next to Louis as Louis worked his oar. "They're a mile and a half away from us, maybe a bit more," he said.

"Any change to the way their sail is set, or anything that looks like they're suspicious?" Louis asked.

"No, nothing," Broccáin said. "Nothing that I can see. Are you in need of water?"

Broccáin, Louis realized, was grateful to him; grateful for his having saved Conandil from the sailors on that first night, despite having to forfeit his own freedom to do so, grateful for his not raping her himself, grateful for giving them all a chance to die fighting.

Lord, I'm like some hero of old, Louis thought, but the thought was more irony than self-congratulation.

The two ships continued to converge. "Half a mile, now," Broccáin said, then soon after, "Quarter mile. The heathens are taking in their sail."

"Are their oars coming out?" Louis asked.

Broccáin waited a moment before replying. "No, they're just sitting there," he said.

"Good," Louis said. "They're just waiting for us, it would seem. Are their shields still mounted in the ship's side?"

"Yes."

"Good. I don't think they would be if they thought we were their enemy. They must think this ship is still in the hands of Northmen. They'll expect us to come alongside and speak to them. Tell Áed to do that, just run the ship up next to them and let the archers set in."

It played out pretty much as Louis had hoped it would, as he had planned it would. Another short bit of rowing and suddenly they were alongside the heathens' ship, the carved head of a dragon looming above, the bright painted shields mounted on the rack down the larboard side. As they pulled close someone from the Northman's ship called out and one of the Frisian sailors, who could speak the Northman's language, responded. Louis did not know what was said, but apparently it was good enough for the heathen, who did not seem to question their approach.

Louis and the other rowers pulled their oars in as the two ships came side to side, so close they were thumping together as the waves lifted them. It was then that Louis heard the first note of confusion from the heathens, a cry, loud and demanding, followed by another. He could hear a buzz run through the men on the other ship.

"Archers!" he shouted from his place at the rowing bench, at the same instant that Broccáin shouted the same. Ten bows appeared in the hands of men at the bow and stern, and arrows began to whip across the short distance, and the screaming came quick on their heels. Fore and aft the sailors tossed grappling hooks over the few feet of water that separated the ships and heaved them together.

"Wait to grab your weapons, wait!" Louis shouted to the men on the benches. As before, the timing was the thing, they had to pull their spears at exactly the right moment.

And they did. The heathens were shocked by the archers' attack, had not the least notion it was coming until the first arrows found their marks. A dozen of them dropped bleeding to their deck before they recovered enough to act. Someone was shouting orders and the men were reacting to it, but Broccáin was on the lookout for that man, the master of the vessel, and on his command the archers put three arrows in him before he had even pulled his sword from its sheath.

By then the Northmen were moving, even with their master dead or dying. They came howling over the rails, weapons raised, and Louis shouted, "Now! Now!" and the spears came up from under the benches, just like the time before. And just like that, the heathens died as they came on, caught between the archers at bow and stern and the sudden appearance of thirty wicked spear tips and the sailors wielding axes and clubs.

The fight did not last long. A great, wild burst of activity, screams of battle madness, shrieks of agony as iron pierced flesh, the sticky, slippery feel of blood washing over the deck planks, and then suddenly, calm. Quiet.

The two ships groaned as they worked against one another, rising and falling in the long ocean swells. Men drew labored gasps, some moaning, some muttering in whatever was their native tongue. Louis still held the spear in his hand. He could feel the blood that coated the shaft growing sticky in his grip as it dried. He could hear his own breath in his ears. He looked around at the carnage, the dead Northmen spread out along the deck, and the Irish and a few of the Frisians as well. The iron collar around his neck was pulling at him. The man forward of him had been killed, a sword thrust through his chest, and now his corpse was weighing down the chain.

Then Áed recovered himself. "Put down your spears! All you slaves, put down your damned spears!" His voice was high pitched, near panic. As well he might be.

Louis turned toward the big Irishman. He was holding an ax that looked tiny in his massive hand. He pointed the head of the ax in Louis's direction. "Put down the spear!" he shouted. Behind him an archer drew back an arrow, aimed it at Louis's chest.

For a moment Louis hesitated. He wondered if he could fling the spear into Áed's heart before the archer loosed his arrow. Probably not. He dropped the spear clattering to the deck.

Another time, he thought.

Once again the Frisian sailors went from man to man among the heathens lying on the deck. Those who were dead they stripped of clothes and shoes and weapons and tossed their corpses overboard. Those who were wounded they killed and did likewise. Then they climbed aboard the heathens' captured ship and pulled up the deck boards to see what their prize held. Louis could only listen from his place on the rowing bench. But whatever they found, he knew from the shouts of triumph, the howls of pleasure, that it was good.

Áed and his men were some time in searching their new-captured ship and disposing of the dead and eating and drinking what they found aboard the Northmen's vessel. Almost as an afterthought they gave food and water to the rowers. Áed made a point of describing to Louis what riches had been found in the Northmen's bilges. He thanked Louis for his help in its capture, expressed his regret that Louis would share in none of it, and assured him he would be lucky if he lived long enough to be sold as a slave.

When he was done with that, Áed stepped up onto the afterdeck and looked forward. "We must be off, bring all this to Brunhard," he said to his sailors. "Take half these slaves, set them at the oars on this new ship. Brunhard will have both vessels. And take this sorry bastard"—he pointed at Broccáin—"and put him back in chains where he belongs."

Two of the sailors grabbed Broccáin and pinned his arms behind him. The dead man in the neck collar behind Louis was unshackled, his blood-soaked body tossed overboard, and Broccáin was chained in his place. Others of Áed's men set to unfastening a line of slaves and shifting them to the other ship alongside.

"Good," Áed shouted, looking over the two ships. "Now," he began, but he was interrupted by a shout from one of his men standing on the afterdeck of the new-captured ship and looking aft.

"Áed!" the man called. "There's another one, another damned ship! To the north! Making right for us!"

Áed turned and took three steps to the after end of the ship and looked astern. He stood motionless for some time, studying whatever it was coming at them. Finally he turned and Louis could tell from the look on his face he did not like what he had seen. He looked off to the horizon, looked up to the top of the mast, then began to issue orders to the Frisian sailors in a loud voice.

"Another one of these filthy Northmen, they're like maggots crawling from a corpse!" he shouted. "This one's bigger, pulling more oars. There's no wind, so we must use our oars too, and by God we'll have to row like the devil is after us, because you can bet he is!"

Louis could hear the fear in Áed's voice. Even if they abandoned one of the captured longships, put all the rowers aboard the other, they would still be hard pressed to get away with the exhausted and unmotivated Irishmen at the oars. If the wind came up and they all set sail it would be even worse; the larger ship would no doubt be the fastest of the three.

There was no fear in Louis. A moment before, before Áed had spotted this new ship, Louis had felt nothing; not despair, not hope, not one thing. But now he felt something stirring in his breast. Because the ship astern was a second…no, a third chance for him, and even a sinner like Louis could see that it was a gift from God.

Chapter Twenty-Six

I counsel thee, Stray-Singer, accept my counsels,
they will be thy boon if thou obey'st them,
they will work thy weal if thou win'st them:
look not up in battle, when men are as beasts,
lest the wights bewitch thee with spells.
The Counseling of the Stray-Singer

Starri Deathless called down from aloft. "*Dragon* and *Fox*, it looks like," he said. Harald, standing at the bow, had turned and looked up at the sound of Starri's voice. Now Starri reached over and grabbed the forestay and swung himself onto it. He hung from the rope and made his way down, hand over hand, to where Harald stood, dropping lightly to the deck.

"I could see them pretty clear, now," Starri continued as if there had been no break in the conversation. "They were rafted together, but now they've seen us and are heading our way."

"Hmm," Harald said. He could feel the disappointment creep in. If these were indeed the other ships of his father's fleet there would be no fighting that morning. And now there would be the question of who was in command of the three of them: Harald, Thorgrim's son, or Fostolf, oldest of the three of them, or Thorodd Bollason, senior to Harald in age, senior to Fostolf in the length of time he had been with Thorgrim.

These were not questions that Harald had any desire to address. Annoyed as he was at having *Blood Hawk* foisted on him, he realized he was enjoying his independent command.

"You think it's *Fox* and *Dragon*?" Harald said, knowing that he was hoping for a different answer this time. "You didn't sound so certain."

"It's them," Starri assured him. "I can always recognize any ship if I've seen it a few times. Faces too, you know. If I see someone two or three times, their face is etched in my mind like carvings on a rune stone."

"Hmm," Harald said, his mind elsewhere. He turned and looked south once more. He could see the two ships clearly, even from the level of the deck, and they certainly did look like *Dragon* and *Fox*.

"Seems they failed to find Brunhard," Harald observed with a bit of relish. "Wonder why they're wandering around here and not out chasing that bastard."

There was nothing to do but wait until the three ships were within speaking distance, so he turned and walked back to the afterdeck, standing beside Hall who had sailed with them and who now held the tiller. Starri followed him and stood beside him, looking forward past the bow at the approaching vessels.

"Wonder what they're doing," Starri said offhandedly, but his words echoed Harald's thoughts. The two ships were about a mile off and bows-on to *Blood Hawk*, coming straight at them, as one would expect. But they were also moving apart, opening up the space between them, as if they meant to come along either side of *Blood Hawk*. Which was also not entirely strange, but still Harald felt something nagging at him.

"I suppose they want to put some room between them," Harald said. "Less chance of some stupid accident like running into one another or fouling each other's oars."

"I suppose," Starri said. They continued to watch *Fox* and *Dragon* approach. All of *Blood Hawk*'s oars were manned now and the big ship was moving fast through the water, quickly closing the distance to the two oncoming ships.

"I don't think those two have all their oars manned, do you?" Harald asked.

Starri took a moment to consider the two ships. "No, they don't. Hard to tell from here, but it looks as if there are oars missing. On both ships."

"Maybe they got in a fight with Brunhard?" Harald speculated. "Lost men?" Despite himself, Harald felt a certain pleasure at the idea that these two might have fought a battle without him and lost. And at the same time he felt a flush of guilt for feeling that way. And still the uneasy feeling gnawed at him like a rat at a beef bone.

"Maybe," Starri agreed. Normally Harald would expect Starri to be upset at the thought of a fight taking place without him, but this time he sounded more thoughtful than upset, which was unusual for Starri. "They're making a poor show of rowing, I can tell you that."

He was right, and Harald realized that that was one of the things bothering him. There was an uncoordinated quality to the rowing. It was adequate, sure, the ships were moving in the right direction, and with reasonable speed. But Harald could see the wandering snake-like quality of the their wakes, as the men at their tillers worked to keep the ships on course, fighting the unbalanced force of the oars. He would expect Norse warriors, bred to this sort of thing, to do better.

"Maybe they suffered a lot in the fight. A lot of wounded men," Harald offered.

"Maybe," Starri said. There was no more than half a mile between *Blood Hawk* and the others now, and it was clear that *Fox* meant to come up on *Blood Hawk*'s larboard side and *Dragon* on her starboard.

What else would they do? Harald thought. It was a perfectly reasonable way for the two ships to approach. But still it made him uncomfortable. There was something about the way they were coming at *Blood Hawk* he did not like, in the same way that one might recognize aggression in someone simply walking toward them.

Can a ship be rowed in a threatening way? Harald wondered. *Does that make any sense?*

But then Starri spoke, Starri who could see things others could not. "I don't know, Broadarm. There's something about these ships I do not like."

"I know," Harald said. "I feel it as well. But I don't know what it is."

"Neither do I," Starri said. "But I think the gods whisper to you, the way they whisper to your father."

"Hmm," Harald said. He had never thought that, and he found it interesting that Starri did. But there was no time to explore that idea.

Harald ran his eyes over the men at the oars, which was most of the men aboard the ship. Few of them were wearing their weapons, since the weapons were awkward when rowing, but every man's weapons were within arm's reach, because Northmen did not care to be any farther than that from their iron and steel. The shields were all mounted on the shield racks along the sides and could be snatched up as quickly as the swords, spears and battle axes.

He looked south once more. A quarter mile of water between *Blood Hawk* and the others. He could see individuals now, men standing on the afterdecks of the two approaching ships. He could see brown and yellow hair above white faces, could make out beards, tunics of red and brown and green. Nothing at all unusual.

"Thorodd Bollason is master of *Fox*, is he not?" Starri said.

"Yes," Harald said. "At least he was when he sailed off, after *Sea Hammer* beached with her sail on fire."

"I don't think that's Thorodd Bollason on *Fox*'s afterdeck," Starri said.

"Who is it?"

"No one I recognize. Sure, even I can't make out a face over this distance, and maybe I'm wrong. Some of these men who joined us not so long ago. I don't know them well. But Thorodd Bollason I know, and I know that's not him."

Harald nodded. He could not tell what words the gods were whispering but he could hear the volume increase. He stepped forward, a decision made.

"Listen, men," he called in his most commanding voice. "You at the oars can't see, but *Fox* and *Dragon* are pulling for us, and they mean to run up on either side. They're friends, our fellows. Unless there's something wrong, which there might be." He was stumbling now with his words, talking too much. Explaining. Thorgrim would not have explained, would have just given orders. But in this case Harald knew he had to explain. Or maybe not. Maybe he should just give orders.

"I want you to be ready for whatever happens," Harald continued, changing to a more direct course. "Be ready to turn the ship sharp if need be, be ready to grab up your weapons and fight. Your shields are in the racks. Grab them up, too. Just be ready for my orders."

There, that was good, he thought. *Not too much talking.*

He rested his hand on the grip of his own sword, Oak Cleaver, which he had not removed despite having done his time at the oars. Oak Cleaver was the fine Ulfberht that his grandfather, Ornolf the Restless, had carried, and which had come to Harald on Ornolf's death. There was no physical object that Harald loved more than Oak Cleaver.

"No, that is certainly not Thorodd Bollason," Starri said. "And the man on *Dragon*, that's not Fostolf, I don't think."

Harald frowned and squinted. What had happened here? Who was in command of these ships? Friends? Enemies?

Enemies, Harald decided. Whoever they were, they were no friends of the men on *Blood Hawk* and they were not coming to talk. Decision made, doubt banished. There was nothing Harald hated more than uncertainty, but that was over. He felt a great weight come off him. He knew what to do now.

"Stand ready at the oars!" he called forward, and his mind was moving fast now and he did not feel the need to explain, only instruct, and he expected his orders to be obeyed as if he were telling his own arms and hands what to do. "Ready…"

Fox and *Dragon* were less than fifty yards ahead now and closing fast, not because of the awkward, ungainly strokes of their oars but because *Blood Hawk* was powering down on them. The two ships were altering course again, closing in like two fingers pinching *Blood Hawk* between them. They were not going to come close, they were going to smash into *Blood Hawk*'s sides, snapping their oars and *Blood Hawk*'s oars, and whoever was aboard those ships would come pouring over the sheer strakes, larboard and starboard. They meant to take *Blood Hawk* by surprise, but the surprise would be theirs.

Twenty-five yards of water between them and Harald gave the order. "Larboard oars, hold! Starboard oars, pull! Pull now!"

There was no surprise among the rowers, no confusion. These men knew their work and they did not even have to think about what Harald had said. The oars on the larboard side came down in the water and stopped, the blades creating a massive and sudden drag. Along the starboard side the men leaned back hard, heaving their oars aft. *Blood Hawk* spun ninety degrees where she lay, perpendicular to the oncoming ships and right under their bows, too fast for them to react.

Harald heard the shouts of surprise and confusion from the decks of *Dragon* and *Fox* but he did not understand the words, which sounded something like his own native tongue but were not. Forward, up by the bow, *Fox* smashed into *Blood Hawk*'s oak sides with a crushing, grinding noise. Then, an instant later, and not ten feet from where Harald stood, *Dragon*'s familiar figurehead came looming over *Blood Hawk*'s rail as her stem struck just forward of the steering board.

Blood Hawk rocked back with the impact and Harald saw men on the other ships actually flung forward and land sprawling on the deck, so sudden and unexpected was *Blood Hawk*'s move.

"Weapons and shields!" Harald shouted. "Weapons and shields!" All along *Blood Hawk*'s decks the men abandoned the oars and snatched up the weapons they had set nearby and yanked the shields from the shield rack. Harald saw the man at the third oar starboard side slip his arm through the strap in the back of the shield, and just as he was taking hold of the boss an arrow drove into his chest, flinging him back.

"Archers!" Harald shouted. "Shields up!" Fore and aft the warriors raised their shields, the move accompanied by the thud of arrows burying themselves in the wood. Archers from both *Fox* and *Dragon* were shooting at them. Had the ships come along either side, parallel to *Blood Hawk* as planned, their fire would have been deadly indeed. But as it was, with the two ships bow on, the archers' aim was blocked by their own stems.

Harald heard a scream at his side, so loud and sudden it made him jump. Then Starri pushed past him, a battle ax in each hand. He leapt up onto the sheer strake right where *Dragon* had struck, seemed to balance there for a second and then launched himself onto *Dragon*'s foredeck and disappeared from sight.

"Oh, may the gods take you!" Harald shouted. Once again Starri was going to beat him into the fight, and after he had so cleverly turned things around on the attackers.

Without a thought he raced down the center of the deck, dodging the men there, dodging the mast, and continued on forward, pulling Oak Cleaver as he ran. An arrow made a whirring sound as it passed close to his head, but his only reaction was to shout, "Men on the starboard side, follow Starri! Men to larboard, follow me!"

He leapt onto *Blood Hawk*'s low foredeck without breaking stride and charged over to where *Fox*'s bow was grinding against her hull. An archer onboard *Fox* was following him with the point of his arrow and Harald managed to duck just as the bowman let fly. He saw a blur and heard the arrow pass and realized he had not bothered to grab a shield.

Too late for that, he thought. He straightened and caught a glimpse of the men behind him charging forward, those on the starboard side racing aft to climb aboard *Dragon*. He set his left foot on *Blood Hawk*'s sheer strake and hefted himself up, teetering there on the edge of the ship, and thought, *I'd like to see Starri move better than that...*

Rarely could Harald match Starri's grace, despite being at least ten or more years Starri's junior.

He could feel the press of men coming behind him as he gauged the jump onto *Fox*'s bow. Three, four feet, and already a bowman was drawing on him so he knew he had better jump soon. He pushed off again, screaming as he flew over the gap between the ships, Oak Cleaver raised overhead. His left foot hit *Fox*'s rail and he kept going, hurling himself into the bowman even as the man made ready to shoot.

The arrow was a heartbeat too late. It passed though Harald's tunic as Harald slammed into the frightened-looking archer. They went down together on the foredeck, but Harald, unlike the archer, was expecting it, and he raised himself quick and slammed a fist into the archer's face, feeling the man's nose collapse under the blow.

Harald rolled to his left and up onto his feet in time to see an ax swinging around at him, wielded by a stout, muscular man with only a smattering of teeth showing in his open mouth. The man no doubt expected Harald to leap back, to try and get clear, which would have allowed him to leap forward and take Harald's head clean off.

But Harald did not do that. Instead he stepped toward the man, grabbed the collar of his tunic with his left hand and jerked him close. The ax completed its swing, the man's arm bouncing off Harald's shoulder as Harald brought his forehead down with a powerful snap against the man's face. He felt the man go limp, like his bones had turned to dust, and he let him fall to the deck at his feet.

More of the men from *Blood Hawk* were leaping aboard now and Harald stepped aside to give them room. In the seconds that followed, Harald had a chance to run his eyes over *Fox*, bow to stern, but he still could not understand what was going on.

There were men at the oars, men seated on each of the sea chests, but he recognized none of them. And, more incredibly, they were doing nothing, not standing and fighting, not grabbing up weapons. Not really moving at all.

There had been half a dozen men near the bow. Harald had dropped two of them and the men coming behind had killed the others. There was another ten or so aft, some with bows, some with spears, some with axes. There was one man shouting orders, a big man, his voice approaching hysteria. There was something else about the man that was not right, and Harald could not grasp what it was.

And then he realized. The man was speaking in Irish.

"Get up, you bastards! Get up and fight! Now, you worthless whore's sons!" the man was yelling, the pitch of his voice getting higher and higher with each word.

Then, midships, starboard side, three of the men at oars stood, awkwardly, and Harald could see they were chained together, chained at the neck. *Slaves?* he thought. But who would go into a fight with a crew of unarmed slaves, chained to their rowing benches? It made no sense.

But the slaves were not unarmed. As the men stood Harald saw spears coming up from under the benches, spears gripped in their hands. "Spears! They have spears!" he shouted the warning to the men behind him. But before he or his men could react the slaves who had stood now spun around as best they could and one after the other hurled their spears, not at the Northmen but at the men on the afterdeck.

The big man who had been screaming in Irish fell silent as they turned, his mouth open, his eyes wide. "No!" was the only word he managed to get out.

One of the slaves replied: "We'll see you in Hell, Áed!"

That, at least, was what it sounded like to Harald. And then the rower threw the spear. There was power and skill behind the throw; the man was no stranger to pole arms. The long weapon whipped over the heads of the seated men and drove itself into the Irishman's chest. His eyes went wider still and he staggered back a few feet, dropping the ax he was holding and clutching at the spear as if he hoped to pull it free, as if that might save him. His legs wavered and his mouth hung open and blood came spewing out.

The two other rowers who had stood had also snatched up spears and they threw as well. One missed its mark and sailed overboard but the other found one of the bowmen and embedded its long iron point in his shoulder. He fell howling to the deck, and the sound seemed to bring the rest of the slaves to life. They leapt to their feet and Harald could see that each of them had a spear hidden below their feet, and each of them raised them as they stood.

On either side of Harald men from *Blood Hawk* pushed past, men who had managed to grab up shields on their way, and they formed a sort of shield wall across the foredeck, a defense against the spear-wielding rowers, but they need not have bothered. The Norsemen were not the ones the rowers were after.

The bound men turned aft, spears raised, stumbling and swaying with the encumbrance of the chains around their necks. Some were within spear thrust of the ship's crew, men too stunned to move who were cut down by the points of the rowers' pole arms.

Those slaves too far to reach out with their spears flung them aft, a hail of wooden shafts and iron points. Not all the spears struck home, but enough of them did. The men who had been on the afterdeck died on the afterdeck, spears jutting from guts and chests. One of the slaves, a big man, his hair wild, shouted, "Turn and sit! Hold up your hands!" and the others obeyed him, turning aft toward Harald and the other stunned and confused Norsemen, and sitting down again on the sea chests, hands held open to show there were no weapons there.

Harald turned and looked over the larboard side toward *Dragon*, which had run into *Blood Hawk*'s after end. It was quiet there as well, the fighting over, though how it had ended Harald did not know. But however it had played out, the fight was done; the ships that had once been part of Thorgrim's fleet were now part of that fleet again.

Harald turned to Gudrid, who was standing beside him, shield still raised. "That was without doubt the strangest fight I've ever seen," he said, and to that Gudrid could only nod his agreement.

Chapter Twenty-Seven

With promises of fine drinks
the war-trees wheedled,
spurring me to journey
to these scanty shores.
Eirick the Red's Saga

They dragged Starri Deathless back aboard *Blood Hawk*, though he had mostly calmed down by the time they got him over the rail. Blood was splashed across his face and chest and his hair was in a wild confusion. Hall had one of his arms, a man named Jokul had the other and two more of the *Blood Hawk*'s men had his legs.

Harald was just climbing back aboard over *Blood Hawk*'s bow when he saw them. He trotted down the length of the deck, calling, "Is Starri hurt?" It was not so long ago that Starri had received a near fatal wound in battle. Once Harald had thought Starri could not be touched by any weapon wielded by man, but he had learned then that the berserker was not as invulnerable as that.

"No, he's not hurt," Hall said as Starri shook the men off and stood. Harald stopped in front of the small group. Starri was still holding his twin battle axes, but the insanity was leaving his eyes, and he was returning to whatever state of mind he occupied when he was not in a berserker rage.

"We had to stop him," Jokul said. "He went aboard *Dragon* and killed nearly everyone on the bow before any of us could follow. He started to go after the men at the oars, but they were just chained up, poor bastards. Slaves, I suppose. Anyway, they had no weapons but Starri didn't realize that right off. But we did, and then Starri did, so we went after the men on the afterdeck. They had spears and bows and axes. Cleared them out. But Starri didn't want to stop."

Harald nodded. This was not unusual at all. Some men had to be prodded into fighting. Starri had to be physically restrained to get him to stop. Usually he would be weeping at this point, despairing of the fact that he had not been killed and sent off to his reward at the corpse hall of Valhalla. But he seemed to be taking his survival better this time.

"They had no weapons, you say? The men at the oars?" Harald asked.

"Well, it turned out they did," Hall said. "When the fighting was done we saw they had spears, on the deck at their feet. But hidden near the side of the ship. They could have picked them up and given us a bloody welcome, but they never did."

"Huh," Harald said. "The rowers aboard *Fox* had spears, too. But they used them against the crew who had taken her, not us. They were Irish, the rowers. Are they Irish aboard *Dragon*?"

Hall and Jokul looked at one another. They shrugged. It apparently had not occurred to them to find out. "They're slaves, seems like," Jokul said. "So Irish, most likely."

That was true enough. Behind them, Harald could see more of the men from *Blood Hawk* climbing back aboard. They too had clothing and weapons smeared with blood, though none of them were bathed in it the way Starri was.

"Let's get *Fox* and *Dragon* secured alongside, then we'll find out what's going on. And figure what we'll do next," Harald said.

The men from *Blood Hawk* found lengths of rope under the ship's deck and with that they hauled *Fox* alongside and tied her in place with heavy rope fenders between the ships to keep them from grinding together. *Dragon* was lashed to *Fox*'s side in the same way, so the three ships formed an odd floating island a mile off the Irish coast.

Harald turned to a knot of men standing by *Blood Hawk*'s mast. "Collect up the bodies of the dead. Any slaves dead, get them out of the collars, but leave the others secured. If there are any of our men dead, put them aboard *Dragon,* wounded aboard *Blood Hawk*. The other dead, the ones we were fighting, they can go overboard." Harald did not say to take the valuables from the dead men first; he knew he didn't have to.

The men turned to their work and Harald watched them and thought about the others; Thorodd and Fostolf and their crews.

What had become of them? This Brunhard was a slaver. If he had captured the men he might have put them in chains to join the other captives. Harald hoped that was the case. If the men were enslaved, then they could be rescued.

He did not like to think on the alternative.

Harald stepped across from *Blood Hawk* and back onto *Fox*. The slaves at the oars sat silent, watching him. He walked down the center of the ship, between the lines of rowers. There was one man he was looking for.

He found him just forward of the main mast. The big man who had ordered the others to sit and show their hands, the man whom the others had obeyed. Harald stopped in front of him and looked down. The chained man met Harald's eyes, and his look was defiant, as if daring Harald to do his worst.

Harald regarded him for a moment. His hair was a tangle but his beard was not so long, which suggested it had until recently been neatly trimmed. His face was filthy. His tunic had a rent, and there was dried blood around the torn fabric, but it was not as filthy as the man's skin. The garment was more in the Norse fashion than the Irish, and it looked to Harald like a tunic he had seen one of the men aboard *Fox* wearing. He wondered if these men had taken the clothing from *Fox*'s crew after they had killed them.

"Who are you?" Harald asked the man. He spoke in Irish and he noticed with some small satisfaction the flicker of surprise on the man's face.

"My name is Broccáin mac Bressal," the man said.

"You command these men?" Harald asked, nodding toward the line of chained oarsmen.

"I did. Once," Broccáin said.

"And now you are a slave?" Harald said.

"Before we killed the crew of this ship I was a slave. Now I do not know what I am."

Harald smiled at the answer. In truth he did not know what Broccáin or any of these men were, either. Trading in slaves was a lucrative business for the Northmen, but he was not so sure his father would want the problems that went along with getting a cargo of human beings across the seas to the slave markets. Thorgrim could not seem to get himself out of Ireland; he would probably not relish the challenge of getting these men out of that country as well.

"What happened?" Harald asked. "How do you come to be here? Who are the men you killed?" This time he nodded toward the stern where men from *Blood Hawk* were pulling spears from corpses, searching the bodies for valuables, then tossing them overboard.

"We were taken in battle, most of us," Broccáin replied. "In Dubh-linn we were sold as slaves to a Frisian bastard named Brunhard. He set us to the oars. You chased us…at least I'm guessing it was you…and Brunhard set your sail on fire. When another of your ships attacked us…this one," he added, nodding down at the deck, "Brunhard had his men aboard, armed, and he gave us spears and told us to fight.

"Your ship was taken, and then the second one the same way." At that he nodded toward *Dragon*, tied up alongside. "Then, when you appeared, we convinced the sailors they could not outrun you, but together we could take your ship as we took the others. They were greedy and frightened, so they attacked you as well."

Harald nodded. This made sense. "You had spears," he said. "But you did not use them on us, you used them on the ship's crew."

Broccáin spat on the deck. "Dogs," he said. "We were happy to kill them. Frisian swine. We didn't know what you heathens would do, but we reckoned it could not be any worse than those bastards."

We'll see, Harald thought. "And what became of the crews of these ships? The men you fought?"

Broccáin looked down at the deck, the first time his eyes had left Harald's. Then he looked back up again. "Dead. The lot of them," he said. "Any who lived through the fight, Brunhard had them killed."

Harald looked at the Irishman and shook his head slowly. *All those men*, he thought. He was used to fighting, to slaughter, but to see the crews of two ships wiped away, that was something else.

They could not get those men back, but they could get vengeance for their deaths at least, and that was something. Thorgrim was already set on getting his revenge on Brunhard, and he had not yet even learned of this outrage. They would see that Brunhard paid for it all. Harald hoped the dead could appreciate it.

His men had finished dumping the bodies into the ocean so he called out to them and said, "There are spears hidden here by some of the rowers. Find them and bring them aboard *Blood Hawk*. Search *Dragon* as well."

Harald watched the men absently, his mind elsewhere. Now he had several problems with which to contend. He had three ships and not enough men to row them, unless he kept the Irish slaves. But he was not sure he wanted to do that. Brunhard was somewhere ahead. His father had been counting on *Fox* and *Dragon* to chase Brunhard into *Sea Hammer*'s reach, but those two ships had been taken and the gods alone knew where Brunhard was now.

"Broadarm!" He heard Starri Deathless's voice behind him, buoyant now as the madness had run out of him and in its place the good cheer that came with mayhem and slaughter. He stopped at Harald's side. He was still streaked with blood, a frightening sight, but he had tied his hair back with a leather thong and that was something of an improvement.

"You see, the gods told me to sail with you," he continued. "And there's Thorgrim, floating around in the sea like some wretched log, while we fight like men. And what do we do now?"

Harald nearly said, "I don't know," but he stopped himself. Such an admission was not at all the sort of thing that a man in command would say. So instead he said, "I have an idea, but for the moment…"

He got no further. Starri's face lit up brighter and he pointed to the man seated behind Broccáin and he said in a loud voice, "Say! We know this fellow!"

Harald looked at the man at whom Starri was pointing. "We do?" Harald asked. The man, like the others, was wearing a tunic in the Norse fashion which did not fit him well. His hair was shorter than most, but in the same sort of disarray. He had a week's growth of beard and his face was as filthy as any of the other men. Harald had indeed noticed the man would not meet his eyes, but he had figured it was out of fear of the new master, and not wanting to attract attention or seem defiant.

But the man was looking up now, and there was most certainly defiance in his face, and Harald could see Starri was right. Through the dirt and the beard he could see that he did know this man.

Then it came back to him.

"Louis?" he said. "Louis, from Glendalough?"

Louis stared back at him. He did not speak. But Starri did.

"There, you see, Broadarm! I told you I never forget a man's face or the way a ship looks. Yes, that's him, the Frank, Louis, from Glendalough."

Harald stared at the man, mouth open, a storm of thoughts racing through his head, such a tempest that no thought would take solid form. He had not seen Louis in many months. He pictured him leaping out of their hiding place and running toward their enemies who were in pursuit, to expose them and ruin the trap Thorgrim and the Irish bandit Cónán had set. The last time he had seen Louis the Frank he was mounted behind one of the Irish men-at-arms who had been hunting them down and riding off.

It all came back as he looked at Louis sitting on the sea chest, looking back at him without a hint of regret or fear. "You son of a bitch!" Harald growled. He pulled Oak Cleaver from his sheath, a fast, practiced move, swept it up over his head and down at Louis's skull.

But Louis had anticipated the move, apparently, and with both hands he snatched up the chain that hung loose from his neck to Broccáin's and held it up. Oak Cleaver came down on the chain and stopped inches from the top of Louis's head. Louis tried to wrap the chain around the sword, to control the blade that way, but Harald jerked his arm back, jerked the blade clear. He set his left foot forward, ready to thrust the tip through Louis's heart when he felt Starri's hands on his arm, heard the man's voice in his ear.

"Hold there, Broadarm, hold! There's no honor in cutting down a man in chains! Let us be reasonable here."

The absurdity of Starri Deathless telling him to be reasonable broke through the dark fury like sparks from a flint and steel. Harald let his body relax. He lowered Oak Cleaver but he did not sheathe it. And in the place of the fury came a great curiosity.

"How do you happen to be here?" he asked. "Were you taken in battle, too?"

It was Broccáin who answered. "He's here because he saved my wife."

Harald shifted his eyes from Louis to the Irishman. Broccáin continued. "My wife, Conandil, was taken when we were. Brunhard's men were going to rape her. Louis was aboard because he had paid for passage to Frisia. He stopped Brunhard's men. For his pains, Brunhard knocked him out and made him a slave as well."

Conandil? Harald thought. Of all of Broccáin's words, the name leapt out at him. He had known a Conandil. Could it be the same woman? How strange was this, to keep meeting people he had thought to never see again.

I have been in this country too long, he thought, and once again he realized he was echoing his father.

A puff of wind caught his long yellow hair and whipped it around in his face. He brushed it aside as he looked to Broccáin and then Louis, but that motion, brushing his hair aside, had set something else whispering in his head. And then the whispering turned into a word.

Wind.

Harald turned from the men on the sea chests and his head reflexively turned in the direction from which the wind was blowing. From the north and east, with a cold touch to it. He realized that in the time his mind had been taken with the fighting and the things that followed, the sky had turned to a milky white, an unbroken dome of gray overhead from horizon to horizon.

They had enjoyed a long stretch of good weather. Too long. Those spirits of Ireland that controlled such things were not often so generous, and now they were done. Harald had indeed been in that country a long time, long enough to understand the workings of the weather there. He knew that this gray dome would not be breaking up soon. It would not be breaking up until it had played host to its unwelcome brethren, the rain and the wind.

Wind... Harald thought again. That changed everything. Harald made his thoughts fall into order, like setting a group of warriors into a shield wall. They had to catch up with Brunhard. They had to make certain Brunhard went where they wanted him to go. How best to do that?

"Broadarm?" Starri said, pulling Harald from his silent thoughts.

Harald looked down at Broccáin and Louis once more and said, "We'll see to you shortly, there are more pressing things to do. Come along, Starri." Then in a loud voice called, "Men of *Blood Hawk*, to me, come to me."

He stepped over *Fox*'s low rail amidships and back aboard the much bigger *Blood Hawk* and the rest of the men came quickly behind. "Here's what we'll do," he said, speaking to the assembled crew, a much smaller contingent than would normally be aboard the longship. "The wind is getting up, and that means Brunhard will be sailing," he said. He wondered if he was once again explaining too much, but he did not have time to consider the issue so he went on. "We'll never catch him under oars, and I don't think *Fox* or *Dragon* could catch him, either." The smaller ships could keep up with Brunhard's fleet, certainly, and could probably out sail them, but to make up the distance they had lost so far, Harald did not think was likely.

"We'll have to sail *Blood Hawk*," he continued. "We'll take the sails off *Fox* and *Dragon* and sew them together. It will not be a pretty thing, but it will work. And we'll set up some new shrouds that will bear the weight."

"What of the other ships, *Dragon* and *Fox*?" someone called out.

"And these Irishmen, these slaves?" another asked.

"Let's see to the sails and shrouds, and then I'll tell you my plan for that," Harald said, though what he really meant was that they should get to work on the sails while he tried to think what he would do next. "Go!"

The men scattered, some swarming over the lowered yards to unbend the sails from the smaller ships, others fishing out twine and needles with which to sew the sails together. Two men ran a thin rope along the top of *Blood Hawk*'s bare yard to measure the length so they might figure how much the two sails from the smaller ship would have to overlap to make them the proper length for the bigger vessel.

Harald watched with satisfaction as the men fell to their various tasks. These were experienced seafarers. They had crossed oceans to get where they were on the coast of Ireland. They knew what to do without Harald's supervision.

"Starri, would you go to the masthead and have a look around?" Harald said next. The last thing he needed was a surprise coming from the sea. And Starri nodded and grabbed onto one of the shrouds and headed aloft with all the effort of a man falling into bed.

Very well, now I must think, Harald thought. He had to sort the random heap of ideas in his head so that he might examine them. He looked over the three ships rafted together, moving in the odd way of ships bound to one another. The wind was already rising a bit and setting them down on the Irish coast, a lee shore, but they were a couple miles off at least and in no danger for some time.

What is the most important thing? Harald asked himself, by which he meant, what would his father, Thorgrim, consider the most important thing. *Get Brunhard*, Harald concluded. *Run him down.* After the incident with the flaming arrow, Thorgrim Night Wolf's every thought would be directed toward vengeance on the Frisian who had tricked him so.

That meant the ships *Fox* and *Dragon* were secondary. And the slaves as well. Thorgrim did not even know about the slaves. In truth, if he had known that Brunhard's cargo was mostly slaves Harald doubted his father would have bothered to try to plunder the ships in the first place. Thorgrim owned slaves, had dealt in slaves before, but generally he thought the business not worth the bother. It took a certain kind of man to make a living as a slaver, and Thorgrim was not that sort.

Harald found himself smiling at the irony. All this for something Thorgrim would not have wanted in the first place.

And even as that thought came to him, Harald came to a decision. He climbed over *Blood Hawk*'s side and onto *Fox*'s deck, then strode along to where Broccáin and Louis were still sitting, chained and waiting.

"Broccáin," Harald said. "You Irish, you seem to have learned how to row a ship."

"We have," Broccáin said. "Not a skill we've wished to know, but we have."

"Here's what I'll do," Harald said. "There's a beach to the north of here. I'll unchain you and your men and let you row these two ships to the beach. You run them ashore and you haul them up on the sand as far as you can and you tie them to whatever you can tie them to. Then you're free to go. Head off along the shore, make your way back to your homes."

Broccáin looked at Harald and did not speak at first, and Harald knew the man was considering this, wondering what trick was being pulled. "That's it?" Broccáin asked. "You'll just let us go?"

"That's it. I have other things I must worry about. You can have the spears the Frisians gave you as well, so you won't be without arms." It would seem to Broccáin that Harald was doing him a great kindness, but in truth Harald had little choice. He had to catch up with Brunhard before Brunhard slipped past *Sea Hammer*, and that meant he would have to leave the two smaller ships behind in any event. They could never keep up under oars, and even if they could, Harald did not have enough people to man them.

This way, the ships would be run up on the beach and there was at least the possibility they would be waiting there if and when he and Thorgrim came back for them.

"You're not concerned we'll just row away with your boats, then?" Broccáin asked.

Harald shrugged. "You can if you wish. The wind's getting up and soon it will be blowing you hard on shore. Unless you're fine ship handlers there's a good chance you'll be wrecked on the rocks. I'd suggest setting the ships in the soft sand, and quick as you can."

Broccáin nodded. This made sense to him.

"One other thing," Harald said. "Louis stays with us." He knew that Thorgrim would not be pleased if he discovered that they had Louis from Glendalough in their hands and then let him go.

Broccáin frowned. He looked back at Louis and then up at Harald. This was a dilemma Harald had anticipated. Broccáin had a certain quality about him; Harald guessed that he was one of these minor nobles with whom Ireland was overrun. He said that Louis had saved Conandil from Brunhard's men. A man of honor would not abandon the man who had saved his wife from such a fate, and Broccáin struck him as a man of honor.

"I don't know what your fight is with this man," Broccáin said. "But I see you'll not let him go, and my pleading for him won't change that. Very well. But I'll stay with you as well."

"You'll leave your people...to stay with the Frank?" Harald asked.

"Yes," Broccáin said. "And because Brunhard has my wife, still. I would never go safe ashore and leave her to that fate."

"Good," Harald said. "I understand that."

"Another thing," Broccáin said before Harald could turn and leave. "My men, many of them are warriors. Skilled fighting men. If you want them, some of them or all of them, to go as well, they'll do as I say."

This was something Harald had not considered, but he considered it now. Fighting Brunhard and his men had never been a concern. They were a handful of merchant sailors against four longships filled with warriors. But now, through cunning and surprise, the crews of two of those ships had been killed. *Blood Hawk* was undermanned. Even if the Norse warriors were still enough to kill all the Frisians, there was rowing and sail handling to consider. They needed strong arms and plenty of them.

"Very well," Harald said. "Pick your ten best men and they'll come with us. The rest can row ashore." Harald was happy to have the help of the Irish, but he did not need so many aboard that they could be a threat if they chose to be.

He felt the wind on his face again and once more turned his head into it. It was a bit stronger now, and it seemed to have more easting in it. Thorgrim, he knew, had developed a keen sense for the manner in which the winds worked on the Irish coast. He would know exactly what to expect.

Harald's sense for such things was not as keen, the attention he paid to them not as strict. But still he had learned a few things. And from that knowledge he guessed that this wind would only blow harder, and before things got better, they would get quite a bit worse.

Chapter Twenty-Eight

[H]ast thou a friend whom thou trustest well,
fare thou to find him oft;
for with brushwood grows and with grasses high
the path where no foot doth pass.
                                   The Counseling of the Stray-Singer

Sea Hammer was positioned exactly where Thorgrim Night Wolf wanted her to be. That much he knew. He did not know if that was also the best place to catch Brunhard and his fleet before they left the coast of Ireland and headed out across the open water. For that he could only guess.

He stood on the afterdeck and felt the ship moving under his feet, swooping up on the rollers coming in from the horizon, rolling and pitching, fore and aft, side to side. His face carried no more expression than one of the carved wooden figures that adorned the homes of wealthy Norsemen—less, actually—but his thoughts were a great fury of activity.

So far it had played out as he hoped. *Dragon* had sailed off to find *Fox* and go after Brunhard, drive him south and east. He had left Harald in charge of *Blood Hawk*, coming up behind. He had taken *Sea Hammer* far offshore, far enough to get ahead of Brunhard's ships unseen.

Thorgrim had ordered them to sail through the night, not a popular decision. But between Thorgrim standing grim-faced on the afterdeck and the huge Godi making his presence felt in all other parts of the ship, no one felt much inclined to make vocal objection.

There had been little wind, which was just as well. Being at sea at night, with all the unseen spirits and creatures that lurked in the depths, was troubling enough. To also know that the wind is setting you down on an unseen lee shore or perhaps blowing you beyond the sight of land was just another level of concern that no one relished.

But as it was they were under the power of the oars, and Thorgrim kept them at it, pulling with an easy, almost lazy stroke as they made slow progress south. The sky was clear, the stars prominent enough that Thorgrim could keep *Sea Hammer* on course while, hopefully, Brunhard and his men spent the night somewhere ashore.

Brunhard's last night in Midgard, the world of men. Hopefully.

There were many worries on Thorgrim's mind that night, but the cape was foremost. He had been told by various men, knowledgeable mariners, that this cape existed, that it was to the south, and that it was the mark that sailors used to indicate the place where they should turn east and make the crossing to Wales. But he had never seen that piece of land himself.

He was concerned now that he might not recognize it, despite having been told it was unmistakable. He was afraid he might miss it in the dark, or, worse yet, pile up on the rocky crags rising unseen from the night sea. He did not sleep that night.

But when dawn came, it brought with it a great wave of relief. There, to the south and west, was the cape: long and low, sweeping out into the sea at a near right angle to the north-south running coast of Ireland. Unmistakable.

"Vestar," he called out to one of the men on the crew, one of those not at the oars at that time. Vestar was one of the younger men, wiry, spry and strong. "Get up to the masthead and tell me what you see."

Vestar nodded and without further word grabbed onto the shroud and headed aloft, gripping the tarred rope with hands and feet. He was quick and the climb seemed all but effortless, though it lacked Starri's manic enthusiasm. And Vestar, young and able as he was, lacked Starri's eyesight. Most mortal men did.

Thorgrim watched Vestar climb, but his thoughts were with Starri. When Starri had opted to go with Harald, Thorgrim had been struck by an odd riptide of emotions. Surprise, for certain. All loyalties aside, Thorgrim did not think Starri would opt to stay aboard the ship that was lumbering along under oars, probably a day or two behind any fighting that might take place.

But Starri had felt something in his gut, and that in turn made Thorgrim wonder what was happening aboard *Blood Hawk*, if their journey was as dull as he had thought it would be. He wondered if all was well with them.

As the surprise had ebbed, relief came in its place. Starri, barely domesticated, could be a genuine bother. One never knew what he would do or say, and his ramblings could get tiresome. And all of that was exacerbated on a sea voyage, when Starri was trapped on a relatively small vessel with little to do.

But in the end, relief was not what Thorgrim felt. He missed Starri. He actually missed the man's unpredictability. Starri kept him sharp, he realized, kept him on edge. There was no chance for complacency when Starri was aboard. There was always a sense of anticipation, wondering what the berserker would say next.

And of course there were the more practical considerations. There were only a few things that Starri was good at, such as fighting and going aloft as lookout, but for those things there was no one better. No one even close.

Thorgrim pulled his eyes from the low green cape off the starboard bow and looked aloft. Vestar was settling in at the masthead and Thorgrim gave him a few moments to scan the horizon. He was about to call up when Vestar called down.

"I see nothing, Thorgrim!" he called. "No sails, anyway! The cape is to the south west, and I can see the shore beyond that. Nothing on the water at all, that I can see."

"Very well," Thorgrim called. "Stay up there for a while; come down when you're tired." Starri, of course, could remain aloft for hours, but it was asking too much of another man to do the same.

He turned back to his silent contemplation of the headland. It rose sharply up from the sea and then leveled out into a long, flat arm of land tending off to the west; not jagged and threatening as much of the Irish coast could be, but more pacific and inviting. Much of that coastline seemed to be fringed with beaches, Thorgrim had noticed, a good and convenient thing, though beaches could be as deadly as rocks to wooden ships when they were flung onto the sand by massive pounding seas.

They were still some distance away from shore, ten miles or so, it seemed. The base of the cape was not visible from *Sea Hammer*'s deck, and the eastern shore of Ireland was lost beyond the horizon.

This was where Thorgrim wanted to be. With their sail furled Brunhard would not see the ship until he was too far from land to pull some clever trick along the coastline he apparently knew quite well. They would meet on the open ocean. And while Brunhard might consider that his territory, he would soon discover his mistake.

Thorgrim turned to Godi, who was standing at the other side of the aft deck. "Godi, let the men have their breakfast and some ale. We can leave off the oars for now. I think we're about where we want to be."

"Very good, Thorgrim," Godi said and he ambled off forward, giving orders as he went. Thorgrim could see the expressions of relief on the men's faces as they slid the oars inboard through the oarports and laid them out lengthwise along the top of the sea chests. They had been rowing leisurely, but it was still rowing, and it was still hard labor.

The momentum came off the ship and she turned slowly broadside to the waves as she drifted, but the motion was still not so bad. The seas were coming in in slow, lazy rollers and not very high, giving *Sea Hammer* an easy, cradle-like rocking side to side. Thorgrim suspected half the men would be asleep in ten minutes. The others ten minutes after that.

Let them sleep, Thorgrim thought. With luck they would need their strength, and soon.

I should sleep as well, he thought next.

As soon as the thought came to him he realized how very tired he was. He had spent the night pacing the deck, scrutinizing the stars, staring off toward the west for some sign of land: a fire on a beach, the flash of waves in the moonlight breaking against the rocks. He had strained his ears to hear anything that might indicate if they were safe or if they were standing into danger.

He looked aloft at Vestar, still clinging to the masthead. He fought down the urge to call out. Vestar was no fool, he would have called down if there was anything to see, and Thorgrim's calling to him might be looked on as a lack of confidence, both in Vestar and in himself.

Instead he turned to speak to Harald, who, if he was not busy with one thing or another, would generally be seated on the edge of the afterdeck. Thorgrim had actually opened his mouth to speak before he remembered that Harald was not there, that he was off on *Blood Hawk* somewhere far beyond the watery edge of sight.

It was Failend sitting there, wearing her boy's tunic and leggings, her thick brown hair tumbling down her shoulders. She sensed Thorgrim's looking at her and she looked up at him and smiled and he smiled back. "You should sleep, Thorgrim," she said. "You've stood the deck all night."

"All the men have been up all night," Thorgrim said.

"No," Failend said. "The others slept when they could. You are the only one who's been awake all this time."

Thorgrim nodded and looked out to sea once more. He sensed Failend standing and then she was at his side. The top of her head was about level with his shoulder and he looked down at her. She was a beautiful girl, and strong, clever and hard when she had to be hard. He cared for her very much. But she had not long been part of his life.

"Is there something I can get you?" she asked. There was a touch of concern in her voice, and Thorgrim guessed she had picked up on this strange mood that had come over him.

"A cup of ale would be welcome," Thorgrim said.

Failend gave a faint smile. "A cup of ale it shall be," she said and headed off forward where the barrel of ale was stashed. She was light on her feet and now that she had found her sea legs moved easily despite the odd rolling of the ship.

Thorgrim watched her go, but his thoughts were still with Harald. He felt a sadness wash over him, much as he had when reflecting on Starri's absence, but much more profound than that.

It was more than two years since they had sailed from Vik aboard Harald's grandfather's ship. More than two years, and Thorgrim could count on his two hands the number of days they had been apart in that time. He himself had grown two years older, two years grayer, two years and many battles worth of broken down.

Harald, too, had been changed in those two years, but he was moving in quite the opposite direction.

He had been a boy when they had sailed, barely able to serve his time at the oars. He had never been in a fight beyond brawling with his older brother or some of the other boys on the farm. But that boy was gone now.

In his place was a man, several inches taller, many pounds heavier, with muscular arms and shoulders, long blond hair tied behind his head, thick and calloused hands. Sometimes his eyes were still those of a curious boy, and sometimes they were those of a warrior who had seen more bloody fighting than most would see in a lifetime. Together they had fought for their lives against men and the sea. They had been destitute and surrounded by enemies. They had been, and were now, in possession of great hordes of silver and gold.

But they were not together. Thorgrim had sent Harald off to take command of *Blood Hawk*.

He sighed and looked out toward the north, toward where *Blood Hawk* should be, almost as if he expected his son's ship to come up over the horizon. And indeed he knew that in his heart he was desperately eager for that to happen.

Did I make a mistake, sending Harald off in Blood Hawk? Thorgrim wondered. What he had told the boy was the truth. Harald was born to be a leader, but first he had to learn a leader's lessons. He had to have command of a ship and its crew. He had to learn that preference should not be shown to one's self or one's kin.

Failend returned, a cup of ale in her hand. She passed it to Thorgrim and as he took it he realized he was as thirsty as he was tired, and he wondered where his mind had been that he should not even be aware of himself. He thanked her and drained the cup.

"Godi," he called and the big man came walking aft, his steps a little unsteady on the rolling deck. "I am going to sleep some. You may let the men do the same, if they wish. You, too. No one slept much last night. Send a man up every hour or so to have a look around for Brunhard or for one of the other longships."

Godi nodded. "You look like you could use some sleep, Thorgrim," he said, half grinning.

"I feel like I could use a sword thrust through my heart," Thorgrim said. "I'm not sure anything less will do me much good."

He pulled out one of the bearskins he kept stored under the afterdeck, shoved it against the side of the ship in a big pile, leaned against it. He closed his eyes and the swooping and rolling of the ship seemed even more pronounced. He lowered his chin to his chest to keep his head from swaying and soon he was fast asleep.

What woke him, he was not sure. Some time had passed, a substantial amount of time. The sun, which had been near the eastern horizon when he had gone to sleep, was now nearly overhead. Godi was standing beside him, shaking his shoulder. The motion of the ship had changed. It was more pronounced now, the rolling quicker, livelier.

"What is it, Godi?" Thorgrim asked, but in his mind he heard two names: *Harald? Brunhard?*

"It's the wind, Thorgrim," Godi said. "The wind's come up a bit while you've slept."

Thorgrim took his eyes from Godi's bearded face and looked up. The tail ends of the lashings holding the sail to the yard were dancing in the breeze. The sky had turned from the light blue of a clear dawn to a uniform gray that stretched to every point on the horizon. The sea now picked up that color as well, gray like unpolished steel.

He turned and faced in the direction from which the wind was blowing, felt the breeze move over his skin and ruffle his hair and beard. Thorgrim considered himself a mariner, even more than he did a warrior or a farmer. He loved every aspect of seafaring. Much of it was fairly simple: the way a ship moved under sail or oar, the effect of current and wind on headway, the manner in which the mast and sail was supported by the rigging.

But weather was another thing, a vastly more complicated thing, and so Thorgrim reveled in the study of it. Predicting weather meant vigilance and observation, noting the size and types of clouds, the direction and strength of wind, the behavior of birds at sea or animals on shore. It meant remembering all of that and looking for patterns and recurring phenomena. It meant learning to trust instincts. And even with all that, it was still generally a pretty imprecise thing. But not always.

"It will be blowing harder soon," Thorgrim said with absolute certainty. "When the wind comes around easterly like this, it means it will blow harder."

"And a lee shore," Godi said.

"A lee shore," Thorgrim agreed. "But we are far enough now that it is no great concern."

No great concern for now, Thorgrim thought. He knew how quickly such things could change.

Sea Hammer took a wicked roll, enough to make Thorgrim and Godi and Failend stagger and nearly fall, their arms and legs coming out in a comical manner to steady themselves.

"We can't wallow in the trough of the waves anymore," Thorgrim said. The rising wind had brought with it a bigger sea. *Sea Hammer* was no longer rocking with an easy motion but rolling with increasing force and violence. "Let's set a sea anchor. That will hold us stern to the seas and slow our drift. We'll remain here, see if Brunhard shows up."

"I'll see it done," Godi said and headed off forward. Soon the men had wrestled out a length of strong rope and lashed some spare boards to the end. That would be set over the stern, and as it dragged through the water it would keep *Sea Hammer* perpendicular to the rollers.

The sea anchor was lowered over the side and the rope paid out, then made fast to a cleat near the stern. As the tension came on the line, *Sea Hammer* turned a quarter circle where she sat, turned her sharp stern into the oncoming seas, and suddenly the entire motion of the ship changed. Rather than the flaccid and listless rolling side to side, now she was being lifted by the stern, pitched forward just a bit, then the stern was sinking as the seas passed under and lifted her bow high. There was something more alive and deliberate about the motion, and it buoyed Thorgrim's mood a bit.

And then there was nothing left but to wait.

Forward, some of the men were sleeping, some eating their midday meal, some sharpening weapons or talking and laughing among themselves. Thorgrim could feel his impatience mounting. Waiting was a big part of his life. It was a big part of the lives of any warrior or seafarer. But that did not mean he liked it.

"Vestar!" he called forward and the young warrior who was sitting on the foredeck with some of his fellows stood and made his way aft.

"Up aloft with you, see what you can see," Thorgrim said. Vestar nodded, swung himself into the shrouds. A few moments later he was settled at the masthead.

For a long time he said nothing. *Sea Hammer* pitched and yawed, giving the man aloft a wild ride and making his job that much harder.

"The headland's no closer!" he shouted at last. "I can't see..." Then he paused and the pause did not go unnoticed. Fore and aft heads turned to the masthead.

"Sails!" Vestar shouted. "I see sails...I think. Pretty far off....I'm not certain... Looks like...one, two...three!"

Thorgrim nodded to himself. Vestar could be wrong, of course. He had not been so certain about what he had seen. But Thorgrim knew that anyone in Vestar's position would be shy about making a definitive statement, unless he was more certain than he was letting on.

And Vestar was not wrong, Thorgrim was sure of it.

Ah, Brunhard, you bastard, I have you now, he thought, and even as the words formed in his head he heard the volume of the wind build, heard its note grow sharper in pitch.

Chapter Twenty-Nine

O'er the sea from the north there sails a ship
With the people of Hel, at the helm stands Loki;
After the wolf do wild men follow….
　　　　　　　　　　　　　The Poetic Edda

Any given piece of rope will bear only so much strain before it parts. It will come straight and tight, like an iron bar. It will stretch and grow narrower and make little popping noises. If it is wet, the water will be squeezed out like ringing out a cloth.

And then suddenly, unpredictably, it will part. At some point along its length it will break with an audible and often destructive force, snapping back, injuring or killing anything in its path.

That was how Brunhard viewed luck. A lot of weight could be put on luck if it seemed to be holding. It could be stretched. But, as with a rope, one had to take great care to not stretch it too far.

Brunhard had a good sense for that. He had a unique ability to see when his luck was reaching the point of blowing apart. It was what had kept him alive all those years and made him a wealthy man, as well. And he knew he was reaching the breaking point now. He could hear the popping sounds, see the water squeezing out.

"Aloft there, what do you see?" he called out peevishly. The slaves were still rowing *Wind Dancer* despite the breeze picking up from the north east. They were not moving very fast. In part this was because there were not as many slaves, some of them having been sent off aboard the captured longship, and in part because Brunhard did not want to go fast. Not yet.

"No ships or sails astern of us, Master Brunhard!" the man sitting at the masthead called down. They had sent him up in a loop of rope so he could remain there longer than he might if he was just hanging on. Brunhard wanted eyes aloft. He wanted information the very moment it was to be had.

"Are you just looking astern?" Brunhard called back. "What lies ahead of us?"

He watched the man kick off the mast and swivel around still hanging from the rope. He seemed to be having fun with his acrobatics, and that annoyed Brunhard even more.

"I see the cape, Master Brunhard! To the south, ten miles, perhaps! The coast seems to be just beach. No rocks and no ships there!"

I know the coast is all beach here, you damned idiot, Brunhard thought. He knew every inch of this coast. That was not his concern right now.

He was concerned about the longships, both the one he had captured and the one they had been trying to capture. *Wind Dancer* and the other ships had set their course south to get away from the stalking Northmen. The captured longship with Áed, Louis, and the Irish slaves aboard had set its course north to intercept them and spring their trap.

Brunhard had been moving slow as he headed for the cape. The plan had been for Áed and his men to capture the second longship and then turn south and rejoin the merchantmen. They would transfer the plunder into *Wind Dancer*'s hold, redistribute the slaves who had survived, and then leave Ireland astern, making the crossing to Wales once they had raised the cape above the horizon.

They should have seen the sails of Áed's ships to the north by now, if all had gone according to plan. The sun was just past its zenith, the day was getting on, and yet there was no sign of them.

How damned long does it take to kill a bunch of heathens? Brunhard wondered. But of course there were many things that might have gone wrong. The treacherous Irishman Broccáin and Louis the Frank might have succeeded in leading a mutiny and taken the ship. Áed and his men might have captured the Northman and decided to sail off and keep the plunder for themselves. The ship might have sprung a leak and sunk.

Or, the worst of all possibilities, the heathens might have killed Áed and his men and taken the ship back. That was the scenario that most worried Brunhard. Not that he cared about the lives of Áed or any of his other men; he didn't, save to the extent that they were useful to him. But if the heathens had taken back their ship, then they might now be coming after *Wind Dancer* and the others. The warrior crew of even one longship, even a small one, would be too much for the few men who sailed Brunhard's merchantmen.

Silef, the most trusted of all Brunhard's sailors, was at the tiller, only a few feet away. "We should have seen Áed and the ships by now," he offered, the only man aboard who would have dared give Brunhard his opinion. And even Silef's opinion Brunhard did not welcome, at least not in that instance. Silef was unlikely to think of anything that Brunhard had not already thought of himself.

"Yes, I know," Brunhard said, trying by the tone of his voice to indicate that further discussion was neither needed nor welcome, but Silef went on anyway.

"Áed might have run off. Or he might have been killed."

"Yes," Brunhard said.

"If he was killed, the heathens might be in our wake, even now," Silef said. "And even so, that's only two of the heathens accounted for."

"What? What do you mean?"

"Well," Silef said. "There were four of the bastards after us. We captured the one. The second Áed went after this morning. But there were still two more. And those two were the big ones."

Brunhard frowned. He hadn't thought of that. "One of them I wrecked," he said and even he could hear the defensive tone in his voice. "Sail on fire? You must have seen it; it was quite spectacular."

Silef coughed and spit phlegm over the side. "I saw the sail on fire," he said. "I didn't see it wreck."

"Well, of course it wrecked! Swept right into the rocks!" Brunhard said, but even as the words left his mouth he felt an uneasy sensation in his gut. Because Silef was right. They had not seen it wrecked.

"Very well, it wrecked," Silef said. "That still leaves one more out there somewhere."

Brunhard felt the rope of luck pull tighter, heard the popping sounds increase. He looked up at the masthead, out astern of *Wind Dancer* and then out to weather. Nothing. Nothing but land to starboard, and open ocean in every other direction. But of course the lookout would have told him if that was not the case. And if he failed to tell him, Brunhard would have flayed him alive on the foredeck.

"We have a breeze now," Brunhard said, ostensibly changing the subject though in fact he was addressing the immediate concern. They were moving slow and doing so on purpose. That was the proper thing to do if Áed was trying to catch up with them, but it was the worst possible choice if the Northmen were in their wake.

"Yes, the breeze is getting up," Silef prompted. "Maybe we should make some use of it."

And with that, Brunhard came to a decision. *To hell with Áed and the Northmen and their ship and plunder*, he thought. His luck was stretched too tight. He had the slaves that remained aboard his ships, he had his cargo, and most of all he had the plunder from the one longship. That was enough. More than enough to make this perhaps the most profitable voyage of his life. He was a greedy man, and he knew it, but he was not so much of a fool as to let that greed destroy him.

"Let me take the tiller. You see to getting the sail set," Brunhard said, stepping up and taking the oak bar as Silef surrendered it. He looked up at the masthead. "Aloft, there! Take a last good look around! We're going to lower you down so we might set the sail!"

In a moment the ship, which had settled into the monotonous work of rowing slowly south, was a riot of activity. Oars were run in and stacked, lashings on the sail cast off. The lookout was lowered to the deck and the halyard to raise the heavy yard was stretched along.

"Anything?" Brunhard asked the lookout as he came aft.

"No, Master Brunhard," the man said.

"Well, to hell with them, we're done waiting," Brunhard said, the words really directed at himself, since he was not in the habit of explaining anything to the near worthless men who manned his ships.

"Yes, Master Brunhard," the lookout said. Brunhard made a dismissive gesture with his hand and the lookout scurried off forward.

Brunhard watched him go and his eye fell on the slave girl, the wife of the Irishman, Broccáin. He wondered if she would understand what it meant that they were setting the sail, if she would realize they were leaving her husband behind, that she would be off to the slave markets without him.

The men should have their chance at her tonight, he thought, *and they'll be glad of that*. But he felt the breeze on his face and heard the first snapping of the sail as it was let loose from its lashings and he thought, *Or maybe not.*

The wind was filling in from the northeast and becoming more easterly, and the sky, which had been clear at dawn, was overspread with clouds now. In Brunhard's experience in those waters that generally meant the wind would be getting stronger before it died again. Maybe much stronger.

Perhaps we should run the ships ashore for the night, he thought, but he could not shake the realization that there was at least one, maybe two longships out there, and he did not know where they were. There were rivers and inlets and various hiding places along much of the Irish coast, but not here. Here there was just a long, almost straight stretch of beach, where Brunhard's ships would be easily seen by any passing vessel.

There was a harbor just north of the cape, the mouth of a river, but the sandbars there were tricky and shifting. There was a better than even chance his fleet would run up on those and there the Northmen would find them, helpless to even run.

Time to leave, Brunhard thought. He knew it in his gut. It was time to leave the coast of Ireland astern, head off across the sea, make his was to Frisia. He would be back in Dubh-linn next summer, but for now his time was out. High winds, foul weather did not worry him too much. It was a short crossing. They had only to survive the night and they would see the shores of Wales the following day.

"Haul away!" he heard Silef shout, and the men began to heave on the halyard, and the slaves as well, those who could lay hands on the rope. The yard rose off the gallows and was swung athwartships as the sail spilled out and bucked and twisted in the breeze.

Brunhard looked astern. *Galilee* and *Two Brothers* were also setting sail, following *Wind Dancer*'s lead. He looked ahead. The cape was visible to him now, a low, dark line along the southern horizon that disappeared suddenly as if the end had been cut off with a knife. They were close enough now.

He pushed the tiller away from him, just a bit, turning *Wind Dancer* a bit more easterly. He would keep easing around to the east so they passed within a few miles of the end of the cape. From there he knew he had to keep as easterly a course as he could. That would not be so very easterly in this wind, but the coast of Wales was a broad target. He was unlikely to miss it.

Silef had the beitass rigged out over the larboard side and a half dozen men were hauling the corner of the sail down to the end of the spar. More men were heaving the starboard sheet aft. The sail, full of wind now, bellied out to leeward and *Wind Dancer* heeled over, the water rushing down her side. Brunhard took a deep breath. He loved this. Usually it made him deeply happy. But his mind was filled with too many worries just then for him to get much pleasure from the set of the sail, the feel of the ship underfoot.

He looked up at the masthead, considered sending the lookout back up. The man had been getting quite a ride before. Now it would be much worse as *Wind Dancer*, sailing nearly as close to the wind as she could get, began pounding into the seas.

To hell with the lookout, Brunhard decided. He didn't need a lookout. He was going to sea, leaving the land astern, leaving the damned Northmen and the damned Irish in his wake. There was only empty sea ahead, and he didn't much care what was behind.

He nudged the tiller some more, bringing the bow around even more easterly. As *Wind Dancer* lifted on the waves he could see the cape more clearly, that familiar headland. There was always a play of emotions when he saw that point. Trepidation, because they were leaving the land now and heading out into the unpredictable sea, where strange and mysterious things lived, and storms could come from nowhere. But there was optimism as well. Because that cape meant he was bound away for Frisia. Home.

It was right about then that Brunhard would usually swear he was done with sea voyaging, that once he set shore in Frisia he would wander no more. He had riches enough. Why did he put himself through this?

This was his ritual every time he sighted the cape, but this time, he realized, it was different. This time he really was done. He had the Northmen's plunder and Louis's casket in his hold, and that was a great store of wealth. The men on the crew might think they were going to share in it—Brunhard had assured them they would in order to retain their loyalty—but once they reached Frisia they would find out to their sorrow that the silver was Brunhard's, and Brunhard's alone.

They might get the wages they were owed for the voyage, or they might not, but they would not get even the smallest share of the silver.

He looked astern. *Galilee* and *Two Brothers* were smaller than *Wind Dancer* and their masters less skillful in ship handling and already they were struggling to keep up.

"Silef!" Brunhard shouted forward. "Luff the sail a bit, let these lazy, incompetent bastards gain on us!"

Silef nodded, eased the tack on the larboard side, spilling wind from the sail. *Wind Dancer*'s motion through the water changed noticeably and her speed dropped off and soon the two smaller ships had drawn to within a hundred yards. Brunhard waved to Silef and half a dozen men hauled the sail taut again and the ship slowly began to regain her speed.

And so it went as the day wore on and the three ships plunged along, making as much easting as they could. That meant a course closer to southeast, but that was good enough for Brunhard. Sometime before dark they would come about, and near the middle of the night they'd come about again and, come morning, that should put them right where they wanted to be.

It would not be a pleasant night, but Brunhard and the sailors were used to that. And at least it was not raining, and there was little indication it would start soon. Not that it would matter all that much. The spray thrown up as the bow pounded into the seas had already soaked them nearly through.

Silef sent one of the trusted men aft to relieve Brunhard of the tiller, and Brunhard, realizing how weary he had become, relinquished it willingly. He stepped over to the weather side of the small afterdeck and leaned against the side. His body was motionless but his eyes were everywhere, running over the set of the sail, gauging how far astern the other two ships had fallen, judging their distance to the cape and the amount of leeway they were making, whether or not they were in danger of being blown down on the land.

We're fine, fine… he thought. They would weather the cape with ease on that heading, stand out into open water. By the time the sun went down they would be out of sight of land.

He shifted his gaze to weather, staring off in the direction from which the wind was blowing. A wave passed under the bow and lifted it high, obstructing the view forward. Then the stern went up and Brunhard looked out toward the horizon. And he gasped. And he felt his stomach tighten.

And then the stern came down again and the horizon was lost to sight. "Silef!" Brunhard roared. "Send the man with the sharpest eyes aloft! I thought I saw a ship to weather!"

Silef acknowledged with a wave, called an order to one of the men, and a moment later the man was climbing up one of the weather shrouds. With the sail set he could easily stand on the yard and hang onto the mast and have as comfortable a perch as a man might find aloft on the pitching and rolling ship.

There was silence fore and aft, but nearly every eye was turned toward the masthead, as if watching the lookout would make his report come quicker or more accurately. Brunhard was just about to call up in frustration when the lookout called down.

"It's a ship! A mile, maybe a little more! No sail set. Might have oars out, I can't see for certain!"

A ship? Brunhard thought. *A ship?* He frowned. *Of course there's a ship, we're on the damned ocean,* he thought. It could be any sort of ship. The chances were that it was a merchantman that would turn and run like the devil was after him at the sight of their three sails.

But he found no comfort in that thought. And he could not shake the memory of how the heathen who had been plaguing them had taken his ship offshore just a few days earlier and waited for them to put to sea before he pounced. It made Brunhard more angry than frightened to think that he could have fallen for the same thing a second time.

Brunhard turned to the man at the tiller. "Fall off, some," he shouted. The man pulled the tiller toward him and *Wind Dancer* began to turn to starboard, her bow swinging away from the wind. "That's good, hold her there!" Brunhard said. He looked astern. *Two Brothers* and *Galilee* were following behind.

There... Brunhard thought. They would run more south, skirt around this bastard, and then they would see if he was a hunter or if he was prey.

"Master Brunhard!" the lookout called down. "The ship is setting sail!"

Damn! Brunhard thought, though he kept that to himself. This was not good.

Perhaps he's trying to get away from us, he thought next, then admonished himself for even thinking such a thing. He knew it was not true, and while he was happy to lie to anyone else for any reason, he knew it was pointless, worse than pointless, to lie to himself. This was the heathen, and he was lying in wait, and now he was coming for them.

And that presented several problems. If they had been close in to land, Brunhard was sure he could have found some means of slipping away. But now they were several miles out, with nowhere to hide. The longship would be faster than his ships. And, more importantly, he was to windward of them. That meant he could sweep down as he chose, herd them like sheep. They were trapped between the Norsemen to windward and the coast of Ireland to lee.

Damn him! Brunhard thought, but still he held his face expressionless. And then he thought of something else. *There's only one of him...* And with that thought an idea began to form.

"Silef!" he shouted forward. "I'm going to luff, so I might speak to the other ships!" Silef waved a hand in acknowledgement. Brunhard turned to the helmsman. "Luff up, meet here. Don't put the sail aback or I'll rip your heart out."

The helmsman nodded and slowly turned *Wind Dancer* to larboard, turning her bow back into the wind. The weather edge of her sail began to shake and twist, and then the rest of the sail seemed to collapse as the wind blew down either side of the oiled wool cloth. The ship's forward motion slowed and she began to wallow as her momentum fell away.

Brunhard looked astern. The two smaller ships behind were still forging ahead, their masters understanding that Brunhard's maneuver meant he wanted to speak with them. When they were no more than fifty feet downwind they too luffed up, coming to as much of a stop as a ship on the ocean could come to.

"There's a ship, some heathen bastard most likely, to windward!" Brunhard shouted, using all of his considerable volume to be heard over the distance and the sound of flogging sails and the wind humming in the rig.

"They'll try to run us down!" he continued. "We'll run for the coast, try to get into the shallows at the river to the west of us! You go ahead, I'll hang back and try to fend him off!"

The masters of the other vessels waved their understanding. "Now, go!" Brunhard shouted and aboard *Two Brothers* and *Galilee* the tillers were pushed over, sails pulled aback, and the ship's bows turned away from the wind as the sails filled again. Hands on the ships hauled at the braces, pulling the yards around square to the ships' keels, trimming the sails to allow the vessels to run straight downwind, back toward the Irish coast.

"Fall off, now," Brunhard said to *Wind Dancer*'s helmsman. The man pulled the tiller toward him and the ship's bow began to swing away downwind. Forward, Silef already had the braces cast off and men standing ready to pull on his command.

"Master Brunhard!" the lookout called again. "The ship to windward has her sail set now, and she's making right for us!"

"Let him come," Brunhard said, speaking to himself.

The Northman would come for *Wind Dancer* because she was the biggest of the three. And Brunhard would make it even more tempting by staying behind, letting the other ships take the lead. He would wait until the longship was nearly alongside, then spin around, head to windward, let the heathens sail right past. If he did that, then maybe the heathen would go after the other two, rather than get into a long chase to weather in that rising wind.

"Worth a try," Brunhard muttered to himself. It would mean the loss of the other ships, their cargoes of slaves and goods, and the men aboard. But it would also mean that Brunhard himself would escape with his life and his treasure. And as it happened, those were the only things about which Brunhard cared in the least.

Chapter Thirty

A third I know: if sore need should come
of a spell to stay my foes;
when I sing that song, which shall blunt their swords,
nor their weapons nor staves can wound.
                                    The Song of Spells

A fleet of ships always put Thorgrim in mind of a wolf pack: each individual swift and deadly, moving as one, acting as one, the whole so vastly more powerful than the numbers alone would imply. Thorgrim loved sailing in a fleet.

This was something different, but it was good, too. They were one ship, alone. Not a wolf pack. Now they were the lynx: stealthy, patient, silent. They were not sweeping their prey in front of them, they were waiting motionless and concealed. Waiting for their victims to get within striking distance. Waiting to pounce.

The distant ships were closing with them, getting closer to the spot where the rolling seas concealed *Sea Hammer* from sight. They had no lookout, Thorgrim guessed, or if they did he was blind, because there was no sign of alarm as the ships stood on.

*Wait…wait…*Thorgrim thought. No need to spring on them yet, not when they were so actively aiding in their own destruction.

Vestar was still aloft, still looking out, and now he called, "The one ship, the big one, in the lead, it's falling off now!" Thorgrim jumped a bit, the sudden cry startling him in his sharp concentration.

Falling off, turning away from the wind. Changing course. There was only one reason he might do that.

"That's it, they've seen us," Thorgrim said to no one in particular. Then he shouted forward, "Get the sea anchor in! Set the sail!"

And that was the end of stalking, and the signal to pounce. Every man had been braced, ready for Thorgrim to give that order, muscles taut, ears sharp. They moved, fast and efficient. The line streaming out over the stern was hauled in, hand over hand. The sail had been lashed to the yard with a series of loops that required only one tug of the rope for the whole thing to fall away, letting the sail spill from the yard.

"Haul!" Godi shouted, but the men on the halyard had been waiting for the word, and even before he could speak that single syllable they were pulling on the thick rope. The yard, already athwartships, now rose quickly up the mast, the sail bucking in the wind, as men to larboard and starboard hauled back on the sheets.

For most of the day *Sea Hammer* had been wallowing in place, but now she began to move. The yard was not yet up to the masthead, the sail not yet properly filled, but the long, narrow hull was starting to surge forward as if the ship, like the men aboard her, had just been waiting for the moment when the hunt would begin.

"The one ship's luffing up!" Vestar called down from aloft. "The other two ships are coming up with her! They're luffing as well!"

Thorgrim turned his eyes from the lookout to the seas beyond the bow. *Sea Hammer*'s stern rose on a wave and he could see the distant sails, three white squares a mile or more away, but his eyes were not sharp enough to take in more.

And then they were lost to sight as the stern came down again. *Luffing...* Thorgrim thought. Brunhard was passing orders to the masters of the other vessels. No other reason they would do that. Because flight was their greatest concern now, their only defense, and killing the ships' forward momentum by luffing would only thwart that effort. But Brunhard was a clever one, and he would sacrifice a few moments of time for the chance to implement some plan.

Plan all you like, Thorgrim thought. *It will do you no good.*

Sea Hammer's sail reached the top of the mast and Godi called out, "That's well! Make the halyard fast!" The ship was really moving now, her speed nearly as great as it could be in that wind and sea. She no longer felt as if she was at the mercy of the waves, but rather that she was brushing them aside. The lean bow was cleaving into the seas, sending spray high on both sides. She was moving faster than the waves were rolling now, driving through the backs of the rollers, surging over them, bow high, then dipping down and slamming into the shallow trough and surging into the next ahead.

Thorgrim felt his lips turn up in a smile. He could see his men forward were already half-soaked by the spray, but they were smiling, too, reveling in the power of the ship underfoot, the straining sail overhead, the vengeance that would soon be theirs.

Brunhard had turned. Thorgrim could see him now, and not just at the crest of the waves, but most of the time, save for when *Sea Hammer*'s stern dipped far down into the troughs. They were closing, and they had their eyes on the merchant ships, which had turned west and now were running for all they were worth back toward Ireland.

No safety for you on the high seas, Thorgrim thought. This was what he had intended. Get Brunhard away from the coast he knew so well. Lure the prey away from its familiar warren and get it in the open. He looked beyond Brunhard's ships to the coast off in the distance. Three, four miles. Brunhard would never reach the shore before *Sea Hammer* ran him down.

Godi came ambling aft, his big, wide face split in a grin. "Your gamble has paid off well, once again, Thorgrim!" he shouted. "I must remember to never game with you if there's silver at stake!"

Thorgrim smiled, though he was never very comfortable with praise, and particularly not fond of it while the chase was still unfolding. He would never say such a thing himself because he was sure it would bring bad luck, and he hoped Godi's saying it would not do the same.

"Have you divided the men up?" Thorgrim asked, changing the subject.

"Yes," Godi said. "Twenty for the big ship, ten each for the smaller ones."

Thorgrim nodded. They had worked this all out in the long hours waiting for Brunhard to make his appearance. They wanted all three ships, not just one, and that would take some clever maneuvering. The plan was to come alongside the first ship they overhauled, grapple just long enough to get a gang of warriors aboard, then cast off and go for the next.

Godi had divided the men of *Sea Hammer* into three divisions, one for each. It would not take many men to vanquish the handful of sailors they could expect to find on Brunhard's ships. It was coming alongside in those seas, and in that rising wind, that would present the greatest problem.

"Very well," Thorgrim said. "It won't be long now."

And it was not, though it was certainly longer than Thorgrim had anticipated. Brunhard's ships were fast, and Brunhard a good seaman. Thorgrim was willing to admit as much, to himself at least. Brunhard had outfoxed him before, nearly wrecked his ship, disabled *Sea Hammer* by putting her sail to the torch. He had made Thorgrim work hard for the vengeance he would now take, but that would make the vengeance all that much sweeter.

"I wonder where *Fox* and *Dragon* are," Godi observed, and Thorgrim realized he had all but forgotten about the other vessels, so intent had he been on how he alone would take Brunhard down.

"That's a good question, Godi," Thorgrim said. He looked up at the masthead. Vestar was still there so Thorgrim called out, "Vestar! What of Brunhard's ships? And do you see anything of *Fox* and *Dragon*?"

A pause as Vestar swept the horizon. He was sitting on the yard, hugging the mast, which must have been an easier seat to keep, but his ride was wilder now, with the ship plunging and bucking as it charged through the seas.

"Brunhard's still running like a dog!" Vestar called with undisguised glee in his voice. "Heading right for shore, but he's not above half a mile ahead! He won't make it! I see nothing of the other ships!"

"Very good! Keep an eye out for them!" Thorgrim called. He felt an uneasiness in his gut and he tried to ignore it.

Fox and Dragon don't matter, he told himself. *Harald is aboard Blood Hawk and she's under oar so he'll be lucky to catch up to us by nightfall.* Few of the men on the other two ships had been with him long. He did not know many of their names. He supposed he should consider every one of his men's lives as valuable as any other, and he did, mostly. Except for Harald.

He'll be along... Thorgrim thought.

It was ironic, and Thorgrim knew it. It was he who put Harald in grave danger by taking him a'viking. But he felt sure that letting Harald spend his days as a farmer, and never know any other life, would do him no favors. A farmer's life could be a good life, a safe life. For Thorgrim's older son, Odd, it seemed to work fine. But it would drive Harald to madness. And farmers, Thorgrim was sure, did not spend the rest of days in Odin's corpse hall.

"Here's that bastard Brunhard!" Godi said, pointing toward the bow. Thorgrim pulled himself from his thought and looked. They were close now, and they no longer had to be on the crest of a roller to see the ships in the distance.

"He's letting the smaller ships get ahead of him," Thorgrim said. "Sure his ship, the bigger ship, is the faster. See how he's spilling wind from his sail."

"Is he protecting them?" Godi wondered. "Holding his own ship back to let them escape?"

"Perhaps," Thorgrim said. "It would be a brave thing to do." He was about to add that he doubted that Brunhard would do such a thing, but he stopped himself. The truth was that he knew nothing of Brunhard, nothing at all. He might be the bravest ship's master on earth. Just because he, Thorgrim, had come to hate the man did not mean Brunhard was a coward.

"It looks as if that bigger ship will be the first we'll catch," Godi said. "I'll see that the men who are told off for that one are ready to go. Grappling hooks, too."

Thorgrim looked at Godi, up at Godi, at his big, honest face. They had not known one another beyond a year, had met fighting side by side at a place called Tara. They had been through many things together since that time. He smiled.

"Thank you, Godi," he said. Godi nodded and headed off forward to see that the men were ready when the fighting began. Thorgrim crossed over to Bjorn, who had the tiller. "You probably would rather get in on the fighting," he said. "I'll take that."

Bjorn, who did indeed prefer fighting to steering, willingly gave the tiller over to Thorgrim. Giving Bjorn his wish, however, was not the reason Thorgrim had taken the steering oar.

This was going to be a tricky thing, coming up alongside Brunhard's ship. And Brunhard, Thorgrim knew, was clever. He was not going to simply sail on and let the Northmen run him down. He would have some trick ready, and Thorgrim guessed it would be some maneuver, some way he would try to squeeze out of the trap. He might possibly try and turn right under *Sea Hammer*'s bow, head off upwind, hope that *Sea Hammer* would go after the smaller ships and let him run to safety. That would explain why he had let the smaller ships take the lead.

Are you that much of a treacherous bastard? Thorgrim wondered. Brunhard's ship was not much above a half mile ahead now. He would find out soon enough.

Chapter Thirty-One

In gusts of wind, that chillful
destroyer of timber planes down
the planks before the head
of my sea-king's swan.
Egil's Saga

For weeks Conandil had lived with terror that was ongoing and visceral. It waned some during those times when the ship did not seem in any imminent peril, or when the Frisian sailors seemed to be occupied with other things, not paying any attention to her or to Broccáin. But then something would shift and the terror would be back in all its soul-rending constancy.

The worst was when Broccáin and Louis had sailed off. They were the only men aboard who might offer her any protection, though she knew full well there was not one damned thing they could do, really. They were both in chains, both as vulnerable to Brunhard's whims as she was.

Still, their absence made her feel like she was on the edge of a cliff. By the time it was clear to her and to Brunhard that they were not coming back, the terror had dulled into an ugly, numbing hopelessness. She listened to Brunhard passing the orders to get the ships under sail, to make all speed for the cape and the open sea, and she felt everything slipping away.

But for all her despair, a part of Conandil's mind remained active and observant. It was just the way she was: fascinated by anything new or unfamiliar. When she encountered anything like that she had to find out what it was, how it worked, what it meant. That was why she was so good with language. Her curiosity was like a hunger, and it could never be sated.

Brunhard's ship was just such a puzzle. She had been on ships before, but only briefly, and both times as a captive of Northmen. Marched aboard Brunhard's ship, she had been terrified and confused, her whole world just madness and uncertainty. But despite the fear she had watched the sailors at their work, had listened to the strange language they spoke—not Frisian, which she was familiar with, but the language of the sea. Words she had never heard before, but whose meanings she divined as she followed their labors with her eyes.

Seafaring, she soon learned, consisted of quite a bit of monotony. When the ship was sailing, or being driven by the arms of the slaves, there was little to do. That was certainly true for Conandil, whose only duty had to do with giving food and water to the men. When she was not doing that she tried to be as small and inconspicuous as possible, crammed into a corner near the front of the ship—the *bow*, she had learned—while hoping none of the sailors would notice her and decide it was time to take their pleasure.

During those times she remained generally motionless, less likely to attract attention, but her eyes and ears were active, taking it all in. She developed a good, basic understanding of the workings of the ship, how the wind and the sail interacted, the effect that the waves had on the vessel as it moved through the sea. When she heard an order, she knew what it meant, and she knew what the sailors would do even before they did it.

And so, when Brunhard ordered his ship to turn up into the wind and let the sail flog, Conandil had a pretty good idea of what he was doing.

He'll need some way to escape, she thought. She had heard the lookout report the ship farther out to sea, just sitting, waiting. She had seen the look on Brunhard's face, the surprise and the touch of fear.

They're waiting for you, Brunhard, you bastard, and you know it, she thought.

As Conandil expected, the two other ships came up close to Brunhard's and they, too, let their sails spill the wind to stop their forward momentum. Brunhard called for their masters to turn and sail for Ireland. He assured them he would keep his own ship back, try to protect them as best he could. Then they filled their sails, turned their ships, and plunged off to the westward.

Conandil frowned and kept her eyes on Brunhard as Brunhard, in turn, shifted his gaze from the land a few miles beyond the bow to the place astern where this unknown ship was coming for them.

Now, what are you about? Conandil thought. She was buoyed to hear that Brunhard's plan was to run for the Irish coast. She and the others might not be any freer there than they were at that moment, but remaining in Ireland was certainly preferable to the open sea, or the Frisian slave markets. As long as they were in Ireland, they had a chance.

But she doubted very much that Brunhard felt that way, and she certainly did not believe his noble-sounding words about hanging back and protecting the smaller ships of his fleet. She had been watching Brunhard as closely as she had been watching the working of the ship. His concerns did not extend beyond the limits of his own skin.

Aft, the helmsman worked the tiller side to side as he fought to keep the ship running downwind. The motion had changed dramatically with the change of course. Now, rather than pounding into the sea, the ship was twisting and rocking fore and aft and slewing side to side in the building waves. The wind, which seemed to have been howling just moments before, now seemed to drop away, but Conandil understood that was just because the ship was moving with the wind, not against it.

No one seemed to be paying her any attention, so she rose slowly to her feet to get a better look around. The long, low shoreline of Ireland, looking gray green in that muted light, was stretched out beyond the bow and not so far away. The sight of it gave Conandil another flash of hope.

She turned and looked astern. She could see the Norsemen's ship behind them now. It had its sail set, which apparently it had not before, which was why it had been so hard to see. The sail had on it a checkered pattern and Conandil was fairly certain it was one of the four Norsemen's ships that had chased them days before. At least, the sail appeared similar to that other one.

She stood motionless, pressed against the side of the ship, but her mind was rolling, pitching and yawing as much as the vessel underfoot. She looked at the Northman astern. Mostly just the sail was visible, though she had occasional glimpses of the hull on those moments when both vessels rose on a wave at the same moment. She was no judge of the speed of ships, but she knew that longships were reputed to be fast, and she did not think Brunhard would make it to the coast before the heathens in their wake ran them down.

Conandil looked at the Norsemen's ship. *So what will you do?* she wondered. Her eyes moved to Brunhard, who was also looking behind him at that moment. *And what will you do?*

The answer, at least for the time being, was nothing, nothing beyond what the two ships were doing already. The Northman did not alter course, just stayed directly behind them, getting closer as the sun, just visible behind the clouds, began to drop into the west. Brunhard continued to run hard for the coast, his two ships a few hundred yards ahead of him, their sails straining in the following wind.

"Silef!" Brunhard shouted down the deck. "Check the sheets away some! Spill some wind!"

Conandil watched intently as the men moved to the ropes made fast near the back end of the ship. She had an idea what they were about to do, but she was not certain. She watched as they untied the ropes, taking great care to not untie them all the way, but rather leave a loop around the wooden bar to which they were tied.

Those are very tight, with this wind, Conandil thought. Those particular ropes, the "sheets" apparently, were holding down the bottom corners of the sail. She could see the enormous pressure that wind was putting on the ropes. It was clear that if the sailors lost control of one of them then the sail would fly up in complete confusion.

But the sailors were skilled at their work and they did not lose control. Instead they eased the lines away, just a few yards, letting some of the wind spill from the sail and slowing the ship up a bit.

This is how he lets the other ships keep ahead, Conandil realized.

"Good!" Brunhard shouted. "Sheet home!" Now, with considerable effort, the men at the sheets hauled away, pulling back the few yards of rope they had just let out.

Interesting, Conandil thought. It was like much of the workings of the ship, interesting but of no obvious use to her. The sailors tied the sheets to their wooden bars again and the four vessels, Brunhard's three and the longship in their wake, settled once again into their race for the shore, silent save for the creak of the rigging, the pounding of the seas on the hull.

It was some time later that Conandil, still standing at the bow, thought, *Brunhard will lose this race...* She knew she was right. The longship, relentless in pursuit, had come up behind them, yard by yard, close enough now that Conandil could see the ship's hull clearly, the tall, curved wood of the bow, crowned with some frightening carving, the long, low sweep of the ship bow to stern. She had seen longships with shields mounted on the sides, but this ship did not have them and Conandil guessed they had been taken off in preparation for fighting.

Interesting, Conandil thought, and her mind began to arrange the facts in logical order. She knew three things, based on what she could observe. One was that the Northmen would most certainly overtake Brunhard's ship. The second was that Brunhard would not try to fight them when they did. The third was that Brunhard did not intend to give himself up to the Northmen. In the best of circumstances one could expect little mercy from heathens. If these were indeed the same ones whom Brunhard had tricked earlier, it would go even worse for him.

So he has some other way to escape, some trick planned... Conandil concluded. And it was only a few moments later, as Brunhard began to issue orders, that the plan began to reveal itself, like the sun rising above the horizon.

"All right, you bastards, listen to me!" the Frisian shouted forward, and all the sailors' stood and turned aft, eager to hear their fate.

"This damned heathen, he's right on our ass, as you can see!" Brunhard continued. His usual, jovial tone was gone now, and in its place anger that Conandil guessed was masking real fear. "He'll come up alongside us, along our starboard side, would be my guess. Here's what we'll do. Once his bow is up with our stern, we'll swing right around up into the wind, close-hauled. We'll sail off to weather and he'll sail right past us, and if we have any luck at all he won't follow us, but instead go after those poor bastards ahead of us, *Two Bothers* and *Galilee*."

Conandil could see heads nodding among the crew. She was not entirely sure what it was that Brunhard was planning. It seemed he had some plan to get the heathens to attack the other ships and leave him alone, which sounded like the sort of thing he would come up with. Whatever it was, the other sailors seemed to approve.

"We'll have to move quick and sharp," Brunhard continued. "Let us have hands to the sheets, tacks and braces. Run the beitass out over the larboard side, but be ready to shift it in an instant! Go!"

And the men went. They moved fast, taking position at the ends of various ropes, grabbing up the heavy pole that lay on the ship's deck and thrusting it out over the larboard side. The longship was not more than one hundred feet astern of them now, reminding them of the urgency of their situation.

Conandil could feel the tension on board, the sense of waiting to spring, all things hanging in balance. Brunhard's eyes were shifting to the ship coming up hard astern, and to the men standing ready and to the two slave ships beyond the bow.

He'll sail right past us...that's what Brunhard said. The plan seemed to be growing clearer to Conandil, like a fog lifting off a hilltop. From what she could understand of the sailors' talk, Brunhard would wait until the last instant and then turn his ship quick, try to sail off, hope the Northmen would go after the other two.

Will it work? She had no idea. *Do I want it to work?* That was a bigger question. Would she and the other Irish captives be better off with the Northmen or with Brunhard?

There was no way to know. But she did know that if their fate was in Brunhard's hands, then their lives would be hell, no better, until they died some miserable death. Her husband was gone, likely dead. One way or another, her life as she had known it was over, her one real taste of happiness and security ripped away. But if she was going to hell, she was taking Brunhard with her.

Five feet from where she stood was the barrel of dried fish from which she had been feeding the rowers, and on top of that was a knife. It was a simple thing, a wooden handle, a heavy iron blade ten inches long and wickedly sharp. She had used it to cut up the fish nearly every day since they had been underway.

"Get ready!" Brunhard bellowed. Conandil looked from the knife to the stern of the ship. The Northman was almost on them now. She could see men standing at the Northman's bow, leaning around the stem on which was mounted the cruel-looking figurehead: big men, bearded men, men holding swords and axes and ropes with grappling hooks. Not more than twenty feet separated the bow of the longship and the stern of the slaver.

"Ready!" Brunhard shouted again, and Conandil thought, *Yes, I am.*

She crossed the five feet of deck on two long bounds and snatched up the knife. She turned and looked aft. No one noticed, so intent were they on the jobs they had to do. She raced aft and that at last drew some attention. She saw men look up in surprise, heard Brunhard shout, "What in hell?"

Silef was there, blocking her way, arms spread wide like he was trying to herd a flock of ducks, but Conandil did not slow. She led with the knife as she raced aft, a knife Silef apparently had not seen since he made no move to avoid it as she drove it into his gut. His eyes went wide and he hunched forward and made a strangling noise, but Conandil did not wait to see him fall. She jerked the knife free as she ran, felt the blood warm on her hand. She screamed. Not a scream of fear or pain or anger, but a war cry. A war cry of her people.

It was a terrifying sound. She could see the men standing by the starboard sheet go wide-eyed, take a step back, confused and shocked. She took two steps past the rowers' benches toward the men standing there. The first in line, a sailor of many years from his look, recovered even as Conandil came at him. He reached out with a hand to seize her wrist, but like Silef he too underestimated Conandil's skill and speed and resolve.

The knife came down on the outstretched hand, a powerful downward sweep of the blade and Conandil saw fingers flying free. The sailor shrieked, stumbled back, slammed into the man aft of him who stumbled as well.

But the sailors were not Conandil's target and she was done with them. She turned quick. Right in front of her was the sheet, straining against the wooden piece to which it was tied. It looked like an iron bar and as she slashed at it with the knife she hoped it was not as strong as that.

It was not. Not at all. Indeed, the ease with which it parted surprised her. The first cut severed the rope halfway through and as she drew the blade back to slash again the fibers began to shred, right before her eyes. She was still cocking her arm to strike when the sheet let go with a loud bang and the sail flew off in a wild confusion.

"Oh, you bitch!" she heard Brunhard roar. "Get that bitch!"

But no one was listening. The sail, untethered from the sheet, beat wildly in the wind, once, twice, and then it too began to shred, tearing into long streamers that thrashed and twisted on the yard like serpents. Conandil heard someone scream, felt the ship turning underfoot as it slewed sideways in the seas. She felt it leaning, leaning to starboard and she was suddenly afraid she would topple right over the rail and be flung into the sea. She reached out her arm and the rower nearest her, her fellow Irishman, fellow slave, grabbed her hand and pulled her inboard.

She looked aft and she sucked in her breath. The seas were rising up on either side of Brunhard's ship as the vessel dipped down into the trough between them. And as it did, the longship, now perpendicular to Brunhard's vessel, came surging over the top of the waves. Conandil was actually looking up at the underside of the longship's bow, narrow and dripping, as it soared over the stern of Brunhard's ship.

Then the wave passed under and Brunhard's ship rose and the longship fell. It dropped onto the afterdeck of the slaver with a crushing sound and the noise of wood splintering, men screaming, and the relentless wind and sea roaring on every quarter.

Chapter Thirty-Two

With its chisel of snow, the headwind,
scourge of the mast, mightily
hones its file by the prow
on the path that my sea-bull treads.
Egil's Saga

They were nearly up with Brunhard's ship, and Thorgrim could feel his spirits soaring. The tiller was quivering in his hand with the pressure of the following seas on the steering oar, the sail was belly-full and straining at the sheets, the waves lifting the ship and pushing her on.

The men were ready to go. Gathered near the bow, swords and axes poised. Godi had a coil of stout line in his hand, a grappling hook hanging from the end. "I think Brunhard's going to swing away sharp," Thorgrim had said to him as they closed with the Frisian ship. "I think he's going to try and run off upwind. You be ready with a grappling hook. As soon as we're close enough, you hook into him like a fish; don't let him get away."

Now Godi was ready, and it would not be long, the length of one or two more waves, before *Sea Hammer's* bow was up with Brunhard's stern. Wild seas, two ships barely under control, a fight and plunder and vengeance in the offing, it did not get any better than this.

Failend was at his side now, bow in hand, a quiver of arrows over her back. "I can drop their helmsman, easy," she said. "Would you like me to?"

"No, no!" Thorgrim said, speaking loud over the wind. "We don't want Brunhard to lose control of the ship now, not right under our bow like that! Once we've grappled you can start taking them down, but not before Brunhard's ship is under control."

Failend nodded.

"And listen here," Thorgrim said. "Look for the one giving orders, that will be Brunhard."

"And I should shoot him first?"

"No, don't shoot him at all. He's for me. Any plunder we get, you all can have. But Brunhard's mine."

Failend nodded. "Don't shoot Brunhard. Very well," she said and hurried off forward.

Sea Hammer's bow went down, her stern lifted high and Thorgrim was looking down the length of the deck, down at Brunhard's fat merchantman less than a ship-length beyond the bow and low down between the seas. Their oars were stowed, of course, but still there were rowers' benches filled with men, which was odd, but Thorgrim did not have time to think on that now. The wind had piped up even since this chase had begun, the skies overhead growing darker, more brooding, but Thorgrim's heart was singing the song of the sailor, the song of the warrior.

On the rise of the next wave, and he's ours, Thorgrim thought.

Then something changed. It changed so fast Thorgrim did not even know at first what it was. The outline of Brunhard's ship was suddenly different, and Thorgrim thought the Frisian was starting his turn and he was about to call out to Godi when he realized that was not it.

It was the sail. The larboard sheet had let go, the sail was blowing free, flogging and whipping in the strong east wind.

"Brunhard! What…" Thorgrim shouted, but he could not even finish that brief exclamation. Brunhard's ship dropped into the trough between the waves and it slewed around to larboard, driven sideways by the following sea. In an instant Thorgrim went from looking down the starboard side of Brunhard's ship to looking at her broadside as she turned ninety degrees and right under *Sea Hammer*'s bow.

"Oh, by the gods!" Thorgrim shouted. His hand tightened on the tiller, ready to pull it toward him to try and turn *Sea Hammer* out of the way, but there was no time for that. He held the steering board straight and had a sudden thought that his ship might pass right over Brunhard's, just bump over it like bumping over a rock just below the surface.

Maybe... Thorgrim thought. And then the wave lifted Brunhard's ship up, right under *Sea Hammer*'s bow, just as *Sea Hammer*'s bow was coming down off the same wave. *Sea Hammer* surged over the crest and dropped on Brunhard's ship like a sledgehammer.

Thorgrim felt the impact in his hands and legs. He was tossed forward, twisting around the tiller, flung to the deck as if Odin himself had flicked him away. As he went down he heard the sound of rending, crushing wood, the shouts of men in shocked terror, the screams of men standing on Brunhard's afterdeck crushed like bugs.

Thorgrim hit the deck and tumbled off the edge of the afterdeck and fell another foot to the main deck below. The sounds of shouting and the crush of wood on wood were even louder by the time he came to a stop. *Sea Hammer* was moving differently now, no longer driving ahead with purpose but wallowing, twisting. The sounds of the keel working against Brunhard's ship sounded like the moans of a dying beast.

Hands on the deck, Thorgrim pushed himself up and regained his feet. He ran forward, pushing his way past the men who were themselves just standing again, or untangling themselves from the sea chests.

Thorgrim had never in all his years of seafaring seen anything like this. *Sea Hammer* had come down on the afterdeck of Brunhard's ship and remained there, as if it were grounded on a rock, except the rock was twisting and plunging, rising and falling with the seas. The two ships had spun around in the wind and waves like a leaf floating on a stream. *Sea Hammer*'s checkered sail was aback now, the wind pressing on the forward side of the cloth. Thorgrim could hear the forestay strain and pop under the pressure.

"Harald!" he shouted and then corrected himself. "Godi, get some men, get the yard down! Don't worry about swinging it fore and aft, just get it down!" They were in trouble now; Thorgrim did not know if either ship could still float, and the pressure on the sail was not helping things.

Godi called the names of a few men, and they raced aft to do as Thorgrim had instructed, with others joining them. Thorgrim reached a place near the bow where his ship and Brunhard's were crushed together. He stopped and forced himself to take it all in, to assess this bizarre situation.

"Oh, by Thor's ass…" he said. The two ships were ninety degrees to one another, all but locked together. A cluster of warriors stood near *Sea Hammer*'s bow, apparently uncertain whether or not they should still follow their original instructions to board and take Brunhard's ship, uncertain about the wisdom of jumping the ten feet down to the deck of the merchant ship below them, a ship that might sink in the next instant.

Thorgrim was not concerned about that. Brunhard was not going anywhere, and the possibility of *Sea Hammer*'s sinking was more of an immediate concern than the Frisians were. "You men!" he shouted. "Get these deck planks up! Let's see what damage we have!"

The men abandoned their place at the rail and grabbed onto the deck planks, which were just laid in place and not fastened down. They lifted them and tossed them aside and Thorgrim looked down into the hold. He could see where some of *Sea Hammer*'s planks had been stove in with the impact. He did not know if his ship could still float on its own without Brunhard's vessel holding it up, but he did not think so. Not for long, anyway.

"Ahhh!" he shouted in frustration.

He turned and strode to the larboard rail, looked down at the merchant ship on which they rested. Her sides were crushed nearly to the level of the deck where *Sea Hammer* had come down on her. The ship was bucking in the swells, twisting and jerking as if trying to get out from under the weight of the longship, and water was washing over her deck boards, cascading side to side. Thorgrim could not tell if this water had come in through the crushed sides or if the merchant ship's planks were stove below the waterline. If Brunhard's ship went down, *Sea Hammer* might well sink right on top of her.

His eyes traced along the deck. There were men lining both sides of the ship; those he had seen seated at rowing benches, larboard and starboard, and others lying in a tangle on the deck and thrashing their way upright again. The rowers were hairy and unkempt men with torn and filthy clothing. Thorgrim could not understand why they just sat there, why they didn't rush to get away from the vessel threatening to crush them all. Then he saw the chains.

Slaves! he thought. *Brunhard's a slaver!* It had never occurred to him that Brunhard's cargo was human beings, that the wealth Thorgrim hoped to plunder from the Frisian merchant consisted of Irish slaves. He smiled, despite himself.

All this trouble... he thought. *All this trouble...and now my ship will sink under me... all for slaves.* Thorgrim had no interest in slaves. He had no interest in trying to keep a cargo of miserable Irishmen alive all the way to the slave markets across the seas. He couldn't even manage to get himself and his men clear of the Irish shore.

The gods do have their fun with me... he thought.

His eyes moved to the bow of Brunhard's ship. The men there were not slaves. They were the ship's crew, and they were most certainly getting clear of the Northmen and the ship that was twisting and grinding on top of them.

Which one of you is Brunhard? Thorgrim wondered, and then it occurred to him that Brunhard might well have been crushed under *Sea Hammer's* keel, and that thought brought with it a wave of disappointment.

He studied the Frisians at the bow of the merchant ship. They stood huddled together, save for one man who stood apart from them with a posture that was part arrogance, part defiance. He was not as tall as some of the others, but he was broad, powerful looking, with a thick beard and a grand head of hair. His tunic was a deep green color, finer than the clothes that any of the other men huddled there were wearing.

You are Brunhard, you son of a bitch, aren't you? Thorgrim thought.

Everyone aboard the Frisian's ship seemed to be frozen in place by the shock of what had happened, the very real possibility that they would all be drowned in the next moment. All but one. Thorgrim could see someone hurrying aft, moving with purpose, threading their way past the rowers and the benches to where *Sea Hammer* lay across the sheer strake. His eyes moved to that person and he saw it was a woman. And she in turn stopped and looked up at him, and for an instant their eyes met.

She was ten feet below him and fifteen feet away. There was a look of surprise on her face and Thorgrim, too, felt an odd sort of wonder in his gut, and he thought, *Haven't we met before?*

Conandil watched, mouth open, eyes wide, hand still gripping that of the man who had pulled her inboard, as the longship's bow dropped onto the slave ship's afterdeck.

She saw fleeting images: the dripping planks of the ship overhead, the look of terror in the helmsman's face as he stood, struck to immobility by fear, at the tiller. The same with the two sailors beside him. Brunhard, with presence of mind enough to move, flinging himself forward and out from under the coming blow.

Then the longship and the slaver had come together, the one rising, the one falling, and the impact had sent Conandil flying across the deck. She felt a shock of pain as her arm and shoulder struck the planking, felt at least one man falling on top of her, felt the chains that held the rowers to the benches whipping her in the tangle of fallen people.

There was a scream, cut short. *The man steering*, Conandil thought. There were shouts of surprise and terror, and the shouts were not Frisian alone. She could hear the Norsemen shouting as well, and though she could not make out the words, she recognized the sound of panic and fear.

She opened her eyes. Her head was resting on the deck and she could see the arm and back of the man who had fallen across her. She could see the underside of the rowers' benches and the far side of the ship. She could see the bare feet and tattered leggings of the sailors as they ran to the bow, as far from the threat of being crushed by the longship or skewered by the Northmen as they could get.

She moved her arm to make certain it would still function. She felt a wave of pain, but she could move it nonetheless, and it was her left arm, not her right. The man lying across her was struggling to get free, but he was chained and she was not so she struggled out from under him, put her right hand on one of the benches and pushed herself to her feet.

The longship had crushed the sides of Brunhard's ship and now it was resting on the deck, sitting in a wide and spreading pool of blood. It looked like the ship itself was bleeding, but she knew it was the men who had been standing there, and who were now pulp as the longship continued to grind.

That was not what I expected to happen, Conandil thought.

The ships dropped down between the waves, twisting against one another, the grinding, rending noise they made almost unbearable. A gush of water flooded in around where the Northman's ship had crushed the Frisian's side and ran like a small flood over the deck planks and cascaded into the open hold amidships.

Will we sink? Conandil wondered. There had to be great damage done to both vessels. Maybe they were sinking now. She looked around for something that might float, something that she could hold onto and perhaps drift back to the shore.

Her eyes fell on the chains. The men, still bound one to the other, were struggling to untangle themselves, to get upright again. Each one had an iron collar around his neck that closed with a hasp. The chains, secured to the deck near the bow and stern, were run through each hasp, preventing them from being opened. If the ship went down, these men, these Irishmen, most of whom had been taken with her, most of whom she knew, would go with it.

Conandil looked toward the slave ship's bow, but no one seemed to be paying her any attention. Their eyes were on the Northmen, the warriors on the deck of the ship that rested on theirs, and on the ship itself, and Conandil guessed they, too, were wondering if they would be going down in the next few moments. But that did not mean they would stand idle while she undid the end of the chains and set the slaves free.

But the other ends of the chains were aft, feet from where the longship was grinding into the merchantman's deck, and no one seemed very eager to be there.

The knife with which she had slashed the rope was lying on the deck at her feet and she snatched it up and stuck it through the thin leather belt she wore around her waist. She pushed her way through the struggling men to the center of the ship, where it was clearer, and stumbled aft to where she knew the chains were made fast. The two ships shifted in the rising seas and she looked up to see if the longship was going to roll over on her and crush her as it had the men on the stern.

There was a man at the longship's bow, one of the Northmen, looking down at her. Well-proportioned, not tall but not short, with dark hair tied back and a beard that was also dark, but softened with visible gray. Their eyes met and once again Conandil was brought up short by the shock of what she was seeing.

Thorgrim Night Wolf? She had been a captive of another Northman, a man named Grimarr, kept alive because she alone knew where their stolen hoard of treasure was hidden. Thorgrim had joined with Grimarr, but he was not an animal like Grimarr was, not the beast so many of those Northmen were. In the end she had escaped by seducing Thorgrim's son, Harald, and running off while he slept.

Could he really be here, now? she wondered. Yes, of course he could. But he was not her concern, not her chief concern.

She pulled her eyes from his and ran aft, nearly to where the longship was resting on Brunhard's deck. The chains that held the two lines of men, larboard and starboard, were fixed to an iron ring in the deck, secured by a bent iron rod. Conandil dropped to her knees and grabbed the rod and twisted it one way, then the other, trying to work it loose. A wave lifted the ships and dropped them again and the longship twisted and groaned and Conandil looked up in terror, but it did not seem likely to come down on her.

Water burst through the smashed section of the slave ship's side and washed over her where she knelt, soaking her up to mid-thigh, but she kept her hands on the iron bar, kept working it back and forth. The ship rolled again and she felt the bar come loose. She pulled and it slid free and the chains fell free of the ring.

Conandil leapt to her feet, chains in hand. She ran to the nearest man and she could see the relief on his face as she drew the chain through the hasp on the neck ring. The last link came clear and the ring fell open and the man pulled it off and flung it away, leaping to his feet and helping Conandil get the next man free.

They moved toward the bow as quick as they could, setting each man free in turn, the captives themselves clapping onto the chain and pulling it through the hasps. At the bow, Brunhard and the sailors were fishing the spears and bows and arrows out from the places under the deck they were stored, readying themselves for the rush of now-free men they feared would come for them.

It was a fear well justified. The last of the captives pulled his neck ring off and then someone shouted, "Get them! Get those whore Frisians!" It was a man named Colgan, one of Bressal mac Muirchertach's house guard, and his words were met with a cheer and a rush aft, all thoughts of imminent drowning lost in the frenzy of revenge.

But the Frisians and Brunhard would not sell their lives cheap. Spears leveled, bowstrings nocked with arrows, they crammed back into the tight V at the far end of the ship and braced for the rush. They would lose in the end, but they would make a lot of bloody corpses before they did.

"Wait! Wait!" Conandil shouted. "Colgan, wait! Wait, you men who serve Broccáin mac Bressal!" She felt a stab of anguish as her husband's name came off her lips, a flash of anger that he had been taken from her. He could have commanded these men. His word would have been law. To them and to her. She wanted it that way again.

But that name, an invocation of home, the man those men-at-arms had served, the man who had become rí túaithe after the death of his father, had the effect Conandil had hoped for. The Irishmen stopped, well short of the reach of the Frisian spears. They stopped and some kept their eyes on the hated slavers forward, and the others looked to Conandil.

"Listen," Conandil said, loud enough to be heard by all the Irishmen. "Brunhard has done a lot of hurt to the Northmen, and they'll want their revenge. And we want them to set us free, not sell us as slaves like Brunhard would do. Maybe if we keep Brunhard as a hostage they'll make a bargain with us."

It was not very likely, and she knew it. Mostly she did not want her people to rush into the tips of the spears, did not want them slaughtered now, after they had lived through so much. And maybe if they had Brunhard, and threatened to cut his throat before the Northmen could, then Thorgrim Night Wolf might be willing to strike a deal.

There was silence fore and aft. No one moved, except to catch themselves from tripping as the ship lifted and fell below them. The wind was louder now, blowing Conandil's hair sideways, whipping her cheeks. The longship was grinding into the stern of Brunhard's ship with the ugly sound of pending disaster.

And then Colgan took a step back, and then another, and the men beside him did the same.

"Very well, Conandil," Colgan said. "Maybe you're right. And for the name of Broccáin mac Bressal we'll heed your words." All together they stepped back, opening up the space between themselves and the sailors at the bow. Two bands of angry and frightened men, their eyes fixed on one another, each waiting to see what the other would do next, from where the next threat would come.

And then one of the Frisian sailors shouted, the words shrill and filled with surprise and fear piled on fear. He shouted, "Look! Look!"

He pointed over the starboard side of the ship, and everyone looked in that direction.

One hundred feet away, the larger of Brunhard's two other ships lay sideways to the seas, completely out of control. The sail was edge-on to the wind and flogging like mad. The deck was a mass of struggling men, fists and arms and weapons rising and falling. The slaves, apparently, had gotten their hands on the crew.

And now their ship was out of control and directly downwind.

From dead silence, Brunhard's ship burst into a roar of voices, dozens of men all shouting at once. The men moved as best they could on the heaving deck away from the starboard side. They grabbed hold of anything solid, looked around for some means to shield themselves. Because Brunhard's ship, and the longship crushing down on it, were both about to slam into this other vessel, and there was not one thing anyone could do to stop it.

Chapter Thirty-Three

War-oak of the helmet god,
I now wield but a bucket,
No sweet wine do I sup
Stooping at the spring.
　　　　　　Eirik the Red's Saga

Thorgrim Night Wolf was kneeling in the shallow hold forward, chisel in one hand, mallet in the other. Armod was beside him, handing him the bits of cloth.

"Another, another," Thorgrim said and Armod put a strip in his open fingers. Thorgrim did not know where the cloth was coming from—old sacks, sail material, torn up clothing—but he hoped it might keep *Sea Hammer* afloat, at least for a while.

The two ships dipped down into a valley between waves. *Sea Hammer* made the groaning, grinding noise that had already become familiar to their ears. A wide section of planking was stove in, the wood shattered around the clench nails that normally held one plank to the other. Thorgrim could see the planks by his knees flex and open. He shoved the cloth in, pounded quick with the edge of the chisel, then pulled the chisel free and the gap closed up with the motion of the ship.

I'm kidding myself... he thought. There was virtually no possibility that these pathetic strips of cloth were going to keep the ship sealed tight if they slipped free of Brunhard's ship, or if Brunhard sunk under them. But he had to do something. And maybe his *ad hoc* caulking would hold long enough for them to slip a cloth around the outside of the damage to further impede the inflow of water. Maybe.

"Another cloth!" Thorgrim called and Armod passed another strip.

It was astounding to Thorgrim that Brunhard's ship was still afloat. The Frisians were good shipbuilders, he knew, and merchant ships were often stouter built than longships, having less need to be fast and nimble. But still he was impressed. And as he worked at the seams he asked the gods to keep Brunhard afloat just a bit longer, just long enough to get *Sea Hammer* on the beach and to keep Brunhard breathing so Thorgrim could put a sword through him.

He reached up, fingers spread, mouth open to call for another strip of cloth when he was cut short by a wild cry from on deck. "There! There! Look to leeward!"

The tone was one that was not to be ignored. Thorgrim dropped his tools and leapt out of the hold, ran to the larboard bow. His eyes swept over Brunhard's ship below. The men chained to the benches seemed to have got loose and now there was some sort of stand-off forward.

"There, Thorgrim!" It was Vestar, standing on the sheer strake, one hand on the stem for balance, and pointing downwind. Godi was there as well and he stepped aside as Thorgrim came up.

Thorgrim followed Vestar's outstretched arm. The smallest of Brunhard's three ships had sailed clear of all of them. It was running off to the south, close-hauled, heeling far over and plunging through the seas. She had already put a mile or more between herself and the rest, and Thorgrim doubted she would stop until she reached Wales.

But that ship was not the problem.

The other ship, not Brunhard's, but the second largest, was no more than one hundred feet downwind and drifting out of control. She was sideways to the seas, her sail flogging and useless. Thorgrim had a glimpse of men struggling on the deck, the familiar look of a great and disorganized brawl.

"Looks like the slaves there are putting up a fight," Godi offered.

Godi was right. The slaves had somehow got their hands on the crew and they were taking their revenge. The sailors, fighting for their lives, had given up trying to sail the ship and now it had turned broadside to the rollers, right in the path of *Sea Hammer* and Brunhard's ship.

No one had seen it until that moment. A crisis turned all eyes inboard. No one would think to look out to sea with *Sea Hammer* ready to sink under them.

"Get the oars down off the gallows, pass them around." Thorgrim gave the orders sharp, loud and fast. "Two men to an oar. If Brunhard sinks when he hits then we'll likely sink as well. But we may be able to float holding the oars, float back to shore, and hope to live through the surf."

He looked beyond the second merchantman to the Irish coastline to the west and he was stunned to see how fast they had drifted down on it. When they had first begun their chase of Brunhard's fleet the land had been no more than a thin dark line on the horizon. Now it was a mile and a half under their lee, no more.

The high ground and the stands of trees were visible from *Sea Hammer*'s deck, and Thorgrim was sure he could see the white plumes of the surf as it smashed onto the long stretch of beach. As long as the ships floated they would live, but once they were in the grip of that surf they would be tumbled and pounded and smashed like Thor's hammer Mjölnir was coming down on them. If they made it that far, then they would likely be killed in the last hundred yards between them and safety.

The men around Thorgrim moved like birds lifting off from a field, running aft and shouting to the others to help get the oars down. Thorgrim watched the merchant ship in their lee and tried to think what more they could do. Cut the mast free, drift on that? Maybe take this third ship, if it was less damaged than Brunhard's or *Sea Hammer*?

Possibly...

The ships dipped low between rollers and then up again, and there was the merchantman, now fifty feet downwind, no more. The men on her deck had finally seen this new danger, the two ships locked together and coming down on them fast. Thorgrim could see panic along the deck, men running to get out of the way, as if there were any place they could run that was safer than any other.

"Stand ready!" Thorgrim shouted. He gripped the edge of the sheer strake hard. The seas lifted *Sea Hammer* and Brunhard's ship and flung them forward and then they were rising together with the other vessel, the rollers driving them together. Thorgrim had a glimpse of the men on Brunhard's ship running to the larboard side, and then they struck.

The second merchantman was nearly parallel to Brunhard's ship when they hit. The impact was sudden and profound, as if the ships had struck rock. Once again Thorgrim was thrown forward, but this time he fetched up against *Sea Hammer*'s side and managed to stay on his feet.

Not so the men below him, on Brunhard's ship, who were mostly thrown to the deck and over the rowing benches as the ships struck, the force of the impact greater than they had expected. Wood ground on wood, strakes and rigging gave way as the ships came together. Thorgrim felt the fabric of *Sea Hammer* quiver under his feet. He felt the vessel shift, drive forward, scrape and tear farther onto the deck of Brunhard's ship until her bow overhung the far side of that ship and the deck of the second merchantman as well.

He heard a groan, like someone in great pain, the sharp crack of a line parting under pressure, the shouts of his men behind him. He spun around in time to see the last of the shrouds on *Sea Hammer*'s starboard side part under the shock of the sudden impact. Overhead the mast began to lean toward him, coming down like a tree cut most of the way through, its fall gathering momentum.

Thorgrim pushed himself off the sheer strake and took three quick strides aft, but it was clear he could not run faster than the mast and yard were falling. He stepped up on a sea chest and leapt off it, leapt aft as if diving into the sea. He came down hard on the deck, turning to hit the planks with his shoulder, rolling and letting the momentum dissipate as his body turned over, then over again.

He rolled to an upright position, coming up on one knee. He felt something hit the back of his head and he ducked and saw the larboard mainsheet come flying past. He watched in horror and amazement as the mast tilted forward, the heel tearing up the mast step and the deck around it as it came down.

The mast was pine, forty-five feet tall and more than a foot across at the base. It fell with greater and greater speed toward the deck, then dropped with full force right across the section of bow where Thorgrim had been standing, smashing the sheer strake and the three strakes under it like they were made of dried reeds.

The yard, which had been lowered when they first hit Brunhard, did less damage but it still managed to shatter the sheer strake to larboard and starboard as it came down athwartships. The sound of wood grinding on wood was louder now, doubled with the three ships locked together and spinning in the seas.

Then the mast came to rest and there was a strange quiet, as if all the men on the three ships were waiting to see what would happen next, holding their breath for fear of disturbing the careful equilibrium that had settled over the drifting wrecks. But that did not last long.

A shout from Brunhard's ship, some harsh words in the harsh Frisian tongue. Thorgrim sprang to his feet and ran to the larboard side and looked down at the ships below him.

Someone aboard Brunhard's ship—probably Brunhard himself—had decided to use the moment's stunned confusion to take command of the situation. Brunhard's sailors who had been huddled toward the bow of the ship were charging aft, spears leveled, axes held over heads. They were screaming, and Thorgrim guessed the screams were from terror and their desire to terrorize the men they were attacking.

But the Irish slaves did not seem very terrorized, and that surprised Thorgrim. It took a trained and a disciplined man to stand fast in the face of an attack such as that, the sailors charging aft, leaping over the rowing benches, brandishing weapons when the slaves had none. He would have expected a panicked flight, but instead the slaves braced for the onslaught, prepared as best they could, grabbed up buckets and shattered bits of wood, anything with which they could defend themselves.

The two hoards, the sailors and the slaves, came together like opposing tides, slamming into one another. Thorgrim saw one of the slaves go down in a plume of blood. But he saw another deflect the oncoming point of a spear, knock it aside, grab the shaft and pull it from the sailor's hands, spin the weapon around and drive it into the gut of the man who had held it seconds before.

Well done... Thorgrim thought. These slaves were not ploughmen and herdsmen who had been swept up in some raid, he could see that, but he did not have time to give it any further thought. He ran forward to where the mast had fallen across *Sea Hammer*'s rail. The blow had reduced the strakes to kindling, right down to the deck. Even if the planks that Thorgrim had caulked with cloth managed to hold, *Sea Hammer* would ship so much water through this gap in her sides that she would still most likely sink.

The three ships, locked together like some massive raft, were spinning as they drifted, turning in the millrace of the mounting seas. Thorgrim half turned until he could see the shoreline, a mile off, no more, the breakers on the beach clearly visible. The wind, blowing hard and building, had kicked up a big surf, the seas breaking a hundred yards or more from the shingle. That was where they would die, in the surf, if the ships did not sink under them in the next few minutes.

Godi was beside him, and Vestar. "This is bad," Godi said.

Thorgrim took his eyes from the shore and looked down into the hold where he had been working just moments before. The gray light of the late afternoon was illuminating the space. Thorgrim could see the planks opening and closing as the ships ground together, the bits of cloth he had pounded in there spitting out. The impact with the second ship had driven *Sea Hammer* further onto Brunhard's ship and done more damage to the hull.

"It's bad," Thorgrim agreed. *Sea Hammer* was done for, and that meant they needed another way off, another way to shore. He looked back at Brunhard's ship. The fighting had spread over most of the forward end. It was not like shield wall on shield wall, or two armies taking the field. It was more like a brawl in a mead hall, a wild melee of dozens of men flailing at one another.

And Brunhard's ship, Thorgrim could see, was in even worse condition than the men were. Water surged back and forth over the decks as it rolled and groaned under *Sea Hammer*'s weight. The sides were smashed in and the deck under the longship's bow likely buckled. Once again Thorgrim was amazed that the ship was still floating at all, and he could not imagine it would for long.

But the second merchant ship, the one that had slammed hard against Brunhard's side and was still pinned there, was another matter. The upper strakes were caved in where she hit, and one of the shrouds was swinging free, but the vessel did not seem to have suffered much beyond that. It was still seaworthy, it seemed, or seaworthy enough to get Thorgrim and his men to safety.

"That ship, the one we hit," Thorgrim said, pointing. "We're going to take that and sail clear. *Sea Hammer* and Brunhard's ship are going up on the beach. There's nothing we can do to stop that. We'll see if there's anything left of them after they do."

Godi nodded. Thorgrim turned to his men, gathered aft. They seemed frozen in place, like rabbits unsure if they should remain still or bolt. They did not know what would happen next. And neither did Thorgrim. But Thorgrim, at least, had the presence of mind to try and make happen what he wanted to happen.

"Come on, you men!" he shouted. "We're going to take that second ship, the one that still swims! See you have your weapons in hand!"

He could see relief wash over them. There was nothing that frightened men needed more than direction and a job at hand, the chance to actively attempt to save themselves rather than simply wait for death to come. And not death in battle, which they would welcome. Death by drowning—cold, dark, prolonged and pathetic—the death they dreaded most.

With a nod toward Godi he took the two steps to where *Sea Hammer*'s mast lay across her shattered side. He stepped through the gap the spar had left in its wake and looked down on the deck below. It was a five-foot drop to Brunhard's ship, and a clear place amidships between the rower's benches. Thorgrim pushed off and jumped.

He hit the deck with his soft leather shoes and dropped to his knees as he did. The ships rolled and a flood of water came from the gap that *Sea Hammer* had opened up and drenched Thorgrim to mid-thigh. He stood quickly and darted forward, making room for the next of his men.

The slaves and the sailors were still at it, still fighting, struggling for possession of the few weapons aboard. There were dead men and wounded men strewn over the rowing benches and jammed in the corners of the ship, and water rushing side to side with each heavy, sick lurch of the vessel.

The one in the green tunic, the stout man with the big beard, the one Thorgrim had guessed was Brunhard, was all the way forward, an ax in hand, conspicuously keeping clear of the fight.

Brunhard... Here was the man who had burned *Sea Hammer*'s sail, nearly wrecked the ship once. Succeeded the second time. Had eluded Thorgrim and humiliated him and now would likely be the death of him and his men.

I'll kill you, you whore's son, Thorgrim thought and he was suddenly overwhelmed by the urge to race forward and drive his sword through the man. It was pointless, an indulgence, but he would be dead soon anyway. Why not allow himself that?

"Thorgrim!" It was Godi at his side. "The ship is drifting away, we should go!"

Thorgrim pulled his eyes from Brunhard. The three ships were still turning as the wind and seas drove them toward the Irish coast. *Sea Hammer* and Brunhard's ship were locked in a death grip, but the third ship was just jammed against Brunhard's side, and nothing was holding it but the pressure of the seas. And now, as the ships swung around, the gap between Brunhard's ship and the other merchantman was opening up.

"Come, you men!" Thorgrim shouted, and headed across the shattered deck of Brunhard's ship, pushing the struggling men out of the way.

One of Brunhard's sailors, his face streaked in blood, mouth and eyes open wide came charging out of the press, a spear lowered and leveled at Thorgrim's gut. Thorgrim's sword was still in its scabbard; he had not intended to remain long enough on Brunhard's ship to need it, but now he did and it was too late to draw it.

He was still running along the deck when he saw a shattered section of wood lying at his feet. He snatched it up, never breaking stride, and realized it was part of *Sea Hammer*'s sheer strake. He swung it down at the iron spear point, catching the shaft of the weapon a foot back from the tip and knocking it clear, spinning the surprised man holding it half around.

Thorgrim, still moving, brought the broken strake backhand over his shoulder and swung it forward, catching the man on the side of the head and tossing him aside. Another step. He could see the gap between the ships was wider now, the second ship drifting away. Three feet between the ships, space enough that Thorgrim was not entirely sure he could clear it.

Then suddenly he was falling, the deck under his feet dropping away as Brunhard's ship rolled to one side, listing despite the weight of *Sea Hammer* pressing down on it. The motion of the sea and the great volumes of water that rolled around below were driving the merchantman down at last. Thorgrim staggered and a surge of water rushed in over the fractured stern, a breaking wave surging down the length of the deck.

Thorgrim was already struggling to regain his feet when the force of the water bowled him over, dropped him to the deck again and the cold seas flooded over him, pushing him like eager hands. He had an image of the men behind him falling as well, massive Godi coming down on top of one of the rowing benches, Bjorn and Ulf tumbling to either side of him.

He spit out a mouthful of water, stood as the boarding sea drained away. Once again the deck was a tangle of men, some dead, some wounded, some knocked down by the seas, some still fighting. And the second merchant ship, the ship on which Thorgrim planned to carry his men to safety, had drifted clear away. Twenty feet of water separated it from the side of Brunhard's ship.

"Oh, you whore's son!" Thorgrim shouted. He looked around for a rope, a grappling hook, anything to snag the ship and pull it back. But there was nothing. Just chaos and struggle on Brunhard's deck.

The ship gave another sluggish roll under their feet and groaned, a dull and weary groan, and Thorgrim knew its time was nearly up. *Sea Hammer* would not swim long once Brunhard's ship sank away, but it was still better than the dying merchantman. Better to go down on the ship he loved than this despised Frisian washtub.

"Back to *Sea Hammer!*" he shouted. "There's nothing here, we're done!" Twenty-five feet now between the second merchant ship and Brunhard's, and the space was opening wider, any hope of boarding that ship entirely gone.

Thorgrim could hear his men climbing back aboard *Sea Hammer* but he did not take his eyes from the deck of Brunhard's ship. The fighting was all but over. Brunhard's sailors had retreated back to the ship's bow, spears held level to fend off any further attack. The slaves were clustered amidships, also holding what weapons they had managed to snatch up. Both groups of men were considerably diminished. The dead and wounded lay on every quarter, and the water rushing over the deck planks was tinted red.

Then he saw the girl, the one he had noticed earlier, the one who had set the slaves free. She was looking directly at him. Their eyes met once again and suddenly Thorgrim knew who she was.

The thrall! he thought. *Grimarr's thrall!* He could not recall her name, but Harald would remember. He had saved her from Grimarr and she had escaped from them on the beach. He remembered now.

Thorgrim took a step back, a quick look over his shoulder. Godi was pulling himself up onto *Sea Hammer* and that meant he, Thorgrim, was the last. He turned, reached up, grabbed hold of the splintered strakes where the mast had done its damage. With a grunt he hoisted himself up and through the rent in the ship's side. Hands grabbed his tunic and, to his silent irritation, pulled him the rest of the way.

I'm not a doddering old cripple yet, he thought, but he kept the complaint to himself. He stood. The men of *Sea Hammer* were clustered near the bow, some looking at Brunhard's ship twisting and sinking below them, some looking at the second merchant ship drifting beyond reach, some at the breakers pounding on the beach now less than half a mile under their lee.

This will be a close thing, Thorgrim thought. They had little time before they were in the surf, and many things could change by then. They were broadside to the waves now, which was not good at all. It meant *Sea Hammer* would be rolled as her keel hit the sand and all her men would be dumped into the sea. But she might turn again, swing bow-to. Brunhard's ship might hold them up. Or it might sink under them. *Sea Hammer* might end up on the bottom before she ever reached the shore.

He thought about the oars again, about trying to float in on them and dismissed the idea. He could see the surf better now and he realized how big it was. It would kill them all. Better to try to ride the sinking ship in.

"We should get an anchor out over the stern," he said, turning to Godi, and then his eyes moved to the stern and to the open ocean behind and, despite himself, he gasped in surprise.

There was a sail there, and not far off. Not like any sail he had ever seen. One half of it was striped red and white, the other a weathered gray. It was set and drawing, bellying out in the gale-force wind, seemingly on the verge of blowing apart. The ship below it was driving through the seas, plunging into the waves, bucking up like a horse wild with fear, twisting and rolling as it made its heedless and reckless way toward the drifting vessels.

And Thorgrim knew perfectly well what ship it was. *Blood Hawk*.

Chapter Thirty-Four

A thirteenth I know: if the new-born son
of a warrior I sprinkle with water,
that youth will not fail when he fares to war,
never slain shall he bow before sword.

The Song of Spells

The sail driving *Blood Hawk*—two sails, really, hastily stitched together—was one of the ugliest, most ungainly things Harald Broadarm had ever seen. And now, ironically, his father's life and the lives of all the men aboard *Sea Hammer* depended on that sail.

The sail was filled and straining at the sheets. Too much sail for the strong and building wind blowing from the east. Under any other circumstances Harald would have reefed the sail by now, or more likely taken it in entirely and run under bare poles. In any other circumstances he would not be charging down on a lee shore, driving his ship as hard as he could into the most dangerous of circumstances.

"What do you see?" he called up to Starri Deathless, who was getting a wild ride indeed at the top of the mast. The seas were rolling in, high and fast, but *Blood Hawk* was driving along even faster, racing up the backs of rollers, launching her bow out over the trough, then plunging down with a great welter of spray and an impact that made the whole ship shudder.

When that happened the taut sail would collapse and hang limp, just for an instant. And then the bow would rise and the wind would fill the sail again with a powerful jerk. The sheets would snap tight and the mast and shrouds would groan and Harald would grit his teeth and wait for the entire sail to blow apart. Which it had not done yet. But he knew it could not take that sort of abuse for long.

"*Sea Hammer*'s still there, and the other ship!" Starri called down. The motion at the masthead was so extreme that Starri had to pause in his reports and wait for a few seconds of calm to shout down to deck, something Harald could not recall his ever having to do before. "I can see a third ship!"

Starri stopped speaking as *Blood Hawk* surfed down a wave and slammed her bow into the next wave ahead, then rose again, shaking off the tons of water. "I thought they were fighting, but maybe they've struck one another!" Starri shouted next.

Hmmm, Harald thought. He squatted down on his heels so he could look forward, under the edge of the billowing sail. He could see the ships in the distance. Not as well as Starri could, but he could see them. They had no sails set, and it seemed as if they had been locked together at least since Starri had first spotted them. Harald had assumed they were fighting, that Thorgrim had managed to run Brunhard down and come alongside the Frisian, board the ship and slaughter the men aboard. But now he was not sure.

Harald straightened and turned to Louis the Frank who was standing next to him. Broccáin was there as well, but somehow the Irishman seemed more out of his depth in that instance than did the Frankish man-at-arms.

At first Harald had kept Louis in chains, but Broccáin had insisted that was not necessary, and that Louis, who was an experienced warrior and who knew Brunhard better than any of them, might be of help. So Harald had relented and set the man free. For the time being.

"What do you think?" he asked, speaking in Irish, a tongue foreign to both of them but their only common language.

Louis shrugged. "I would have thought they were fighting, but I cannot think it would take Thorgrim so very long to kill Brunhard and his men. There's not so many of them, and they are not warriors."

Harald nodded. "Maybe," he said. "I just can't tell what they're doing."

"It doesn't matter what they're doing," Louis said.

"What do you mean? Why doesn't it matter?" Harald was quite ready to take offense at this, quite ready to put Louis back in chains.

"I mean, that is your father's ship. I know nothing of ships, but I heard you say it's in danger of going ashore, which would be bad. That I can understand. So you must go help them, as fast as you can, which you seem to be doing. It doesn't matter what Thorgrim's up to. It does not change what you must do. You must get to him no matter what."

Harald nodded again. That made sense. Louis was right. It really didn't matter. Regardless of what was happening with *Sea Hammer*, he would continue to drive *Blood Hawk* toward her, just as fast as he could.

There was something about Louis that Harald liked, despite himself. He had not really noticed it before, when Louis had been their prisoner. But the man had a calm and professional air about him, even though he was fairly young. He had the quality of a man who had seen enough fighting and danger that it no longer ruffled him, of one whose mind remained calm and clear regardless of what was going on around him.

Like Thorgrim. Like the way he himself hoped to be one day.

"Broadarm!" Starri shouted. "*Sea Hammer*'s dismasted! The mast has fallen over!"

Harald felt his stomach twist. He thought he might be sick. His greatest fear now was that he had come too late, that his father and the rest would drown in the surf before he could reach them, and he would spend the rest of his life thinking about the moments wasted stitching the sails together, giving the Norse dead as proper a sea-burial as he could.

"Have they struck bottom, do you think?" Harald shouted. That would be the most obvious reason for the mast to fall. If the ship had come to a sudden, jarring stop, her keel striking the bottom as the water grew shallow, the whipping motion could well bring the rig down. Harald had seen it before.

"No!" Starri called. "They're still some ways from the shore! Maybe they hit that other ship!"

It doesn't matter, Harald thought, unconsciously echoing Louis's words. "Starri, you can come down now!" he called aloft.

There was a pause, and then Starri called, "Very well!" with a decidedly disappointed tone that surprised Harald. He had thought he was doing Starri a favor, allowing him to leave the wildly swinging masthead, but the berserker apparently did not see it that way. Harald thought about changing his mind, letting the man stay, but he feared that would make him look indecisive, so he kept his mouth shut.

Overhead, Starri reached out and grabbed onto a shroud. He swung himself over just as *Blood Hawk*'s bow slammed into a wave that made the ship shudder and Starri, who was trying to wrap his legs around the shroud, took a wild swing fore and aft. It occurred to Harald that Starri could actually fall. He had never really thought about it before, just as he had never considered the possibility that Starri could be gravely wounded in battle until he was. There was no law set by the gods that said Starri could not fall from the rigging and die.

But he didn't. He let his body swing back and forth once, twice, and then he caught the shroud with his legs and came sliding down, going quickly hand over hand. He dropped to the deck and with a few quick steps joined Harald and Louis and Broccáin on the afterdeck.

"So, Broadarm, what is your plan?" he asked. There was a smile on his face, his previous annoyance apparently forgotten. It seemed that here on deck, with the ship sailing just on the edge of control, the urgency of their task, the danger of rushing down on a lee shore, there was exhilaration enough even for Starri Deathless.

"We get to *Sea Hammer* as fast as we can, see what's going on, see what we can do to help," Harald said. "Keep *Blood Hawk* out of the surf if we're able."

Starri nodded vigorously. "That's a good plan, Broadarm," he said. "A very good plan."

They were half a mile away now, but the seas had grown so big that they still obscured *Sea Hammer* and the others when they rose up around them. Harald could see the tiny shapes of men scrambling around, but he could not tell what they were about. He could see the ships turning as they drifted toward the shore. The third ship, the one Starri had reported from aloft, was visible now.

That's one of Brunhard's ships, Harald thought. Not the biggest one. *Sea Hammer* seemed to be entangled with the biggest one. That was the second largest, and like the other two it seemed to be drifting out of control.

What by the gods could have happened? Harald wondered, but he kept the question to himself.

"By the gods!" Starri shouted. "They're like drifting wrecks! What could have happened?"

Harald shook his head to indicate that he did not know. Louis and Broccáin said nothing. They did not speak Starri's tongue.

Overhead the ugly lash-up of a sail collapsed again as the ship rode down the front of a wave, quivered as the bow struck, then snapped full as the bow came up again and the wind filled the oiled wool cloth. Harald would have loved this, and Hel take the danger, if he had not been so worried about his father, and so concerned that the sail would blow out before they reached him.

But they did not have long to go. *Sea Hammer* and the merchant ships were drifting fast toward the beach and the killing breakers, but *Blood Hawk* was moving faster still, living up to her namesake, swooping over the seas, driving relentlessly toward its prey.

Then Harald realized that in his concern for the present moment he had not considered what he would do once he reached *Sea Hammer*, how he could save his father and the others.

He looked out to the east. The wind had built to a near gale, the gray seas cresting white and building in height. And worse, it was blowing directly on-shore. They would have to get a line to *Sea Hammer* and tow her away from the breakers, but they would never do that under sail. If they tried to sail off that lee shore with *Sea Hammer* in tow, both ships would be driven onto the beach.

Oars, then, Harald thought. They would have to sail down to *Sea Hammer*, pass a line, get the sail in and pull her to safety with the oars. He looked at *Sea Hammer*, crippled-looking with her mast lying at an angle across her deck. *Why aren't you rowing, Father?* he wondered. *Why haven't you tried to row free of the surf?*

He stepped up to the edge of the afterdeck. "Listen here, you men!" he shouted and all the men of *Blood Hawk* who had been crowding along the starboard side, which gave them the best view of the drifting ships, now turned and looked aft.

"We're going to grapple *Sea Hammer* and tow her clear of the surf!" Harald continued, trying to sound as commanding and self-assured as he could. "We can't sail clear of the coast in this wind, we'll have to row, and it'll be a hard pull. We'll sail right down on *Sea Hammer*, get the sail down and oars out right together. We'll send a line over and row clear. Understood?"

Heads nodded all along the ship's side.

"Good. Get the oars down now, and get them ready to run right out the oarports on my word!"

The men moved to do as instructed and Harald watched them and considered his next problem. There was only one man aboard whom he trusted to throw the grappling hook from *Blood Hawk*'s bow to *Sea Hammer*'s stern, and that was himself. And there was only one man he trusted to take the tiller for so tricky a maneuver, and that was also himself. But he could not do both.

"Gudrid!" he shouted and Gudrid left off pulling an oar from the gallows and stumbled back to the aft deck, any movement tricky and awkward with the ship pitching and rolling as it was.

"Can you throw a grapple far and true?" Harald asked. He did not know Gudrid well, but he had been impressed with what he had seen so far, and Gudrid was well made and powerful-looking.

"As well as any man, I reckon," Gudrid said, a good answer as far as Harald was concerned.

"Very well. Get the grappling hook and the best length of line aboard. I'll bring the ship in as close to *Sea Hammer* as I dare. You take your place here," he said, pointing to a spot just forward of the afterdeck. When I tell you to throw, you throw, because that's as near as I'll be able to get. Then you make the line off to the cleat there and we'll tow *Sea Hammer* clear."

Gudrid nodded and there was nothing in his expression that gave Harald pause. "I'll do as you say," he said, gave a bit of a smile, then turned and headed forward.

A quarter mile now separated *Blood Hawk* from the others. Harald relieved the man at the tiller, took the heavy oak bar in his own hands. He wanted to get the feel for the ship's motion, to get a sense for how she would respond in that wind and sea. He had, after all, less than two days' experience aboard her.

"You know, Broadarm," Starri said. He was standing behind Harald, standing on the edge of the sheer strake and gripping the tall sternpost. In circumstances such as this Starri could not bear to remain on deck.

"What, Starri?" Harald said, giving the tiller a twist to ease the ship up the back of the next wave.

"I think *Sea Hammer* is actually on top of Brunhard's ship!"

"On top of Brunhard's ship?"

"Yes! It looks to me as if her bow is resting right on Brunhard's stern. Now how by the gods did they manage that? Ha! Thorgrim Night Wolf never fails to surprise!"

On top of Brunhard's ship...Harald thought. *What has happened here?* But Louis was right. It did not matter. All that mattered was keeping *Sea Hammer* out of the surf.

And that would be a close thing, Harald could see. The ships were drifting fast. They were as close to the outer edge of the breakers as *Blood Hawk* was to them. And that meant that by the time *Blood Hawk* arrived, she, too, would be perilously close to shore. He looked at his men, standing along the centerline of the ship, the tips of their oar blades resting in the row ports, ready to run out.

I hope you bastards know how to pull, and pull hard, he thought.

Gudrid came aft, a coil of rope in his hands, a grappling hook tied to one end. He laid the line carefully on the deck and started looping a smaller coil over his hand. There was a thoughtful and competent quality to what he was doing and it gave Harald confidence, a thing he realized he was greatly lacking at the moment.

"Look, that other ship's drifted clear!" Starri cried and Harald shifted his eyes from Gudrid to the ships just past the bow. He could see them clearly now, and it was only when they and *Blood Hawk* were both between waves that they were blocked from view.

The ships had turned a half circle. Whereas before Harald had been looking at *Sea Hammer*'s starboard quarter, now he was looking at her larboard side. And he could see that Starri was right. *Sea Hammer*'s bow was actually resting on Brunhard's stern.

That's not going to make things any easier, Harald thought. And then he saw the third ship, Brunhard's other ship. It must have been caught up in that whole mess, but now that the two ships had turned in the seas it had drifted free. But it was still out of control and being blown toward the coast like the other two. And now it, too, would be in *Blood Hawk*'s way.

"Get ready!" Harald shouted. "When I give the word, let the yard come down on a run and haul the sail up! Just let it come down athwartships!"

The men positioned at the various lines waved their arms to indicate they understood.

"Gudrid! Ready?" Harald shouted and Gudrid, a couple yards away, nodded his head.

One hundred yards to *Sea Hammer* and Harald could see men on her deck and men on the merchantman's deck, but he could not tell what any of them were doing. Brunhard's ship was well down by the stern, but it was not clear if *Sea Hammer* was pushing it down or if it was sinking from the damage it had sustained. No matter. He didn't care about Brunhard's ship.

But that thought led to another. *I wonder if Sea Hammer is damaged as well, where she rests on Brunhard's ship? Maybe she'll sink if I pull her free...*

Fifty yards and Harald could see that the man he thought was Thorgrim was indeed Thorgrim. He was standing at the stern, gripping the sheer strake with one hand, the sternpost with the other, and watching them come on. They could have called to one another if not for the wind that was blotting out any sound from beyond *Blood Hawk*'s deck.

They halved that distance and Harald could see that his father was indeed yelling something, but the words were whipped away to leeward. He could see Godi like some giant carving standing at Thorgrim's side.

"Stand ready, Gudrid, I'm about to turn!" Harald called, and Gudrid nodded again, but his eyes were fixed on his target, his body poised to throw, and he did not speak or move beyond that.

Blood Hawk hurdled down on *Sea Hammer*, rising on the waves, pounding down, and every bit of Harald wanted to turn the ship now, but he gauged the distance and he waited. Gudrid would have one chance only, he could not miss, and Harald had to get *Blood Hawk* close enough that he wouldn't. If he did miss, if he had to haul in the line and throw again, they would all be in the surf before he was half done.

And then the moment was right. Harald could feel it in every fiber. "Sail, down!" he shouted and the men at the halyard cast the line off the cleat and let the yard fall fast in a controlled plummet, while others hauled the buntlines to draw the sail up the yard.

"Oars!" Harald called next and the men at the oars, tensed and ready, ran the long looms out of the oarports and threw themselves onto the sea chests as Hall called the rhythm.

"Now, Gudrid! Now!" Harald shouted. The calm had deserted him in the frenzy of the moment. Gudrid drew his arm back and whipped the grappling hook around in a sideways throw. The dark iron hook made a lovely, clean arc through the air, sailing over the thirty-foot gap between the ships and right over *Sea Hammer*'s sheer strake. Some of *Sea Hammer*'s men leapt clear of the flying metal as others snatched the hook up.

"Pull!" Hall shouted and Harald felt the blades of the oars bite, felt the ship respond as he pushed the tiller over, turning *Blood Hawk*'s bow into the wind and seas.

Now he could hear Thorgrim's voice, just audible despite his being not more than twenty yards away. Harald swiveled around to see him.

"Harald!" he shouted. "I'm going to cut you loose! You can't help us!"

"No!" Harald shouted back. "We'll tow you offshore!"

Thorgrim shook his head, the motion exaggerated so Harald could not miss it. "We're stove in! We'll sink if we come off Brunhard's ship!"

The distance between the vessels was opening up. Gudrid had looped the line over *Blood Hawk*'s cleat and was slowly paying it out, but taking up the tension as well. He knew better than to let the strain come on the line suddenly and risk its parting.

"Don't cast off the line!" Harald shouted. He did not know what to do, but he only knew that he could not stand letting *Sea Hammer* drift free, not after all this. Then he had a thought.

"We'll ease you through the surf!" he shouted. "You'll go sideways if we don't! We'll pull you straight!" Already the distance between the ships was so great that Harald was not sure his father had heard, but he knew full well the dilemma with which Thorgrim was wrestling. He did not want to put Harald and *Blood Hawk* in danger. But he also did not want to toss away a chance to save the lives of the men aboard *Sea Hammer*. Not a choice that any man would want to make, so Harald decided he would make it for him.

"Pull!" Hall shouted again and again the men leaned back against the oars, heaving the blades through the sea, pushing the ship away from the shore and right into the wind and waves. Rowing against that would have been hard even without the two ships hanging on the tow line. With them there, Harald was not sure it was even possible.

"Pull!"

He looked astern. Gudrid had finally taken a few turns around the cleat, hitching the tow rope in place. The line was rising up out of the water as the strain came on, and *Sea Hammer* at the other end was turning toward them, turning stern into the waves rather than broadside to. If she had any hope of making it through the surf she would have to remain turned that way. If she was sideways to the seas she would roll and be torn apart.

Thorgrim yelled something across the distance, but Harald could not make out the words. He looked astern again, expecting to see his father bring an ax down on the tow rope and cut *Blood Hawk* free. But neither he nor Godi had moved, and Harald guessed he was choosing to let Harald try to save his men.

"Pull!" Harald looked down over the side, and back past the stern to see if there was any wake, if *Blood Hawk* was making any progress at all. He thought perhaps she was making headway, but he could not tell for certain, and if she was, it was not much.

It was not for want of trying. Harald could see the men's faces were already turning red with the effort. Gudrid had taken up an oar now, which meant every man aboard but him and Starri was rowing.

"Look here, Broadarm, look here!" Starri shouted from his perch on the sheer strake just behind Harald. Harald glanced up, saw Starri pointing over the starboard side, and he followed Starri's arm.

The merchant ship, the second one, the drifting one, was one hundred feet away off the starboard side. It had come clear of *Sea Hammer* and Brunhard's ship and was spinning off on its own. What the men on that ship were doing, Harald could not tell. He could only see a few men moving, and they looked to be hurt or stunned. Whatever they were doing, it did not involve sailing the ship.

But it did not matter to him, because that ship posed no threat to *Blood Hawk*. Until now.

The ship's sail was still set, and it had been alternately flogging and coming aback. But now, as the waves spun the ship around, her stern came up into the wind and the sail filled with a snap. The ship heeled a bit as it surged forward, moving with building momentum, driving right for *Blood Hawk*'s side.

"Pull! Pull! It'll run us down!" Harald shouted. One more wave, or two, and the ship would be right on top of them, and then they, too, would be dragged onto the beach.

"Cut *Sea Hammer* away!" someone shouted from forward. "Cut it away!"

"Shut your mouth and pull!" Harald shouted back. He would not let his father go. He would hold on and guide the longship through the surf, and even if the ship was broken up, the men, and his father, would live. Or they would have a better chance at living, anyway.

"Pull!" The word had not left his mouth when he felt *Blood Hawk* leap forward with a jerk, the oars driving her fast through the water. He turned and looked behind. The tow rope to *Sea Hammer* was gone, and Harald knew with certainty that his father had cut it, condemning himself and his men to the surf so that Harald and *Blood Hawk* could escape.

But he was too late. Even as *Blood Hawk* surged ahead, the big seas lifted the merchantman and flung it with willful malevolence at her starboard side. It rolled toward them, rolled over the oars, snapping most of them off at the oarports. And then with the cruel fickleness of the gods, the ship spun away from *Blood Hawk*, never even touching the longship itself, but leaving it crippled and helpless and right on the edge of the breaking seas.

Chapter Thirty-Five

A ninth I know: when need befalls me
to save my vessel afloat,
I hush the wind on the stormy wave,
and soothe all the sea to rest.
                    The Song of Spells

Thorgrim Night Wolf wanted to weep with pride for his son. He wanted to sing a skald's song to the world about the boy's boldness, his seamanship, the way he commanded *Blood Hawk* and drove her with a reckless courage right up to the edge of the surf. He was stunned by the beauty of how they had taken in the sail, run out the oars, threw a line to *Sea Hammer,* all as if it was some well-practiced dance performed in the safety of some great hall.

And at the same time he wanted to cuff the boy on the back of the head and give him a good dressing down for being so heedless of his own safety and the safety of the men and ship under his command. He, Thorgrim, was a hypocrite and he knew it. It would not have occurred to him to fault another man for risking his life that way, but the thought that Harald might die to save his father was unbearable.

"He may be too close to shore already," Godi said, standing at Thorgrim's side. "If he tries to get us safe through the surf he may get pulled in himself."

Great hulk of a man that he was, a brutal killer in battle— Thorgrim had seen him decapitate men with his battle ax as if he were swatting an insect—Godi could be surprisingly soft-spoken and diplomatic. He was using those traits now, pointing out in the mildest of terms that Harald and his men were likely to find themselves meeting the same watery death as the men of *Sea Hammer.*

"He can't get us through the surf the way he thinks he can," Thorgrim said. "The rope isn't long enough. Two ropes wouldn't be. He'd be swept in himself."

He bent over, picked up an ax that had been dropped on the deck near where he stood. "I'll let him pull *Sea Hammer* around so we're stern-to the seas and then I'll cut him loose. They should still be far enough offshore that they can row clear, if the men break their backs and pull like sons of bitches."

The rope lifted from the waves as *Blood Hawk*'s oars dug in and the longship began to claw its way to windward. The yard was down and the sail, or what Thorgrim had realized was actually two sails, those from *Dragon* and *Fox*, was hauled up to it, the few loose folds snapping in the on-shore wind.

"Now we'll see," Thorgrim said. He had his doubts that Harald would even be able to turn the longship and the waterlogged merchantman she rested on. He was not sure *Sea Hammer* would remain floating long enough for him to try.

They heard a groan forward, a deep, agonizing sound and the deck vibrated under their feet as the rope began to exert pressure on *Sea Hammer*'s stern. The vessel shifted enough to make them stumble and they turned and looked forward.

Sea Hammer was turning, pulled by Harald's tow line, her bow pivoting where it rested on the stern of Brunhard's ship. The second merchant ship had drifted clear and now she was to windward of the sinking vessels, closer to *Blood Hawk* than she was to *Sea Hammer*.

Then everything changed again. The stern of the second merchantman was caught by the seas and spun around and her sail filled and bellied out. Every man aboard her seemed to be dead or wounded; no one was making any effort to control the ship. But with the sail full she surged forward as if manned by a spirit crew, not away from *Blood Hawk,* as Thorgrim had hoped she would, but toward his son's ship.

"Oh, Hel take that bastard!" Thorgrim shouted. He took two quick steps aft and brought the ax down on the tow rope. The strands parted with a cracking noise and the rope snapped back over the water and *Sea Hammer* began to turn sideways again.

But Thorgrim's eyes were not on his own ship, they were on Harald's, and before he could say another word the drifting vessel rolled over *Blood Hawk*'s starboard oars. Thorgrim could see the ash looms shatter; he could see *Blood Hawk* start to turn broadside to the seas.

"Harald…you should not have come for me," Thorgrim said.

They were still more than one hundred yards from the beach, the waves cresting and starting to break over the rails of *Sea Hammer* and Brunhard's ship, when they finally struck bottom.

Thorgrim and Godi were making their way forward, stumbling over the madly swinging deck, when a roller, larger than the rest, lifted the two ships up high as it raced for the beach. And then it dropped them, dropped them fast, and Brunhard's ship struck the sand with a heavy thudding noise and the rending of wood and the shouts of the men clinging to the sides of the ship.

Thorgrim and Godi were flung to the deck and they felt *Sea Hammer* roll and twist under them. Their eyes met and Thorgrim wondered if he looked as wide-eyed with shock as Godi did. The next wave lifted them, flung them farther in toward the beach, and once again Brunhard's ship slammed down on the sandy bottom and *Sea Hammer* drove farther onto the half-sunk hull.

"She'll break up fast now," Godi said and they stood.

"We both will. Once Brunhard sinks, we sink too, and what's left gets tossed onto the beach."

They raced forward to where the rest of the men stood crowded around the bow, holding on to whatever they could grab. Beyond that, they were doing nothing, because there was nothing they could do. Nothing beyond holding fast and waiting to see what would happen, if they would make it through the surf or if the ship would break up under them.

They struck a third time, much harder, because the water was growing shallower with every yard they were driven toward shore. Brunhard's ship twisted under them, rolled partway on its side, and suddenly the motion of *Sea Hammer* was different, as if she had been freed from some encumbrance.

"Brunhard's breaking up!" Thorgrim shouted. He looked over *Sea Hammer*'s rail and as he did he saw the first of the men from Brunhard's ship come swarming up through the hole the fallen mast had made in her side. The man had wild hair and wild eyes and terror on his face. He seemed oblivious to everything save for the need to get off the dying merchant ship and onto the dubious safety of *Sea Hammer*.

He had not yet squeezed through the gap when the next man began following him through, and more came on the other side of the mast, and still others farther forward, hauling themselves up over the sheer rail.

Thorgrim saw one of his men raising a battle ax and he shouted, "Hold! Let them come!" There was no point in trying to stop them. They would all be dead in the surf soon enough.

For a fourth time the seas lifted the vessels and dropped them, and this time *Sea Hammer* struck as well, with the stern of Brunhard's ship all but broken up under them and only the forward section still afloat. Thorgrim could hear the crush of the hull striking bottom and felt the shudder like it was his own death rattle. *Sea Hammer*, no longer pinned to Brunhard's ship, was starting to turn broadside to the waves, and once she did that she would be rolling like a log and that would be the end of her and the end of them.

Then he heard Bjorn shout, "Here, look at this!" and, to Thorgrim's surprise, the words did not seem to suggest yet another looming disaster, but rather a reason for hope.

Before he had thought it through, indeed before he had thought of anything at all, Harald Broadarm gave the order: "Set the sail! Now! Set it now!"

The men obeyed. The rowers on the starboard side, who now mostly held shattered lengths of oars, tossed them aside and raced to take up the halyard and cast off the buntlines and man the sheets. The men to starboard, whose oars were still intact, ran them inboard, dropped them across the sea chests and raced to help. By the time they were hauling like madmen to raise the yard, Harald still had not figured out why he had given that order.

They needed the ship to move, that much he understood. A ship that had no forward momentum was helpless, completely at the mercy of wind and sea. The oars gave them the most control; they could row in any direction they chose. Not so with the sail. Their course would be limited, and it was likely that they would never be able to claw their way off this lee shore. But they could try. With the sail set they could steer for the open sea.

No, Harald thought. *I can't abandon Sea Hammer...*

And then at last he understood what had been bubbling below the surface, the plan that had formed in some part of his mind that was deeper than conscious thought. The plan that the gods had whispered to him.

The yard was halfway up the mast now, the sail flogging as the wind blew down either side of the cloth. Harald pulled the tiller toward him and hoped the rippling sail was giving them enough headway that the steering board would bite.

It was. *Blood Hawk*'s bow began to swing slowly around, downwind, turning toward the beach and the heavy surf breaking over it.

The sail filled as *Blood Hawk* turned and Harald felt the ship surge forward, felt the tiny tremor through the oak bar in his hands. She was alive again, a wild creature barely under control.

This was why Harald had given the order to set sail: he needed power, he needed drive. He could not let this ship be tumbled helpless in the seas, her men flung to their deaths in the roiling water. If she was going ashore then he would drive her ashore, like a man whipping a stallion into a run.

From his place at the tiller he yelled forward. "We're going to run her up on the beach!" he shouted. "Ride the waves in! And we'll go along *Sea Hammer*'s side and we'll snatch them all up!"

He could see grins among the men forward, nodding heads. They were caught up with the spirit of the thing, the mad recklessness of it. It might be insane but it was insanity of their choosing, not madness thrust upon them. They liked it.

"There you go, Broadarm!" Starri shouted from behind him. "That's the bold move! That's what pleases the gods!"

Harald felt a bit of a smile come to his lips. This was good, that Starri approved. Sometimes Starri did not like to take risks at sea, because he feared the gods would not look favorably on a death by drowning as they would on a death in battle. But this, Starri seemed to think, was a death worthy of a warrior's spirit.

Harald called forward, "Ease those sheets some!" and the men at the sheets eased them away and the bottom edge of the sail lifted a bit and now Harald could see under the sail and out past the bow. A wave was racing under *Blood Hawk*'s keel, but *Blood Hawk* was moving nearly as fast as the wave, surfing along under the driving power of her odd-looking sail. Harald pushed the tiller forward, struggling to keep the ship stern to the wind, as the seas like some evil force tried with all their might to turn her sideways and roll her over.

Sea Hammer was just ahead, maybe four ship lengths away, and Harald could see that for the first time in many days they seemed to be getting a bit of luck. Brunhard's ship was breaking up, striking the bottom now, and it had loosened its grip on *Sea Hammer*'s bow. Now the longship had turned stern to the waves, perpendicular to the beach, positioned perfectly for Harald to run up alongside.

He could see only one problem with his plan. They could bring *Blood Hawk* alongside *Sea Hammer*, but they could not stop. *Blood Hawk* was moving much faster than his father's half-sunk, waterlogged ship. She would go tearing past, and the best that Thorgrim and the others could hope to do was leap aboard as she did.

But there was nothing for it. There was nothing more that Harald or any man could do.

Another sea lifted them and flung them toward the beach. They wallowed down between waves then came charging up the back of the next, the bow driving out into open air then dropping again and sending spray high on either side.

"When we come alongside *Sea Hammer* we'll ease the sheets!" Harald shouted forward, making his voice as loud and deep as he could. "We'll ease them just for an instant, then haul them in again! I need every man on the sheets!"

They moved. They staggered across the pitching deck and formed themselves up into two lines nearly all the way aft, right where the two sheets were made off to the cleats on *Blood Hawk*'s side. Easing the sheets would slow *Blood Hawk*, just a bit. Enough, Harald hoped, to make it easier for the men of *Sea Hammer* to jump across.

But they still needed the sail's drive; they could not live long without the forward momentum. The sheets would have to be hauled in again, quickly, so the sail would catch the wind. That would be no easy task. The blowing gale was putting a tremendous amount of pressure on the sail. It would take the effort of every man to pull it in again, and even then Harald was not sure it would be enough.

"Ready!" Harald shouted. They were one set of waves away from *Sea Hammer*'s side. Now Harald could see that it was not luck that had turned his father's ship stern to the seas; they had thrown an anchor over the stern. He could see the anchor line now, running taut from the after end of the longship and disappearing into the water.

Blood Hawk rose on a wave and Harald's eyes and every bit of his conscious mind were on *Sea Hammer*'s starboard side, like an archer lining up a target. This would not be pretty and it would not be gentle. In those winds and seas there was no way to ease alongside. The best he could do was to smash *Blood Hawk* into the larger ship and hope for the best.

He could see his father now, and Godi, and the rest of the men in a line along the deck and he hoped that that meant they had divined his purpose. They would have a few heartbeats worth of time, no more, to get aboard *Blood Hawk* and the dubious safety of the intact ship.

"Ready…now! Ease the sheets!"

Larboard and starboard men unhitched the heavy ropes from the cleats, but they knew better than to just let them go. Instead, they slacked the ropes away fast, letting them snake around the cleats, easing them off, quick but controlled.

The sail bellied out and lifted, bellied and lifted and Harald felt the speed coming off the ship, but with the speed went control as well. He pushed the tiller away, swinging *Blood Hawk* toward *Sea Hammer* which was now no more than a dozen feet forward of the larboard bow. He saw the men of *Sea Hammer* bracing to jump and he knew they understood his intention.

But not just the men of *Sea Hammer*. There were others, more men than had sailed with his father.

Brunhard…Harald thought. Brunhard's men must have climbed aboard, knowing that their own ship was sinking fast. *No matter…if we live we'll sort it out on the beach.*

Blood Hawk and *Sea Hammer* rose together, lifted by the same wave, *Blood Hawk* surging ahead, her bow driving right at *Sea Hammer*'s stern. Harald pulled the tiller hard toward him, swinging the bow away before it slammed headlong into his father's ship. *Blood Hawk*'s larboard side ran down *Sea Hammer*'s starboard and then the two ships slammed together with a crushing, keel-shuddering impact. *Blood Hawk*'s sheer strake was crushed and *Sea Hammer*'s upper planks collapsed at the beam in a horror of shattered oak.

But the men were jumping. Forward along *Sea Hammer*'s side the men were putting their feet on what was left of the sheer strake and launching themselves across to *Blood Hawk*, falling in heaps on the wet deck planks. Amidships, others were able to simply step across as the two ships ground alongside one another.

He could see Thorgrim, standing back from the ship's side, nearly all the way aft, and he had a sudden fear that his father would not jump at all, that he would insist on riding his ship in to their mutual death.

Failend was by Thorgrim's side, and Harald saw his father push her forward. She took two quick steps, got a foot on the sheer strake and leapt. She looked to Harald like a bird, flying over the space between the ships and coming down in a flurry of hair and tunic and leggings

"Father, jump!" Harald shouted, but instead Thorgrim grabbed Godi by the arm, jerked him forward, put a hand on his back and shoved him toward the rail. It was a symbolic gesture, Harald knew; if Godi did not want to be moved then Thorgrim was not going to move him. But Thorgrim would never leave *Sea Hammer* unless he was the last living man aboard. He could picture his father and Godi arguing over who should go last and he felt a flush of anger at that. He could only hope that they would decide and move in the next fifteen seconds, because after that it would be too late.

Right down the line, bow to stern, men leapt from the shattered side of *Sea Hammer* onto *Blood Hawk*, sweeping by. Harald could feel his ship starting to turn under him, the seas starting to turn it sideways.

"Sheet in the sail! Sheet it in!" Harald shouted and the men standing ready at the sheets began to haul away, leaning into the pull, legs braced, arms straining. The men of *Sea Hammer*, just come aboard, saw what was happening and they, too, joined in while Brunhard's men and those Harald guessed were the Irish slaves stood watching.

The sail, bellied out until it was nearly horizontal, was hauled back down foot by foot and the effect was immediate. *Blood Hawk* began to surge ahead even as the last men leapt across the space between her and *Sea Hammer*.

And then it was just Godi and Thorgrim as *Blood Hawk*'s stern drew up alongside that of *Sea Hammer*. Harald looked over at his father across the twenty feet that separated them, each to his own ship. Godi took two lumbering steps toward the edge of the ship, stepped up onto the sheer strake, still intact at the after end, and jumped.

It was a clumsy jump but Godi had a lot of weight to get airborne. He came over *Blood Hawk*'s larboard side and hit the deck with his right foot and managed to stay upright as he stumbled amidships. Harald looked over at *Sea Hammer*. Thorgrim was at the side of the ship. He had run forward a few feet but now the curve of *Blood Hawk*'s hull meant the space between the ships was wider, too wide for Thorgrim to jump. They would sweep past and leave his father behind.

"Harald!" Godi shouted and Harald shifted his eyes to the big man, just recovered from his leap. "Turn to starboard! Starboard!"

And Harald did. Once again he acted without thought, just knowing somehow that Godi was right, that turning to starboard was what he had to do. He thrust the tiller forward and *Blood Hawk* sheared away from *Sea Hammer*'s side, and as she did her stern swung in close to the very spot where Thorgrim stood.

Godi was taking no chances that Thorgrim might decide his place was with his dying ship. He took two quick steps to the larboard side and reached a massive arm across the narrow gap between the ships, grabbed a fistful of Thorgrim's tunic and half pulled, half dragged him over, with Thorgrim himself giving the minimum of help with the effort.

Thorgrim's landing aboard was even less spectacular than Godi's as he all but fell in a heap on the deck, Godi's hand still holding him by the collar. Harald could not help but smile, and then he felt *Blood Hawk* shift again under him and he turned his attention back to the tiller and the ship's heading.

They were still sheeting in. The sail was pulled halfway home, the men still leaning into the ropes, fighting for every foot. *Blood Hawk* lifted on a wave and surfed forward, leaving *Sea Hammer* and the remains of Brunhard's ship astern. Harald heaved back on the tiller, fighting to keep the ship stern to the breaking seas.

The wave passed under *Blood Hawk*'s keel and the stern sank down and struck bottom, sending a tremor though the fabric of the ship. The men forward looked wildly around as if looking for the source of the blow. Harald grit his teeth and pushed the tiller forward again.

They were less than a hundred yards from the beach now, the seas rising up on either side of the ship, curling over in tumbling, breaking waves. The stern came up. Harald spared a glance down to see if there was any visible damage, though he knew any stove planks would be hidden by the deck boards.

*Not long now...*he thought. They had only to live through the next few sets of waves and then they would be on the beach, one way or another.

The men were hauling in the last few feet of the sheets when the stern came down again, hitting with considerably more force, making Harald stagger and cling to the tiller for support. The sail collapsed, just for an instant, then snapped out with the full force of the wind behind it and with a crack like a whip it blew apart, seeming to dissolve into so many tendrils. The lines of men hauling on the sheets tumbled backward over the sea chests and along the deck as they suddenly had nothing to pull against. *Blood Hawk* began to turn sideways to the sea.

Harald heaved back on the tiller, trying to bring the stern around, and he met with only limited success. The waves had the ship now, and without the driving power of the sail the steer board had little effect. The helm answered, a bit, the bow swinging back nearly perpendicular to the beach. And then the wave below dropped away, dropped the bow down as if it was an unbearable load. The bow struck the bottom, driving into the sand, and the mast quivered and the shrouds snapped taut and Harald was certain the whole thing was coming down.

He opened his mouth to shout a warning forward, but before he could get the first word out, the waves lifted *Blood Hawk*'s stern and pivoted the ship on her still-grounded bow. In the time it took for Harald to pull the now-useless tiller toward him, the ship turned sideways to the breakers. The incoming wave reared up over the larboard side, curling and menacing, and then broke against the ship and dropped its tons of water down onto the deck.

Men, oars, weapons, sea chests, they were all swept away in the massive onslaught of water, crashing over the deck planks and surging across the ship, tumbling all in front of it. *Blood Hawk* staggered and rolled in a sluggish, heavy way, near half filled with water. The next wave lifted her—she was parallel to the beach now—and tossed her forward. She struck again, not on her bow or stern this time but on the full length of her keel. Harald felt the blow up through his legs and in his teeth as he alone remained upright, holding fast to the tiller.

The next sea lifted the ship sideways, lifted and rolled her, and Harald felt her going over, her keel still fast in the sand, the waves pushing her from below like a man turning a table over. He held to the tiller and did not know what to do because there was nothing at all he could do except stand there as his ship rolled in the waves like a log.

Then the keel came free from the sand, the grip of the sandy bottom broken, and *Blood Hawk* lifted again as the next wave flung her in toward shore. She rolled back to an even keel, rolled beyond that, and the next wave broke onto her deck, filling her even beyond what the first wave had done, knocking down those men who were just now struggling to stand.

She lifted again and again she was flung toward the beach, and Harald wondered how long she could endure this pounding, when she would just roll or break up. He knew what was coming and he held fast to the tiller as the ship's keel slammed down onto the sand. He could hear wood breaking that time, something below giving way.

He was used to the rhythm now: hit, lift, roll. He saw the next wave coming on and he waited for it to pick the ship up and roll it again, maybe clean over at last. He saw the water breaking along the larboard side, saw it rushing past the bow. *Blood Hawk* rocked a bit, but she did not move.

Harald looked out to sea. He looked toward the land. The waves had cast *Blood Hawk* so far up the sand that she was now beyond their reach, too far from the deep water for the rollers to lift her any more.

They were ashore. And they were still alive.

Chapter Thirty-Six

Spear-wielder, my brooch-goddess
is born to an inheritance.
Egil's Saga

Conandil figured she had only one thing left to live for, and that was killing Brunhard the slaver.

As Broccáin mac Bressal's wife, Conandil had tasted the first real happiness she had ever known, and Brunhard had helped crush it and turn that all into an endless nightmare. He had taken her freedom, given his men leave to rape her. He had killed her husband. She had actually saved Brunhard's life, convincing the freed Irishmen not to kill him and the other Frisians. In return, Brunhard and his men had attacked them the first opportunity they had, had killed half their number at least.

Conandil figured that any reason she once had to live was gone now, and she was ready for it to be over. She just had one last task to perform.

They had been in a stand-off, Brunhard's men and the Irish, each keeping to their patch of deck, weapons held ready, when the ship first struck bottom. Conandil felt the hull come down as a wave passed under it, a motion she was accustomed to, but then the bottom hit, making the half-sunk ship shudder in a way that seemed as if it would fall apart at any moment.

The Norsemen's ship was still resting on the stern, and when Brunhard's ship hit, the longship came down on it like a hammer blow, crushing the aft end further, letting the water flow even more freely on board.

Conandil was crouching a short ways behind the mast, the crowd of Irishmen who had survived the fighting formed up between her and the Frisians at the bow. No one was speaking or moving, but when the ship struck, Conandil heard curses and gasps and even a few screams. She could see the men look wildly around, eyes wide in fright, the terror like a physical presence.

The ship hit again and the deck under the longship buckled and the Irishmen shifted nervously. Conandil could see they were looking for a place to run. But there was only one option: the heathens' ship. She could see eyes turning that way, could almost hear the desperate choice in each man's head—stay aboard the slaver as it broke up, or fling themselves into the lair of the Northmen.

When Brunhard's ship struck again, Conandil could feel it start to come apart underfoot, as if it no longer had the strength to hold itself together. And that decided things for the men on board. As if following a single command, they turned and rushed aft, scrambling to get to the Northmen's ship while it was still within reach. The Northmen might kill them all, or they might not, but the sea would most certainly swallow them up, given the chance.

Conandil was caught up in the rush. All of her thoughts had been centered on killing Brunhard, but when the men began to run aft, she ran with them. They crowded in the stern, swarming around the side of the longship, some pulling themselves up through the gap made by the falling mast, others leaping up and grabbing the edge of the ship and hoisting themselves over.

She stood in the middle of that crowd, not even certain she could reach up high enough to grab a handhold, not sure she wanted to. And then she felt hands on her arms and waist and she was hoisted up and men already on the longship reached down and pulled her aboard.

Another wave lifted the ships and dropped them and she felt the longship grind against the dying slaver below. She looked around to see how the Northmen would react to this invasion of their ship, but they seemed not to care, and Conandil guessed they had more pressing things to think about. She had assumed the Norsemen's ship was mostly intact, save for its resting on Brunhard's ship, but she realized that might not be the case. Perhaps it was mortally wounded as well. Perhaps they were no safer aboard her than they were on the slaver.

She pushed her way through the press of men to a place in the clear, where she could see better. The Frisians were following the

Irish onto the Norsemen's ship and Conandil thought, *This won't end well for you, you Frisian dogs. Irish or Northmen, someone will kill you all.*

But neither Northmen nor Irish seemed too worried about the Frisians just then. Except for Conandil. She was still thinking about them, and about Brunhard. She was not worried about making it to shore because she really didn't care about her life beyond the next five minutes. There was just the one last task to finish.

The knife she had snatched up to cut the sheets of Brunhard's sail was still in her belt and she pulled it free now. She felt certain that she could cut Brunhard down right there, right in front of his own men and everyone else, and no one would give one damn about it. No one seemed to be giving much thought to anything but his own personal survival.

The Northmen had retreated to the stern, the others, the Irish and the Frisians, huddled together near the bow getting as far from the Northmen as they could. She ran her eyes over the men, peeking through the clusters, trying to find Brunhard. He would certainly be hiding among the Frisians; he would know both the Irish and Northmen wanted him dead. But she could not see him there.

Cautiously she moved to the larboard side, shifting the angle of her view, but still no Brunhard. There was some commotion aft, something happening that sent a wave of excitement through the Northmen, but Conandil did not know what it was and she did not care.

She inched forward, closer to the bow. She could see the Irishmen and the Frisians in their discreet groups, standing clear of one another, both terrified and uncertain. But no Brunhard.

Could he have stayed behind? Conandil wondered. She turned quick and looked down at the half-sunk hulk of Brunhard's vessel. And there he was.

Brunhard had stayed behind, but he seemed to have no intention of dying with his ship. He was on his knees as far forward as he could get, as far from the water that washed over the deck as possible, and he was working fast. He had six oars and he had lashed them together to form a square with an X running diagonally from each corner. He had lashed loose planks to the square as a sort of deck and tied a long rope to the frame, with a baulk of wood made fast to the other end, for what reason Conandil could not imagine. But she knew perfectly well what the rest of it was—a raft to float him to the beach.

It seemed a flimsy affair for the massive breaking waves that were pounding the vessels and rolling in toward the shore, but it was probably the best he could do in the short time he had, and it was something that would float, something to which he might cling. Something that might bring him safe to shore and give him the chance to run off, and that meant it was something he could not be allowed to have.

Conandil ran to the gap in the Norsemen's side left by the falling mast, slipped through the open section and dropped easily to the deck of Brunhard's ship. The after end of the merchantman was half sunk, the water nearly up to her waist, but there was still deck below on which to stand.

A wave surged over the shattered side and hit her like a fist, knocking her down. She snatched at a rope that was twisting in the water, prayed that it was made fast to something. She tried to stand but felt herself swirled off by the powerful sea, slamming hard against the side of the ship, submerged, pinned by the water. She pulled furiously at the rope but found only slack. Her lungs were bursting but she could not push herself off against the force of the water.

And then the rope came taut and she was able to pull against it, pull herself away from the ship's side. She got a foot down on the deck and pushed herself upright, coming clear of the sea, gasping for breath. Then, perversely, the ship rolled the other way and the water drained off and Conandil made her way forward, uphill, up to the bow where Brunhard was struggling with the last lashings of his raft.

She reached around behind her and was relieved to find the big knife still secure in her belt. She pulled it free, settled the grip in her hand. Brunhard's back was to her and he had not yet seen her coming. She took a step, and another, moving cautiously, but with the great roar of the wind and the pounding of the seas, the creaking of the half-sunk ships, the yelling of the men, she knew that the sound of her steps would not give her away.

Brunhard's shoulders were rising and falling, his arms seemed to be flailing as he worked the lashings around and hauled them tight.

Time's up for that, you bastard, Conandil thought. She took another step. Brunhard's back was hunched and his eyes were down.

Conandil turned the knife so the flat of the blade was horizontal. One thrust, right between the ribs, right into his foul heart.

She hoped he would stand at that moment, turn and look into her eyes, so that he would know who had killed him. She hoped that her face would be the last thing he saw on earth, the instant before he found himself kneeling in judgment before the throne of his maker.

Three more steps, then two. She drew the knife back and the ship took another drunken lurch. Conandil stumbled sideways, getting her right foot under her, catching herself the instant before she fell to the deck, but the movement was too great to be missed. Brunhard gasped and leapt to his feet, turning as he did. His eyes were wide, his mouth open, a dark hole in the midst of his thick and streaming beard.

Brunhard looked at Conandil, looked around to see if there were others, then looked back at Conandil. And he smiled.

"Ah, dearie, if you've come to get humped by Brunhard, it's not a good time!" he exclaimed. "Meet me on the beach, would you?"

Conandil felt the rage well up in her, doubling and tripling. She took a step forward, moving with caution, the knife held low and in front. Brunhard stepped back and he was still smiling, still looking on this whole thing like some grand joke, the way someone might tease a kitten that thought it was engaged in a genuine hunt.

There were many things Conandil wished to say to Brunhard, but she could not speak the Frisian language as well as she could understand it, so she held her tongue and took another cautious step. *The knife will say everything that needs saying*, she thought.

"Come along now, you little Irish whore," Brunhard continued, still smiling, his eyes still holding Conandil's. "Put the knife down like a good girl."

Conandil made a growling sound and took two steps forward, leading with the knife. Brunhard dropped to a knee and with his left hand he swept Conandil's knife arm aside and with his right he snatched up a spear that was lying on the deck. He never took his eyes from Conandil as he grabbed the weapon, and Conandil realized he had known all along that the spear was there.

Brunhard stood quick, thrusting the spear as he did, but Conandil leapt back, two, three, four paces, clear of the black iron point. Brunhard pulled the spear back and advanced on her, and she stepped back again. Spear against knife, the Frisian was still smiling as he took little jabs at Conandil, driving her back. "Do as I say, my dear," he said. "My men will be disappointed if I gut you like a fish."

Conandil felt the ship under her lifting on a wave, felt that sickening twist in her stomach as the vessel swooped up from below. She stopped retreating, held the knife ready, waiting for Brunhard to make his move. But she could see no way of getting past the point of his spear, and it occurred to her for the first time that it might be her, and not Brunhard, who died on that deck.

She didn't mind death. But the thought of Brunhard killing her, and living to speak of it, was intolerable.

The wave passed under and the ship began to plunge downward again and Brunhard made his move. He took a lunging step forward and thrust with the spear and there was nothing that Conandil could do in that instant but watch the deadly tip come flying in at her.

Then Brunhard's ship struck the bottom. It hit with tremendous force, a great crushing noise, the scrape of keel on sand, the sound of the Northmen's ship grinding into the stern. And Brunhard stumbled.

Conandil, eyes fixed on the spear tip, saw it swing wildly to the side as Brunhard struggled to keep his feet. She heard him grunt, a curse form on his lips. But she was moving by then, moving like a stoat: small, quick, deadly. Her left hand knocked Brunhard's spear aside and she advanced on him even before he had recovered his footing. Brunhard stood, tried to draw the spear back, and then realized Conandil was already too close for that weapon. He dropped it and was swinging a fist at Conandil's head when her knife came sailing in, the blade still horizontal, right past his half-raised hand, right into his chest at just about the spot that his heart, if he had such a thing, would be found.

Brunhard seemed to freeze in place, save for his eyes and mouth that flew open wide. He was looking right into Conandil's eyes, but she was not certain he saw her, or anything at all. He made a little choking sound and blood erupted from his mouth and ran like a spring down his wet beard and over his tunic.

She pulled the knife free, ready to stab again if she had to, but she did not. Brunhard sunk to his knees, eyes and mouth still open, though Conandil could not tell if he was still alive. She put a foot on his shoulder and pushed. Brunhard flopped over sideways and twitched a bit, but did no more than that.

Conandil looked at his motionless body, the blood pouring from the rent in his chest and mixing and swirling with the seawater that ran over the deck. She thought she would feel more pleased than she did.

The ship struck bottom again and Conandil could see the deck buckling side to side, as if the ship had broken its back. She could see it was being torn apart. She looked out toward the shore. Ireland. A hundred yards away, no more, but the surf was massive and deadly and she knew she would drown as soon as the ship under her fell apart.

She had been ready for death, ready to go to her maker, once she had sent Brunhard on ahead of her. But now she was not so sure.

The sight of Ireland, her land, the hills dull green in the muted light of the late day overcast, worked on her mind. For all her troubles, she was not sure there was any place she wanted to be more than her Ireland. It was so close. But she could not reach it.

And then she looked down and saw Brunhard's raft.

Epilogue

Hard is it on earth, with mighty whoredom;
Axe- time, sword-time, shields are sundered,
Wind-time, wolf-time, ere the world falls;
Nor ever shall men each other spare.

The Poetic Edda

Thorgrim embraced Harald. He wrapped his arms around the boy and hugged him tight and kept hugging until he had to consciously tell himself to let go. The words he wanted to say were an inchoate jumble in his head and he could not form them into anything like what he wanted to express, so he just hugged his son and hoped that would answer.

Starri Deathless, Godi, Failend, Vestar, Armod, Olaf Thordarson, they all hugged and slapped one another and marveled at the fact that they were still alive and the ship under their feet was mostly intact. There was some commotion forward, shouting, a struggle among the others who had jumped aboard *Blood Hawk*, but they paid no attention. They did not care. There were tales to tell, stories to hear, good news and bad to recount. They were together again, this small handful of Northmen, the survivors, and they wished to take pleasure in that simple fact.

Then, when the first great tide of words began to ebb, they hopped down off *Blood Hawk*'s low side to the sandy beach on which she rested. They walked around the bow of the ship so they might get an unobscured view of the three vessels still out there: *Sea Hammer* resting on the remains of Brunhard's ship, and the smaller merchantman still bashing and jolting its way toward the beach.

The Irishmen had gone up the beach, near to where the sand yielded to crumbling cliff walls. They had dragged the Frisian sailors, screaming and thrashing, with them. Thorgrim could hear shouting in two languages, neither of which he understood. And then came a long, sharp scream, a cry that bespoke considerable pain and terror. The Irish were beginning the work of revenge.

"Brunhard's men didn't treat the Irish thralls very well," Harald said. "I'm thinking they're paying the price for that now."

"Was Brunhard among them?" Thorgrim asked. "Do they have him there? Brunhard's the one I want."

"No," Harald said. "I asked among the Irishmen. Just after we came ashore. They said Brunhard was not aboard *Blood Hawk*. And I could see no one who looked like a ship's master among the Frisians."

"Hmm," Thorgrim said. He wondered if Brunhard had drowned. That would be too bad. As for the other Frisian sailors, he did not care in the least what became of them. He knew they would not be anyone's problem for very much longer.

The Northmen walked to the water's edge, right at the point where the crashing waves could reach no higher, and looked out to sea. *Sea Hammer* had swung broadside to the waves and was down by the bow. Thorgrim could picture the water pouring in through the stove—in planks there, his pathetic attempts to caulk the seams with strips of cloth all washed away by now.

The seas lifted the longship and flung her toward the beach and then she came to rest again. She would make it ashore, he could see that. The question was whether she would be in one piece or a thousand, if there would be enough of her left to repair or if she would be good only as a source for scrap wood to make *Blood Hawk* seaworthy again.

There was almost nothing left of Brunhard's ship. They could see that her keel had broken and what was left of her hull was quickly coming apart. A big sea crashed over her side, swept her decks, and the men on the beach could see something floating free, though what it was was not entirely clear. It was flat and frail looking, some sort of odd lash-up. The wave lifted it and tossed it forward and they could see there was something on it, but whether it was a person or a bundle of some sort they could not tell.

"Starri, can you see what that is?" Thorgrim asked.

Starri took a step forward, squinted at the distant object. "No part of a ship that I can tell," he said at last. He watched for a bit more, as wave after wave flung the thing closer.

"I think it's a raft," Starri announced at last. "Some kind of raft lashed together, and someone riding on it."

That pronouncement brought a murmur of interest to the crowd. "Maybe it's Brunhard," Harald said. "Maybe he thought to make up a raft to get ashore."

Another murmur. "You might be right," Thorgrim said. "He's a clever one. But if this is him he'll find he's too clever for his own good health. He'd have been better off staying with the ship."

They watched with mounting curiosity as the raft drifted in toward shore. As it came closer they could see that there was a sea anchor trailing behind which served to slow the raft down and keep it from tumbling in the waves.

"That was well done," Godi said. "Whoever's on that raft would have been dead by now if they hadn't thought to put that sea anchor out."

The raft was halfway to shore when the rest of Brunhard's ship began to come apart in a serious way. The forward end tore clean off right at the beam and began tumbling and breaking up in the waves. The smaller of Brunhard's ships, which had been drifting farther off, was driven into what was left of the larger one and the lot of it was pushed farther and farther toward shore.

The raft was not so far off now, and half a dozen men ran out into the surf and up to their waists where they could grab hold of it and the person riding it in. Thorgrim was certain by now that it was Brunhard. No one else had shown such creativity when it came to saving their own hide.

But it was not Brunhard. He could see that even as the men reached the raft and steadied it and helped the passenger off. As far as he could tell it was not a man at all. It was a woman, and a slight one at that, smaller even than Failend, he thought. One of his men scooped her up in his arms and carried her through the water toward the safety of the beach. And then he remembered. Grimarr's thrall.

Thorgrim heard a voice cry out behind him. It spoke one word. "Conandil!" And then the man was running, one of the Irishmen, running down toward the surf and the man carrying the woman in through the waves.

"Who's that?" Thorgrim asked Harald, nodding in the direction of the raft. He did not specify whom he meant. He meant all of them.

"The woman is named Conandil," Harald said. "Same name as the one who was Grimarr's thrall, but I don't know if it's the same woman."

"It is," Thorgrim said. "I saw her face."

Harald nodded. "The man is her husband, Broccáin. He came to fight with us, hoping to get his wife back."

Thorgrim nodded. Such a strange intertwining of people and things and events.

Knee high in the surf, Broccáin took Conandil from the man who was carrying her and brought her the rest of the way to the beach, hugging her close as he bore her in his arms. Thorgrim recognized this as the sort of thing that he would find pleasing if he were given to being pleased by this sort of thing. Instead he made a grunting sound and turned toward Harald.

"There's work to do," he said. "The sun will be down soon, and we don't know who saw us come ashore. Any of these petty kings with some band of cripples they call men-at-arms might think we're as vulnerable as lambs right now. We'll need to get men posted."

He ran his eyes over the men who stood on the beach with them, half the number of men who had sailed from Vík-ló; the crew who had been sent off in *Blood Hawk* or his own men from *Sea Hammer*. The men from *Fox* and *Dragon* were dead, according to Harald. Some of the living he did not recognize but guessed from their appearance that they were Irish slaves. Or maybe slaves no longer. Thorgrim was not sure. He hadn't yet decided.

"Get some of your men…" he continued, when his eyes stopped on one of the Irishmen, standing a ways back and looking as if he did not care to be seen. Something about his face caught Thorgrim's eye. Something about the way he stood, the frame of his body.

*I know you, too…*he thought.

"Yes, Father?" Harald said. "Get some on my men…?"

Thorgrim did not answer. He stared into the man's face and then the man lifted his head and stared back, unabashed, defiant.

Louis…

It was Louis the Frank, their prisoner from Glendalough. The one who had betrayed them, ruined their perfectly laid trap, run off with the Irish men-at-arms who were hunting them.

"Son…of…a…bitch!" Thorgrim said, his voice growing in volume with each word. He drove forward, pushed the men in his way aside, his arms reaching to grab the Frankish bastard by the throat. As he moved he registered the fact that Louis was not backing away, was not flinching or cowering, but rather standing fast, standing ready to fight.

Then Thorgrim felt hands on his shoulders, hands on his arms and he was brought up short. He twisted to get free, but it was Harald and Godi who had got hold of him, and few mortal men were likely to break their grip.

"Let me go!" Thorgrim demanded. "It's that whore's son Frank!" But they held fast and the first rush of fury subsided and he shook them off and they let him.

Thorgrim turned to Harald. "He was on *Blood Hawk*. Did you know he was on your ship?"

Harald's pink cheeks flushed further and he opened his mouth. Harald was not the sort who was quick with a reply in such circumstances, nor was he a very adept liar, and so he stammered a bit and then said, "I had him in chains at first, Father, but he was a help to us. He knew Brunhard, better than any of them, and he helped us in finding him."

"Good," Thorgrim said. "Maybe his God will look with favor on him for that. But I won't." He turned back to Louis, who was still standing his ground, still looking as defiant as a man in his battered state could look. Thorgrim pulled his sword, Iron-tooth, from its scabbard and pointed the tip at Louis. "Someone give him a sword and we will finish this."

Someone among the Northmen handed Louis a sword and Louis took it up with the ease and confidence of deep familiarity. He took a step back, making room to fight, brought his left foot back a bit, his right forward, held the sword low and in front of him. Right and left the men stepped away, clearing a place on the beach.

Thorgrim took a step forward, brought Iron-tooth up so the tip was pointing at Louis's neck, five paces away. "I didn't get to kill Brunhard," he said, "but at least I can kill you. And in truth, that will be a sweeter thing." He knew that Louis could not understand his words, but that didn't matter. He would certainly understand his meaning.

And Louis did. He moved like a sudden gust of wind, fast and silent, his sword darting forward at the end of a long lunge. The tip might well have driven five inches into Thorgrim's chest if Thorgrim had not been tensed and ready. But he was, and he stepped back and knocked Louis's incoming blade aside and countered with a thrust of his own.

Louis had leapt back the very instant he saw that his lunge would miss, and though he was not in the best place to counter Thorgrim's stroke, it was good enough. With a flick of his wrist he knocked Thorgrim's blade out of line, then drew his own back over his shoulder. He swept it down again in a powerful backhand blow, but Iron-tooth was there to stop it. The blades struck, the sound of steel on steel ringing out over the beach, silent now save for the pounding surf.

Both men held their swords in that manner, crossed, pushing one against the other, then both stepped back again. And then, darting like a mouse, Failend was between them, her hands up, turning left and right to shift her gaze from one to the other.

"Enough!" she said, and her voice carried surprising power coming from so small a woman. "You have crossed swords now, but now you are done." She spoke in the Norse tongue, and then again in Irish.

Thorgrim took another step back and he frowned with confusion. "Failend, what is this about?" he asked.

"I will not stand by and see one of you kill the other. Or, more likely, you kill one another. It's stupid and pointless and I won't have it."

Thorgrim pointed his sword at Louis. "I know you've not forgotten how he betrayed us. Ruined the trap we had set for the men hunting us down."

And Thorgrim had not forgotten that Louis had been Failend's lover. He was not jealous. He was too old for that sort of nonsense. But he did think it was coloring her view of things.

"Betrayed us?" Failend said. "He was your prisoner. *I* was your prisoner. What loyalty did he have to you? How would you have acted if you were prisoner to another?"

Then Louis began to speak. He spoke Irish and he spoke to Failend, the words as angry-sounding as Thorgrim's. Thorgrim could not understand it, but he was pretty sure he knew what the Frank was saying, could almost hear his protesting Failend's interference in a matter of honor.

Failed turned her back on Thorgrim and spoke to Louis, and Thorgrim could hear the same biting tone. Women, he knew, could often see things in a way he could not understand. It was as if they were able to climb to some place where men could not go, and it gave them a perspective that men could never get.

She turned away from Louis, back to Thorgrim, switched back to the Northmen's language. "Louis wants only to be free of Ireland and to get to his home. You want only to be free of Ireland and get to your home. You two have nothing to fight about."

Thorgrim lowered his sword. Here was one of the most irritating things about a woman's perspective. It often made sense, even when Thorgrim did not want to admit as much.

"Why do you care about this?" Thorgrim asked. "Why should you meddle in our affair?"

That question seemed to throw Failend off a bit, though Thorgrim could not tell if it was because she had not thought about her own motives, or if because she thought the answer so obvious it was not worth asking the question. Whichever it was, she frowned and seemed to need some time to come up with her reply.

"Why can't I stand here and watch you two do this?" she asked. "Can't you see why not? Even beyond the sheer stupid waste of it all?"

Thorgrim nodded. He did not reply. But he understood.

Failend took a step closer. "By God, Thorgrim, don't we have enough to do now? Hasn't there been death enough?"

Thorgrim looked around. The men were watching in silence. What they thought of all this he could not tell. To the east, nearly up on the beach now, was the half-sunk and shattered remains of *Sea Hammer*, the flotsam that was once Brunhard's ship, and the second merchantman, run up on the sand, tilted on her side, showing off her crew of dead and wounded men.

Blood Hawk was heaved up on the sand, and she was damaged as well. How much, Thorgrim did not know. His two other ships, *Dragon* and *Fox* were somewhere off to the north. He had barely enough crew to man all those ships. He had no sails for any of them. They were in an unknown country surrounded by people who were strangers to them, but who they could be fairly certain would want them dead.

And then Thorgrim came to a decision. There was no real thought in it, he was just going by instinct now, doing the thing his heart told him to do. He turned Iron-tooth around and slid the blade back into its scabbard.

"Tell Louis he will live. For now, anyway," he said to Failend. He turned to the others. "We have work to do. A lot of work to do."

And it was true. Once again they had to gather up the wreckage and piece it together and hope that this time, this time, the gods would finally grant them leave to go.

Would you like a heads-up about new titles in The Norsemen Saga, as well as preview sample chapters and other good stuff cheap (actually free)?

Visit our web site to sign up for our (occasional) e-mail newsletter:

www.jameslnelson.com

Other books in *The Norsemen Saga*:

Glossary

adze – a tool much like an ax but with the blade set at a right angle to the handle.

Ægir – Norse god of the sea. In Norse mythology he was also the host of great feasts for the gods.

Asgard – the dwelling place of the Norse gods and goddesses, essentially the Norse heaven.

athwartships – at a right angle to the centerline of a vessel.

beitass – a wooden pole, or spar, secured to the side of a ship on the after end and leading forward to which the corner, or clew, of a sail could be secured.

berserker – a Viking warrior able to work himself up into a frenzy of blood-lust before a battle. The berserkirs, near psychopathic killers in battle, were the fiercest of the Viking soldiers. The word berserkir comes from the Norse for "bear shirt" and is the origin of the modern English "berserk."

block – nautical term for a pulley.

boss – the round, iron centerpiece of a wooden shield. The boss formed an iron cup protruding from the front of the shield, providing a hollow in the back across which ran the hand grip.

bothach – Gaelic term for poor tenant farmers, serfs

brace – line used for hauling a **yard** side to side on a horizontal plane. Used to adjust the angle of the sail to the wind.

brat – a rectangular cloth worn in various configurations as an outer garment over a *leine*.

bride-price – money paid by the family of the groom to the family of the bride.

byrdingr – a smaller ocean-going cargo vessel used by the Norsemen for trade and transportation. Generally about 40 feet in length, the byrdingr was a smaller version of the more well-known *knarr*.

cable – a measure of approximately 600 feet.

clench nail – a type of nail that, after being driven through a board, has a type of washer called a rove placed over the end and is then bent over to secure it in place.

clew – one of the lower corners of a square sail, to which the **sheet** is attached.

curach – a boat, unique to Ireland, made of a wood frame covered in hide. They ranged in size, the largest propelled by sail and capable of carrying several tons. The most common sea-going craft of mediaeval Ireland. **Curach** was the Gaelic word for boat which later became the word curragh.

derbfine – In Irish law, a family of four generations, including a man, his sons, grandsons and great-grandsons.

dragon ship – the largest of the Viking warships, upwards of 160 feet long and able to carry as many as 300 men. Dragon ships were the flagships of the fleet, the ships of kings.

dubh gall – Gaelic term for Vikings of Danish descent. It means Black Strangers, a reference to the mail armor they wore, made dark by the oil used to preserve it. *See fin gall*.

ell – a unit of length, a little more than a yard.

eyrir – Scandinavian unit of measurement, approximately an ounce.

félag – a fellowship of men who owed each other a mutual obligation, such as multiple owners of a ship, or a band of warriors who had sworn allegiance to one another.

figurehead – ornamental carving on the bow of a ship.

fin gall – Gaelic term for Vikings of Norwegian descent. It means White Strangers. *See dubh gall*.

forestay – a rope running from the top of a ship's mast to the bow used to support the mast.

Frisia – a region in the northern part of the modern-day Netherlands.

Freya – Norse goddess of beauty and love, she was also associated with warriors, as many of the Norse deity were. Freya often led the **Valkyrie** to the battlefield.

gallows – tall, T-shaped posts on the ship's centerline, forward of the mast, on which the oars and yard were stored when not in use.

gunnel – the upper edge of a ship's side.

hack silver – pieces of silver from larger units cut up for distribution.

halyard – a line by which a sail or a yard is raised.

Hel – in Norse mythology, the daughter of Loki and the ruler of the underworld where those who are not raised up to Valhalla are sent to suffer. The same name, Hel, is sometimes given to the realm over which she rules, the Norse hell.

hird – an elite corps of Viking warriors hired and maintained by a king or powerful **jarl**. Unlike most Viking warrior groups, which would assemble and disperse at will, the hird was retained as a semi-permanent force which formed the core of a Viking army.

hólmganga – a formal, organized duel fought in a marked off area between two men.

Haustmánudur – early autumn. Literally, harvest-month.

hirdsman – a warrior who is a member of the **hird**.

jarl – title given to a man of high rank. A jarl might be an independent ruler or subordinate to a king. Jarl is the origin of the English word *earl*.

Jörmungandr – in Norse mythology, a vast sea serpent that surrounds the earth, grasping its own tail.

knarr – a Norse merchant vessel. Smaller, wider and sturdier than the longship, knarrs were the workhorse of Norse trade, carrying cargo and settlers wherever the Norsemen traveled.

league – a distance of three miles.

lee shore – land that is downwind of a ship, on which a ship is in danger of being driven.

leeward – down wind.

leech – either one of the two vertical edges of a square sail.

leine – a long, loose-fitting smock worn by men and women under other clothing. Similar to the shift of a later period.

levies – conscripted soldiers of ninth century warfare.

Loki – Norse god of fire and free spirits. Loki was mischievous and his tricks caused great trouble for the gods, for which he was punished.

longphort – literally, a ship fortress. A small, fortified port to protect shipping and serve as a center of commerce and a launching off point for raiding.

luchrupán – middle Irish word that became the modern-day leprechaun.

luff – the shivering of a sail when its edge is pointed into the wind and the wind strikes it on both sides.

Midgard – one of nine worlds in Norse mythology, it is the earth, the world known and visible to humans.

Niflheim – the World of Fog. One of the nine worlds in Norse mythology, somewhat analogous to Hell, the afterlife for people who do not die honorable deaths.

Njord – Norse god of the sea and seafaring.

Odin – foremost of the Norse gods. Odin was the god of wisdom and war, protector of both chieftains and poets.

oénach – a major fair, often held on a feast day in an area bordered by two territories.

perch – a unit of measure equal to 16½ feet. The same as a rod.

Ragnarok – the mythical final battle when most humans and gods would be killed by the forces of evil and the earth destroyed, only to rise again, purified.

rath – Gaelic word for a **ringfort**.

rod – a unit of measure equal to 16½ feet. The same as a perch.

ringfort – common Irish homestead, consisting of houses protected by circular earthwork and palisade walls.

rí túaithe – Gaelic term for a minor king, who would owe allegiance to a high king.

rí ruirech – Gaelic term for a supreme or provincial king, to whom the **rí túaithe** owe allegiance.

sceattas – small, thick silver coins minted in England and Frisia in the early Middle Ages.

seax – any of a variety of edged weapons longer than a knife but shorter and lighter than a typical sword.

sheer strake – the uppermost plank, or strake, of a boat or ship's hull. On a Viking ship the sheer strake would form the upper edge of the ship's hull.

sheet – a rope that controls a sail. In the case of a square sail the sheets pull the **clews** down to hold the sail so the wind can fill it.

shieldwall – a defensive wall formed by soldiers standing in line with shields overlapping.

shroud – a heavy rope stretching from the top of the mast to the ship's side that prevents the mast from falling sideways.

skald – a Viking-era poet, generally one attached to a royal court. The skalds wrote a very stylized type of verse particular to the medieval Scandinavians. Poetry was an important part of Viking culture and the ability to write it a highly regarded skill.

sling – the center portion of the **yard**.

spar – generic term used for any of the masts or yards that are part of a ship's rig.

stem – the curved timber that forms the bow of the ship. On Viking ships the stem extended well above the upper edge of the ship and the figurehead was mounted there.

strake – one of the wooden planks that make up the hull of a ship. The construction technique, used by the Norsemen, in which one strake overlaps the one below it is called *lapstrake construction.*

swine array – a Viking battle formation consisting of a wedge-shaped arrangement of men used to attack a shield wall or other defensive position.

tánaise ríg – Gaelic term for heir apparent, the man assumed to be next in line for a kingship.

thing – a communal assembly

Thor – Norse god of storms and wind, but also the protector of humans and the other gods. Thor's chosen weapon was a hammer. Hammer amulets were popular with Norsemen in the same way that crosses are popular with Christians.

thrall – Norse term for a slave. Origin of the English word "enthrall."

thwart – a rower's seat in a boat. From the Old Norse term meaning "across."

Ulfberht – a particular make of sword crafted in the Germanic countries and inscribed with the name Ulfberht or some variant. Though it is not clear who Ulfberht was, the swords that bore his name were of the highest quality and much prized.

unstep – to take a mast down. To put a mast in place is to step the mast.

Valhalla – a great hall in **Asgard** where slain warriors would go to feast, drink and fight until the coming of **Ragnarok**.

Valkyrie – female spirits of Norse mythology who gathered the spirits of the dead from the battlefield and escorted them to **Valhalla**. They were the Choosers of the Slain, and though later romantically portrayed as Odin's warrior handmaidens, they were originally viewed more demonically, as spirits who devoured the corpses of the dead.

vantnale – a wooden lever attached to the lower end of a shroud and used to make the shroud fast and to tension it.

varonn – springtime. Literally "spring work" in Old Norse.

Vik – an area of Norway south of modern-day Oslo. The name is possibly the origin of the term *Viking.*

wattle and daub – common medieval technique for building walls. Small sticks were woven through larger uprights to form the wattle, and the structure was plastered with mud or plaster, the daub.

weather – closest to the direction from which the wind is blowing, when used to indicate the position of something relative to the wind.

wergild – the fine imposed for taking a man's life. The amount of the wergild was dependant on the victim's social standing.

yard – a long, tapered timber from which a sail was suspended. When a Viking ship was not under sail, the yard was turned lengthwise and lowered to near the deck with the sail lashed to it.

Acknowledgements

As with any book, thanks are due to many. Steve Cromwell came through once again with one of the finest covers in the series (in my somewhat humble opinion) and once more Alistair Corbett's magnificent photography helped make the look even more dramatic. Thanks to Alicia Street at iProofread and More for correcting my poor spelling, a grammar. That's to my long-time agents Nat Sobel and Judith Weber and all the good folks at Sobel Weber Associates for all their great work in getting Russian, German, Spanish and audiobook versions of the Norsemen Saga.

And to Lisa, for keeping the rest of it together...